They Fought the Clandestine War Before the War—and Only One Side Could Win It

CARLOS GUNTHER ROBLES: Code name Jaguar, he's a crack engineer, assassin and saboteur. With a hundred men like him on Germany's side, the war would be over in six months . . .

J. EDGAR HOOVER: The tough-dealing FBI chief had a plan to thwart Germany, enrich his country and capture one of the bureau's most wanted criminals. Now he has to make it work . . .

ADMIRAL WILHELM CANARIS: The chief of intelligence for the Nazi high command directed a daring plot. His agents would destroy the Panama Canal—and keep Germany a major threat in the Americas for years to come . . .

WILLIAM STEPHENSON: Britain's master spy and the man they called Intrepid would do anything for king and country—even allow himself to be dangerously outmaneuvered by his own American allies . . .

HARRY FOX: They called him bootlegger, murderer, thief. The FBI wanted him behind bars—and to carry out the mission no other man could handle . . .

Praise for Charles Robertson's **Directive Sixteen**

"Major historical figures and explosive events from a little-known period of World War II . . . a colorful cast of fictional characters and an imaginative plot . . . a revealing, intriguing thriller."

—Justin Scott, author of *Rampage*

Books by Charles Robertson

Directive Sixteen
Strike Zone

Published by POCKET BOOKS

STRIKE ZONE

CHARLES ROBERTSON

POCKET BOOKS

New York   London   Toronto   Sydney   Tokyo   Singapore

This book is a work of fiction. Names, characters, places and incidents are either the product of the author's imagination or are used fictitiously. Any resemblance to actual events or locales or persons, living or dead, is entirely coincidental.

An *Original* Publication of POCKET BOOKS

POCKET BOOKS, a division of Simon & Schuster Inc.
1230 Avenue of the Americas, New York, NY 10020

ISBN: 0-671-61154-2

First Pocket Books printing May 1990

10 9 8 7 6 5 4 3 2 1

POCKET and colophon are registered trademarks of
Simon & Schuster Inc.

Printed in the U.S.A.

STRIKE ZONE

CHAPTER 1

Kirkuk Province, Iraq; October 15, 1941

A full moon hung across the midnight sky. The night was clear, the air was cool. Amir Hoshewi lay motionless, his body pressed against the cold, hard ground. A truck passed not fifty yards from where he lay. He could hear the voices of the British soldiers, their laughter racing across the clear night air. He waited until the sounds told him that the truck had passed and then slowly raised his head to look. Amir spat in the direction of the departing truck and drew a finger across his throat.

When he was sure that the military patrol had gone, he once again directed his attention to the oil storage tanks and derricks of the Kirkuk oil fields that sprawled across the flat, rocky plain almost a mile from where he lay. He was looking for some movement. Movement that would indicate that the man he knew only as Jaguar was on his way back.

The huge Kirkuk oil fields, discovered in 1927, were among the world's largest producing fields. Controlled by the British, and directly connected by pipeline across the Syrian desert to Haifa in Palestine and Tripoli in Lebanon,

1

Kirkuk was the most important source of oil to the British military forces in North Africa.

Amir could not help but marvel at the immensity of the complex. The rounded tops of the oil storage tanks glistened like jewels in the moonlight. The steel derricks, thrusting up out of the barren land, reminded him of the spires of the holy mosque he had seen on a boyhood trip to Baghdad.

As he had been instructed by his leader, Mullah Mustafa Barzani, Amir had brought the Jaguar here to the great Kirkuk oil fields of northeastern Iraq. Traveling after dark, in three nights they had covered the more than sixty miles from Barzani's camp in the Zagros Mountains in Sulaymaniya Province on the border of Iran. They had established an encampment almost five miles away from the oil fields, where they stayed during the day. At night, for four consecutive nights, Amir had brought the Jaguar to this spot, where large outcroppings of shale rock provided cover from prying eyes. From here the Jaguar had timed the frequency of the military patrols, smiling with satisfaction at the clockwork punctuality of the British soldiers, and sketched the details of the complex. He had seemed particularly interested in the size and number of the oil storage tanks. On the third night the Jaguar had left Amir at this same spot, made his way alone across the one-mile stretch of rocky ground, and disappeared inside the oil complex. He had returned several hours later. As usual, he had said nothing.

On this, the fourth night, they had loaded almost four hundred pounds of explosives onto their pack animals and made the journey from their encampment in the hills. They had staked and tethered the animals several miles away and then made two trips to carry the explosives to their position a mile away from the oil fields. Amir was covered in sweat; the Jaguar seemed barely winded by the effort.

They waited until the patrol had passed, then the Jaguar slung one of the explosive-filled knapsacks across his back, and, without a word, made off for the oil complex. Amir wondered who was this strange man who had not spoken one single word to him in three days. Although he had been told nothing, Amir assumed that the Jaguar was European and that he worked for the Germans, who had promised a Kurdish national homeland once the British were driven out of Iraq. More than that he did not care to know.

The man's name was Carlos Gunther Robles, and he was an Argentinian. Born of a German mother and an Argentinian father, he was a passionate believer in the destiny of Adolf Hitler and his National Socialist Workers Party. He wore the rough wool clothing of the Kurdish peasants and the red and white checked turban of the Barzani tribe. He was tall and dark-haired and his face was deeply tanned from his many weeks in the harsh Iraqi sun. Robles's expression had rarely wavered in the time that Amir had known him. He did not smile, indeed, he barely acknowledged that Amir existed, and his eyes, blue as a cloudless sky, gave no clue as to what lurked behind them.

Amir watched him for a time, but soon the Jaguar had disappeared into the darkness, and Amir rolled over onto his back and watched the stars. Amir was a young man, little more than twenty, and part of a Kurdish nationalist group committed to the establishment of an autonomous Kurdish state in northeastern Iraq. For that purpose the Kurds had allied themselves with the pro-German military faction under the leadership of Rasheed Ali al-Gailani, who had sworn to rid Iraqi soil of British dominance. In May of that year Amir had taken part in the uprising that had toppled the Iraqi government and established Rasheed Ali as the new ruler of Iraq. Rasheed Ali had been encouraged by the Germans in his endeavor, and soon after taking control of the country he had declared war on the British. Unfortunately, the Germans did not send the assistance they had promised, and the British, with only a small, but well-trained, army at their disposal, quickly reestablished control of the country. Rasheed Ali had been forced to flee to Iran, and the Kurds had moved deeper into their hiding places in the mountainous regions of Kurdistan. Many of the insurgents, including Amir's brother, had been captured and executed by the pro-British government. Amir felt no particular animosity about these acts of barbarism—the Kurds

3

were well-acquainted with this type of oppression—and he knew that had his side prevailed, they would have meted out the same punishment to their enemies.

It had been whispered in the Kurdish encampment that Amir's brother had broken under torture and had revealed Barzani's hiding place. Troops had been dispatched, and if not for an informer within the government, the Mullah Mustafa Barzani himself might have been captured and hanged. Amir had felt the cold stares of his people, heard the whispered curses as he passed by, and sensed the coldness of the great man himself. But Amir had remained silent and proud, and in the end the great man had relented and entrusted Amir with this important mission against the British. He was to render all assistance possible to this foreigner. His heart had soared when he realized that his time of trial was over.

Amir jumped up with a start to find the Jaguar standing over him, one hand on the handle of the hanjar that was tucked into the scarves he wore wrapped around his waist. Heart pounding in his chest, Amir's hand went to his own dagger as he stepped back. Robles looked at Amir with disdain and then slung the next knapsack over his shoulders and started back toward the oil fields. Again, Amir watched him disappear into the night.

When he returned next time, Amir was alert and waiting for him. He did not want it reported to Barzani that he had been derelict in his duty. He helped Jaguar with the next knapsack and gave him a reassuring pat as he again started back.

This time Jaguar was gone for a long time, and Amir watched the British patrols pass twice before he returned. Amir lifted the fourth knapsack, but the Jaguar shook his head and indicated that he was finished. They divided the remaining explosives between them and started back toward the foothills, where they had left the animals. There they loaded the remaining explosives onto the pack animals and began the long trek back to the Kurdish encampment in the mountains.

There were still several hours of darkness left and the

night was cold, but Amir thought only of the warm greeting he would receive when he returned from this apparently successful mission. Now the stares and whispers would be stopped for good.

They rode side by side, and Amir noted that every few minutes the Jaguar would look at his watch. Finally he reined in his horse and turned back to look in the direction from where they had come. *"Ravestan,"* he said, and Amir stopped, also, and waited.

They did not have to wait for long. First there was a flash of light, and then almost immediately the dark rumble of explosion raced toward them across the barren plain. The first rumble was followed by another and then another and continued until the sounds were indistinguishable. The noise rolled over them like great peals of thunder while the light grew in intensity until it was almost like sunrise.

Amir let out a long cry of exultation. This would surely be a mission that would reestablish his courage in the eyes of Barzani's followers. The women in camp would no longer treat him with disdain. The children would treat him with renewed respect. He looked at the Jaguar so that they might share the joy of this dual victory, but saw only the same expressionless face that he had seen for four consecutive days. Then he saw the pistol in the Jaguar's hand, and his own expression changed from joy to bewilderment and then to sudden comprehension.

The Jaguar spoke to him in his own Kurdish dialect. "Amir Hoshewi, this is from Mullah Mustafa Barzani," he said, aiming the pistol. "The debt must be paid."

Amir opened his mouth to protest, but the bullet was quicker than his words. A hole appeared where his left eye had been, and he fell backward across his horse. He lay facedown in the dirt.

Robles calmed his horse, slowly dismounted, and walked toward the motionless form. He stood over Amir for a moment, then, using his foot, turned him over onto his back. Amir gave a low moan. The Jaguar shook his head in disappointment, sorry that the job was not yet done. He picked up Amir's turban, which had fallen beside him. The turban had unraveled, leaving only two long, twisted strips of cloth. Robles shook out the twists and used the cloth to cover Amir's face. Then, confident that the blood would not splatter, he held the pistol against Amir's temple and pulled the trigger. The Kurd gave only a mild twitch.

Robles remounted and gathered in the reins of the other animals. With the great fire that he had started lighting his way, he moved on to the east. He had successfully completed both tasks. One, a relatively minor favor for a favor. The other might easily influence the outcome of the war in the Middle East. He looked back over his shoulder at the light beyond the horizon and knew that this fire would burn for weeks.

For the first time he allowed himself a small smile of satisfaction.

CHAPTER 2

A chill November wind gusted across Bendler Strasse, stirring the leafless trees that lined the street, and scuttled down a side street to the Landwehrkanal. The two guards on duty at the main door of the row of town houses that housed the headquarters of German Military Intelligence shielded their faces against the dirt and debris that swept past them. One of them looked at the cold gray sky. "Winter," he said knowingly. "It won't be long now." The other merely nodded and straightened his greatcoat. They were expecting an important visitor, and he wanted to be ready.

Inside, on the fifth floor, Admiral Wilhelm Canaris stoked the small fireplace in his office. He added a small shovelful of coal to the flames, probed the glowing embers with a poker, and then stepped back to admire his handiwork. He rubbed his hands together in front of the fire as if in joyful anticipation. He wanted the room to be warm when his visitor arrived.

Although he rarely wore his uniform to the office, Admiral Canaris was in full uniform today, in honor of his distinguished visitor. Canaris was a small man, with a long face and sad, penetrating eyes. At fifty-three, he was the head of the secret intelligence service of the German High Command, otherwise known as the Abwehr. He went to his desk and sat. For at least the tenth time that morning he looked at his watch while drumming his fingers on a stack of unopened reports. His distinguished visitor was already fifteen minutes late.

The red light above the door went on, a signal from his aide that his visitor had arrived. Canaris stood up and came out from behind his desk, straightening his tunic and bringing himself to attention. The door opened and Grand Admiral Erich Raeder, commander-in-chief of the German Navy, strode into the office.

Raeder paused long enough for his aide to slip his naval greatcoat from his shoulders, dismissed the aide with a short wave, and acknowledged Canaris with a curt nod. "Please sit down, Admiral," Raeder said, indicating the chair behind Canaris's desk.

Both men sat, Raeder placing a briefcase at his feet, and waited until the aide had left the room and closed the office door.

Raeder smiled. "So, Willi," he said, "how are things with you?"

Canaris tapped the stack of reports on his desk. "Busy, as usual, Admiral."

Although Raeder was twelve years older than Canaris, the two were close friends. Raeder, in fact, had persuaded Hitler in 1935 to appoint Canaris to his position as chief of military intelligence. Raeder looked around the room. This was the first time in the six years that Canaris had held this position that Raeder had ever visited him in his office. The office itself, he thought, was rather small for a man with such an important position. It was paneled and lined with bookshelves, more like a banker's office, or a lawyer's, than the office of one of the most important military figures in Nazi Germany.

Canaris broke the brief silence. "This is indeed a rare honor for me, Admiral. I would have been more than glad to come to Bendler Strasse."

"Sometimes I think the walls have ears at the Bendler Block."

The Bendler Block was the name used for the row of squat, ugly buildings on Bendler Strasse that housed the headquarters of the High Command of the Army, Navy, and Defense Ministry. Bendler Strasse was only a short walk from Abwehr headquarters on Tirpitz Ufer.

"And how are things with the High Command?" asked Canaris.

"There seems to be a growing rumbling of discontent with the Russian campaign. Our forces are advancing everywhere, and there still are high hopes for a speedy victory, but this, if you remember, was a campaign that was to be over within six to eight weeks. So far the Russians, although absorbing tremendous losses, show little sign of capitulation."

The Abwehr had grievously underestimated the strength of the Russian Army at the start of the campaign. Canaris's intelligence agency had estimated approximately 240 Russian divisions; already there had been more than 360 Russian Army divisions reported in the field.

Both Raeder and Canaris had lobbied against Hitler's Russian venture; Raeder because he would have preferred to complete the conquest of the British before embarking on any new campaigns, Canaris because of a long held and firmly rooted fear of Russian capabilities. Events of the past two months had demonstrated that both men had been correct.

"But," Raeder went on, "the Führer is still confident of victory before the worst of winter sets in."

"Did someone inform the Führer," Canaris said, "that winter begins early in Moscow?"

"I am sure," Raeder said, "that the Führer is well-aware of the hazards of the Russian winter."

"Winter," said Canaris. He could almost hear the howl of the wind and see the frozen corpses piled like cordwood on the snow-covered plains of Russia.

"This visit," Raeder said, "was prompted by a meeting with Hitler yesterday. The Führer was very pleased about the latest escapade of your agent in Iraq. He believes that it will take the British at least six months to recover their oil-producing capacity, and by that time the war in that region will have been successfully concluded."

"Yes, the Führer called me the other day to personally congratulate me on that."

"Well, he is still talking about it," said Raeder. "You have scored a very important victory for yourself and your organization, my friend."

Both Canaris and Raeder knew that there were forces within the Nazi government working to take control of the Abwehr away from the military organizations that it served. Canaris was determined to protect the independence of his agency and the power of his position.

"You must tell me a little something about this agent of yours that the Führer is so enthralled with. He called him the Jaguar, I believe, and told Ribbentrop that if he had a hundred such men, the war would be over in six months."

"If only that were true."

"Tell me about him."

"Of course," Canaris said. He reached into his lower desk drawer and removed a thin file folder. He opened the file and laid it on his desk in front of him. "His name is Carlos Gunther Robles, and he is thirty-three years old. His father is Argentinian, of Spanish descent; his mother of German descent. His maternal grandfather, Gunther Reitmann, emigrated from Düsseldorf in 1880 to Capetown, South Africa, where his mother was born in 1885. Her father and two of her brothers were killed fighting the British during the Boer War." Canaris looked up. "One of the brothers was hanged by the British."

Raeder nodded.

"Apparently, the family lost everything in the war," Canaris went on. "In 1904 the remnants of the family— mother, daughter, and one surviving brother—emigrated to Buenos Aires. The daughter was nineteen. There she married into a wealthy Argentinian family. The girl was apparently very beautiful. She bore two daughters and a son. The son, Carlos Gunther Robles, attended the university at

Barcelona, where he received a degree in engineering. He did postgraduate work here in Germany at the Kaiser Wilhelm Institute in Dahlem. He is employed as a construction engineer by the Santeros Construction Company with offices in several South American capitals and in Madrid. Santeros is involved in many worldwide construction projects, giving Robles easy access to many countries that are closed to other agents."

"I understand that he has had other successes, similar to his destruction of the Iraqi oil fields."

Canaris allowed a small smile to crease his usually impassive face. "Yes. He was responsible for the diamond mine disaster in South Africa last year. Hundreds of workers killed and diamond production brought to a standstill for several months. Of course, there have been other, smaller, successes over the past two years."

"The Führer has asked me to speak with you about a special project for your agent. One for which he feels Jaguar is especially well-suited, and one that could have far-reaching implications for the future course of the war."

Canaris was wary of Hitler's schemes, but said nothing.

"At the present time," Raeder said, "the Führer feels that the Americans are the biggest thorn in our side."

Canaris thought that the Russians were a considerable thorn.

"Roosevelt has the best of both worlds. He sits back while the British and Russians do his fighting for him. Just last month he signed an accord with the Russians to give them all possible help in the war against us. He sends supplies and makes brave speeches . . ."

"Good God, Admiral," Canaris said, "surely Hitler is not going to declare war on America. Bad enough that we attacked the Russians before terminating the war in the west, but to initiate hostilities with the Americans while the Russians are still a formidable opponent is"—Canaris lowered his voice to a whisper—"madness."

"I assure you, Hitler has no intention of attacking the Americans. The Japanese will do it for him."

"I'm not sure I understand."

Raeder smiled. "As you know, for several months the Führer has tried to convince the Japanese to join the war against Russia. A war on two fronts would place the Russians in an extremely difficult position."

Canaris resisted the impulse to remind Raeder that Hitler had placed Germany in exactly that same position.

Raeder went on. "Unfortunately, the Japanese remain unconvinced that a campaign against the Russians is in their best interest. They view themselves, quite properly in my opinion, as a Pacific power and have little interest in challenging the Russians on land. They see the United States as their main adversary and are more interested in removing the Americans as a threat to their designs in the Pacific."

Canaris nodded. He was beginning to see where this conversation was leading.

"The Führer, feeling that the best way to keep the Americans out of our hair is to have them involved in a war with the Japanese, has decided to encourage the Japanese with their Pacific plans."

"It would be very difficult for the Japanese to challenge the United States. Any war in the Pacific would of necessity be a naval one, and the U.S. Navy is considerably larger than the Japanese."

"Quite true," Raeder said, "but Japanese Ambassador Oshima had some very interesting observations about the matchup of naval forces. Although the U.S. outnumbers the Japanese in battleships seventeen to twelve, only nine of the U.S. ships—none of them built after 1921—are in the Pacific. The other eight—including the only two modern ships in the American Navy—are with the Atlantic Fleet."

"My information is that the Japanese have only ten battleships."

"Oshima told me, in strictest confidence, that the Japanese have completed the construction of two monstrous ships of almost seventy thousand tons, each with nine eighteen-inch guns."

Canaris was surprised. Although it had been rumored for years that the Japanese were building a new class of battleship, ships of such proportions were unheard of.

"He showed me photographs of the ships," Raeder said. "They are incredible. Twice the size of even the latest American battleships, and more than a match for any ship afloat. The Americans are in for quite a surprise when these two monsters appear over the horizon."

"What about aircraft carriers?" asked Canaris.

"The Japanese have eight; the Americans seven. But, once again, only four of the American carriers are in the Pacific. In cruisers the matchups are even more in the Japanese favor. The Japanese have thirty-five cruisers to the Americans thirty-seven, but half of the American cruisers are assigned to the Atlantic." Raeder made a palms-up gesture. "So it seems that the vaunted American naval superiority in the Pacific is merely a myth. The Japanese certainly do not believe it."

"Apparently, the problems of a two-ocean navy are more than the Americans can bear," Canaris said.

With that Raeder reached into the briefcase that he had placed at his feet and removed a rolled-up map. He unrolled the map on Canaris's desk, placing paperweights at all four corners to hold it in place. "This, my old friend, is where you and your 'Jaguar' enter the picture."

The map showed Central America with the southern portion of Mexico in the upper left corner and the northern tip of Colombia at the lower right. Canaris looked at the map. His sad eyes looked up at Raeder. "The Panama Canal," he said simply.

"Exactly," Raeder said. "The Panama Canal is what makes the Americans a two-ocean naval power. Next to the British Navy, the American Navy is the world's largest, but it is divided somewhat unequally between two oceans. The Atlantic Fleet is smaller, but contains the navy's two most modern battleships; the Pacific Fleet is larger, but antiquated. The Japanese feel that their navy is superior in every way to the American Pacific Fleet—more aircraft carriers, more modern battleships, and certainly more combat experience." Raeder leaned forward and pointed at the map. "The Japanese soon intend to engage the American Pacific Fleet in a major battle that the Japanese are certain will be resolved in their favor. Before the Japanese involve themselves in the war, they intend to eliminate the U.S. Pacific Fleet as a threat to their ambitions in the Pacific."

"And how," Canaris asked, "do they intend to achieve this remarkable feat?"

"Oshima was rather vague as to the method, but he seemed quite confident that the Japanese can destroy the Americans with one decisive victory. He seems very interested in anything we can tell him about the British attack on the Italian Fleet at Taranto."

Canaris nodded. In November of 1940 British naval aircraft, while losing only two planes, had sunk half the Italian Fleet while it sat at anchorage. Canaris was aware that the Japanese had been gathering as much information about the British method of attack as they could. "I think you will see a similar effort on the part of the Japanese," he said. "They have a penchant for the unexpected, undeclared initiation of hostilities. It is very much in keeping with their philosophy."

"You are, perhaps, correct. I had forgotten that the great Japanese naval victory over the Russians in 1905 was an unannounced attack on their fleet while it rested at anchorage. Hostilities were commenced without a declaration of war." Raeder shrugged as if that formality were of no importance. "Whatever method they choose, the Japanese are quite confident that they can similarly annihilate the American Fleet."

"Their confidence is certainly commendable," said Canaris.

"The Japanese are certain that they can eliminate the American naval presence in the Pacific in less than two weeks." Raeder looked at his map again. "There is just one thing that concerns them." He stabbed a finger at the Panama Canal. "If the Americans are able to reinforce the Pacific Fleet before the battle is successfully concluded, the Japanese superiority vanishes overnight. The Panama Canal is the only way that this could be accomplished. Using the canal, the Americans can have naval reinforcements in the Pacific in less than two weeks. If the canal is inoperable, it will take more than a month. You—and Jaguar—must stop them."

"By destroying the canal," Canaris said.

"Precisely."

"Do we have a timetable for this project?" Canaris asked.

Raeder smiled. "Our Japanese friends say it is essential that the canal be closed sometime between the first and second week in December. And that it remain closed for at least a month and possibly more."

"Has the Führer given any thought to how this should be accomplished?"

"By explosive device planted at some strategic point in the canal."

"That will take a great deal of explosives."

Raeder said nothing.

"I seem to recall," Canaris said, "that Reichsmarschall Goering bragged earlier this year that his Luftwaffe could close the canal at any time he so decided."

"I think the Führer has finally learned not to take the fat one's boasts too seriously. The Reichsmarschall was noticeably quiet during these discussions."

"Large amounts of explosives will have to be purchased and agents will have to be paid. Such an undertaking will take a great deal of money. Much more than my agency will be able to supply. We have already strained our South American budget to the limit."

What Canaris did not say, but the grand admiral was well aware of, was that the Abwehr was virtually bankrupt in South America. In June of 1941 the American government had frozen all German and Italian assets. This, coupled with a British currency embargo, had made it virtually impossible for the Germans to pay agents in South America or even to bring money into the hemisphere. It was common knowledge in Berlin that the network of long established agents was in danger of collapsing because of a lack of funds.

"The Führer understands your problem, Willi," Raeder said. "All of our remaining funds in Mexico and South America will be placed at your disposal."

Canaris smiled grimly. "Begging your pardon, Admiral,"

he said, "but even if all of the remaining currency were given to me immediately, it would not begin to pay the debts we have incurred, to say nothing of financing an operation of this magnitude."

"Our funds are limited," Raeder said, "but the Italians have agreed to contribute almost one million in American currency, which is presently in the bank of Mexico, and the Japanese, who obviously have much to gain from this venture, will contribute more than three million American dollars from their accounts in Mexican banks." Raeder smiled. "Do you think that your man can accomplish his goal with as much as four million dollars at his disposal?"

Canaris calculated quickly. Half of that amount would pay off his accrued debts and fund his South American ventures for a year. He was sure that Robles could mount an operation against the Panama Canal for much less than the amount that was left. If he played this properly, he could destroy the canal and have enough money to operate agents in South America for the foreseeable future. Five hundred thousand dollars, he thought, should be more than enough for a man as resourceful as Jaguar to buy as many men and as much explosives as were required to destroy the canal. "I'm sure that amount should be quite sufficient," he said.

"You, my friend, are being entrusted with all of the foreign currency in the western hemisphere possessed not only by Germany, but by Italy and Japan as well. After this there is no more. The price of failure will be high."

"I understand, Admiral."

"Very well, then. Instruct Jaguar to return to South America to await further instructions. Arrangements are already underway to have the money ready for his use. You will, of course, be in charge of how, and in what amounts, it is to be distributed to him. I would suggest that the money remain in German hands for as long as possible. I would not want to hand over such a substantial amount in one lump sum."

"Agreed, Admiral," said Canaris. "I think an initial payment of . . . say . . . five hundred thousand dollars should be more than sufficient to get the plan underway.

Then my man in Buenos Aires can dole out the remaining funds as needed."

"I think that would be best," Raeder said.

It would also be best, Canaris thought, to have the funds under his control at all times. "I will see to it that Jaguar is contacted right away."

CHAPTER 3

As always, Robles was on guard. He took nothing for granted. At the time of the appointed meeting he waited in a café across the street from the railway station until the German exited onto the Avenida da Liberdade. Every few minutes the German removed his hat and looked at his watch, and Robles smiled at the ridiculousness of this prearranged identification signal. Robles watched him and the others who passed by for at least ten minutes before he decided that it was safe to cross over and introduce himself. By that time the German was already irritated by his tardiness.

His name was Colonel Hans Meister, and he was an Abwehr officer who had come from Berlin to meet with Robles. He was tall and in his late forties with fine-chiseled, aristocratic features. He wore a dark, heavy overcoat over a wool suit and a gray wide-brimmed hat. If the essence of intelligence work was to be inconspicuous, thought Robles, then this one was in the wrong profession.

Meister saw Robles as he approached him from across the avenue. The German identified Robles from the photograph

18

in his file at Abwehr headquarters but did not allow that flash of recognition to register on his face. Instead, he looked beyond Robles to assure himself that the man was not being followed. After introducing himself with a coded phrase that Robles had been told to expect, Meister suggested that they walk along the Avenue toward Edward VII Park, which had been named for a visiting British monarch.

The park was almost a mile away, and for most of the time they walked in silence. The Avenida da Liberdade reminded Meister of the Champs-Elysées before the war. The sidewalks were teeming with smiling pedestrians, and the thoroughfare itself was jammed with vehicular traffic. Paris, he thought a little sadly, was not such a happy city these days.

When they were in sight of the park, Meister, speaking in German, said, "The admiral sends you his warmest greetings, and I am to pass along to you the heartiest congratulations from the Führer himself on your latest venture."

"I am always happy to serve Adolf Hitler," Robles said.

Meister turned his face away so that Robles would not see his smile. With enough fools like this willing to die for the Führer, he thought, perhaps he could survive this ridiculous war. "The Führer has personally selected you for what is possibly the most important single mission of the war."

"Personally selected?"

"Yes," Meister said. "If you successfully complete this mission, you will be brought to Berlin for a personal audience with the Führer."

"What does the Führer want me to do?"

"Quite simple, really," said Meister. "He wants you to destroy the Panama Canal. At least make it impassable for a few months."

For a while Robles seemed lost in thought. They were in the park now, on a wide concrete walkway that circled a large fountain. Meister found an empty bench near the entrance. Robles sat beside him while Meister scanned the surrounding area. No one was within earshot.

Neither man paid any attention to the man who had

followed them into the park and selected a seat across from them that was well beyond listening distance.

"Do you think that you can accomplish this?" Meister asked.

"It is an immense undertaking," Robles said. "I would need almost unlimited resources." He did not add that even then the job was probably impossible.

"I am here to inform you that the Führer and the German people are prepared to give you every assistance that you will need."

"That means money," said Robles. "Lots of money."

"At this very moment Abwehr agents in Mexico are holding a considerable amount of money—in American dollars—which they are prepared to make available to you as soon as you return to South America."

"How much?"

Meister smiled. "Considerable. The head of the Abwehr office in Buenos Aires will be in charge of dispensing the funds. You will receive a substantial initial payment in American dollars to finance the operation. The exact amount will be determined later."

Robles nodded.

"More can be provided as required. Also, at the same time you're conducting your operation, other operatives will be performing acts of sabotage all across the Americas. Bridges will be destroyed, military and industrial installations sabotaged; the Americans will learn that we can strike wherever and whenever we choose."

"Does the Führer intend to declare war on the United States?"

"No, but he has decided to give our friends the Japanese an assist with their plans in the Pacific—and to give the Americans something to worry about besides meddling in our affairs in Europe."

"When do we begin?" Robles asked.

"Immediately." Meister gave Robles an envelope. "Inside you will find the name of your contact and the phrase he will expect you to use in identifying yourself."

Robles slipped the envelope into his coat pocket. He

would memorize and destroy the contents in his hotel room. "How much time do I have?" he said.

"You must be prepared to strike between the first and second weeks in December."

"That is little more than one month. I'm not sure it is possible within such a timetable. I will have to purchase an enormous amount of explosives, decide where to plant the charges, and find men who can transport the explosives to the desired locations."

"I can, perhaps, help you with some of those problems. The man you have been told to contact can put you in touch with someone who has access to a large cache of military-grade explosives. Much of what you require may already be in place."

"And if I need anything else?"

"Our consular offices can give you all the assistance you require, and relay any messages to and from Berlin."

"If I am to be successful, I will need the full cooperation of everyone involved. Even then it may not be possible to accomplish such a thing on such short notice."

"I was told that you are a man who can do the impossible. Besides, the timing is dictated by whatever the Japanese are planning, and the Führer has promised to fulfill his part of the bargain."

Robles stood up. "Then I shall leave immediately. The sooner I begin, the better."

The two men shook hands, and Meister watched Robles walk back in the direction from which they had come. He almost felt sadness as he watched Robles hurry off to do his duty for the Führer and for Germany. Men like this do not live for very long, he thought. Meister waited until Robles had left the park before he, too, headed back toward the center of the city.

The man on the park bench across from them continued to read his paper for several minutes until both of them had disappeared. Then he got up, folded his paper neatly, and tucked it under his arm before leaving the park.

* * *

At the British Embassy on Rua S. Domingos a' Lapa the undersecretary to the ambassador stood up when John Simpson was ushered into his office. "Well, then, John, how did it go?"

"Quite well, sir, I think," Simpson said in a high-pitched, nasal whine that was barely distinguishable as speech. "The German you had me follow met with someone outside the railway station. They walked to the park and had a rather interesting conversation about sabotage activities in the Americas."

Simpson was stone deaf, his speech the tortured approximation of a man who had never heard the sounds or patterns of conversation. A Cambridge graduate, Simpson's dreams of a position in the Foreign Service had been thwarted by his disability. He had been forced to take a position with an accounting firm where he had no direct contact with clients and his pained speech was not an embarrassment to the firm. In the spring of 1940, however, a former classmate who now worked for the Secret Intelligence Service had contacted him and made a rather interesting proposal. The classmate who remembered Simpson's lip-reading ability proposed that Simpson take a position with the intelligence service, where he could turn his handicap into an advantage. For the past year Simpson had been assigned to the British Embassy in Lisbon as an aide to the undersecretary, who himself was actually the head of MI6 in the Iberian peninsula. Portugal, neutral in the war, still maintained diplomatic relations with all of the warring nations and was a hotbed of espionage activity. Simpson was kept very busy "listening to" conversations between the various agents of the Axis powers.

"Unfortunately, I was unable to get anything about specific targets, but apparently they are going to make a major effort in the very near future."

The undersecretary strained to decipher Simpson's words. Even after a year he still found it difficult to understand what the man was saying. After a few minutes of effort he smiled kindly. "Well, John," he said, "why don't you write up your report and let me have a look at it? If it's as important as you say, I'd like to get it off in the diplomatic pouch to London on the next flight."

Simpson, frustrated as ever by his inability to communicate, stood up. He gave a simple nod in acknowledgment of the undersecretary's orders and left the room.

CHAPTER 4

The rain had stopped, and the streets around the public market in the old colonial section of the city were suddenly alive with pedestrians. Children played in the puddles left by the sudden storm while the adults, casting apprehensive glances skyward, tried to get on about their tasks before the next deluge drove them indoors again.

The market teemed with the produce of Panama—mangoes, bananas, pineapples, avocados—and with the products brought here from around the world. Multicolored scarves and blouses were sold from pushcarts by native vendors who seemed to belong to an earlier century. Shoppers carried gaily colored straw bags filled with fruits and vegetables and sometimes a freshly killed chicken. Shop owners called to passing shoppers in an attempt to attract them to their wares. Everyone yelled at everyone else. The noise was deafening.

An automobile, a 1939 Packard, windows down against the oppressive heat, made its way slowly through the shoppers and the handcarts on the street. The driver honked the horn to disperse the crowd, but few, if any, paid him any heed. The two men in the backseat did not seem concerned that their journey was laboriously slow. They were deep in conversation and oblivious to much of what went on about them.

One of them was an American. His name was Harrison Fox, and he had lived in Panama for several years. He was the owner of the Panama Club, a popular night spot near the Via España in the heart of Panama City's celebrated entertainment district. His companion was Ernesto Garcia, a Panamanian who was his friend and business partner. Garcia was in his middle forties. His once lean and muscular body had become increasingly soft over the years. Fox was almost ten years younger, and despite the growing inactivity of his life, he still was lean and dangerous looking.

"I just think that now is an especially ominous time, Harry," Garcia said. "You should be very careful."

Fox turned from the window where he had been watching the children splash through the puddles. He smiled. "I thought it might get easier when Arias got the boot."

Less than a month earlier a coup, promoted by the United States, had deposed the anti-American president of Panama and replaced his government with one more friendly to the United States. The former president, Arnulfo Arias, was now in exile in Cuba.

"I don't think so," Garcia said. "Those government officials that we used to bribe are no longer in power. And the new government might feel more pressured to honor an extradition request by the Americans."

Harry sighed. "Here we go again."

The Packard had finally pushed its way through the crowds on the narrow streets and edged its way out onto the more spacious Avenida Central when the driver spoke for the first time.

"I think somebody is following us, Harry," he said.

"You sure?"

"No. But he's been behind us for some time. Every time I turn, he turns."

Harry Fox looked at Garcia, who gave him a knowing look. "Keep an eye on him," Fox told the driver. He turned back to Garcia. "If someone was going to do something, the market would have been the perfect place."

Garcia shrugged. "Unless he's got something planned up ahead." Garcia reached inside his jacket and pulled out a small revolver. He smiled. "Just in case."

"Julio," Harry said to the driver. "Give me the extra pistol."

Julio did as he was told, carefully handing the weapon to the man in the backseat.

Harry took the gun and looked at it distastefully. It was a nine-millimeter automatic, made in Germany. Expertly he pulled back the slide and chambered the first shell. "I hate this kinda stuff," he said.

Garcia grinned. He seemed to be enjoying himself.

"They're still there," Julio said after another turn. "You want me to lose him?"

"No," Harry said. "Let's see what he's up to."

Julio turned the car onto another wide avenue lined with acacias and royal poinciana trees. He kept the car at a steady pace so as not to arouse the suspicions of the men in the following car. The car behind them drew closer and then pulled out into the outside lane.

"I think he's going to pass, Harry," Julio said.

"Give him plenty of room."

The car, a large black sedan, passed them without incident and raced ahead until it was a small speck heading toward the Via Espana. The two men in the front seat had not given so much as a glance in the direction of Fox or Garcia.

Harry Fox looked at the gun in his hand and then at Garcia. "We must be getting paranoid."

Garcia shrugged. "Better safe than sorry."

They rode in silence for a time until Julio said, "You want me to drop you at the club first, or should we stop to pick up Emilio?"

Harry hesitated and Julio explained. "The new man. Emilio? He asked if I could pick him up today and bring him to work. I told you earlier."

Harry sighed and looked at his watch. "You might as well pick him up now. We'll wait in the car."

Moments later Julio turned the Packard into one of the side streets off the avenue. The narrow street was lined with two-story buildings—shops on the ground level and apartments above. Halfway down the street Julio braked hard. "Damn," he said.

Harry looked up. "What is it?" he said, but before Julio could answer, Fox saw the black sedan blocking the road ahead of them. The doors opened and two men stepped out into the street. Both were armed with revolvers.

"Back up. Now!" Garcia said, his voice edged with tension.

Julio threw the Packard into reverse and quickly backed down the street. After only a short distance he slammed on the brakes. "Damn," he said again.

Fox turned to see that their path was blocked by a second car identical to the first. The doors opened and three men jumped out, one of them holding a Thompson submachine gun. Harry recognized the weapon immediately. Back in Kansas City, during the bootleg wars of Prohibition, he'd had many opportunities to witness the Thompson's deadly efficiency. "Damn is right," Harry said softly.

The street was suddenly—almost magically—empty. Where only moments before there had been a bustling side street, with shop owners and patrons everywhere, there was now a deserted, ominous alleyway.

Fox and Garcia did not wait for the men to approach them. Without a word between them, they opened the rear doors of the Packard and both dived out into the street from opposite sides. They easily found cover in shop doorways directly across from each other.

Julio was right behind Fox. They stood back-to-back in the doorway. "I've got these two covered," he said to Harry.

"We'll take the other three," Harry said.

The man with the submachine gun opened up and the forty-five caliber slugs dug heavily into the wall above Harry's head.

"Get the one with the tommy gun first!" Harry yelled across the street to Garcia. He knew that was where the real danger came from. Anyone with such a weapon became an instant killing machine.

Another burst from the Thompson was again several yards above Harry's head. "He's not too good with that thing," Harry said.

Garcia opened fire first, but he was too far away for his small pistol to have any real value. It was enough, however, to send the others scurrying for cover. Harry stepped out from the doorway as they moved away from him and fired one shot at the man with the submachine gun. He missed, adjusted his aim quickly, and squeezed off another round just as his target was about to step inside a doorway.

The man yelped in pain as the bullet struck him in the hip. He went down in the street clutching the wound. The Thompson went flying out of reach.

Harry turned his attention to the two who approached from the other end of the street. To his surprise they were running back toward their car. He looked at Julio, who said, "I didn't even fire a shot." The two men jumped inside their car, and the engine roared to life. In seconds the car went racing down the street. Harry looked across the street to Garcia, who shook his head.

They looked back up the street and saw that the others were also scrambling for their car. The wounded man had his arms around the shoulders of his companions, his left leg dragging behind as they pulled him along with them. Harry fired a single shot well above their heads, and without hesitation they dropped the wounded man and dashed for the car. In reverse, the car careened wildly back down the street as they made their escape.

Harry and Garcia stepped out from their doorways and cautiously moved toward the man who lay groaning in the street. He was a young man, no more than twenty-five, and he looked up, his eyes fearful, as the two men approached. He spoke rapidly in English, looking directly at Harry. "I did not intend to kill you," he said.

"What the hell are you talking about?" Harry said.

"I was only supposed to scare you this time."

Harry nodded, remembering the shots that were well over his head. "This time?"

The eyes darted from one to the other. "Next time—if you didn't listen to reason—I was supposed to kill you."

Harry raised the pistol and aimed at the man's face. "That's too bad," he said.

The man's eyes widened in fear, and he crossed himself. He squeezed his eyes shut and said "Sweet Jesus" over and over again in Spanish.

"Who sent you?" Harry said, although he already knew the answer. "And what does he want?"

The man, relieved to still be alive, opened his eyes. "Viega," he said. "Narciso Viega. I am to frighten you into leaving Panama."

Harry lowered the pistol. "You didn't do a very good job," he said.

Garcia grinned. "Shall we take him to a doctor or leave him until his friends come back?"

The man recovered quickly from his surprise that they were not going to kill him. "I will just wait for them," he said. "I don't want to be any trouble."

Harry and Garcia looked at each other and laughed. They left the wounded man and went back to their car. Julio was standing by the front door. "Nice shooting, boss," he said matter-of-factly. "But I thought I was supposed to be the bodyguard."

Harry smiled and gave Julio the pistol as he climbed into the backseat.

"You still want me to pick up Emilio?" Julio asked.

"He won't be here," Harry said.

"I don't get it," Julio said.

"He set this up," Garcia said. "He was the only one who knew that we might stop by to pick him up. He must be working for Viega."

Julio nodded and got behind the wheel. He looked into the rearview mirror. "I knew we might stop here, boss," he said. "It was me who suggested it."

Harry leaned forward and touched Julio on the shoulder. "Drive, amigo," he said.

Julio put the Packard in gear and the big car moved silently down the street.

"Just like old times, Harry," Garcia said as he watched the street roll by his window.

Harry held up his right hand, fingers outstretched, to reveal a slight tremor. "Not quite," he said. "Nobody's shot at me in some time. I'd forgotten what it's like."

Garcia slapped him on the back. "You were still the same old Harry, my friend. Cool as a cucumber."

Harry looked at the still shaking fingers. "Hardly," he said.

Garcia ignored the comment. "That bastard Viega wants to take over the Panama Club. But it'll take more than that cheap hood to run you out of Panama, Harry." It was more of a question than a statement of fact.

Harry Fox was silent. Narciso Viega, he knew, was something more than a cheap hood. Viega had until recently been a cabinet official in the government of Arnulfo Arias. Until now his attempts to acquire a controlling interest in Harry's business had always been easily rebuffed. Now that Viega was out of power, he had obviously decided to intensify the effort. Despite Garcia's bravado, Harry knew that they were both aware that the game had escalated to a new and much more dangerous level. "I don't know, Ernesto," he said. "You heard what that punk said—this was only a warning. Next time we might not be so lucky."

"We can handle them, Harry. We always have before."

"I'm not sure that I have the stomach for this kind of game anymore."

Garcia nodded sadly, but said nothing. He looked away. Not too long ago, he thought, they would have laughed at what had just happened. Maybe they were both getting too old for this kind of game.

CHAPTER 5

Hamilton, Bermuda; November 6, 1941

Susan Spencer mopped the sweat from her brow and took a look at the clock on the wall of the windowless basement room. She sighed when she realized that she still had more than two hours left on her work shift. Around her, at desks identical to hers, sat young women, all apparently engrossed in reading personal mail. The personal mail, of course, did not belong to them.

Susan Spencer was twenty-three years old and a native of Toronto, Canada. She had come to Bermuda, lured by the prospect of excitement and romance. The idea of working as an intelligence operative at a luxury hotel in a beautiful semitropical climate had certainly had its appeal. Most of the appeal, however, had been the certainty that Bermuda would be teeming with eligible young men in uniform. What she had found, unfortunately, was that most of the men assigned to Bermuda were either married or middle-aged— or both. The young men she had hoped to meet were off at the front with all the other young men. She was here with several hundred young women, mostly Canadians, most of whom had believed, as she had, that they had been assigned to a tropical paradise.

Instead, Susan found herself in a swelteringly hot basement, reading a letter to someone's grandmother in Munich. The chances were one in a thousand—make that ten thousand—that this particular letter was anything other than what it seemed to be. There seemed to be nothing out of the ordinary in the letter, none of the stilted phrases, repetitive patterns, or out-of-context statements that she had been taught to look for. She wondered why the controllers had singled out this particular piece of mail for inspection. Perhaps, she thought, the address was one that had been previously used to send a message to Germany. Reluctantly she read the letter again, not wanting to miss something that had not been apparent in the first reading. Still nothing. She sighed and refolded the letter and placed it back into the envelope and into the pile of previously inspected mail. Someone else would seal the envelopes so that no one would ever suspect they had been opened.

On this, the early shift, Susan was one of thirty young women, called trappers, whose job it was to inspect the personal mail that had been illegally removed from aircraft that stopped to refuel in Bermuda on the way to Europe. The Bermuda operation was part of British Security Coordination's effort to intercept messages between Germany and its agents in the Western Hemisphere.

In order to perpetuate this scheme the Pan Am Clippers, giant flying boats that carried as many as seventy-seven passengers to and from Europe, were routinely delayed by "engine trouble" or "risky weather conditions" on the refueling stops in Bermuda. Those who traveled frequently between the United States and Europe were not long in realizing that the Bermuda stops were always inordinately long. Some American travelers complained to their government about these high-handed and obviously illegal tactics, but under orders from President Roosevelt no action was taken that might have dissuaded the British from their illicit labors.

In the sweaty basement rooms of the Hamilton Princess

Hotel, a round-the-clock procession of agents inspected the thousands of pieces of mail that passed between the United States and Europe each week. Of particular interest was the diplomatic pouch containing messages from the German Embassy in Washington to the German Foreign Office in Berlin. Diplomatic mail was, of course, protected from seizure and inspection by several international agreements that were theoretically still in force, but British intelligence agents routinely opened, inspected, photographed, and then expertly resealed hundreds of German diplomatic documents each week. Suspicious-looking private mail was also expertly opened, examined and resealed. The BSC agents in Bermuda had learned to recognize addresses in Spain and Portugal that were used by German agents in the Americas as conduits for messages to Berlin.

These BSC agents monitored all forms of communication between Europe and the Western Hemisphere. Men and women, hunched over radio monitoring equipment, listened to the shortwave transmissions between German agents in North and South America and their controlling officers in Berlin. Others listened for the faint transmissions from U-boats in the North Atlantic. Most of the radio messages were in code and had to be laboriously decoded by any one of several methods then in use by British intelligence. However, some of the messages—especially those from the U-boats—were encoded by what the Germans called the Enigma machine, a typewriterlike device that encoded messages into an apparently indecipherable labyrinth of meaningless letters. With the help of a captured Enigma machine British Intelligence in Bletchley Park, just north of London, had been decoding German messages since the summer of 1940. With a copy of this device, BSC agents in Bermuda, at what came to be known as "the Bletchley of the Tropics," routinely decoded messages between U-boat commanders and Kriegsmarine submarine headquarters in Wilhelmshaven.

Susan's hair was stuck to the back of her neck, and her undergarments were clinging to her body. She would have given anything to strip off her clothes, go outside, and jump into the waters of the Great Bermuda Sound, which was no more than fifty yards from where she sat. She smiled at the thought. Three weeks ago, she and a young sailor had done exactly that under a bright Bermuda moon on a secluded cove in Somerset. Afterward they had made love on the beach until early morning. One thing about men who spent most of their time at sea, she thought; it made them exceedingly horny. That was three weeks ago, she wailed to herself. She couldn't wait until his ship was back in port. In the meantime maybe she would just go for that nude swim in the sound. That would certainly stir things up around here. She thought again. Probably no one would notice. The other girls wouldn't care, and the pudgy old men who worked down here had probably forgotten what a young, naked body looked like.

She looked up as someone stopped in front of her desk. Case in point. Arthur Parker, her controlling supervisor. Parker was fifty-four, short, bald, and without evidence of a single muscle anywhere on his body. A cigarette dangled from his lips, the smoke making his eyes watery. Parker smoked two packs a day and smelled of sweat, beer, and cigarettes. He was typical of most of the men who worked here. When Arthur starts to look good, she thought, I'm getting out of here.

"'Lo, luv," he said. "If you've finished with these, I'll just take 'em off to the next station."

She was grateful that he was not replenishing the supply of mail in the In box on her desk. "We almost finished?" she asked.

Parker nodded. "Hoping to get the clipper off in an hour or so."

Susan sighed and sat back in her chair. "Good," she said, stretching her arms high above her head.

"Not to worry, luv," Parker said impishly. "Another clipper's arriving in about fifteen minutes."

"Jesus," Susan said, although she knew the clipper schedule as well as anyone. She lowered her head onto the desk. The fan on her desk blew directly in her face, but it was not enough to relieve the oppressive heat. She cushioned her head on her arms for a moment, then looked up at an obviously amused Parker. "I've got to get out of here for a bit, Arthur. The heat's getting to me."

Parker smiled. "Go ahead, then," he said. "Just don't disappear, in case I need you."

"You're a doll, Arthur," she said. "I'll be right outside."

Quickly, before he could change his mind or someone could ask her where she was going, she left the room and went up the stairs to the ground-floor level. She pushed open the back door and stepped out onto the lawn. Pink and glistening in the bright Bermuda sun, the Hamilton Princess Hotel sat on the edge of Hamilton Harbor where the harbor opens up into the Great Bermuda Sound. Regal in its colonial splendor, the hotel seemed untouched by distant war, but most of the rooms were either empty or requisitioned by the intelligence agents of British Security Coordination.

Susan walked across the lawn to the water's edge, where spread out before her were the sparkling blue-green waters of the Great Bermuda Sound. On the other side of the sound, dazzlingly white, were the houses that dotted the tropical green hillsides of the far shore. Directly to her right was the New York Clipper, one of a series of giant seaplanes that spanned the globe for Pan American Airways. The clippers were presently one of the few methods of passenger transportation between the Western Hemisphere and war-ravaged Europe. The great aircraft was tethered to the long dock that led directly to the property of the Hamilton Princess. As the plane bobbed gently at anchor, Susan could see several men reloading the mail sacks and luggage, which had been removed for inspection.

The cooling breeze off the water was incredibly delicious, and Susan unbuttoned the top buttons of her blouse and held the fabric away from her body, allowing the wind to caress her. For one brief moment she considered her earlier thought about stripping herself naked and leaping into the water, but it was, of course, only a thought.

Susan kicked off her shoes, sat on the edge of the bulkhead that separated the lawn from the harbor, and put her feet into the water. She could feel her body temperature drop. Looking around the sound, it was easy to see what had made her choose this assignment. This was one of the most beautiful places that she had ever seen. She had even been here before the war, and her remembrance of that time made today's reality even more difficult to bear. But at least for now she could close her eyes and enjoy the tranquility of the moment.

Even before she heard the sound, Susan felt the vibration of the incoming clipper from somewhere off in the distance. She knew that it would soon be time to get back to work.

The late afternoon silence of Hamilton Harbor was shattered by the arrival of the Lisbon Clipper. At first there had been only a distant drone, but soon the growl of the four Pratt and Whitney engines grew to an ear-shattering roar as the great Boeing 314 flying boat, wings glinting sunlight, swooped in low across the sound. Then the clipper banked into a tight circle that brought her directly into the wind. The huge plane touched down gently in the blue-green water and, after a brief run toward the opposite shore, turned left and began to taxi toward the Hamilton Princess.

The plane was tied up across from the New York Clipper, and the passengers, all of whom were men, filed out onto the dock, squinting in the bright sunlight. Robles and the other passengers were taken by launch to the Royal Bermuda Yacht Club, where drinks were served on the terrace overlooking the harbor. Refueling, they were told, would take little more than an hour, and then they would be on their way to Baltimore, the clipper's final destination. Robles wondered why they had not been taken to the Hamilton Princess, which was directly across from where the clipper was berthed. Instead, they had been ferried at least a mile away from where their plane had landed. From the yacht club, he noted, they could not see the clipper. Some instinct told him that there was a reason for the delay and for keeping the passengers together and isolated from the aircraft.

An hour later the travelers were informed by one of the flight crew that "a minor oil leak in number two engine" would be the cause of a further delay. The postponed departure, it was promised, would be a short one. In the meantime, the twenty-two travelers were invited to dine at the yacht club.

After dinner the disappointed passengers were informed by the clipper's second officer that the problem with the aircraft was somewhat more serious than had at first been anticipated. Repairs could not be made until morning, necessitating an overnight stay in Bermuda. The passengers let out a collective groan, but under the circumstances no one voiced any vociferous complaints. Arrangements had already been made for them to spend the night at the yacht club's guest quarters, where, they were assured, every effort would be made to guarantee their comfort.

Robles cursed under his breath. It was now impossible for him to make his connection from Baltimore to Havana, and from there on to Panama City.

Moments later a British officer appeared on the scene. He wore a white shirt, with navy blue epaulets at the shoulder which identified his rank, white dress shorts, and white socks worn to just below the knee. The officer cleared his throat and waited until he had the attention of the group. "Good evening," he said in a loud but pleasant voice. "I am Lieutenant-Commander Groves, and I am a part of His Majesty's naval defense forces in Bermuda." He looked around the room as if expecting questions. There were none. "You realize, of course, that Bermuda is an important British naval outpost. Consequently, it is my duty to inform you that you are restricted to these premises until your scheduled departure."

There was a murmur of dissent from the passengers and someone asked, "Can't we even go for a walk?"

Groves smiled pleasantly, but his tone was firm. "I'm afraid not. Anyway, the shops have already closed, and none of the hotels are offering any sort of service that might interest you. However, we have given special permission for the bar here at the yacht club to remain open until midnight. We hope that you can pass the time pleasantly and be on your way by morning."

"What about our luggage?" someone asked. "A change of clothing might make our stay more pleasant."

"I'll see what I can do," Groves said, "but I wouldn't count on it." He was gone before there were any more questions.

The passengers looked at one another with bemused acceptance. Robles, always suspicious of anything that was out of the ordinary, pretended nonchalance when one of the passengers gave him a quizzical look. Whatever was happening, he thought, obviously had to do with the aircraft. Perhaps the British were using the clippers to smuggle items into or out of America. Tonight, under cover of darkness, he would try to find out what was going on.

Lieutenant-Commander Groves, who was the station chief of British Naval Intelligence, Bermuda, looked up at the officer who stood in front of his desk. "Sit down, Tommy," he said.

Lieutenant Tom Whitson, Groves's second in command, took the offered seat. "You got a good look at him, then?" he said.

"Yes," Groves answered. "I just wanted to see the bastard for myself. From the description sent by the Lisbon station, I'm quite certain that this Robles chap is our man."

"What do you think he's up to?"

"Maybe nothing." Groves looked at the message that had been delivered by one of the crewmen aboard the Lisbon Clipper. This was one of the methods by which the British Embassy in Lisbon communicated with the Bermuda outpost. "Says here that he was observed talking with a known German agent. We are to search his belongings for any contraband—weapons, explosives, radios, and the like—and, if we find anything, detain him here."

"Explosives?" Whitson said warily. "Shouldn't we inform the boys that there might be explosives in his things?"

"Already done," Groves said.

"And if we don't find anything?"

"Send him on his way, I suppose. We'll let BSC know that he's on his way in to Baltimore. They'll alert the FBI. The Americans will have to take it from there. Have you asked the girl to meet us here?"

Whitson was about to answer when there was a knock on the door. "That would be her now," he said.

"Come in, please."

Susan Spencer opened the door and entered Groves's office. "You wanted to see me, Commander?" she asked.

"Sit down, Miss Spencer," Groves said.

Nervously Susan slid into a seat. She wasn't at all sure why she had been called here. Perhaps her discontent with her working conditions had been noted and Groves was going to give her the old king and country speech. To hell with that, she thought.

"Let me get right to the point, Miss Spencer. I have an assignment which I would like to offer you."

Oh, shit, she thought. I'm being canned and sent back to Canada.

"There is a gentleman here today—arrived on the Lisbon Clipper—who apparently has contacts of some kind with German Military Intelligence," Groves continued. "We have detained his flight for the usual reasons"—he smiled —"with which you are obviously familiar, but we thought that we might use the time for a double purpose."

"I'm not sure I follow you," Susan said.

"We'd like you to strike up a conversation with this man. Perhaps elicit some information from him as to his intentions. An attractive young lady like you shouldn't have any problem interesting a gentleman traveler."

Susan smiled. This was the first time that Groves had referred to her as attractive. He was a little old for her, and he was married, but he was one of the better-looking men here. "What do you want to know?"

"Oh, anything. Where he's from . . . Where he's going . . . What he's up to . . . What he was doing in Lisbon . . . Any sort of information might be helpful."

Susan nodded. This seemed easy enough, and she was always eager to please. "All right."

"According to his passport," Groves said, "he's been doing a lot of traveling over the past two years. Places like Spain, North Africa, South Africa, the Middle East. SIS seems particularly interested in what he was doing in Iran." He looked at his notes. "He's even been to a few places in occupied Europe. You might ask him what he's been up to." He smiled. "We don't expect him to tell you that he's a spy or anything, but perhaps if we had a little more information about him, it might help us in our investigation."

"I'd be glad to help out," Susan said. Since her arrival in Bermuda, she had hoped for something more interesting than reading other people's mail. At the very least, the evening would be more exciting than what she had planned.

"Wonderful," Groves said. "He's over at the yacht club. Perhaps this evening you could make your way over there and look him up."

"How will I know him?"

"I've had a look at him," Groves said. "Perhaps I could meet you over there for a drink later. When he arrives, I'll point him out to you, and be on my way. I think you'll find him rather good looking. He's about thirty-five . . . dark hair . . . athletic type."

Susan had expected some fat, balding German. She smiled. "I think I can handle this."

"Yes," Groves said, smiling. "I thought of you right away."

That evening most of the twenty-two clipper passengers gathered in the bar at the Royal Bermuda Yacht Club. Earlier they had been assigned rooms, and Robles found that he was sharing accommodations with a salesman from a Pittsburgh steel manufacturer. The salesman, whose name was Frank Johnson, was a backslapping, handshaking, wise-cracking dynamo who was on his way home from an apparently successful sales meeting in London with a purchasing agent for the British government. Within ten minutes he had told Robles his entire life's history. Robles told enough about himself to satisfy Johnson's almost insatiable curiosity. When Johnson suggested that they visit the bar, Robles agreed in the hope that Johnson would find someone else to bore with his interminable stories.

"Might as well enjoy our stay in Bermuda," Johnson said as they walked down the stairs to the ground-floor level. "Can't do anything about it anyway. I was talking with one of the other passengers—Wilkins from Houston, sells petroleum products. He flies this route all the time, and he says that since the beginning of the war, he has always been delayed in Bermuda. Sometimes he flies the longer route—Lisbon to Africa to Brazil to Washington—and his planes are never delayed. Makes you wonder, doesn't it?"

"I hadn't really thought about it." Robles himself usually took this more southerly route from Europe to South America, but he had been unable to book passage on such short notice. Why, he wondered, was the Bermuda stopover the source of delay?

"And another thing," Johnson said. "They've got guards all over the damn place—front, back, and even out on the grounds. Makes you feel like a prisoner. What the hell do they think we're going to do?"

"I can't imagine," Robles said.

The bar was part of a large room dotted with small round tables and a baby grand piano in a corner near the entrance. Obviously, in peacetime the bar had been a pleasant place to spend an evening listening to music and enjoying a quiet drink. Already there were several customers there who were not a part of the clipper group. Robles quickly scanned the room. There was little there that interested or concerned him.

Robles and Johnson took seats at the yacht club bar and ordered drinks. There was a guard posted at the front entrance of the Royal Bermuda Yacht Club, presumably to make certain that none of the visitors left the premises. The guard spent most of his time talking to a young Bermudian who worked at the front desk. From his seat at the bar, Robles observed the man for a short time and decided that he was neither attentive to nor concerned with his task. He probably does this every time the clipper is in, Robles thought, and doesn't expect very many problems from the collection of businessmen who travel the trans-Atlantic route. Robles sipped his drink and waited for the opportunity to leave.

Johnson, with the trained eye of the traveling salesman, also scanned the bar. He immediately picked out two young women who sat alone at a table just a few feet from the bar.

"Opportunity knocks," he said. "Whaddya say we give those two a chance?"

"I don't think so," Robles said. He had barely given the women a glance.

"The little one with the dark hair seems to be giving you the eye," Johnson said.

Robles pivoted on his stool. The two women were indeed looking their way. The one with the dark hair was especially good looking. She smiled and raised her glass in a brief salute. Robles turned back to the bar. "I don't think so," he repeated.

"C'mon" Johnson said. "This could make our little delay very pleasant."

"Why don't you go ahead?" Robles said. "I think I'll just go back to the room. I haven't been feeling well."

"Suit yourself," Johnson said and picked up his drink and approached the two women.

That should keep him busy for a while, Robles thought, and immediately got up to leave. He went to the stairs and instead of going up to his room, he went down to the basement. There, he soon found what he was looking for—a door that led to the rear. He opened the door and stepped outside. The moonlight illuminated the waters of the sound. Immediately he saw the figure turn to face the direction from which the noise had come. Damn, he thought, another guard.

"Who goes there?" snapped the guard.

Robles hesitated. He was still in the shadows where he could not be seen and could easily close the door and quickly return to the bar. But that would arouse suspicions. "Just trying to get some air," he called.

"Not here you don't," the soldier said. "This area's off-limits to civilian personnel."

"Sorry," Robles said. "I'll just go back inside then." He held his breath.

"Righto," said the soldier. "Off with you, then."

Robles closed the door and made his way back upstairs to the ground floor. There had to be another way out. He walked through the lobby. The guard was still there. Still inattentive, but, nevertheless, still there.

"Glad you came back," a voice behind him said.

He jumped a little and turned to see the girl from the bar. He wondered if she had been looking for him or had just happened to be here in the lobby when he returned. Robles was not a man who believed in coincidence. He said nothing.

"Feeling better?" she asked.

"Pardon?"

She looked back over her shoulder in the direction of the bar. "Your friend said you weren't feeling well."

He remembered. "Oh. I'm fine. Just a little airsickness, perhaps." He took a good look at the girl for the first time. She really was good looking—large suggestive eyes and full pouting lips that she had covered with a deep red lipstick. She wore a snug-fitting blouse and skirt in an obvious attempt to accentuate her figure.

She shivered a little under his relentless stare. In a moment he had made her feel naked. For the first time she was not sure if that was good or bad. "Coming back into the bar?" she asked.

"I don't think so."

She touched his arm. "C'mon. We could have some fun. It's boring on this bloody island."

Robles was vain enough to think that women found him attractive, but wise enough to be wary whenever they threw themselves at him. After all, he thought, if she's looking for a good time, there are other men inside who would be much more receptive to her overtures.

"If you're bored with this place we could always try someplace else," she added.

"That would be most enjoyable," he said, "but I'm afraid that I and the other passengers are under a military block-ade for the evening."

The girl smiled. "I can help you run the blockade," she said.

"How?"

"I'll talk to the guard. Tell him that we're going to my place. He'll understand."

"And where is your place?"

"I have a room at the Bermudiana—just across the street . . . and a bottle of Johnnie Walker."

Robles looked around the room. His training and natural inclination told him to be cautious, but he was certain that her interest in him was sexual. She might also have other interests, but if she could get him out of here, it might be worth the risk. He smiled. "Let's go."

She touched his arm. "I'll talk to the guard," she said. "Wait here."

He watched her as she left. He, of course, wondered what authority she had to countermand the guard's orders that none of the passengers should leave the yacht club.

Her room at the Bermudiana was actually a two-room suite on the second floor, a small sitting room and a fairly large bedroom with two double beds. A french door in the living room led out to a small terrace. Another door in the bedroom led to a bathroom.

"How does a working girl afford such accommodations?" Robles said.

She laughed. "Every hotel on the island is empty. You can get a room for a song."

Robles wondered why then had the clipper passengers been roomed at the yacht club. "It's very nice," he said, sitting on the couch.

"I'll make you a drink," she said, and when he nodded she went to a small bar near the french door. "I'm glad you're here," she said, calling over her shoulder. "You don't know how boring it is here." She opened the french door. "There's always a nice breeze in the evening. By the way, my name's Susan—Susan Spencer."

He had no reason to hide his real name. "Carlos Robles," he said.

"I hope it's true what they say about Latins," she whispered loud enough for him to hear.

While Susan made him a drink, she began to pepper him with questions. Most were the usual "get acquainted" type questions—Where are you from? What do you do? How do you like your job? Robles answered them truthfully, but incompletely. He had found that one was less likely to be tripped up by the truth. She seemed genuinely interested in his travels, and he told her that his job required that he make several European trips each year.

Robles answered her questions and pondered his predicament. He wanted to get out of here as quickly as he could so that he could make his way to the clipper to see what, if anything, was going on at the airplane. The girl obviously had other intentions. He watched her. She was attractive—nice legs, good slim body. He sighed. Business before pleasure, he thought. Perhaps he could conclude his business at the clipper and come back.

Susan brought him his drink and sat next to him on the couch. As she sat, she hiked up her skirt and crossed her legs, momentarily revealing a generous portion of thigh. Robles, knowing that the display had been for his benefit, smiled and began to regret that he had more pressing problems than how to spend the evening with a beautiful young woman. He knew that his Abwehr controllers would be very interested in what was going on with the Lisbon Clipper. Why, for instance, was the clipper always delayed in Bermuda and not anywhere else? It was not enough that he should merely voice his concerns to the Abwehr. He wanted to be the one to tell them what was happening. He took another look at Susan Spencer and could see the willingness in her eyes. He was torn between what he saw as his duty and what was a potential evening of pleasure. A smile crossed his face. Perhaps if he played his cards right, he could have it both ways.

Susan continued to pester him with questions. She was enthusiastic and seemed genuinely interested in his job and his travels. Robles assumed that it was her way of making conversation, but her persistence was becoming tiresome.

He gave her his glass, and she went to get them both a refill. "What about you?" he asked in an attempt to deflect her persistent interrogation. "What are you doing here in Bermuda?"

Her cover story was well rehearsed. "My family moved here several years before the war started," she said. "My dad owns a shop on Front Street. I work at the Bank of Bermuda."

"Bermuda seems like a nice place to live."

"Used to be—before this stupid war. Without tourists the place is dead. There's absolutely nothing to do." She looked into his eyes, dark, mysterious pools that seemed to beckon her. "Absolutely nothing to do," she repeated.

Robles smiled.

She returned with the drinks. He certainly was handsome, she thought, and quite charming and intelligent. Susan was quite certain that whoever had informed the intelligence services about Robles must have been mistaken. She couldn't imagine what it was that Groves wanted to find out about him. She knew what she wanted to find out. She was feeling a little tipsy now and wondered if he would make the first move or if she would have to be even more obvious. Groves had told her to get information—he hadn't said how. She imagined herself naked on her bed anticipating the moment of penetration. For king and country, she thought, and giggled a little at her foolishness.

Robles looked at her strangely, and she realized that she was a little drunk. Perhaps she should get back to the business at hand. In an effort to regain the initiative she made her first mistake. "I really envy all those exotic places you've been to," she said. "Morocco . . . Madagascar . . . Iran. What's it like?"

Although his expression did not change, Susan realized her mistake immediately. Robles had told her about Morocco and Madagascar, but it had been Groves who had mentioned Iran. "You did say you'd been to those places?"

He did not want her to know he had caught her mistake.

"Yes. I've been to all of them."

"You've been to so many places that I have a hard time keeping track."

"I do, too, sometimes."

She gave a small sigh of relief. No harm done. She was tiring of all these questions anyway. It was time to put first things first. "You probably have women waiting for you every place you go," she said, leaning forward to rest a hand on his knee.

He smiled, allowing her to draw her own conclusions. He had lost all interest in her. He was now certain that she was a British agent. What intrigued him more than anything else was how had they known about him? Obviously they did not know much, or they would not have sent this stupid girl to question him. But the fact that they knew anything at all was quite disturbing.

Susan was unaware that the game was over. "Play your cards right," she said, "and you could add Bermuda to the list." Her hand moved from his knee to the inside of his thigh.

He took her arm by the wrist and removed her hand from his leg. "This has been most pleasant," he said, "but I must be going now."

Susan started to speak, but he was already on his feet.

"I have an early day tomorrow, and a long trip ahead of me."

Susan was almost dumbfounded by the sudden turn of events. "Are you sure you can't stay?"

He was already at the door. "Good-bye," he said, "and thank you for a pleasant evening."

The door closed behind him and he was gone.

"Shit," Susan muttered. What had gone wrong? She was sure that things had been progressing nicely. What the hell had happened?

Robles left the Bermudiana and immediately went around to the back of the building. He kept to the shadows and the trees and made his way across the expansive grounds at the rear of the hotel. He crossed a wide street and the backyards of several expensive homes. Except for the barking of a few dogs his passage went undetected. He paralleled Pitts Bay Road until it snaked north. Here he crossed quickly and hid himself in the bushes by the side of the harbor.

Across a short inlet sat the Hamilton Princess, and there, moored in the inlet, was the Lisbon Clipper. The plane was illuminated by the row of lights that lined the dock, but the aircraft itself was not lit, and there did not seem to be any activity in the area. Robles settled down to wait.

The night had grown chilly and he was just about to end his vigil when a movement at the end of the dock caught his attention. Two men were moving a small trolley of some kind—one pushing, one pulling—towards the clipper. The trolley was piled high with what appeared to be luggage. They stopped at the clipper, and the one who had been pushing walked out onto the short stabilizers beneath the wing and pounded on the fuselage with his fist. Almost immediately a door opened and a third form appeared. Robles heard voices but was unable to discern what was being said. After a moment or two of this unintelligible conversation the two men on the dock began to unload the trolley and hand the contents to the man who was inside the clipper. When the trolley had been emptied, the process was reversed and the man inside began to hand out what appeared to be large canvas sacks to the men on the dock.

Mail sacks, Robles thought, and immediately knew what was happening. The British were inspecting all of the mail that was routed through Bermuda. He knew that German Embassy documents from North and South America were routinely shipped on the clippers, and obviously, the British had access to an enormous amount of classified material.

He smiled. The Abwehr would be very glad to hear what was happening here in Bermuda. Obviously, the Americans had to cooperate with the British in this endeavor. There would be an immediate international outcry when the details of this were revealed. An outcry that would be enough to embarrass the Americans and put a stop to this business.

Robles waited until the two with the trolley had gone and the door of the clipper had been closed before he made his way back across the road and once again into the backyards off Pitts Bay Road. He retraced his steps and found himself behind the Bermudiana.

In passing, he looked up at Susan's window, thinking momentarily that he might pay her a surprise visit and finish what they had started. He saw a shadow silhouetted on the sheer drapery that covered the french door. She was still awake. Then he saw another shape. She had company! She doesn't waste much time, he thought. He had been gone less than forty minutes.

One of the shapes moved closer to the door and Robles ducked into the shadows behind a tree. The curtains parted, and Susan stepped out onto the veranda and looked across the lawn. A man followed her onto the veranda and Susan turned to face him.

"I'm sure you did everything you could," the man said. "I'm just a little bit surprised that you couldn't find out more about him."

"I'm sorry you're disappointed," she said. "I did the best I could. Maybe I'm not cut out for that kind of work."

"Perhaps not," the man said. He looked around the grounds. "We shouldn't be talking out here," he said. "Let's go back inside."

Robles waited a few minutes, then emerged from his hiding place. He stood below Susan Spencer's veranda and listened. All that he could hear was the low murmuring of voices. He reached up, grabbed the floor of the veranda, and effortlessly hoisted himself up. He silently pulled himself over the rail, waited for a moment, then padded softly to the door opening. He was just in time to hear the man bid Susan good night. Robles whispered a silent curse. He had wanted to hear what they had to say about him. There were other ways to find out, he thought. He reached into his jacket pocket and touched the knife that he kept there.

He watched her through the thin drapes. If she had turned, she would have seen him, too, but he did not care. He waited until she went into the bedroom, and then he stepped inside and closed the door. She was gone for several minutes, and he could hear her moving about in the bedroom. He took a seat near the door and waited for her to come back. When she did come back, she had changed into a robe and was brushing her hair.

At first she did not notice that someone was in the room, and then she looked up and saw him sitting in the chair. At first she was startled and covered her mouth with her palm, but then she smiled. "You came back," she said.

"Yes," he said simply. "I thought we should talk."

"How did you get in?"

He pointed in the direction of the french door.

Susan was too excited by his reappearance to be concerned that he had clandestinely entered her apartment. "D'you want a drink?" she asked.

"I'd like that," he said.

She brought him his drink and sat next to him. "Well. What should we talk about?"

He finished half his drink in one swallow. "I'm really not much of a talker," he said. He placed the glass on the table and put his left arm around her shoulders.

Susan smiled and moved closer.

He put a hand behind her head, and she, thinking he was about to kiss her, closed her eyes and turned her face toward him. Instead he reached into his pocket and withdrew a knife, touching the small button so that the blade sprang erect. He grabbed her hair and forced her head back, exposing her neck. She froze as he touched the point of the blade to her throat.

"Not a sound," he said. "Is that clear?"

Susan's eyes were wide with fear. She nodded once.

"When I ask you a question you will whisper your answer. And you will answer truthfully everything I ask you. Is that clear?"

Susan nodded again. She knew right away that Groves had been right about him.

She was not terribly brave. She told him everything. She told him about the clippers and the mail inspection. She told him about the radio interception stations. Told him that he had aroused suspicion when he had been seen with a known German agent. If she had known about the Enigma machine she would have told him about that, too. She was foolish enough to hope that cooperation would save her.

He could not, of course, allow her to live.

When he finished questioning her, she looked at him, her eyes pleading with him. She had come here to this backwater of the war, looking for romance, never thinking that her life would be in danger. He would have preferred to let her live because he felt no particular animosity toward her, but he could not. He had his obligations, and he had a job to do. It was as simple as that. He placed the point of the knife on the fleshy part of her chin, between the neck and the point of her chin and gave one savage thrust upward. Her mouth opened in surprise, and he actually saw the blade drive up into her brain. Her eyes rolled back into her head, and she slumped forward. His instructors at the Abwehr school at Quentz Lake, who had taught him this technique as a substitute for slashing the jugular, had told him that death would be almost instantaneous and that there would be very little blood. He was glad to note that they were correct.

He scooped her up, marveling at how light she was, carried her into the bedroom, and rolled her body under the bed. She would not be discovered for at least a day. By then he would be in Panama.

Robles turned out the lights and left the way he had come in.

CHAPTER 6

New York City; November 7, 1941

The two men on the New York-to-Washington train sat quietly while the train pulled out of the tunnel into the bright sunlight of early afternoon. The older of the two was William Stephenson, a Canadian businessman, who had been designated by Winston Churchill to establish a British intelligence service, known as British Security Coordination, in the United States. Stephenson was forty-five and a hero from the first war. He was sad-faced and rather nondescript, the kind of man that few would give a second glance. Behind this inconspicuous demeanor, however, lurked a sharp intellect and a fierce determination. His code name, Intrepid, was ideally descriptive of the man.

"Nasty business in Bermuda last night," Stephenson said. "Apparently, someone murdered one of our girls—a trapper."

"Did they catch the killer?" his companion asked.

Stephenson shook his head. "By the time the body had been found, the killer had left the island. Took the clipper to Baltimore and disappeared."

Both men made sad faces of resignation and turned their

attention to the morning newspaper. In their almost matching gray pin-striped suits they might have been investment bankers on their way to a Washington meeting. They were in fact British intelligence operatives on their way to Washington to meet with J. Edgar Hoover, the director of the Federal Bureau of Investigation.

They sat in silence for a short time until, finally, Stephenson looked around and closed his newspaper. The car was almost empty, and although no one sat within earshot, he spoke softly. "No matter what we think of Hoover," he said, "we've got to have his cooperation. He has the ear of the President, and apparently, Roosevelt trusts him as he trusts very few others." Stephenson looked away for a moment and watched the landscape rush past his window. "Besides," he said finally, "he gets the job done. We've got to give him credit for bringing down Arias in Panama. He said he'd do it, and, apparently, that's exactly what he's done."

One month earlier, on October ninth, word had arrived from Panama that the pro-fascist government of President Arnulfo Arias had been overthrown by a coalition of his cabinet ministers and that a new president, Ricardo Adolpho de la Guardia, had already been installed. Stephenson was well aware that Hoover's FBI had been most responsible for encouraging the Panamanians to overthrow their elected president.

The other British agent nodded reluctantly as if unwilling to give Hoover his due. His name was Wilfred Smythe, and he was a member of Stephenson's British Security Coordination staff, which operated out of offices at Rockefeller Center in New York City. Smythe was in his late thirties, with dark, slicked-back hair and a deceptively youthful face. Before the war he had worked in a London bank. This morning he had been asked to accompany his boss to Washington for a conference with the FBI director, who had promised "information regarding a matter of vital interest to British security."

"And now," Stephenson went on, "it seems that Mr. Hoover has discovered the source of the German funds that we have been so concerned about."

"Did he say how he found out?"

"No. Only that the money is in Mexican banks and that he believes the amount is in excess of four million American dollars."

"Four million dollars," Smythe said wistfully.

"As you know," Stephenson said, "in June of this year the U.S. government froze the assets of Germany and Italy that were held in American banks, and about six weeks later did the same to the Japanese."

Smythe nodded.

"Apparently, after what happened to the Germans and Italians, the Japanese figured that they were next. According to Mr. Hoover, the Japanese were able to transfer close to three million dollars in American currency out of the country before Roosevelt shut them down. Right now the money is in the Bank of Mexico in Mexico City along with another million that the Italians have been keeping there. It seems that the Italians and the Japanese intend to turn over most of this money to German Abwehr agents in South America."

"It makes sense," Smythe said. "American currency is the best method of payment in South America, the Germans are out of money and can't get any into the country because of our currency blockade, so they get their Japanese and Italian friends to turn over available funds to them. With that kind of money the Germans could finance their South American operations for several years."

Stephenson nodded. "That's why we have to make certain that this money does not fall into enemy hands. I am prepared to ask Mr. Hoover for his assistance in"—he searched for the proper euphemism—"appropriating these funds."

"Do you think that Hoover is likely to agree?"

"I'd rather deal with Bill Donovan at COI, but Hoover has put himself in the picture and we can't afford to disregard someone with his influence."

The COI, Coordinator of Information, was a new governmental department established by President Roosevelt in July of 1941 to gather facts about various aspects of the war situation. It was a department headed by a hero of the last war, Bill Donovan, and one that duplicated the intelligence functions of the War Department and of the FBI but reported those findings directly to the President and not to either of those other organizations. The Pentagon was dismayed by what was seen as an encroachment of its function, and Hoover was nettled by the fact that the President seemed to be making an end run around what had become an FBI prerogative.

"As usual," Stephenson said, "we'll have to treat Mr. Hoover with kid gloves. Let him see the benefits to himself and the United States; show him that this could be a feather in his cap; and last, but not least, let him think that there is absolutely no risk to his agency."

"Is that possible?" asked Smythe.

Stephenson smiled. "I'm going to propose to Mr. Hoover that we steal the money from the Germans without their ever being aware that it has been taken."

Smythe turned to his boss, a question forming on his lips, but Stephenson had already turned his attention to his newspaper and seemed instantly engrossed.

The FBI offices were on the Pennsylvania Avenue side of the Justice Department Building that occupied the entire block between Ninth and Tenth streets and Constitution and Pennsylvania avenues. Although supposedly a section of a much larger Justice Department, the FBI, because of Hoover's longevity and influence, had already begun to dominate its supposed master. The building was one of Washington's most daunting edifices. In some ways the gray granite structure—blunt, imposing, efficient—mirrored the man who ruled this fiefdom as surely as any medieval despot had ruled his kingdom. To his men and his supporters, J. Edgar Hoover was the epitome of strength and incorruptible dedication to duty; to his enemies and detractors he was the proof that power and corruptibility were synonymous.

Stephenson and Smythe left the elevator at the fifth floor and walked down a terrazzo-tiled corridor. The walls were lined with display cases that were mute testimony to the bureau's proficiency: Dillinger's revolver, Pretty Boy Floyd's machine-gun, photographs of various gangsters under arrest, and myriad newspaper headlines touting the excellence of the FBI. Photographs of Hoover were everywhere. Everything was for the glorification of the director.

"He's certainly not shy about tooting his own horn," Smythe whispered.

After a relatively brief wait, the two Englishmen were granted an audience with the great man himself. They were ushered into Hoover's large office, where the director introduced them to one of his men, who rose from his chair and offered the British agents an unnecessarily firm handshake.

Every FBI agent Smythe had ever met had engaged him in just such a masculine ritual. Bone-crushing handshakes, he thought, must be the first course in an FBI agent's training at the FBI Academy in Quantico, Virginia.

Hoover's hands, however, were soft and delicate, and he rarely shook hands unless forced to do so.

Except for the hands, the FBI director was a bulldog of a man, short, squat, and tenacious. He was a lawyer who had only briefly practiced law before his appointment as a special assistant to the attorney general. He had then served as the head of the General Intelligence Division of the Department of Justice, providing information that assisted Attorney General Palmer in his campaign against suspected communist radicals in the labor movement. In 1921 Hoover became the assistant director of the Federal Bureau of Investigation, and only three years later, at the age of twenty-nine, was appointed director. Now forty-six, J. Edgar Hoover was in charge of the most powerful investigative agency in the United States.

Hoover had done his job diligently—and, some would say, too well. He had attacked mobsters, criminals, radicals, and subversives with uncommon zeal. In the process his FBI had become one of the most respected—and feared—law enforcement agencies in the world. At the same time Hoover himself, because of his penchant for collecting compromising information about prominent figures in American life, became one of the most feared and hated figures in the government.

After welcoming his British guests, Hoover sat back in his chair, hands behind his neck, while Stephenson offered his congratulations on the recent events in Panama. Boosting Hoover's already inflated ego was one of the tasks that BSC agents were required to perform. Hoover's cooperation with the BSC was so vital to British interests that Stephenson's organization often gave much of the credit for their own work to the FBI and to J. Edgar Hoover. The British, however, had nothing to do with the Panamanian coup.

"Arias," said Stephenson, "was a definite threat to the security of the hemisphere. You and your men took care of it in magnificent fashion."

Hoover smiled. He did not dispute the Canadian's interpretation of the events.

In 1940 Dr. Arnulfo Arias, the president of Panama, had been elected overwhelmingly in a campaign in which he had promised to renegotiate the terms of the 1903 Hay–Bunau–Varilla treaty between the United States and Panama. That treaty had promised American sovereignty in the Panama Canal in perpetuity and had given the United States the right to intervene in Panama to defend the canal and to maintain order in Panama City and Colón. The United States had in fact intervened in Panama in 1907, 1917, and 1918. In 1936 the United States had given up this "right" to intervene in Panamanian politics but maintained the right to consider the Canal Zone as American territory. Arias had publicly proclaimed that he wanted the United States out of Panama and that he wanted Panamanian control of the canal. He had also declared his sympathy with the goals of Nazi Germany and for a brief time had opened his arms wide to the agents of the Axis powers. Because of the strategic importance of the Panama Canal, this situation had worried many officials in the governments of the United States and Great Britain.

The British, concerned that the Germans might use Arias to establish a foothold in the Americas, appealed to Franklin Roosevelt. After some deliberation, Roosevelt turned to J. Edgar Hoover, who controlled a considerable pool of agents in South America. The approach was tentative, the question vague: Was there anything that could be done about what was considered a potentially dangerous situation? As usual, Hoover needed no definitive instructions and had done his job exceedingly well. In Panama discreet inquiries had been made, promises offered, and assistance given. In a relatively short time Hoover's men had accomplished the director's stated goals: get rid of Arias and establish a government that is friendly to the United States.

"Well," Hoover said matter-of-factly, "I did it. I said I'd get rid of that Nazi Arias and that's exactly what has happened." He smiled smugly. "I think I've saved the United States of America—and Great Britain—from a great deal of trouble down the road."

"You certainly have, Director Hoover," agreed Stephenson. "And we are all very grateful for that fact."

Smythe, as were his instructions from Stephenson, smiled and nodded pleasantly at everything Hoover said.

Hoover turned again to the man who sat to his right. "Special Agent Trump here is assigned to the American Embassy in Panama City. Trump is as much responsible as anyone for our success in Panama."

Trump gave a toothy approximation of a smile. He was in his mid-thirties, tall and thin. In a futile attempt to disguise his baldness he had combed his hair across the ocean of exposed skin between the shores of hair on either side. Smythe noticed that Trump seemed to mimic the mannerisms of Director Hoover, smiling, scowling, glaring, in adoring emulation of his chief.

Next to Franklin D. Roosevelt, J. Edgar Hoover was the most powerful man in Washington. Criminals, labor leaders, and politicians grew exceedingly nervous at the mention of his name. There were many in high places in Washington who would have liked nothing better than to send Hoover packing, but there were few who would dare voice such an opinion. For almost twenty-five years Hoover had dedicated himself to rooting out all manner of corruption in American life. Now, with half the world in flames and the rest tinder for the fire, Hoover had turned his attention to another threat—spies.

The director of the FBI was convinced that there was a massive effort on the part of Nazi Germany to infiltrate and subvert the governments of several Latin American countries. The German effort in this area was actually rather minuscule, but Hoover, who saw plots and subversion under every rock, was certain that the Germans hoped to make South America a base for their future plans against the United States. In this delusion he was encouraged by the British, who hoped to make Hoover an ally in their struggle against Germany. British Intelligence—under Stephenson's direction—had established a large operation in New York City from which they hoped to keep track of any and all German activities in the Western Hemisphere, and this office bombarded Hoover with a constant stream of intelligence information about German operations—some real and some imagined—in the Americas.

"We've solved one problem," Hoover said, "but the whole of Latin America is one seething caldron of subversion. There are Germans and German agents everywhere. In Brazil alone there are almost one million persons of German extraction. The German National Socialist Party has more than thirty thousand members in Buenos Aires. Uruguay is a hotbed of German activity, with close to fifty thousand active members of German clubs of one type or another."

Stephenson nodded agreeably. Most of this information had been supplied to Hoover by the BSC. As with most of the information given to Hoover, it was a careful compilation of fact and exaggeration. There were indeed many South Americans of German extraction, but most were descended from Germans who had emigrated from Germany in the last century, and while there were many who had fallen under the spell of the charismatic German leader, the majority had never expressed any interest in a German takeover of their respective countries. The British assumed, and hoped that Hoover would join in their assumption, that every South American of German extraction was a potential agent of Nazi Germany.

"And let's not forget," Hoover went on, "that, until recently, most of the airlines in South America were run by Germans and most of the planes were flown by German pilots." He gave Smythe his famous baleful glare. "Those planes could easily have become bombers and been used against the interests and even the territory of the United States."

What Hoover was referring to was the fact that until 1940 the Colombian national airline, Scadta, had been operated by Germans. What he did not say was that eighty percent of the airline had been owned by an American company, Pan Am, whose chairman fiercely opposed the Roosevelt Administration's attempts to remove the Germans from influential positions with the airline. The United States had bullied Colombia and Pan Am into firing all of its German personnel in February of 1940. In July of 1940 the name of the airline had been changed to Avianca.

Now it was Smythe's turn to smile—and with good reason. He himself was responsible for the information about the German connection with several of the South American national airlines.

Stephenson nodded to Smythe, who reached into the briefcase he had placed at his feet. "We've brought you something else that might interest you, Mr. Director," Smythe said. "It is a map that was recovered, by one of our agents in occupied France, from the body of a Gestapo general." Smythe smiled knowingly so that Hoover would understand how the German had met his fate.

He handed the map to Hoover, who unfolded it carefully as if it were a holy relic.

The map showed South America, but instead of the usual configuration of countries it showed the continent divided into five larger areas. The text was in German.

Hoover looked up at Stephenson.

"Apparently," Stephenson said, "Hitler intends to divide South America into five German-dominated zones. There are handwritten notes on the map," he said, pointing, "that indicate where the Germans intend to build naval and air facilities."

"The President will be very interested in this information. I'll see that he gets it this afternoon."

Stephenson and Smythe maintained their blank expressions. Although both were convinced that the map gave an accurate portrayal of Hitler's intentions in South America, they were also aware that the map had been created by British Intelligence in London.

Hoover opened his desk drawer and carefully placed the map inside. He smiled. "Perhaps it would be better if I told the President that this map has come into my possession through another source. There are some at the White House who might be suspicious of its origins if I say that you gave it to me."

In this particular case Stephenson preferred that Hoover take all the credit for the acquisition of the map. "As always, Mr. Director, however you wish to handle this information is fine with me."

Hoover got up out of his chair, his smile replaced by the usual perpetual frown. "All right," he said, "let's get down to business." The director hiked up his trousers and assumed a pugnacious stance. "I've got your report here," he said, picking up a file folder on his desk, "that claims the Germans are up to something in South America. Although it's rather vague, the report claims that large amounts of funds are to be transferred to German agents all across South and Central America and that major acts of sabotage are planned in the very near future."

"That is correct," Stephenson said. "Additionally, we have sources who tell us that the German espionage network in South America is close to bankruptcy. Agents have not been paid and are threatening to cease operations if monies are not forthcoming." Stephenson paused, hoping Hoover would follow his lead.

"My sources tell me," Hoover said, "that the Japanese and Italians are about to solve that problem with a little gift of four million dollars to the Germans."

"That's what I've been afraid of," Stephenson said.

Hoover smiled enigmatically. "What do you suggest we do about this?"

Stephenson sighed. Hoover was making this as difficult as possible. "Perhaps," he said, "if we were to prevent the transfer of this money, we could shut down the Germans in South America. At the very least, we would deal a major blow to their espionage network. But first we'd have to know when and how the transfer is to be made."

"I've got a contact on the inside—a bank officer—who has been keeping an eye on the situation. Just yesterday he informed me that within hours of each other, the Japanese and the Italians issued withdrawal orders for most of the funds." Hoover grinned. "They've asked for the money in new fifty-dollar bills. Easier to transport," Hoover explained. "New bills take up much less room than used money. Four million dollars in new fifties would fit easily into two suitcases. They have also requested that the money be delivered to the German consular offices in the port city of Vera Cruz. Apparently, as you suspected, they intend to take the money to South America."

"Then the funds have not been released yet?"

"No. The Mexicans needed time to put together that amount in American funds. The new fifties are being shipped from Houston."

"Could your contact delay release for as long as possible?"

Hoover grinned. "I've already asked him to do just that. I think we can hold them off for five or six days—perhaps a week."

Stephenson calculated rapidly. "What we'd like to do," he said, "is intercept those funds shortly after they leave the bank and make sure they do not fall into enemy hands."

"You mean steal them?" Hoover asked.

"Something like that."

"I thought you might have such a plan in mind. I have also assigned an agent to the bank. He will follow anyone who picks up the money."

"Would you—the FBI—have any objections to such an operation?"

"As long as the FBI and the United States government are

not implicated in such an action"—Hoover paused—"and if the FBI was a partner in the operation."

"Partner?" Stephenson asked.

"As an organ of the United States government, the FBI could not possibly take part in the theft of funds legally owned by another country, especially when such funds are deposited in a banking institution maintained by a third country with friendly relations with the United States."

"What, then, do you propose?"

"That your organization perform the operation but under the control of the FBI."

"And the money . . .?"

"All turned over to the U.S. Treasury."

Smythe stifled a sigh. Almost four million in American currency would be a marvelous bonus to the British government's hard-pressed economy.

"Unless, of course," Hoover went on, "you're more interested in obtaining the money than in denying its use to the Germans."

"Of course not," Stephenson said, looking, for a moment, at Smythe. Both realized that Hoover had backed them into a corner. They also realized that if the operation went wrong, it was the BSC and not Hoover's FBI that would take the blame. If, however, the operation succeeded, Hoover would reap the credit and the American government would benefit by almost four million dollars. Stephenson forced a thin smile. "We are always glad to work with the cooperation of the FBI."

Hoover thumped a fist on his desk. "Good. My man Trump will be in charge and will be responsible for bringing the money back to the United States. Your men will work directly with him. Is that understood?"

"Perfectly, Mr. Director," Stephenson said. "I wonder if I might offer a suggestion?"

"Go ahead."

"Rather than simply stealing the money, perhaps it might be better to replace the money with counterfeit currency."

"I'm not sure I follow you."

Stephenson leaned forward. "This could be a marvelous

opportunity to expose the entire German spy apparatus in South and Central America. We steal the money, replace it with counterfeit currency, wait a reasonable amount of time—perhaps until some of the counterfeit begins to show up—then we claim that the Germans are paying their people with counterfeit money. On the one hand we expose most of the people who are working for the Germans, on the other we make it virtually impossible for the Germans to get anyone to ever work for them again."

"What assistance would you need from us?"

"The U.S. Treasury Department and the FBI are world-renowned for their operations against counterfeit currency; I have been told that the FBI has the world's largest collection of counterfeiting plates. We would require the use of the best of those plates, and enough ink and paper to print four million dollars worth of American money."

"Impossible," Hoover said. "Currency of that quality would link the FBI—and the U.S. government—too closely with this operation. Once the Germans discovered that their money was counterfeit, they'd know that the U.S. was somehow involved. You will also want to consider the implications for your government if something goes wrong. Counterfeiting the currency of a neutral state could have serious consequences throughout the hemisphere. The U.S. government would have to make a strong protest, as would the Mexicans. This plan of yours could start more problems than it solves."

"I'm sure you are quite right," Stephenson said.

"What we need," Hoover said, "is someone who has no connection with either of our governments."

The room fell into silence until Special Agent Trump coughed into his hand. Hoover looked at him sharply. "You have an idea?" he asked.

Trump nodded. "Perhaps, Director, I might have a solution to the problem."

"Let's hear it," Hoover said.

"The man who passed the best counterfeit money that we've ever seen is still at large. . . ."

Hoover's face darkened. "Fox."

". . . He presently lives in Panama," Trump continued. "He almost certainly has access to counterfeit currency and might be persuaded—with the proper inducement—to participate in this venture."

Hoover did not appear to be listening. The famous jaw jutted forward. "I want him caught. I want him brought back here."

"I'm not sure I understand," Stephenson said. "If you know the whereabouts of this man—why is he still at large?"

"Because," Hoover said angrily, "until recently Panama was a place that gave sanctuary to fugitives from American justice."

"For a price," Trump added. "We've tried to extradite him several times in the past three years, but he was always able to pay off the right people."

"And what," asked Stephenson, "would be the proper inducement to get this man to help us."

"The changed political climate in Panama might persuade him that extradition is a likely possibility," said Trump. "If we promised him a full pardon, I think he would come in on our side."

Hoover snorted. "A pardon? Never!"

Again, Trump was apologetic. "I said, *if* we promised him a pardon, Director. We don't actually have to grant him one. As a matter of fact, if we involve him in this operation, it may be easier to arrest him when it's over."

Smythe sat up in his chair, the distaste evident on his face, but a quick look from Stephenson dissuaded him from saying anything.

Hoover grinned. "I like that, Trump. Use the son of a bitch and then drag him back here to stand trial for his crimes."

"What exactly did Fox do—besides counterfeiting?" Smythe asked.

"He's a murderer, a bootlegger, and a thief," Hoover said, "and I want him brought to justice."

"But," said Stephenson, "you think he can be persuaded to help us?"

Hoover grinned and Trump followed suit. "Yes," Hoover said. "One way or another, we'll persuade him."

"We'd have to move quickly," Stephenson said. "The Germans will want to get their hands on that money as soon as possible."

"As I said, I already have an agent at the bank. Special Agent Trump can be on the next plane for Panama," Hoover said.

"I'd like Colonel Smythe to accompany him," said Stephenson. "He'll be in charge of our end of this little game."

"Fine with me," Hoover said, "just so long as he knows who's in charge."

Smythe and Stephenson gave the director identical frozen smiles.

"Of course, Mr. Director," Stephenson said. "My man is at your service."

Hoover sat back in his leather chair. He looked at Trump and nodded appreciatively. "This just might be a very profitable venture. Screw the Germans, keep the money, and capture one of our top priority criminals. I like it already."

CHAPTER 7

Panama City, Panama; November 8, 1941

The young American woman stopped just inside the front entrance of the Panama Club, letting her eyes quickly scan the room as if she were looking for a familiar face. The place was somewhat less than she had hoped it would be, but much more than she had feared. The room was large and high-ceilinged, and there was a long mahogany bar to her right, where the bartender had halted his glass polishing to watch her carefully. In front of him, dotted about the room, were individual tables. To her left was a small bandstand and a dance floor. Through a wide opening at the rear of the room she could see part of another room, where there were several gaming tables. The piano player gamely kept at his keyboard, but no one was paying him any attention. All eyes were on the woman at the door.

The ceiling fans swirled in gentle symphony.

Her name was Victoria Gansell, and to the hundred pairs of eyes that had turned to watch her, she looked as if she had just stepped down from a movie screen. She was dressed in white, skirt, blouse, man-styled jacket, and a wide-brimmed hat. She was astoundingly beautiful—blond hair, blue eyes, long slender legs, a narrow waist, and, beneath the blouse, a subtle hint of magnificent breasts. Each feature of her face approached perfection, but there was a quality of sadness in her eyes that was at variance with the rest of her.

She sensed the stares, but seemed oblivious to the attention. A few years earlier she had appeared in several Hollywood films, and the stares were a reaction with which she was quite familiar. It had, however, been quite some time since her presence had inspired this kind of response. Lately she had even begun to wonder if, perhaps, her power had begun to wane. After the disappointments of the last few years it was reassuring to know that it had not. She had imagined herself in just such a scene as this in at least a hundred motion pictures, but the roles had always gone to someone else while she had had to be satisfied with minor roles, bit parts, or, more often than not, no part at all. If this were indeed the movies, she thought, the piano player would stop playing and the room would fall into a suspenseful silence. Close enough, she thought, suppressing a smile.

The taxi driver who had brought her here entered with her suitcases and placed them beside her. He leered at the gawking faces as if he expected some special acknowledgment for bringing them this beautiful creature.

"Thank you," she said.

The driver seemed reluctant to leave. He backed away slowly, his head bobbing. *"Gracias, señorita,"* he said several times.

A man approached her warily. He was short and stocky with jet-black hair, a thick mustache, and a pleasant, open face. He spoke to her in English. "Good evening, señorita," he said, "My name is Ernesto Garcia, and this is my place. Perhaps I could be of some assistance."

"Your place?" she said. "I thought Harrison Fox owned this place."

"Ah, you are a friend of Harry's?"

"Maybe. Is this his place or not?"

Garcia grinned. "Yes. Harry is . . . how would you say . . . the majority stockholder of this enterprise. I am merely a minor partner. You are here to see Harry, then?"

She nodded.

"And may I tell him who is here?"

She smiled nervously. "Victoria. Victoria Gansell."

"Such a beautiful name, for such a beautiful lady," Garcia said. "Perhaps, Miss Gansell, you would like to sit down and have something cool to drink while I let Harry know that you are waiting."

Victoria looked at her suitcases, but Garcia snapped his fingers and someone approached to take them away. He led her to an empty table and helped her into a seat. A waiter appeared. "The señorita is a friend of Señor Fox. See that she gets whatever she wants." He leaned forward. "I will be back in just a moment."

Before she could thank him, he was gone.

Harry Fox got up from behind his desk. "Here? You mean she's downstairs in the bar?"

Garcia nodded. "Harry," he said, "this one is more beautiful than any of the others. This one is the most beautiful woman I have ever seen. She should be in the American motion pictures."

"She was," Fox said. He walked to the window that looked down on the bar.

"I sat her near the bar—at the front," Garcia said.

Fox parted the curtain and looked out. He let out his breath slowly when he saw her. "She sure is a looker," he said.

"You want me to bring her upstairs?" Garcia asked, but Fox was already lost in thought, staring at the woman in the room below.

He had first met her almost five years ago at a Hollywood party given by some people he knew who, after Prohibition ended, had gone from the whiskey business into motion pictures. She was one of perhaps twenty beautiful young women—starlets, he remembered they had been called— who were there as adornments, but there was something about her that made her stand out from the rest. There was an innocence about her, a vulnerability that he wondered if only he could see. She had come to Hollywood from some small town in Texas to make her fortune in the movies, but had quickly discovered that Hollywood stardom was only for the chosen few. Bright, fresh, beautiful faces like hers were commonplace in this celluloid fantasyland.

That night he had rescued her from some fat, cigar-smoking, clammy-handed, self-styled producer who promised that he could make her a star. After that they had become friends and then lovers. She had clung to him then as if she needed his protection from the wolves who preyed on innocents, but he knew that he could not save her. She had wanted him to stay, he remembered, but that had been impossible. He had his own troubles, and could never stay in one place for very long. He had seen her several times over the next few years. Sometimes she was with someone, sometimes she was not and they could pick up their relationship where they had left it, but he was always saddened by the changes in her. The beauty was still there—that would never change—so was the vulnerability, but the innocence was gone.

"You want me to bring her upstairs?" Garcia said again.

"No," Fox said. "I'll go down."

Victoria watched him come down the stairs and make his way toward her. He hadn't changed much since the last time she had seen him, and she hoped that he would think the same of her. He was tall, with light brown almost blondish hair that was thinning slightly above the temples. He moved with the same confidence that she remembered, a gliding, athletic swagger that bordered on arrogance. She sipped her drink to disguise her nervousness. "Well, Harry," she said when he reached her table, "are you surprised to see me?"

"Surprised is hardly the word."

"I suppose I should have asked if you were 'happy' to see me."

He bent over and kissed her. "Very happy." He sat across from her. "How in the hell did you get here?"

"I was working in Havana." She gave an involuntary shiver as if the recollection had chilled her. "That didn't work out too well, but I met a guy who had his own plane. A

Texan. He said I brought him good luck at the tables. He offered to take me anywhere I wanted to go, although I don't think he figured I'd say Panama." She looked around. "Here I am."

Harry could feel the tension in her voice. "How are things, Vicky?"

Her voice was steady, but her eyes betrayed her. "Not so great, Harry. I've been on a downward spiral for the past few years. Done things that I wish I . . ." Her voice trailed off. "Sometimes I wish I could go back home to Texas. I was happy there. My mother's still there. She'd take me back, even after all the heartache I've given her."

"It's not easy to rebuild those old bridges," Harry said.

"Tell me about it. There's a lot of water under this bridge."

"What brings you to Panama City?"

Victoria smiled. "I know it was over a year ago, but the last time I saw you, you offered me a job. I just wondered if that offer was still good?" She finished her drink while she waited for his response.

Harry motioned to the waiter to bring her another. He stared into her eyes, saw the uncertainty, sensed the desperation. "The offer is still good. Anytime you want it."

"Well, seeing that I've got less than a hundred bucks to my name, I guess now is as good a time as any."

"You're on the payroll as of now," he said. "Take a couple of days to get settled. Start whenever you want."

Her face began to crumble, and she almost lost her composure. She touched his arm. "Thanks, Harry. I always had you pegged as an okay guy."

"The last time I saw you was in Vegas. You were working at one of the new casinos. I thought things were going well for you."

The sadness was back in her eyes. "Same old story, Harry. Just like Hollywood. Talent is a dime a dozen. They want more than talent. Every job has strings attached. I got tired of the strings." She looked at him, her eyes misty. "There aren't any strings attached to this job, are there, Harry?"

"It's just a job, Vicky. There isn't a job in this whole

world that's worth making you do what you don't want to do."

She brightened as if a weight had been lifted. "You got someone right now?" she asked. "A girl—a woman. Are you with anyone? I don't want to get in the way."

Harry grinned. "Not at the moment," he said. "You have found me, as they say, unattached."

Victoria sipped her drink, eyeing him over the top of her glass. "Can you find me a place to stay? For a few days. Until I get settled."

"You can stay here if you like. I have an office and some rooms upstairs."

"You stay here?"

"Sometimes. I have a house outside Panama City, but I stay here a couple of nights a week." Fox stood up and made a signal to a young boy, who appeared almost immediately. "Pedro will take your bags and show you to your room. Get yourself settled. I've got a few things to take care of now. We'll have dinner later and we can talk."

She watched him go and allowed herself a small sigh. Maybe things would be all right now for at least a while.

She had always been beautiful and like most beautiful women had thought that her beauty would be her salvation. Somehow, as is sometimes the case, it hadn't worked out as she had hoped. Early on, everything had come easily to her. As a young girl her looks had made her popular, and she was unfamiliar with either loneliness or rejection. She had been "Miss Everything" in her hometown in Texas and during her two-year stint at the University of Texas. She had been catered to, admired, coddled, envied. She had beauty, talent, and brains. What more could she want? She wanted more.

In 1935, at twenty-two, she had gone to Hollywood to find fame and fortune. There she found that she was one of a thousand like her. At times it seemed that everyone was twenty-two and beautiful and had come to Hollywood to find the same dream. She had made the rounds of auditions and casting calls, and for a time things seemed to be going her way. In a relatively short time she had secured minor roles in several B movies and was being considered for a larger role in a motion picture being produced by MGM and starring Clark Gable. Here she had found her first hint of rejection. The role had gone to someone else. This was perhaps the turning point in her life. From there everything had seemed to go downhill, as if one failure had opened the floodgates of a reservoir of constant rejection.

Surprised and hurt, she had made subtle inquiries as to why she did not get the coveted role. It was impossible to believe that the other girl had been more talented or more beautiful or just simply luckier. Hadn't luck always been with her? Her agent, somewhat casually, suggested that perhaps she hadn't slept with the right people. Until then it had not occurred to her that the path to success started in the bedroom, and she refused to even consider such a possibility. But, as time went on and she saw others getting the roles that she wanted, she found that she had to alter her position. In a last-ditch effort to give herself a chance at stardom, she made herself available to those who could best promote her faltering career. For a time the strategy seemed to work, and she was able to secure a few minor roles in a few forgettable pictures. But still the better roles eluded her, and in time even the minor roles were not coming her way with any regularity. She found that she had joined a coterie of young women who desperately held on to their hopes of stardom. They attended parties and premieres on the arms of agents or producers, but they were intended merely as decorations. Victoria learned quickly that promises made in bed were rarely honored and that there was always another starlet willing to take her place. She tired of making love to fat old men who smelled of whiskey and cigars.

Outside it was raining. Harry Fox lay back in bed, took a deep drag on his cigarette, and thought about Victoria. She was two doors away, down the hall, and he suspected that if he knocked on her door, she would welcome him with open arms. During dinner her old confidence had reappeared, and he could tell that she felt safe here. He hoped that it had something to do with him, but perhaps it was just being away from the environment that had caused her so much pain. In any event he would not pressure her, would not make her feel that she owed him anything. Where she had been, everyone wanted a piece of you for every small favor. She would not get that from him.

The room was in semidarkness, the ceiling fan swishing gently above his head.

He heard a scraping at his door and automatically sat up in bed and reached into the open drawer of the night table and took out the small pistol that he kept there. He knew that Julio was on guard downstairs and no one would get past him without killing him.

The door opened slowly, filling the room with light from the hallway. He saw Victoria framed in the doorway. She wore a long, white silk nightgown. "You awake?" she whispered.

He slipped the pistol under his pillow. "Yes."

She came in, closing the door behind her. She paused by the side of the bed to let the nightgown slip from her shoulders and fall to the floor. Naked, she climbed in beside him, pulling the sheet up over her shoulders.

"You don't have to do this," he said. "I hired you because I needed a singer and you can sing. And because you're a friend."

"Hold me . . . please," she said softly.

He turned toward her and pulled her close to him. She was trembling, almost as if she were crying, but there were no tears. They held each other for a long time without speaking until she felt his hardness against her leg. She reached down to touch him. "Hello, again," she whispered into his ear. "It's been a long time."

She draped a leg across him and guided him inside her. "I've missed you," she said.

They made love as if they might never see each other again, hands moving, bodies thrusting, mouths locked together. He wanted to tell her that it was all right now, but he wasn't sure that it was, and so he said nothing.

After, they lay side by side, breathing deeply, neither wanting to say anything that would end the moment. In the faint light Harry watched her as she stared at the ceiling. She felt his eyes on her and turned to look at him. "What do you see when you look at me?"

"The same thing as always. The most beautiful woman that I've ever seen."

"Still?"

"Some things don't change."

"I wish that were true."

"Look," he said, "I don't know what you've been up to this past year—and I don't want to know. I only know that it didn't make you feel good. But you're still the same person that I met years ago in California. Inside"—he tapped a finger on his chest—"you're still the same."

In the moonlight he could see the tears glistening on her cheeks.

"I tried to kill myself in Vegas three months ago," she said without any trace of emotion.

He did not know what to say, so he said nothing. He reached for her and pulled her to him, holding her as tight as he could.

"But I didn't have the guts to pull it off," she said.

"You should have come to me sooner."

"I was going to be a star, Harry. Everybody said so. I couldn't go back home as a nobody." She pulled herself away from him and sat up. "Got a cigarette?"

He gave her one and lit it for her, watching her in the harsh light of the match. The shadows and her tear-streaked face played tricks, and he saw for the first time how terrible things had been for her. "It'll be all right now," he lied.

She blew smoke at the ceiling. "I always feel safe when you're around, Harry. Why is that?"

He didn't answer.

"Sometimes I think you're the only decent guy I've ever met in my whole life. That couldn't be true—could it?" She went on before he had a chance to say anything. "That's why I came here, I guess." She put her hand on his arm. "Can I stay for a while, Harry? Just till I get myself together?"

"Stay as long as you like."

"No. As long as *you* like. When you want me out of here,

just let me know and I'm gone. I'll cook for you, wash your shirts, make love any time you want it."

"I don't need anybody to cook for me or wash my shirts," he said.

She laughed and put her head on the pillow next to his. "That's good. I'm not too good at that anyway."

"After you've been here for a while, you might not be so anxious to stay."

"It can't be worse than Vegas or Havana," she said.

"Don't be too sure about that."

Victoria felt something beneath the pillow, reached under, and pulled out his pistol. "What the hell is this for?"

He took it from her and put it back on the night table. "Insurance," he said.

"What kind of insurance?"

"Panama City adjoins the Canal Zone which is officially U.S. territory. There are people who would like to turn me over to the American authorities in the zone. And there are people in Washington who would like to get me back there."

"For what? I know you told me once that you were a bootlegger during Prohibition, but I can't believe that the government is still after you for that."

"More than that," he said.

There was something about his tone that frightened her. "You don't have to tell me. I don't care what it is. Forget I asked. It's none of my business."

He ignored her plea. "Maybe you won't think I'm the most decent guy you ever met if I tell you."

"So don't tell me."

"They're after me for two things—besides the bootlegging. One—for the murder of a city councilman in Kansas City almost fifteen years ago. And two—for currency violations, passing counterfeit money almost eight years ago."

Victoria was silent.

"Aren't you going to ask me if I did it?"

"I know you didn't do it," she said. "I know you wouldn't kill anybody."

"It's a tough world out there," Harry said. "Don't be too sure of anything or anybody. Besides, the FBI doesn't have to prove that you did it, they just have to catch you and say that you did it."

"I don't think a gun will stop the FBI," Victoria said.

"Probably not, but there are people here in Panama City who would like to see me leave the country—either in a pine box or in the custody of the U.S. government—so that they could take over this place. I've got a pretty good business here; it's very popular with the 'norteamericanos' who work in the zone. We serve good food, good drinks, and provide good entertainment. People have a good time while they lose their money at the gambling tables. The gambling profits alone are enough to make some people want me to vacate the country."

Victoria took a deep drag on her cigarette. In the red glow her face was almost without expression.

Harry looked into her eyes. In the faint light he could tell nothing from what he saw there. "Sure you want to stick around?"

"You said you needed a singer, didn't you?"

Harry pulled her close. "I'm glad you're here. For however long."

She pulled his face down to hers. "Just hold me," she said, kissing him. She wondered what she was getting herself into.

CHAPTER 8

Ernesto Garcia burst into Harry Fox's upstairs office. "I think we got trouble downstairs, Harry."

Harry looked at Victoria, who sat in the chair across from him, and then turned to Garcia. "What kind of trouble, Ernesto?"

"Government trouble. Two guys in the bar say they're looking for you. One of 'em says he's with the FBI. Says he knows you."

Harry went to the window that looked down into the bar and pulled back the curtain. It was early in the day and only a few tables were occupied. "Trump," Harry said. "You two stay here while I go see what the bastard wants." He saw the look of alarm that had spread across Vicky's face and added, "Don't worry, they can't touch me here."

Victoria went to the window and peered through the curtain. She watched Harry head downstairs and walk across the barroom floor toward the two men who sat at one of the back tables. "What do they want him for?" she asked Garcia.

"Many things."

"Did he really kill someone?"

"Harry didn't tell you that he killed someone, did he?"

"Not in so many words, but that's one of the things they're after him for, isn't it?"

"Perhaps."

"What happened, Ernesto? I know Harry wouldn't kill anyone."

"Victoria," Garcia began sadly, "maybe you don't know Harry as well as you think you do. If Harry had to kill someone—perhaps a man who deserved killing—he would do it without a second thought."

"You mean, he did kill someone?"

"He has never admitted that to me—or to anyone. All I know is that when Harry was a young man his father owned a bar in Kansas City. When Prohibition came, his father did what everyone else did and sold liquor illegally. Everyone did it and no one seemed to care. For a time the father was very successful, but then some Kansas City politician—a councilman, or something—decided that he wanted to become a partner in Harry's father's business. Harry's father refused, and very soon after that he was raided by the police, who closed him down. Two weeks later the bar reopened under new management. Harry's father was sentenced to three years in jail, but unfortunately, he died after less than a year. Some time later, perhaps a month or two, the councilman was having an after-hours drink in what was now his place of business when someone who must have had a key to the back door came in and shot him three times in the head. The police suspected Harry, but, because the killing had all the earmarks of a mob hit, they were unable to prove that he had anything to do with it."

Victoria felt a sudden chill and wrapped her arms around herself. "What do you think the FBI wants?" she asked.

"They always want something."

Harry Fox pulled back a chair and sat across from the two men who sat silently waiting. "Special Agent Trump, this is indeed an unexpected pleasure," Harry said. He looked at Wilfred Smythe, who, caught in the glare of the obvious animosity, seemed uncomfortable. "I don't believe I've had the pleasure of meeting your friend."

To Fox's and Trump's surprise, Smythe stood up and extended his hand across the table. "Wilfred Smythe," he said, shaking Harry's hand. "Colonel Wilfred Smythe."

"Colonel?" Harry asked. "Is this a new FBI rank, Trump?"

"Smythe is not with the bureau," Trump said.

"I'm with British Security Coordination in New York City," Smythe said.

"You're a long way from home, Colonel."

"I'd rather you called me Smythe—or Wilfred, if you prefer."

Harry nodded. "OK, Smythe." He turned his attention back to Trump. "What can I do for you, Trump?"

"We were wondering," Trump said, "what you thought of the new political situation here in Panama."

"I didn't care much for Arias, but he was elected by his own people. I guess his biggest mistake was thinking that the U.S. government would let these people decide things for themselves."

"My question was not an invitation to discuss international politics," Trump said sharply.

"Pardon me," Harry said. He nodded to Smythe. "Lots of people travel all the way from New York just to hear my opinions on the political situation in Central America."

"What I really wanted to know," Trump said, "was how you thought the new government might treat an extradition request."

"I guess they'd probably dance to whatever tune you played."

Trump smiled from ear to ear. "Precisely what I was thinking."

"Although if it was extradition you were after," Harry said, "you'd probably be over at the Presidential Palace talking to de la Guardia instead of sitting here chewing the fat with me."

Smythe jumped in to salvage an obviously deteriorating

situation. "The reason that I have asked Special Agent Trump to bring me here, Mr. Fox, is that I was hoping that you might be persuaded to perform an invaluable service for His Majesty's government."

Harry spoke to Smythe, but his eyes never left Trump's face. "Now, why in hell would I want to do that, Colonel? It's been months since His Majesty invited me for tea."

"Well," Smythe began, "Director Hoover has mentioned the possibility of a . . ." The lie stuck in his throat. "Perhaps Agent Trump could explain."

Trump had no problem with the lie. "Director Hoover has suggested a full pardon for any and all crimes if you cooperate fully in this matter."

"Who does J. Edgar want me to kill?"

"Nothing like that," Smythe said hurriedly. "Actually we—the British government—want you to steal something, and then replace it with a substitute so that no one will know that it has been taken."

Harry sat back in the chair and looked from one to the other. "Why me? Contrary to what some people think," he said, looking directly at Trump, "stealing is not exactly my main line of work."

"How about counterfeiting?" Trump asked.

Harry's face hardened. He leaned forward, elbows on the table. "Let's get down to it. What is it that you people want?"

"I'm afraid," Smythe said, "that until you decide whether or not to help us we can't tell you any more than we have. You'll just have to trust us."

Harry stood up. "It's been nice talking to you, gentlemen. I wish you luck with whatever little game you've got planned, but I think you're going to have to count me out."

Smythe looked to Trump for help, but the FBI man only scowled.

"Enjoy your drinks," Harry said. "They're on the house." He spoke to Trump. "And good luck with that extradition thing."

In silence they watched him walk away.

Smythe spoke first. "Interesting fellow."

Trump glared at the Englishman. "I'm gonna nail his hide to the barn door."

Harry was making drinks from the cabinet in his office. Victoria, who already had a drink in her hand, sat on the leather sofa across from Harry's desk while Garcia paced the room.

"Counterfeiting?" Garcia asked.

"We didn't get to the details," Harry said, handing Garcia a drink, "but it had something to do with counterfeiting."

Garcia laughed and dropped into the leather chair in front of the desk. "The FBI wants you to do some counterfeiting for them? I like that, Harry. I like that a lot."

Harry sat and put his feet up on the desk. "I don't know what the FBI has to do with it. Seems more like the British want the help, and the FBI is just along for the ride."

"But they offered you a pardon, my friend?"

"I wouldn't trust Trump as far as I could throw him."

Victoria chimed in. "But a pardon, Harry. No more running. No more hiding out."

Harry looked around, waving an arm to encompass the room. "I kind of like it here."

"Someday, Harry," she said, "you might want to go home."

"Victoria is right, Harry," Garcia said. "Someday you may grow tired of this place, and everyone should have the right to go home. Besides, with this new government, who knows how long you will be welcome here?"

Harry sipped his drink. His eyes were full of doubt.

Garcia broke the somber mood with a loud laugh. "I could always speak to my cousin, Domingo. He has contacts with the kind of terrible people who make this counterfeit money."

Harry smiled and raised his glass in salute. "I'm sure he does."

Victoria sensed that there was something secret between the two men but knew that it would be fruitless to pry. She wondered if she would ever know what kind of a man Harry Fox really was.

There was a knock at the door and Harry said, "Come."

The door opened and a young man entered. He was Roberto Garcia, Ernesto's eldest son, and he was the maître d' in the downstairs dining room. Roberto was in his early twenties. He was tall and handsome with a pleasant, reassuring manner. "Harry," he said, "one of the gentlemen who was here earlier has returned. He says that he would like to speak with you."

Harry went to the window. "Smythe," he said, "the Englishman."

Wilfred Smythe stood in the center of the room. He held his hat in his hand and looked up at Harry's office. When he saw the curtain part, he gave a brief nod.

"Send him up, Roberto," Harry said and then spoke to Garcia, "Let's find out what he wants."

Smythe seemed uncomfortable when he entered the room. He took a seat but politely refused the offered drink. "I thought that we might talk," he said.

"Talk," Harry said simply.

Smythe looked at Garcia and Victoria. "I had hoped to speak with you in private."

Garcia started to rise, but Harry stopped him with a short movement of his hand. "Señor Garcia is my oldest and most trusted friend, Smythe. We have no secrets. Anything you tell me, I'll only tell him after you've gone. So if you don't want him to know—you'd better not tell me."

Smythe nodded and stole a quick glance at Victoria, who was filing her nails.

Harry smiled. "I'm afraid I couldn't keep a secret from Miss Gansell if I tried."

Victoria crossed her legs and winked at Smythe, who smiled weakly. "I suppose not," he said. He gave a soft sigh of resignation and plowed on. "Mr. Fox, part of my job is to prevent the German infiltration of the South American continent. As part of that operation, the British government has made it extremely difficult for the Germans to acquire currency—particularly American currency—in this hemisphere. The American government has been most cooperative in this regard, I might add. Without money to pay agents, the Germans are finding it very difficult to operate in South and Central America. Quite recently we have been informed that the Germans have been able to acquire a rather substantial amount of American currency. To put it simply, we'd like to stop them from distributing that money throughout their South American network."

"And," Harry said, "you'd like me to steal it."

"Yes."

"And replace it with counterfeit money."

"You are quite astute, Mr. Fox."

"You said earlier that you wanted something stolen and replaced with—I think you called it—a substitute."

"That's correct."

"I don't get it," Harry said. "I can see why you want to steal the money, but why replace it with counterfeit?"

Victoria looked up from her nail filing. "That's easy, Harry. Take the money from the Germans, and they'd probably just get more somewhere. But once the word gets out that they are passing phony money, no one will want to work for them." She gave her best dumb blonde look and winked at Smythe. "How'm I doin', honey."

"Apparently, Mr. Fox, I have been guilty of underestimating you—all of you. Until now I had wondered if Mr. Trump—and Mr. Hoover—were correct when they said that you were the right man for the job."

"It's nice to know that Hoover thinks so highly of me," Harry said. "But why me?"

"The FBI seems to feel that you have some expertise in the counterfeiting of American currency. We need large amounts of counterfeit American money in a hurry."

"Seems to me that the FBI could provide you with all that you want—plates, ink, paper. They've got some of the world's best counterfeit plates locked up at bureau headquarters."

Smythe nodded his agreement. "Mr. Hoover does not

want to implicate the bureau in a highly illegal international venture."

Harry smiled. "I see. He avoids the risk but is ready to take the credit—and probably the profits."

"Something like that," Smythe said.

"I assume that there is some risk involved in this. What do I get out of it?"

Smythe looked down at the floor. "The previously mentioned pardon, for one thing."

"Anything else?"

"If you mean anything monetary, I'm afraid not. Mr. Hoover is insistent that all recovered money be returned to the U.S. Treasury."

"Good old J. Edgar can always find a way to take the fun out of anything."

"You could satisfy yourself with the knowledge that you are helping to make the hemisphere safe for democracy," Smythe said quite seriously.

Harry looked at him, waiting for the punch line. When it did not come he said, "Please, spare me the drivel about democracy. If I get caught—that is, if I'm lucky enough not to get my head blown off—I don't suppose anyone is going to step forward and say that I did it for democracy?"

"I'm afraid not."

"Let me be honest with you, Smythe," Fox said. "I don't print counterfeit money, but I know people who, if the price is right, can print whatever currency you might require. But they won't do it for nothing."

"How much?" Smythe asked.

"How much counterfeit are we talking about, and how soon do we need it?"

"We need somewhere in the neighborhood of four million dollars—"

"Big neighborhood," Harry interjected. "I'd think that a hundred thousand dollars would be a fair price."

Smythe did not seem perturbed by the price. ". . . and we need it within a few days—a week at most," he said.

"You get the okay for the money, and I think we can handle the job," Harry said to Smythe.

"I'm sure that I could get my people to provide half of the hundred thousand," Smythe said, "and perhaps I could persuade the FBI to contribute the rest. After all," Smythe said, "they are getting four million dollars out of this."

"That's up to you," Harry said.

"If I can convince the FBI to provide the money, will you do the job?"

"I'd need to know more about it, but if I think it can be done, I'll do it. Provided I get my pardon."

Smythe stood up. "I'll talk with Trump right away. I'm sure that I can convince him to provide the rest of the money. Can we meet with you tomorrow?"

"Make it the day after. I need the time to talk with some people who might be able to help. I'll be spending the day at my house outside the city. If Trump agrees, bring him there sometime in the afternoon. Maybe we can do business."

CHAPTER 9

In 1941 the Abwehr had several spy rings operating in Panama. Kurt Spengler, who was the local manager of the Hamburg-America Line, and the German consul in Colón, had been the Abwehr's resident director since 1935. Spengler had at least ten full-time and part-time spies in his employ at any one time. On the Pacific side of the canal, various members of the German Embassy staff in Panama City, led by the second secretary Gisbert Lohse along with the usual assortment of informants and part-time operatives, were actively engaged in espionage activities against the United States. The Abwehr suspected that most of these persons were under constant surveillance by the FBI. Robles was warned to avoid contact with any of these groups.

There was a third spy ring which operated out of the offices of the Hapag-Lloyd Steamship Company in Balboa, a suburban district of Panama City that sits at the Pacific entrance to the Panama Canal. This circlet of espionage agents comprised only three members: Heinrich Drexler, the leader of the group, whose position as local personnel director for the steamship company provided him access to all areas of the Canal Zone; Erika Schreiber, Drexler's secretary; and Ludwig Brack, a mechanic and handyman whose skills provided him with easy access to the Zone. This ring, because of its small size and careful operation, was felt to be secure. Robles's contact in Lisbon had given him a phone number and an Abwehr password to allow him to contact the Drexler group.

Robles's first task upon arrival in Panama City had been to find lodging in one of the many run-down rooming houses that dotted the city. He was looking for the kind of place where he could come and go as he pleased without arousing the suspicions of his neighbors. Such places were easy to find in Panama City. He found himself drawn to the canal and limited his search to an area within walking distance of the Balboa Pier. He settled for a small apartment, two rooms in the back of a large apartment building that was shared by several families.

When he felt that he had settled into his rooms, he went for a walk along the Balboa Pier, where ships unloaded cargoes that would be carried across Panama by rail. From the docks Robles could see the wide entrance to the Panama Canal that led to the first set of locks at Miraflores several miles inland. The harbor was filled with a line of ships, each awaiting its turn to begin the trip through the canal. The harbor bustled with activity, but if Robles closed his eyes, he could imagine the approach to the canal deserted, the harbor silent, the canal closed.

After a while Robles turned away from the pier and made his way to the Avenida Diablo, a wide thoroughfare lined with apartment buildings and run-down hotels. He went inside one of the smaller hotels and asked to use the telephone. He would not use the telephone at his own place to make a call. The woman behind the desk looked up momentarily, pointed to the phone, and went back to her magazine.

Robles was at first surprised when a woman's voice answered the phone—he had not expected that—but he dutifully gave the Abwehr code words. "I am expecting the arrival of a package from Lisbon," he said. "I was told to ask for Mr. Drexler."

There was a pause and a sound, as if a drawer had been opened, and then the woman's voice was back. "Is this Mr. Braga?"

This was the correct response. "Yes."

"Your package has arrived, Mr. Braga. It can be delivered immediately or you can pick it up if you prefer."

"I would be grateful if you would deliver it for me," Robles said.

"Very well. Let me check that we have the correct address."

Robles heard the sound of the phone being put down and again the sound of a drawer sliding open. He prepared to write down the instructions that he knew would come next.

In a moment the woman's voice was back. She read him an address, which he copied down, and then he said, "Yes, that is correct. Can I expect delivery by this evening?"

"Yes. Anytime after seven," she said.

They thanked each other and hung up. Robles looked at the address. It was meaningless—a house number and the name of a street—unless one used the proper decoding procedure. When he transposed the numbers in the proper sequence and translated the street name from his one-time pad, he would know where he was to meet his contact.

He put the address in his pocket and left the hotel. The fat woman behind the desk did not look up.

By force of habit Robles arrived early at the address he had been given. It was a small house, wedged between other similar houses, on a quiet street in the Quarry Heights section near Ancon Hill. He took a taxi, getting out a half dozen or so streets before his eventual destination, and walked the rest of the way. There was no chance that he had been followed.

He watched the house for almost half an hour, and when he did not note any unusual activity, he walked across the street and knocked at the door.

Heinrich Drexler opened the door and wordlessly ushered

him inside. Drexler was in his forties, tall, blond, and rather handsome. He appeared nervous. "You were not followed, I trust?" Drexler said.

Robles gave him a baleful look. "No."

The men shook hands and Drexler led Robles into a small but comfortable living room. A young woman, wiping her hands on an apron, came out of the kitchen to join them. She, too, was blond, and quite beautiful. She smiled and eyed Robles appreciatively and removed her apron as if to let him see her figure. She was, Robles estimated, no more than twenty, and he wondered if she was Drexler's daughter.

Drexler had seen the look that passed between them, and he quickly made sure that Robles was made aware of the living arrangements. "This is Miss Schreiber," he said, putting his arm around the girl. "She lives here with me."

Miss Schreiber squirmed out of his grasp, and Robles smiled at the small domestic drama that was unfolding in front of him. She gave Robles a firm handshake. "Erika," she said.

"You are the one I spoke with today," Robles said.

"Yes," she said pleased that he had recognized her voice.

Drexler offered to make drinks, but Robles preferred coffee. Erika went back into the kitchen, and the two men sat across from each other. "The men you are to contact have not yet arrived," Drexler said.

Robles had not expected them to be there yet. His eyes wandered to the kitchen door, where he could hear the girl preparing the coffee.

"In a day or two. As soon as I hear I will let you know." Drexler had been told to give his full and absolute cooperation to this man, but already he did not like the way things were going. "Is that all right?" he said somewhat testily.

"I don't like the telephone contact," Robles said. "Someone could be listening. I think personal contact is better."

"I'm not sure that would be wise."

Robles was well aware that Drexler had been told to follow orders. "Send the girl. We'll meet in a café . . . or something."

Drexler's face hardened. "What else can we do for you?" he asked.

"I need a contact who knows the country. Someone who can put me in touch with the right people. And someone who can contact Abwehr headquarters for me, if necessary." Robles knew that Drexler had an Afu radio set by which he could contact the Abwehr reception station in Hamburg.

"I can do these things for you," Drexler said reluctantly.

Robles expected him to add, "But I won't."

Erika returned with the coffee. She placed a cup in front of each and sought neutral ground in a chair between them. She sipped her coffee, watching both men over the rim of the cup. She listened as they set up a series of codes that would enable them to make initial contact by phone and set up meeting places. It was obvious that Drexler did not like Robles, and she was sure that it was because of her. Erika enjoyed provoking this kind of sexual confrontation, relishing Drexler's jealousies and the fact that he could not resign himself to constant infidelities. Infidelity was not really the correct word, she decided. After all, she had been told to gather information about the Panama Canal and its defenses. In what other way could she be expected to persuade the men she went out with to give her such information? Men always liked to show how important they were, she thought. Especially in bed. She smiled as she half listened to Drexler and Robles. The Canal Zone was the perfect place for someone like her, she thought. There were twenty men to every woman. And now someone new and very interesting had been added. "We have been told of some of your previous exploits," she said to Robles. "Very impressive."

Robles did not answer. He enjoyed watching Drexler's growing discomfort.

"Are we supposed to know why you are here?" Drexler asked.

Robles assumed that they already did know. There were very few targets in Panama worthy of a man with his talents. "Why else would I be here?" he said.

"Do you really think that you can destroy the canal?"

Erika asked, and then giggled like a schoolgirl who had made a mistake.

Drexler gave her a furious look.

Robles smiled. He liked her enthusiasm. "Anything that man builds can be destroyed," he said. "It is merely a matter of applying force in the proper location."

Erika's eyes betrayed her interest in Robles. "I can't wait," she said. "The Americans won't be so cocky then."

Drexler saw the look that passed between them. "You might think otherwise when you see how well defended the canal is," he said almost scornfully. "Two years ago—even last year at this time—the task would have been considerably easier. But the Americans have finally realized how vulnerable the canal is and how vital it is to their security."

"You may be right."

Drexler was anxious to prove that he was. "Our job is to report to Berlin all of the defensive fortifications that have been built in the past two years. Coastal artillery pieces have been installed at the forts that guard the entrances to the canal; the navy conducts continuous surface patrols in the waters adjacent to the canal; there are aircraft warning stations and antiaircraft emplacements at each set of locks; and the garrison—thirty thousand strong—is on twenty-four-hour alert."

"That may well be," Robles said, "but those things are designed to stop air attacks, invasions, or naval bombardment." He looked to Erika and smiled. "Nothing can stop one man who knows what he wants."

"What do you want from us?" Drexler asked quickly, hoping to bring to an end what was for him an unpleasant evening.

"Names," Robles said. "The names of people who can be trusted to help me acquire the things I might need."

"I trust only my own people," Drexler said. "That's why we have been able to operate for so long."

"I was told that you operate with only one other man."

"Correct. Ludwig Brack will help you get whatever you need."

"I will need large amounts of explosives and the manpower to transport them. Can we expect any help from the Panamanian opposition to the government?"

"Don't trust any of the former Panamanian officials. Most of them are corrupt. Money is all they care about."

"I will have money," Robles said. "It can be a powerful inducement to cooperation."

"Viega is the man you want," Erika chimed in. "He's got his sticky fingers everywhere."

"Viega?" Robles asked.

"Narciso Viega," Drexler said. "Until recently he was the commander in chief of the Panamanian National Guard. He still wields considerable influence with many Panamanians. He is the man you want to see about explosives and manpower."

"Do you trust him?"

"He wants the Americans out of Panama. He imagines that he is using us to that end."

"And he can provide the explosives I will need?"

"As you are no doubt aware," Drexler said, "the recently deposed Panamanian government, led by President Arias, was most sympathetic to our common cause. Arias, correctly, anticipated that the Americans would use their influence to remove him from office and substitute someone more to their liking. To prevent this from happening, Arias had determined to hold the canal for ransom."

"Ransom?" Robles said.

"Quite simply, if the Americans ever challenged the Arias government, he wanted to be able to threaten them with the destruction of the canal. To that end, we provided to Arias and his supporters a considerable amount of military-grade, high explosives. It is my understanding that the Japanese have been helpful in this endeavor, also. Consequently, the explosives that you require are already in Panama."

Robles wondered why the plan had not been implemented when Arias had been deposed.

Drexler saw the question behind his silence. "Apparently, the Arias supporters did not have time to put their plan into effect. The Americans took them by surprise."

Robles's expression showed his displeasure with that

explanation. The prospect of failure, he knew, was a daunting adversary. The Panamanians had failed because they did not have the resolve. He did. "And the Arias supporters will turn this cache of explosives over to me?" he asked.

"We can't be certain of that. They will probably demand some sort of payment for the explosives and for their assistance."

"Payment for our own explosives?"

"These people are not like us," Drexler said. He was about to make a derogatory remark about the Hispanic ancestry of the Panamanians when he remembered that Robles was Argentinian. "They want financial profit from their activities," he said instead.

"I want to meet with Viega as soon as possible."

"What else?"

Robles did not look at Erika. "I have a place to stay, but I want a second place—in case I have to leave the first in a hurry."

"You could stay here," Erika said quickly.

Drexler's head snapped around in dismay.

Erika giggled and looked at Robles. "After all," she said, "we only use one of the bedrooms." When Drexler turned away, she made a face that disclosed her dissatisfaction with that arrangement.

Robles was sure that her remarks were intended to inform him of the sexual nature of the relationship and to advise him of her availability. He decided that enough had been accomplished for the evening. He did not wish to turn Drexler against him. He might need the man's help. "I don't think that would meet my requirements," he said, and noted Drexler's sigh of relief. "You will inform me when my contacts arrive," he told Drexler, "and set up a meeting with Viega." He turned to Erika. "In the meantime," he said to her, "you, perhaps, could find me a place to stay. As soon as I collect my funds I will want to move."

Robles shook hands with both and quickly went to the door. "I will call every day until my contacts arrive," he said. "If any meeting is required, you can let me know then."

Drexler opened the door and closed it quickly behind Robles as soon as the visitor had stepped outside. Robles paused for a moment before he walked away from the door. He could hear them arguing before he reached the street.

CHAPTER 10

Late in the afternoon, Harry and Garcia boarded a train for the relatively brief trip across Panama to the city of Colón. For Harry, the trip was not without danger as the Panama Railroad was owned by the Panama Canal Company and its route lay entirely within the Canal Zone and American jurisdiction. As always when he made this journey, Harry wore dark glasses and a wide-brimmed hat. He carried papers that identified him as Ralph Jensen, an American engineer who was presently unemployed and looking for work in the zone. Although security within the Canal Zone was notoriously lax and identification was rarely asked for, Harry had no desire to be detained within the American-controlled zone. He was certain that the FBI would have him on its "restricted" list and that within hours of apprehension he would be on his way back to the States in FBI custody.

As usual, the trip was uneventful. No one asked any of the passengers for identification or to give any reason for being in the Canal Zone. What military personnel they did encounter seemed more intent on flirting with Panamanian women than on worrying about potential saboteurs entering the zone. Less than two hours after leaving Ancon on the Pacific side of Panama, they arrived in Colón on the Caribbean side. From the station they took a taxi to the run-down business district in the center of the city. They walked down a side street and stood across from a small storefront that advertised printing services. Harry looked at his watch. "Let's wait for a bit," he said.

At just a few minutes before closing the two men entered the business establishment of Epifanio Chiari. Chiari was a small, thin man in his late sixties. He looked up as the two men entered, and although he wore glasses, he still squinted to bring the faces into focus. He smiled when he recognized his visitors.

"Harry, Ernesto, my friends," he said warmly, opening his arms to embrace them in turn. "To what do I owe this unexpected pleasure?"

"Epifanio, we have need of your special services in a matter of great urgency," Harry said.

Chiari looked at his watch. "I was just about to close up," he said, going to the door. He turned the lock and pulled down a shade. "Let's go downstairs."

The lower level included three separate rooms: a long, narrow workspace where four printing presses stood, a darkroom at one end, and a separate room used as an office at the other. A young man stood beside the only one of the presses that was in use. The noise was almost deafening.

"This is my stepson, Ricardo!" Chiari said, yelling above the din of the press. Harry and Garcia nodded an acknowledgment and followed Chiari into the small room at the far end.

Chiari closed the door behind them, muffling, somewhat, the noise of the press. He sat at a small desk, and they sat in two wooden chairs. Chiari took a brandy bottle and three glasses from a lower drawer and poured each a healthy portion. He pushed two glasses across the desktop toward his guests. "I must say that I am surprised, Harry," Chiari said.

"Surprised?"

"Yes. You said you would require my services only once and then never again. I've had others tell me the same, but they always came back for more. Somehow I always thought that you would be the exception."

"These are exceptional times," Harry said.

"Well, then, what can I do for you, my friends?"

"I need four million American dollars in fifty-dollar denominations," Harry said.

"That's a lot of money, Harry. And I don't especially like fifty-dollar bills. Even real ones make people suspicious."

"I'll need it in less than a week. Can you do it?"

Chiari looked as if he had been wounded by the doubt implied in Harry's question.

Garcia was quick to jump in. "Harry meant, of course, will you do it, Epifanio."

Harry nodded. "I meant that there isn't much time for such a large job."

Chiari sighed. "It's not a question of can I do this, Harry. I can do a job like this in three or four days. I could make the plates after hours tonight and tomorrow. Prepare the ink and get the paper ready. The shop is closed on Sunday, and I could run all of it in maybe eight or ten hours. But I have managed to stay in business for almost thirty years by never being too greedy. I have found that as long as one does not overburden the monetary system, no one really seems to mind or notice if someone passes a little bit of counterfeit now and then." He smiled. "As long, of course, as the counterfeit is of excellent quality. I am an old man, Harry. I am ready to give up this work and leave the business to my stepson."

"Just one more job, Epifanio. One more big job and then you can retire knowing that you were the best there ever was."

"Four million dollars would bring the Americans down on all of us, Harry."

"Not this time, Epifanio," Harry said. "This job is at the request of the American government."

"Maybe you'd better tell me what this is all about, Harry."

Harry told him the story, and as he did he could see Chiari's interest grow.

When Harry was finished, Chiari smiled. "I would love to put something over on those German bastards," he said. "Even though it has been almost thirty years since I last set foot on French soil, I still consider myself a Frenchman."

Epifanio Chiari was not his real name. He had been born in Marseilles in 1875 and lived there for most of his younger years. He had been apprenticed to a printer as a twelve-year-old and had learned the trade well. Later he had added engraving to his skills. In 1904 he had been convicted of counterfeiting French currency and given the option of a lengthy prison term or serving with the Foreign Legion. He had chosen the latter and served with the legion in French North Africa for seven years, where an enterprising colonel had encouraged him in his quest to create the perfect counterfeit currency. In 1912 he returned to France and continued his education as a counterfeiter. Through the stupidity and greed of colleagues he was again apprehended and this time sent to Devil's Island. After three years he and two others escaped in a raft and made it to the shore of French Guiana. After three years in Brazil he had come to Panama, married a widow twenty years his junior, and opened his own printing and engraving business. From time to time, almost as a matter of professional curiosity, he created what were regarded by many experts as the finest counterfeit bills made anywhere in the world.

"So the great J. Edgar Hoover himself is behind this scheme of yours, Harry?"

Harry nodded.

"But why do you do this, Harry? What's in it for you?"

"One hundred thousand dollars," Harry said. "Shared equally among the three of us, paid upon the successful completion of the job, and Ernesto and I will pay whatever expenses are incurred out of our share."

Garcia added, "And the FBI has promised Harry a pardon. He will be able to go home again."

"Home," Chiari said. "Then I understand completely, my friend. Everyone should have the right to go home someday.

I will show Hoover the best fifty-dollar bills he has ever seen." Chiari laughed. "So good, Harry, that he could use them to pay his agents' wages."

Harry smiled. "Well, that's just it, Epifanio. They can't be that good."

"What do you mean?"

"A few weeks after the money is switched, the FBI wants to be able to identify the German agents who receive the money by letting everyone know that the money is counterfeit."

"Good enough to fool the Germans but with some easily identifiable flaw?"

"That's about it."

"How about if I create a counterfeit bill that is absolutely indistinguishable from the genuine article, but in two weeks would be rejected by anyone who had ever seen a real fifty-dollar bill?"

"You can do that?" Garcia asked.

"I will mix the ink so that in two weeks the greenbacks will begin to turn blue. By the third week not even a child would accept them."

Harry could imagine the consternation of the Germans when their "money" started to turn blue. "That sounds perfect," he said. "I'll get the okay from the FBI tonight. When can you begin?"

Chiari smiled. "I will begin now."

Harry reached into his jacket pocket and removed an envelope from which he removed four crisp, new fifty-dollar bills. "These might help."

Chiari took them and poured another round of drinks. "To success," he said.

"To success."

Chiari began immediately. Harry and Garcia followed him to his darkroom, where he photographed the four fifty-dollar bills. Working quickly and confidently, the old man then made a positive transparency rather than the usual reversed negative. He placed the finished product on a white background and examined it carefully through a magnifying glass called a loupe. "Quite good," he said. He continued to inspect the images on the table and talk at the same time. "The problem with trying to recreate American money," he said, "is in the printing process itself. The Bureau of Engraving uses what is called the intaglio printing process. This process uses huge presses with etched cylinders that are able to deposit relatively heavy amounts of ink onto the paper. This is what gives the feeling of a raised surface to American money. I can approximate that feeling with offset lithography by using a deep etch process, but too much ink and we get smearing, so we must be very careful."

Harry and Garcia were silent, unwilling to break the concentration of a master craftsman at work.

"Of course," Chiari said, "I'll have to use the right paper, an off-white stock that has the feel of currency."

"I have been told," Garcia said, "that it is the paper that is the most difficult thing to reproduce."

"Yes and no," Chiari said, his eye at the loupe, his face still close to the positive transparencies on the table. He had taken a small artist's brush and was delicately applying a small amount of opaquing fluid to several places on the transparency. "It is impossible to exactly duplicate the paper because only one company is allowed to make it, and they, of course, are allowed to sell it only to the government."

"What about the threads that are woven into the paper?" Harry asked.

Chiari yanked several hairs from his head. "Threads," he said, displaying the hairs. "I'll photograph them and include them on the printed paper. They're not real threads, of course, but the only way to tell is to tear the bills apart and examine them through a microscope. I don't think your German friends will take the time to do that."

"I suppose not," Harry said.

"Don't worry, Harry," Chiari said. "These bills will pass a thorough visual inspection by a bank teller. Except for one thing."

"What?"

"The serial numbers. Because these bills are not meant to

be passed individually but handed over in a lump sum, the serial numbers can't be the same. If they were, even a superficial examination would discover that the bills were fake."

"What do we do?"

"Using the individual serial numbers from the four bills you gave me, and the numbers from any other American currency we have available, I can make up any number of different serial combinations," Chiari said. "I can easily print several hundred different versions and run them separately. That's enough so that the duplications won't be noticed."

"Sounds like a lot of extra print runs," Garcia said.

"True, but I'll prepare the numbers and the Treasury Department seal first. Both are green. Ricardo can print them while I'm preparing the front and back of the bills. Then he will print the backs—also green—while I put the finishing touches on the face of the bill. We print the faces over the seal and numbers, let them dry for a bit, cut them to size, and"—he smiled—"we have money that even Mr. Hoover will be proud of."

"You make it sound easy," Harry said.

"Easy? No. But not as difficult as the American Treasury Department would like everyone to think. I could tell them how to make money that no one could counterfeit."

"Why would you want to do that?" Garcia asked.

"Why, indeed," Chiari said. "Why, indeed."

CHAPTER 11

In the early afternoon Smythe and Trump made the drive out to Harry Fox's house in the fashionable suburbs to the east of Panama City. They drove past the two stone pillars and the wrought-iron gate that was opened by a guard with a rifle slung across his shoulder. They parked in front of the large white house, where they were greeted by another armed guard, who led them around the side of the house and onto the back patio, which overlooked the Pacific.

Trump shaded his eyes from the bright glare of the sun and looked around. The rear of the property was built into a steep hillside and looked particularly inaccessible from that side. The patio itself was on several levels, each stepping down away from the house. On the last level, just before the high railing that surrounded the rear of the property, was a small, sparklingly blue swimming pool. Trump drew in a sharp breath when he saw Victoria, sunning herself at poolside. A robe and the top half of her bathing suit lay at her side. She was unaware of their presence.

Trump gave Smythe a jab with his elbow.

Victoria opened her eyes and saw both men, Trump's eyes

wide in astonishment, Smythe's eyes to the ground. She sat up and turned her back as she reached for her robe and slipped it on.

She walked past them without a word and called into the house, "Harry, your friends are here."

As Harry came out of the house to greet them, Trump said to Smythe out of the corner of his mouth, "Who was it who said that crime didn't pay?"

Smythe ignored the comment and shook hands with Fox. "I've brought Special Agent Trump with me," he said, "to tell you that we think that we can do business on your terms."

"Can I get you a drink?" Harry asked as he led them over to some chairs that surrounded a small table.

Both accepted the offer of a drink, and as they sat, Harry made a gesture with his fingers and a young man appeared with three glasses and a pitcher of something cool looking. Harry poured, and when each had sipped the drink he said, "When do you need the money?"

"Four or five days from now," Trump said.

"Monday?"

Smythe nodded. "Can you do it?"

Harry took a sip of his drink. "Yes. My people are ready to go, but we have to start right away." He smiled. "It would be nice if the ink were dry before the Germans touched it. I'll tell my people to begin tonight."

Trump leaned back in his chair. "I will provide authentic Bank of Mexico money wrappers," he said. "I want the money in stacks of one hundred bills each. When we make the switch, we want things to be as simple as possible."

"Good idea," Harry said. "When do I get the wrappers?"

"I'll have them tonight," Trump said. "Be careful with them. There will only be enough to wrap the required amount."

Harry smiled. "Don't you trust me?"

Trump returned the smile. "Quite frankly, no."

"That's fine with me," Harry said. "A little distrust is always good in a business relationship."

Smythe said quickly, "Agent Trump will also have a small sample of government ink—not enough to do the job of course but just to give your people something to try to match."

"Good thought," Harry said. "That should prove very helpful."

"I'll have the wrappers by six o'clock tonight," Trump said. "When can you begin?"

Harry looked at his watch. "The plates might even be ready by now. If you give me the ink tonight, I can have my people start working on the match. Tomorrow perhaps—if the proper paper has been found—we can start printing the money."

"I suppose there is nothing like being prepared," Trump said.

"That's a motto I've learned to live by," Harry said.

"Now we can go over the rest of the plan."

"Just tell me where the Germans have the money," Harry said. "I'll work out the rest of the details."

"This plan has been worked out in Washington," Trump said.

Harry grinned. When Trump said "Washington," it was as if he had a marching band behind him. "Go ahead," Harry said.

Trump leaned forward conspiratorially. "The money will be delivered within the next few days from the bank in Mexico City to the German consulate in Vera Cruz. We have information from a very reliable source that the money will be taken by courier from there to a Spanish freighter for the trip to Buenos Aires."

Smythe was annoyed. The "reliable source" was the British monitoring station in Bermuda which had been intercepting and decoding German diplomatic messages for the better part of a year. As usual, the FBI acted as if they had gathered this intelligence information on their own.

"That ship—the *San Fraterno*—is scheduled to make stops in Limón in Costa Rica, Colón, here in Panama, then Barranquilla in Colombia, before the trip to Buenos Aires."

Harry interrupted. "It would be best to get to the money before they get on board ship. Somewhere between Mexico City and Vera Cruz."

"No good," Trump said. "The Germans are sure to examine the money carefully soon after they take possession."

"The Germans themselves have attempted the forgery of several European currencies. They are sure to be on the lookout for any kind of switch," Smythe said.

"If they discover that it is counterfeit, the Mexican government would be held responsible. We can't have that. We have to wait until the Germans take actual possession and have verified the authenticity of the currency."

"Besides," Smythe interjected tartly, "the usually reliable source reports that the couriers will disembark in Colón, where they will remain for at least one day and one night in order to transfer some of the money to a third party."

"Quite possibly to some of the backers of the Arias government who might be planning to return Arias to the presidency," said Trump.

"Then," Smythe went on, "the couriers will board an Argentinian passenger ship for the remainder of the journey to Buenos Aires."

"So," Harry said, "we make the exchange while they are in Colón?"

"Precisely," Trump said. "The couriers will be on their own in a hotel."

"Wait a minute," Harry said. "Why won't they go to the German Consulate in Colón? With that amount of money, they'd be much safer."

"Our information is," Smythe explained, "that the Germans have been told to avoid contact with anyone from the legation."

"Why?" Harry said.

"The Germans suspect—correctly—that we are watching their employees. They don't want us to discover whoever they are meeting here in Panama."

"Fox, I want you to get some men and some police uniforms," Trump said. "You will have these men accost the

Germans in their hotel room and confiscate the money. The Germans will of course protest that they are traveling under diplomatic immunity. During the course of the discussion, the money will be taken to another room and the switch made. Then your men will make profuse apologies for the misunderstanding and return the money to the Germans." Trump looked pleased with himself. "I will be there to take possession of the real money."

Harry made a face. "I can think of about ten ways to do this easier. We're involving too many people, and the plan seems unnecessarily complicated."

"This," said Trump, "is the plan that has been worked out by Washington. If you do your part properly, I see no chance for failure." He stood up, and Smythe, reluctantly, followed suit.

Harry remained seated. "These couriers are going to be heavily armed, and babysitting four million dollars is apt to make them more than a little nervous. If someone knocks on their hotel room door, they just might shoot first and ask questions later."

"Are you in or are you out?" Trump said.

"I'm in," Fox said reluctantly.

"That's it, then. We'll see you later at your place. You'd better get busy rounding up your people. This whole thing is going to start happening pretty soon."

Harry was already beginning to regret his involvement in this scheme.

CHAPTER 12

Even to someone who routinely handled millions of dollars on a daily basis, it was an awesome sight. The money, green and inviting, was in two large stacks on a long table in the vault of the Bank of Mexico in Mexico City. Between the stacks of money, two women were hunched over the table, like cobblers at the last, meticulously counting each bill. As they worked they moved the bills from one stack to the other so that as one pile grew the other diminished. The only sound in the vault was the whirring of the electric fan that had been placed there to relieve the oppressive heat of the chamber.

Miguel Flores, assistant to the vice president of banking operations at the Bank of Mexico, watched as the two women he had been assigned to supervise counted the four million dollars in American money. The money had arrived from the bank in Houston that morning, and already it was being counted and prepared for transfer. The women first removed the American bank's green wrappers and then, after counting the individual stacks, replaced the wrappers with the gold wrappers of the Bank of Mexico.

Aside from the great amount of currency involved, this might have been a simple transfer of funds from one account to another. The money had originally been held in the accounts of the Italian and Japanese governments, deposited when the Americans had declared that such accounts were no longer welcome in American banks. It was now being transferred into an account held by the German government in Vera Cruz. Until this transfer of funds, the German account had been inactive for several months due to a lack of funds. What made the transfer somewhat unusual, however, was the German request that the Bank of Mexico ship the entire amount in new American fifty-dollar bills. Although American currency was common tender throughout Latin America, it was rather unusual to request such a large amount in cash and in one denomination, and the Bank of Mexico had been obliged to exchange funds with an American bank in Houston. Still, Flores thought, these days there was very little that was normal about international finance. This particular case, however, seemed more unusual than most, and everyone—the Americans included—seemed very interested in what was happening to this money.

The women worked quickly, quietly, and expertly, the money flashing through their nimble fingers as they counted. After rewrapping, the bills were placed at the end of the table, where the women worked. Every few minutes Flores picked up the counted bills and transferred them to a second table where he placed them in short stacks. He placed ten wrapped packets in each stack for easier counting when the women were finished.

When the women were about halfway through the task of counting, Flores looked at his watch. He did not want them to finish too quickly. His boss had told him that the Germans were anxious to have the money transferred as soon as possible after its arrival in Mexico City. His American friends, on the other hand, had said that they would appreciate as much delay as possible. Since his American friends occasionally fortified their friendship with a small contribution to his retirement fund, Flores was more agreeable to their wishes than to anything that the Germans might request. Truthfully, there wasn't too much he could do about delaying the transfer, but he knew that if he could delay the completion of the task of counting and rewrapping until just before closing time, the money would not be transferred until the following day.

"Count carefully, ladies," he said to the women. "These are not pesos you are counting, but American dollars."

The women looked at each other and then at the ceiling in exasperation. If this one would leave them alone, they would have been finished already. Several times he had stopped them and made them recount some of the wrapped packets because he did not think they were thick enough to contain the required two hundred bills. Of course they were always correct. As if that were not enough, he had, several times, interrupted them in midcount with some inane chatter about nothing in particular, forcing them to begin the count again. The job was taking twice as long as it should.

Flores looked at his watch again and smiled. At this rate he was sure that the money would remain here in Mexico City for another day. An armored car and four armed men were standing by to take the money to the train station, where it would be placed in a private car with two armed men for the trip to Vera Cruz. There the money would be withdrawn by the Germans. Flores had hoped that the money would arrive later in the day, but when it had come this early he had insisted that the bank conduct a thorough accounting. He was sure that he could delay the transfer to Vera Cruz for one more day. He wasn't sure why the Americans wanted him to delay handing over the money to the Germans, but his FBI contact had told him that they wanted as much delay as possible. The FBI had already held up the transfer of the money from the American bank for as long as they could without arousing suspicion. They were also very interested in how the money would be transported to Vera Cruz: how it would be wrapped, and how many bills were in each stack.

Finally the four million dollars in American fifty-dollar bills sat on the large table in the center of the vault room.

The women who had done the counting were anxious to be gone. It was almost closing time, and if not for this one they could have seen to their other duties and been ready to leave on time.

"Just a few more moments," Flores said, "and we can all be on our way."

He opened one of the large steel doors that lined the lower shelves in the vault and indicated to the women that they should place the money inside. Wordlessly, they did so, stacking the bills carefully so that they would be sure to fit easily. When they were finished, Flores locked the door and smiled. He thanked them for their efforts, and together they left the vault. If they hurried they could see to their other duties before it was time to leave.

Flores had done his part—whatever that was—by delaying the count as much as he could. Now he would tell his boss that there had not been enough time to finish the job and make arrangements for the armored car to take the money to the train station for the journey to Vera Cruz. His boss would shrug and say, *"Mañana, Miguel. Tomorrow is soon enough."* Then he could tell his FBI contact that he had done his part in delaying the transfer. Again, he wondered why they wanted this done and why they wanted to know how the bills were to be wrapped. Usually the FBI wanted to know about the private accounts of Mexican government officials and businessmen, and they were quite willing to pay him well for this information. That he understood. Such information could always be valuable, and he was sure that the Americans would not hesitate to blackmail the thousands of corrupt officials who stole from their own people. But this—he shook his head in bewilderment—this defied logic. What difference did it make how the bills were stacked and how they were wrapped? He sighed. Americans. One could never tell what it was they wanted. Perhaps it was better, he thought, if he did not know any more than he did now.

CHAPTER 13

On Saturday evening Harry and Garcia made the trip back to Colón to see how Epifanio Chiari was progressing. The print shop was already closed when they arrived, and Chiari's wife opened the door and beckoned them inside. "He's downstairs," she said, ". . . working."

Both Chiari and his stepson, Ricardo, looked up when Harry and Garcia entered the workshop. Ricardo had a rag in his hand and was wiping a solution of some sort across a gleaming silver cylinder that was attached to the most modern looking of the four presses. Stacks of paper were everywhere.

Chiari smiled and came to greet them. "Come, come," he said. "I want you to inspect our work." They followed him into the small office, where Chiari opened the bottom drawer in his desk and took out a small stack of perhaps twenty fifty-dollar bills. He spread them out on the table. "These are just samples," he said. "Don't be too critical. Those that we are preparing to print now will be much better."

Harry picked one up and held it in front of his face.

112

Garcia did the same. They inspected the bills carefully, turning them over, rubbing the paper between thumb and forefinger. Harry placed his bill on the table and picked up another. "These bills are . . ." He paused.

"Magnificent," Garcia said, finishing his sentence for him.

"Epifanio," Harry said, "these are the most incredible counterfeits that I have ever seen. To call them counterfeit does not do them justice."

Chiari broke into a wide grin, the pride evident in his face.

"I want to take some of these with me," Harry said. "To show them to the FBI."

"Of course," Chiari said. "Take what you want." He laughed. "I can make plenty more. Come with me. We were just about to begin a press run when you arrived."

They followed him out to the workroom, where Ricardo was fiddling with the press. He turned a crank and raised a stack of paper into position at the rear of the press. He nodded to his stepfather.

"We are ready, I think," Chiari said, giving the press a quick last-minute inspection. He picked a sheet from the top of the stack and handed it to Harry. On one side were eight reproductions of the reverse side of the fifty-dollar bill. Harry thought that the U.S. Capitol Building had never looked more beautiful. On the other side were eight different serial numbers and the Treasury Department seal. "We will have more than a thousand different serial numbers."

Chiari started the motor for the printing head, allowing the damping roller to contact the plate cylinder. He watched it turn a few revolutions and lowered the form rollers. The plate picked up the image cleanly without scumming, so he started the second motor, sending a stream of paper down the feed board. He allowed only a half dozen sheets to pass through the rollers before lifting the suction cups and bringing a halt to the movement of paper into the press. "Inspection," he said and lifted a sheet from the delivery tray. He held it up to the light, then said to Ricardo, "Registration is off slightly to the left."

Ricardo used what looked like an allen wrench to make a

minor adjustment to the back of the press. Chiari nodded and his stepson started the second motor again. This time only three sheets went through before the procession was halted. Again Chiari inspected the results. This time Chiari himself did the adjustment and let several sheets run through the machine before bringing it to a stop. He held up the top sheet to the light and said, "Perfect."

Ricardo started the motor.

Air hissed as the suction feet picked up each sheet and carried it to the head stops where the grippers pulled the paper into the press. In a fraction of a second the sheet had passed through the rubber roller—image transferred from plate to blanket to paper—and was on its way down the chute, past the ink-drying heat lamps, to the delivery board.

The machine found its rhythm and sang a song of mechanical perfection. Each part of the press—the suction feed, the rubber blanket, the metal plate, the drive mechanism—had its own distinctive music, but the tones combined in a kind of symphonic harmony that was spellbinding. Every half second the suction cups picked up another sheet and began the process that culminated in eight fifty-dollar bills sliding into the delivery tray a half second later.

Harry and the others were almost mesmerized by the machine's rhythmic perfection. They listened as the machine played its music. "Four hundred dollars, four hundred dollars, four hundred dollars," it seemed to sing while they stared in fascination as the press deposited sheet after perfect sheet into the delivery board.

As the four-hundred-dollar stacks grew higher, Epifanio Chiari broke the spell. "After a while the image will not be as sharp," he said above the song of the press. "I have several other plates—all of similar quality—ready to replace this one. Tomorrow I will run these same sheets through the press again."

Harry looked at him, puzzled.

"It will give the ink that raised look that the government gets from the intaglio process. We want a deep, rich image, my friend."

Harry turned his attention back to the growing stack of money. He stared, unblinking and expressionless, as the pile grew.

Chiari laughed. He had seen that same look on the faces of others when beautiful money rolled off the press. He patted Harry on the shoulder. "By this time tomorrow you will be looking at four million dollars."

Harry watched sheet after sheet fall into the tray.

"It's incredible," Victoria said, holding up one of Chiari's fifties. "I can't tell the difference between this and a real one."

"We're about to find out if Trump can tell the difference," Harry said.

They were in Harry's office. It was almost midnight, and Harry had called Trump as soon as he and Garcia had returned from Colón. He was anxious to have Trump inspect the quality of the counterfeit bills.

"How did things go here tonight?" Harry asked Victoria.

She smiled. "Fine. Good crowd, and if I do say so myself, I was in pretty good voice."

Victoria was wearing a red, skintight gown, slit on one side up to the hip and with a plunging neckline. Harry let his eyes run across her body. "And I'll just bet the crowd was here to listen to your voice."

"What else?" she asked.

Word had spread quickly in Panama City that the Panama Club had found a dynamite new singer who just happened to be a Hollywood starlet. The Americans who worked in the Canal Zone and those wealthy Panamanians who emulated the North Americans in their entertainment preferences now made Harry's place—as many of them called it—the first stop on their evening revelry. Such was the hunger for things American that it mattered little that few, if any, could ever remember seeing Victoria Gansell in a motion picture. She was an instant success, and the Panama Club, always one of the busiest night clubs in Panama City, now found itself as the premier hot spot in town.

Even if she had been unable to sing a note or carry a tune, it was worth the visit just to watch her perform. But it didn't take long to realize that she knew her way around a song. It wasn't that her voice was magnificent—it was too raspy and perhaps too limited in range—but she had the ability to wrap herself in a song and make it her own. When she sang, it was as if that song had been written for her and about her. She sang about love gone bad and love unrequited, and her listeners were certain that, as unlikely as it seemed, this beautiful creature had lived through some bad times. Even Harry had to admit that she was damned good.

Harry's only complaint was that during Vicky's two nightly shows, business dropped off in the casino.

Ernesto Garcia knocked at the door, and Harry said, "Come."

Garcia entered with Trump and Smythe following closely behind. Trump, as usual, had a scowl on his face. He saw Vicky and looked her up and down hungrily.

"Working clothes," she said.

"Let's get on with this, Fox," Trump said. "I've got things to do."

"I thought this might be past your bedtime," Harry said. "Doesn't J. Edgar like his agents to get a good night's sleep?"

"You leave the director out of this," Trump said.

"Sorry," Harry said, "I didn't mean to take his name in vain."

Smythe stepped in before the incident escalated any further. "Harry, you said you had something to show us."

Harry went to his desk and opened the top drawer. He removed three fifty-dollar bills and placed them on the desk. "Two are fakes," he said. "One is real. See if you can tell the difference."

Both men went to the desk and looked at the bills. Smythe gave an almost immediate gasp of amazement. "Incredible," he said. He picked one up and felt it carefully. "I can't begin to tell the difference." He looked at Trump, who had still said nothing. "Of course," Smythe went on, "I don't have the same everyday working knowledge of American

116

currency that Agent Trump has . . . but then, neither will the Germans."

Trump took all three bills and examined them carefully, holding them against the desk light, rubbing them in his fingers to see if the ink smudged. He dropped one on the desk. "Forgery," he said disdainfully. He held up the other two and began again his inspection routine. "They are quite good," he said finally and held one out for Harry to look at, "but this one is genuine. The other two are counterfeit."

Harry took the offered bill and looked at it. "Pretty good," he said, handing the bill back to Trump. "How did you know?"

Trump looked at it again. "The quality of the paper—the lack of noticeable threads—and the smell of the ink." He smiled. "American currency has a distinct smell."

"Remarkable," Smythe said. "I had no idea."

"The only way I can tell is by the serial numbers," Harry said.

"Obviously," Smythe said, "it's good enough to fool the Germans."

Everyone looked at Trump. "Yes, it is," he said. "I think it would take an expert to say that this is counterfeit currency."

"Then we have a go?" Smythe said excitedly.

Trump nodded. "Yes. We have a go."

"The rest of the money will be ready tomorrow," Harry said. "I'll pick it up and deliver it to you on Monday morning. Before delivery I'll require half of what was promised to me so that I can make the first installment on the payment to the people who made these bills."

"The British will pay you their half of the commitment," Trump said. "The bureau will pay when all of the money has been recovered. I'll also require that you give me the plates that were used to make these bills. Since Uncle Sam is paying the cost of this operation," Trump said, "it wouldn't do to have your people printing up a few extra million of these for themselves."

"Fair enough," Harry said. "The plates will be delivered with the currency."

"That's it, then," Trump said. "We will see you on Monday with the counterfeit and the plates." He picked up the two bogus bills from the table and put all three in his pocket. "I'll just hang on to these for now," he said.

Harry stepped forward. "The counterfeits you can keep," he said, "but I'd like the real fifty, if you don't mind."

Trump grinned and handed all three bills to Harry, who riffled through them and removed the one he wanted. He returned the other two to Trump. "Don't spend them here," Harry said.

Anger flashed across Trump's face. "These bills go back to Washington," he said and stomped out of the room.

Wilfred Smythe followed him but not before whispering, "Good job, Harry. Well done, indeed."

Harry waited until they had gone and the door had closed behind them. He gave Garcia a wink and said to Vicky, "How about that drink? One for Ernesto, too."

"Sure," she said and moved to the liquor cabinet. "That Trump gives me the creeps," she said as she poured gin into two tall glasses, "but I guess he knows his money. I still can't figure out how he knew which one was real."

Garcia started to laugh and then Harry joined in.

"Somebody going to tell me the joke?" Vicky asked, bringing the two men their drinks.

They clinked glasses. "All three were counterfeits," Harry said.

CHAPTER 14

"It is really quite beautiful, is it not?" asked Ewald Kramer, nodding toward the two large leather suitcases that lay open on the desk of his office. Both suitcases were filled with the American currency that had only just been delivered from Mexico City to the German consular offices in Vera Cruz. Kramer's job was to accept delivery of the shipment and to verify that the currency was genuine. Once that was accomplished, he was to turn it over to the Abwehr for shipment to Buenos Aires. "There is something about money—any kind of money—that is quite awe-inspiring, don't you think?" Kramer was a Foreign Office attaché on assignment from the German Embassy in Mexico City. He was also a resident representative of the Abwehr, although that meant only that he acted as a conduit of information for and from the many German agents who passed through the port of Vera Cruz on their way to other assignments in South and Central America. Kramer was in his early fifties, slightly built, and fairly new on the job.

The two men to whom he had directed his comments looked at each other and then at Kramer. "We are not

119

concerned with such things," one of them said. He was Max Greiser, an Abwehr agent, and the man whose responsibility it would be to see that the money arrived safely in Buenos Aires.

"I did not mean to imply that this money is of any personal importance to me," Kramer said. "Only that it is important to the aims of the Führer and the German people."

Greiser smiled. He enjoyed intimidating faint-hearted fools like Kramer. Before the war it had been fools like Kramer who had prevented Greiser from making the kind of job advancement that he was certain he deserved. Greiser was tall and arrogantly handsome. He wore English-tailored suits, and although he had a wife and child in Buenos Aires, he considered himself something of a ladies' man. Like Kramer, Greiser had once been employed in the foreign service, but had transferred to the Abwehr when war began. The chances for promotion came much more rapidly in military intelligence, he felt, and his facility with languages —especially Spanish and English—could be put to better use. He was presently listed as a special assistant to the chargé d'affaires at the German Embassy in Buenos Aires. In reality he was the assistant to the head of the Abwehr office in Buenos Aires. "Of course not, Herr Kramer," he said. "I did not mean to suggest that you did."

His companion, whose name was Helmut Blaskowitz, was ten years Greiser's senior. He was a large, barrel-chested man with a round beefy face and huge, dangerous-looking hands. Although he had never been in the navy, his diplomatic passport listed him as the assistant to the naval attaché. He was in actuality Greiser's bodyguard. Blaskowitz had once been a street thug in the early days of the Nazi movement in Munich and owed his present position to the attention of several prominent officials in the Nazi party who admired his single-minded dedication to duty—his penchant for violence had done his reputation little harm, either. Blaskowitz smiled at Kramer's discomfort.

Greiser tired of the game. "You have our tickets?" he asked.

"Yes," said Kramer, reaching into his coat pocket and removing some papers. "Your ship—the *San Fraterno*—is presently docked in the harbor. The captain awaits your arrival and will leave as soon as you are ready. You will arrive in Limón on the seventeenth and Colón on the day after." He placed the tickets on the desk next to the suitcases.

Greiser picked up the tickets and slipped them into his pocket without comment.

"You are instructed to disembark in Colón and go to the Washington Hotel, where a room has been reserved for you. On the evening of the eighteenth you will meet with a man who will identify himself by Abwehr code . . ."

Greiser did not say that he had seen photographs of the man he was to meet.

". . . and you will give him five hundred thousand dollars."

"That is a lot of money to hand over to someone I know nothing about."

Kramer was merely passing along instructions. "When that is accomplished you will then board the Argentinian passenger liner *Bahia Grande,* which will be leaving Colón on the morning of the nineteenth. You will arrive in Buenos Aires ten days later on the twenty-ninth of November, where you will be greeted by an armed escort to take you and the money to the German Embassy."

"Sounds simple enough," Greiser said.

Kramer looked at the money. "I don't envy you the task," he said. "I'm glad to be rid of the responsibility of this. If anything happens to that money, there will be hell to pay."

Greiser laughed and Blaskowitz joined him. "Don't worry," he said. "The money is safe with us."

That, Kramer thought, was the kind of arrogance that invited trouble. "I'm sure you are correct," he said, happy that the problem was Greiser's and not his.

CHAPTER 15

The morning sun was already brutally hot. Everything seemed to be affected by the heat, and those who had to be outside moved slowly as if burdened by an invisible weight. Robles sat inside the small café, next to an open window from where he could observe the street. A gaily colored awning provided some small respite from the glare of the sun. From where he sat he could see the railroad station across the Avenida Central as well as observe the passersby. He saw Erika when she was still at a considerable distance, and he had to admit that he enjoyed watching her. She was tall, standing a full head above most of the Panamanians on the street, and walked with an arm-swinging, leg-striding confidence that reminded him of a victorious army on the march.

This was the first time he had seen her since the evening at Drexler's. It had been Drexler who had come yesterday to tell him that the German couriers would arrive that day and to give him instructions about the transfer of the money. Robles fully expected Drexler to do everything in his power to keep the girl away from him. He had been surprised to

122

learn that she would be the one to bring him news of his new living quarters.

He waved when she entered the café, and she smiled and sat across from him. She wore a light cotton blouse and skirt. Her skin was tanned golden. She seemed genuinely pleased to see him, and Robles was certain that they would soon be lovers. The girl meant nothing to him, but she was attractive and obviously available. He did have needs.

"I must confess, I am surprised to see you," Robles said.

"Heinrich was busy and couldn't possibly get away until later. I convinced him that it was essential that you move immediately."

Robles smiled. "Is everything still on for tonight?"

Erika looked around, leaned closer, and whispered, "Yes. The couriers will arrive in the early evening. They are scheduled to leave tomorrow morning."

He knew all of this but let her go on. She apparently enjoyed being part of the intrigue. He watched her carefully. Beneath her tan she seemed flushed with excitement as she talked, whether over the fact that she was part of this operation or that she was here with him, he could not be sure. He let her finish, staring into her eyes as if he were genuinely interested in what she had to say. He did, however, have other things on his mind. "Would you like a drink?" he asked.

She looked at her watch. "I don't have much time. I thought you might like me to take you to the apartment."

Robles could think of nothing that he would like better. "Take the day off," he said. "Spend it with me. I'll tell Drexler I needed you to help me."

Erika bit her lower lip. "I have a date this afternoon with an American naval lieutenant. He provides me with a great deal of information about the canal. I'll be spending the afternoon with him."

Robles felt foolish. Her excitement was not for him but for someone else. "I understand," he said.

She smiled sympathetically. She reached across the table and touched his hand. "We can be at the apartment in five minutes," she said. "I don't have to meet my lieutenant for another forty-five minutes. As long as you give me enough time to wash up and comb my hair afterward, there is no problem."

Robles stood up and offered her his hand. "Let's go," he said.

The room was dark, shades pulled against the heat of the afternoon sun. Harry Fox sat at his desk, feet up, head back, eyes staring at the ceiling fan that swirled above his head. Every few minutes he dabbed at the sweat on his face with a handkerchief. Other than that he was motionless. An untouched drink, ice cubes long since melted, sat within easy reach on the desk.

He had been like this for hours. Everything seemed in order, and yet he had his doubts. The counterfeit money was remarkably good; Garcia had rounded up several reliable men—including his cousin, who was a detective with the Panama City police—and had even acquired some police uniforms. Garcia himself had insisted on leading the men when it came time to make the switch, so Fox knew that the operation was in capable hands. The plan, although not to his liking, was reasonably simple—grab the money, make the switch, give it back. So why was he worried? He shook his head. He didn't like any of it. Least of all, he liked involving Garcia in what was essentially his operation. Harry would reap the benefit of the pardon. Why should Ernesto take the risk? Garcia had laughed away Fox's concerns by pointing out that Harry couldn't very well lead the police raid on the Germans' hotel room. "They might think it strange that a 'gringo' was in charge of a Panamanian police detachment," he had said.

There was a knock on the door. Harry looked up and Victoria stuck her head inside. "Busy?" she asked.

Harry shook his head.

Vicky came in and sat across from him. "You okay?"

"Fine," he said, without conviction.

"You're worried about tonight, aren't you?"

"I just don't like it. I wish that I could take care of the switch myself . . . in my own way."

"But this is how Trump wants it," she said.

Harry scowled. "What is it with you two?" Victoria asked.

"You wouldn't understand."

"Try me," she said. "I want to understand you," she said. "I want to know all about you. You're the most important man in my life, and sometimes I feel that I don't know anything about you."

"It's not Trump," he said finally. "It's people like Trump. People who think they know all about right and wrong when all they know is the law. The law doesn't know anything about right and wrong . . . or about justice."

"You're talking about what happened to your father."

"Ernesto talks too much sometimes," he said.

"Ernesto loves you like a brother," she said.

"And I feel the same about him," Harry said. "We go back a long way. I owe him a lot. Did he tell you why the FBI has been after me for all these years?"

"He told me that your father died in prison and that someone killed the man who was responsible. . . . That's all. He said there was no way they could prove that you did it."

"Running a saloon was the only thing that my old man ever knew," Harry said. "When Prohibition came along, he did what everybody else did and turned it into an illegal speakeasy. In a short time he became very successful— more successful than he had ever been before. This councilman—guy named Frank Maggio—wanted to take over the business, so he pulled a few strings and had my father arrested and convicted and sent to jail. Two months after my old man went to prison, Maggio reopened the saloon. It became one of the more popular spots around town for big shots and politicians." Harry lit a cigarette. "Six months later my old man was dead. Pneumonia, they said. A week later somebody pumped six shots into Frank Maggio. Three in the chest, three in the head. Some people thought that the mob got him; some people thought that Willi Fox's kid got him. Nobody knows for sure."

"They can't prove that you did it?"

"FBI doesn't need proof. They just need to catch you."

"Did he tell you about the counterfeiting?" He smiled grimly. "That one they can prove."

"No," she said.

Harry picked up his drink, saw that the ice had melted, and put it back down on the desk. "During Prohibition I performed a necessary service by importing good quality booze from several South American countries. That's where I first met Ernesto. He was my supplier. I sold several thousand cases a week to some of the best places in the country." He took a drag on his cigarette and let the smoke drift to the ceiling. "When Prohibition ended, I still had a rather large inventory of liquor, but now the big boys moved into the business. The people who knew that Roosevelt would end Prohibition were able to corner the market and force the distributors to buy from them. If the distributors wanted a steady supply, they had to buy only from the major corporations. It was just like what the mob had done during Prohibition. I couldn't find a buyer for my merchandise and had to sell my inventory to one of those companies for about fifteen cents on the dollar. Damn near wiped me out. That's when Garcia bailed me out." Harry smiled at the recollection. "He set me up with some people who made counterfeit American money. I gathered several hundred thousand in counterfeit, used it to buy a warehouse full of liquor from the company who had bought my liquor, and then I sold it very quickly at a cut-rate price to a second company. Before anybody realized that the money was counterfeit, I was out of the country with a few hundred thousand dollars in my bags. Seemed fair to me," Harry said. "I thought justice had been done. The FBI didn't quite see it that way, however."

"So you bought this place and settled down in a kind of"—she searched for the right word—"exile?"

"Exile?" he said. "I like that."

"Now maybe it's over. Maybe you can go home."

He blew smoke to the ceiling fan and watched it dissipate. "Maybe," he said. "Maybe not."

"Why not?"

"Trump," he said. "I don't trust him."

"He promised to get you the pardon if you did this. They can't back out now. Can they?"

"They can do whatever they want. Besides, maybe I don't want to go home."

"I don't believe that."

"Maybe I like it here."

"Then why do this?" she asked.

Harry had no answer. He sipped his drink. It was warm and somehow bitter.

CHAPTER 16

The city of Colón, destroyed by fire during the turbulent times when Panamanians were trying to wrest their independence from Colombia, had been rebuilt and modeled after the old city of New Orleans. Poverty and neglect, however, had robbed Colón of the charm and character of its American counterpart. Colón was run-down and impoverished, and if not for its proximity to the canal and the U.S. Navy's Coco Solo Naval Base and the U.S. Army's France Field the city might simply have ceased to exist. The city's main industry was catering to the pleasures of the American servicemen who frequented its streets every night of the week. In consequence a thriving red-light district of saloons, dance halls, and bordellos had been developed in the city center.

The Washington Hotel was the pride of the city of Colón. The impressive structure, with an imposing Spanish mission style facade and a large, elegant lobby, had been built to house the visiting dignitaries who had come in a constant stream during the construction of the Panama Canal. Like some elegant creature from a bygone era, it was one of the few enclaves of luxury in a city that had gone into an immediate decline after the completion of the canal. Surrounded by palm trees, the hotel sat on the edge of Cristobal Bay, where, on any given day, as many as fifty vessels from around the world waited in turn to pass through the Gatun Locks and begin their transit from the Atlantic to the Pacific side of the canal.

It was already dark when Harry Fox and Ernesto Garcia arrived to wait across the street from the hotel. The night was warm, and the lights from the ships in the bay were like low-lying stars strung across the horizon.

"You're sure everything is all set?" Harry asked.

"Don't worry, Harry," Garcia said. "I told you, my cousin Sebastian will be with us. Nothing will go wrong. It is a very simple plan."

"I don't like it. I told Trump I didn't like it."

"Don't waste your breath, Harry. Trump is a very stubborn man. The kind who always gets his way."

"So where the hell is he?" Harry said, looking at his watch. "His men should be in position already." They had not heard from Trump since Harry had presented him with the four million in counterfeit money earlier in the day. Trump had looked at the money without expressing satisfaction or dissatisfaction with the quality of the bills. "The switch could have been made already."

"He'll be here," Garcia said.

As if on cue, a car pulled up next to them, and Trump and Smythe got out of the backseat. There were two other men in the front.

Trump's face was a grim, official mask. "Everything set?" he said.

"Yes," Harry said. "We've got three men in uniform and two in plainclothes, ready to move on your orders. Garcia will be in charge; the others are waiting at the rear of the building. He and his men will enter the hotel through the rear service entrance, which will be left open, and go up to the third floor using the back stairs."

"And the room?"

Harry pointed across the street to the hotel. "We've taken

the room directly across the hall from the Germans. Third floor, fifth window in from the left. It shouldn't take more than a few minutes to switch the money."

"And you're sure that they have the money with them?" Smythe asked.

Harry nodded. "It cost me fifty dollars to find out that they didn't leave anything in the hotel vault. Whatever they brought is with them in the room."

"I hope you didn't use a counterfeit fifty," Trump said.

Harry smiled. "No."

"All right," Trump said. "I'll take over from here. When my men are ready, they'll signal from the window. You will then send your men to the Germans' room, where they will confiscate the money and bring it across the hall, where my men will switch it with the counterfeit. The head man"—he nodded in Garcia's direction—"will negotiate with the Germans while the switch is taking place. They will, of course, claim diplomatic immunity from such a seizure, and after a few minutes your man will agree with them and allow the money to be returned. He will then depart with profuse apologies, and we will wait for the Germans to leave before leaving with the money."

"What do we do?" Harry asked.

"We wait here until it's all over," Trump said.

"My men are ready," Harry said.

"Then, let's go," Trump said.

Harry hesitated and Trump stopped. "Problem?"

"There are a lot of things that can go wrong with this plan. I'd suggest that we—"

Trump cut him off. "If your men do the job as instructed, nothing will go wrong. If, however, anything does go wrong, don't expect help from my people. Our job is to collect the money and stay out of this." He turned away. "Let's get on with it."

Harry started to speak but thought better of it.

"Don't worry, Harry," Smythe said softly. "Everything will go on schedule."

Harry was silent and Smythe followed Trump.

Trump signaled to the men in the car, and they stepped out into the street. Each carried a large suitcase containing the counterfeit bills.

Harry, Ernesto, Trump, and Smythe waited in silence as the two men carried the suitcases across the street. When the men had disappeared inside the hotel, Harry looked at Garcia, who gave him a wink of encouragement. Harry shook his head. "I don't like this, Ernesto."

Despite his calm exterior, Robles was fidgety. He did not like being in the confines of a hotel room with such a large sum of money, or with the two Germans who had treated him with an obvious lack of respect. Both were Abwher officers and had made no attempt to disguise their reluctance to hand over such an immense amount of money to someone who was not German. Considering the amount of money involved and the importance of the task which he had been assigned, Robles thought that the men were much too casual in their attitude. As far as he could determine, they had taken no special precautions for the safety of the money, which was in two large leather suitcases and sat on the floor between them. They had, he thought, assumed an air of German superiority that precluded anything other than success.

Everything about the arrangements made Robles slightly uneasy. Some sixth sense told him that things were not as they should be.

They were in the sitting room of a rather modest suite. The room itself was large, and there was a second room opposite the front door. Robles had immediately considered all methods of entry and exit.

"You will, of course," said the one who appeared to be in charge, "be required to sign for the amount that is to be given to you."

"Of course," Robles said.

The man had introduced himself as Max Greiser, and he seemed to view the undertaking as somehow distasteful. It was obvious to Robles that the Germans were not aware of his importance to their cause. Greiser did not bother to explain that he was the second in command of the Abwher office in Argentina.

The other had been introduced only as Blaskowitz. He was a big man, with short hair and a red, beefy face, and he had an angry-looking scar on his left cheek. He had said nothing. After the introductions Blaskowitz had opened one of the leather suitcases and begun to count out stacks of fifty-dollar bills on a low table in the center of the room. The bills were still in their bank wrappers.

"There are two hundred bills in each wrapper," Greiser said matter-of-factly. "Ten thousand dollars in each. Fifty stacks comes to five hundred thousand dollars."

Fascinated, Robles watched the German count out the money. It was an awesome display. The German had made ten rows of bills and kept adding to the stacks until each row had five packs of fifties. "Fifty," he said without looking up at Robles.

"Would you care to count it before signing?" Greiser asked.

"That won't be necessary," Robles said, signing the paper that Greiser had placed in front of him on the table. Immediately Robles began to put the money into the leather satchel he had brought with him. He was anxious to conclude this business and be gone from this place. He hoped that the satchel was large enough. He'd had no idea that five hundred thousand dollars would take up so much room.

As Robles continued to fill the satchel, a small noise in the hallway outside made him hesitate for just a moment. He looked at the Germans, but obviously they had heard nothing. An alarm bell started softly clanging somewhere in the back of his brain. Again he heard the noise—like feet shuffling quietly in the hallway. Quickly he finished his task and stood up. "I need to use your toilet," he said.

Greiser motioned toward the other room.

Robles picked up his satchel. "I'll take this with me, if you don't mind."

Inside the bedroom Robles went to the window. Some

inner sense told him that he must be prepared to escape, but there was no safe way that he could descend to the street three stories below. A narrow ledge led to a balcony about fifteen feet away. If absolutely necessary he could get out that way, but it was more risk than he was prepared to take at the moment. He looked around the room, but there was no good hiding place. There was a loud knocking at the outer door, and Robles immediately kicked his satchel under the bed and withdrew his pistol from the holster under his left arm. He waited.

The loud knock startled the Germans into inactivity. It was followed almost immediately by a cry of "Police," and then the door was kicked in. Three uniformed men and two in plainclothes rushed into the room. Both men in plainclothes were armed. All eyes immediately fell on the open suitcase on the table and its mate sitting on the floor nearby.

"My name is Lieutenant Ivaldi," said Ernesto Garcia, waving his pistol at the two Germans. "We have been informed that you are in possession of contraband currency." He nodded in the direction of the suitcase. "My orders are to seize any such currency."

The second man, who stood to one side and slightly behind Garcia, was Garcia's cousin Sebastian Rios. He also aimed his pistol at the Germans and made his face as stern as possible.

"This currency," Greiser snarled, slamming the suitcase shut, "is the property of Germany. We are officers of the German Foreign Service on our way to Buenos Aires. We are diplomatic guests in your country, and as such are immune from such illegal seizures."

"That you can discuss with my superiors at police headquarters." Garcia motioned Sebastian forward toward the suitcases. "Step back, please."

"I protest," Greiser said.

Garcia pointed the pistol at Greiser's midsection. This time his tone was much more menacing. "Step back, please, and raise your hands above your head."

Greiser and Blaskowitz did as ordered.

Sebastian stepped forward and lifted the closed suitcase onto the table. He released the leather straps and opened it. It was filled to the top with packages of fifty-dollar bills, and he released his breath slowly.

The other suitcase wasn't as full. "Where is the rest of the money, señor?" Garcia asked.

"There is no more," Greiser said, but Blaskowitz's eyes involuntarily went to the bedroom door.

Sebastian smiled. "Perhaps there is more in the other room," he said.

Ernesto Garcia went to the bedroom door, opened it, and saw Robles standing next to the opened window, a satchel in his hand. "Stop," he said and raised his pistol.

Without hesitation, Robles shot him once in the chest and Garcia fell back into the outer room. The sound of the shot froze everyone momentarily, and then the three uniformed men turned and ran for their lives. They had been told that there would be no gunplay.

The Germans, hands still in the air, widened their eyes in amazement as Sebastian Rios looked once at his pistol as if deciding what to do, and then he, too, turned and ran.

Robles emerged from the bedroom, stepping over Garcia, the leather satchel in his left hand, the pistol in his right.

Greiser said, "What the hell is going on here?"

"Obviously these men were not the police. They intended to relieve you of your money, and when your embassy registered a protest, no one would have known anything about this matter." Robles looked down at the man he had shot. Garcia was gravely wounded but his eyes were open, and he stared up defiantly at the man who had shot him. Robles aimed the pistol at Garcia's face. "I'd suggest that you two grab your money and get out of here before the real police arrive."

Greiser grabbed Robles's wrist. "I forbid you to shoot this man," he said.

"He saw my face," Robles said.

"If you kill him, every policeman in Panama will be

looking for us." Greiser released the wrist. "You can disappear into the night. We have to get out of this damn country. If you kill him, we could be detained for weeks."

Robles looked down at Garcia and nodded reluctantly. The man was finished anyway. "As you wish," he said. He holstered his pistol and walked to the front door. "The rear stairs are to your left," he said to the Germans, who were frantically pulling together their luggage. "I think that would be your best way out." He turned to the right and was gone.

From across the street Harry heard what had sounded like a single gunshot. Before anyone could speak, Harry had dashed across the street toward the hotel. It was obvious that something had gone wrong. The men had been under strict orders not to fire their pistols.

Harry raced through the lobby, past the elevators, and began to bound up the steps two at a time. As he reached the first-floor landing, a well-dressed man passed him on the way down. He wore an English tailored suit and a wide-brimmed fedora. He carried a light raincoat over his right arm and a large leather satchel in his left hand. The man looked straight ahead, his eyes never wavering for an instant.

Harry slowed as the man passed him. He was too casual, too indifferent to the fact that someone was dashing madly past him on the stairs. Harry was torn between the desire to get to the third floor, where he suspected that Garcia was in trouble, and his suspicion of the man on the stairs. He took one last look at the man, who continued calmly down the stairs, before he renewed his dash to the third floor.

When he arrived on the third floor, Harry found the Germans' room wide open and several hotel guests in the hallway peering into the room. Harry pushed them aside and went inside. He found Ernesto Garcia on the floor. Garcia's eyes were unfocused and staring into space. A young man, the assistant to the hotel manager, stood next to Garcia. He looked bewildered.

"Oh, Christ," Harry said, kneeling next to his friend. "What happened?"

"I don't know, señor," the young man said.

"Did anybody call a doctor?"

"Yes. The doctor is on the way."

"That you, Harry?" Garcia said, his voice far away.

"It's me, Ernesto. Hang on. The doctor's coming."

Garcia grasped Harry's arm and held on to him. His grip was like iron. "Stay, Harry," he said. "I don't want to be alone."

Harry looked at the hotel assistant. "Get out of here," he said, "and get that doctor here." He cradled his friend's head in his arm. "You're going to be okay, Ernesto."

"There was a third man in the bedroom, Harry," Ernesto whispered. "He shot me when I opened the door."

"Did you get a look at him?"

Ernesto nodded.

"Tall, gray suit, dark hair?" Harry asked.

"That's him."

"I saw him on the stairs when I came up." Harry bristled at the memory of how calm the man had been.

"Don't forget that face, Harry. Find him for me."

"Don't worry. I'll find him—we'll both find him."

Garcia smiled. "Sure thing, Harry," he said, and then his head slumped back, and he was dead.

Harry Fox lowered Garcia to the floor. He sat next to him for a few minutes holding Ernesto's cold hands in his. Etched into his brain was the face of the man who had killed his friend. There was a noise at the door, and a middle-aged man with a black bag came into the room. Harry moved aside as the doctor knelt next to Garcia, took one look, and shook his head. The doctor felt for a pulse, but Harry knew that it was a futile gesture.

Harry stood up and went to the door. Trump and Smythe were in the hallway. Trump was talking to the two men who had been in the room across the hall.

Smythe turned when he saw Harry approach. "What does the doctor say?" he asked.

"Too late," Harry said. "He's dead."

Smythe sighed.

"What happened here?" Harry asked Trump. "Did your men see anything?"

Trump said casually. "Your men blew it. Apparently, there was a third man in the room when they went in. He shot one of your men, the others panicked and ran. The Germans—and the money—are gone."

Harry clenched his teeth. "Your men couldn't stop the Germans from leaving?"

"That was not part of the plan," Trump said. He turned to the two men who were avoiding Harry's eyes. "I don't want either of you here when the police arrive." He turned back to Harry. "We had nothing to do with this," he said.

"Nothing to do with this?" Harry said, his anger brimming.

Trump either did not recognize the danger signals or he chose to ignore them. "You were supposed to take care of this," he said. "I'll report to Director Hoover that you couldn't handle the job."

Harry grabbed Trump by the lapels of his jacket and slammed him viciously against the wall. "My friend is dead because of you. Don't tell me I couldn't handle the job. I can handle the job, asshole. Only this time you'll stay out of my way and let me do it."

Trump tried to wrestle himself free, but he was powerless against Harry's fury.

Smythe wedged himself between them and extricated Trump from Harry's grasp. "Enough of this," he said. "We've still got work to do before the Germans disappear with that money."

"Perhaps," Trump said, adjusting his jacket, "but I'm afraid that Mr. Fox's participation is no longer required. We'll find someone else. Someone who can do the job properly."

"Just a minute," Smythe said, surprising everyone with his vehemence. "We don't have time for any of this nonsense. The Germans are boarding that ship tonight." He looked at Trump. "Unless you want to stand on the dock tomorrow morning and wave good-bye to four million dollars, I say, if Harry can get the money back, we let him get on with it." He looked from one to the other. "I'll take full responsibility."

"Very well," Trump said. "I—and the bureau—wash my hands of this whole matter." He turned to walk away, but paused after a few steps and turned back to face them. "Except, if that money is recovered, it will be claimed by the United States government. Is that clear?"

Smythe said grimly, "Yes, quite clear."

When Trump and his men were gone, Smythe turned to Harry. "You're still going after the money?"

"I'm going after one of the men who has the money," Harry said. "If I can recover the money, I will."

"Look," Smythe said. "The most important part of this operation is to deprive the Germans of the use of this money."

"To you maybe," Harry said.

"I'm going with you," Smythe said.

"Did you ever kill anyone?" Harry asked.

"Well . . . no."

"Then stay home. You'd just be in the way."

"I'm determined not to let this venture deteriorate into a personal vendetta between you and the man you're after . . . or, for that matter, between you and Trump."

Harry glared at the Englishman, who struggled against a desire to step back. Smythe managed to hold his ground. "I don't care if you kill all three of the bastards," Smythe said. "Just as long as you first make the switch and let them deliver the counterfeit to Buenos Aires."

"Okay," Harry said. "I'll bring back your goddamned money."

"You'll need the counterfeit," Smythe said. "I'll get it from Trump."

"Keep him out of my way. I don't want to see him."

Smythe nodded.

"Bring the money to the Panama Club tonight," Harry said, then looked back inside the room where Garcia lay. "I've got things to do," he said, "and not much time to do them."

"Good luck," Smythe said. Harry turned and walked into the room to be with Ernesto until the ambulance arrived.

CHAPTER 17

Cristobal, November 19

The Argentinian passenger ship *Bahia Grande* gave three
deep-throated blasts on the departure horn as thick, black
smoke billowed from the single stack on her aftdeck.
Crewmen worked feverishly, preparing to cast off the thick
lines which secured the ship to Pier No. 9 in Cristobal
Harbor as the twin screws gave several preliminary turns,
churning the water at her stern.

The *Bahia Grande* was the pride of the small Argentinian
Passenger Lines. The eleven-thousand-ton ship carried as
many as two hundred and sixty passengers as well as several
thousand tons of dry cargo. Every ten days the ship made
the journey north from Buenos Aires to Cristobal/Colón,
dropping off and picking up passengers along the way at Sao
Paulo and Rio de Janeiro in Brazil; Paramaribo in Dutch
Guiana; La Guaira, the port city of Caracas, in Venezuela;
and Barranquilla in Colombia. In Colón she took on new
passengers, disgorged her commercial cargo, and reloaded
for the reverse trip homeward.

At dockside, next to the gangplank which led into a
double-doored opening in the *Bahia Grande*'s hull, stood

Senior Assistant Purser Reynaldo Obregon, clipboard and passenger list in hand, anxiously peering down toward the end of the pier. He turned and looked up at the bridge wing, which projected out over the side of the ship, from where the officer on duty looked down at him. Obregon shrugged, and the officer on the bridge wing gave a disappointed shake of his head, then turned and called out to someone inside at the bridge. The ship gave three more blasts on the horn, and the screws began to churn in earnest.

Obregon began to walk up the ramp while motioning to the two crewmen who waited inside the gangway that it was time to pull in the gangplank. At that point one of the crewmen pointed to the end of the dock, and Obregon turned to see two cars racing toward his ship. He motioned for the men to wait and returned to his post at the end of the ramp.

The two cars, a Lincoln Continental convertible and a huge Packard sedan, pulled to a screeching halt in front of Obregon. A man stood up in the backseat of the Lincoln and stepped out, then turned to help his wife step out onto the dock. They looked at Obregon expectantly, as if he should applaud the choreography of their maneuver.

Obregon stepped forward and gave a small, formal bow. "Mr. and Mrs. Hollander," he said in his best English, "allow me to extend the greetings of the captain and to welcome you aboard the S.S. *Bahia Grande.* I am the Senior Assistant Purser Reynaldo Obregon, and if there is anything that I can do for you, please do not hesitate to ask."

"I've got bags here to be taken care of," Hollander said. "You'll see to it that they are taken to my stateroom." He handed Obregon his and his wife's passports. "I suppose you'll need these. Make sure they are returned promptly."

"Of course, señor," Obregon said with a clenched-tooth smile. "I will see to it personally."

"Then, let's get on with it," Hollander said and headed toward the gangplank.

Mrs. Hollander paused momentarily as she and her husband passed Obregon. "Thank you," she whispered.

Obregon touched his fingers to his cap and gave a nod that

was a half bow. At least, he thought, the woman understands the necessity of civility. If not for the fact that there had been a call from the American Embassy in Panama City with a request that the *Bahia Grande* await the arrival of a very important American industrialist, Obregon and his ship would have been gone an hour ago. And now this so-called important man arrives without so much as a word of apology and insults an officer of the finest merchant ship in the Argentinian Passenger Lines. Obregon looked up to the bridge where the officer on duty had been watching the vignette below. Obregon shook his head and pantomimed spitting in the direction of the Hollanders, then motioned for the two crewmen at the gangway opening to join him on the dock.

The two drivers were already removing the Hollanders' luggage from the Packard, and the crewmen groaned when they saw the volume of it. There were more than a dozen suitcases and two large trunks and still more coming from the apparently limitless capacity of the large automobile.

Harry Fox, halfway up the gangplank, looked back for a moment and then whispered to Victoria, "Well, Mrs. Hollander, so far, so good."

The man behind the ornate desk wore a white tropical suit and smoked an immense Cuban cigar. His Panama hat rested on top of the desk. Except for this the desktop was empty. When he smiled, which was not often, he revealed uneven rows of poorly spaced and badly stained teeth. He was a large man in his early fifties, a man who at one time had probably been lean and muscular, but that was before the good food, the good times, and the easy job had made him fat and lazy. Now the easy job was gone, but the remnants of the good food and the good times hung around his waist like a lumpy laundry bag. His name was Narciso Viega, and he had been until very recently the minister of defense in the government of Arnulfo Arias. He owed that lofty position to the fact that he had been a former general in the Panamanian National Guard who had supported the now deposed president of Panama.

Narciso Viega eyed the young man who stood in front of his desk. Although he had been told by his German contacts that the man he would meet was one of the top saboteurs in the world, he was not particularly impressed by what he saw. Handsome, yes, but this one did not look like someone who could drive the yanquis out of Panama. Still, he thought, as always, they come to me when they want something done. Although he no longer enjoyed the authority of either of his former positions, he was certain that he was a man who commanded respect.

Robles thought that Viega looked ridiculous, like one of those villains in an absurd American movie.

"So," Viega began, "I am told by mutual friends that you require my assistance."

That, Robles thought, was before you were booted out on your ass. "Yes, Señor Viega," he said. "I am told that you are a man of great influence."

Viega flashed his rotting teeth. "I still have many friends in the army and in the civilian government. And I am sure you noticed when you came here that I still command a band of loyal supporters."

What Robles had seen was a ragtag bag of loafers who lounged around the grounds of Viega's estate.

"How can I help you?" Viega said.

"I need men who will follow orders and not ask questions."

"How many?"

"At least a dozen."

Viega smiled. "That will be no problem."

"I will also need explosives. Lots of explosives."

"These I can also provide. But, of course, the price for such things is very high."

Robles reached into his inside coat pocket and threw a packet of bills onto Viega's desk. Viega picked it up and fanned through it with his thumb, then placed it back on the desk.

"Ten thousand American dollars," Robles said. "Consider it a down payment . . . or a gift to show my good faith."

Viega smiled, opened a drawer in his desk, and swept the

money across the table with his hand so that it fell into the drawer. "Such generosity is unnecessary," he said as he closed the drawer without taking his eyes from Robles. "However, I am sure that my men will appreciate your gift. Since the yanquis forced our president from power, my men have been waiting for an opportunity to strike back." He locked the drawer where the money had gone. Robles knew that the men outside would see very little of it.

"We," Robles said, "both have the same ultimate goal." He knew that this was far from true.

Viega nodded, although he, too, knew that this was an untruth. He assumed that Robles sought the removal of the Americans from Panama so that his friends the Germans could spread their influence in Central America. That was fine with Viega, but his own motives were quite different: eliminate the Americans so that he and his friends could once again rule Panama. To that end he was willing to sell his soul to the devil. This man, he thought, looking at Robles, does not look much like the devil to me.

"If my plan is successful," Robles said, "you and your men will soon return to positions of prominence in Panama."

"I am certain," Viega went on, "that I will be able to provide the explosives that you require."

"I was told that you were a man of infinite resources."

Viega smiled again, clenching his cigar in his teeth. "Might I ask what you intend to use these explosives for?"

Robles knew that Viega already knew what the explosives were for. His German contacts had, more than likely, told him exactly the purpose of Robles's mission to Panama. Besides, there was only one target in the whole country that was worthy of demolition. Viega then, had some other motive in asking the question. "The canal," Robles said. "What else?"

"The canal?" Viega almost wailed. "The Panama Canal is the lifeblood of my country. Why would the Germans think that I would help them—or you—destroy the canal? Without the canal, Panama is nothing."

"The intention is not to destroy the canal, only to close it for a relatively short period of time."

"Perhaps," Viega said, "but to attack the canal will require many men and a great deal of explosives. That could be very expensive."

Robles smiled, happy to have the problem out in the open. "I will need men only to assist me in transporting and placing the explosives. I would expect to pay for everything that I require. I was told that you could provide whatever I would need."

"If the price is right," Viega said, smiling, "anything is possible."

Viega assumed that Robles was aware of the existence of the tremendous cache of explosives and that this was why the Argentinian had been sent to him. When the Arias government had been in power, Viega had been charged with collecting and storing large amounts of explosives at various locations in the Canal Zone and in the canal itself. If the United States ever threatened the rule of Arnulfo Arias, the explosives would be used as a potent threat to keep the Americans at bay. Arias had assumed that the United States government would accept several years of provocation before taking action. He had not reckoned that Franklin Roosevelt, convinced that the United States would soon be involved in the war, was reluctant to leave the strategically important Panama Canal in the hands of someone who was an avowed sympathizer of his probable enemy. When war seemed imminent, Roosevelt took the first opportunity to rid himself of a potential thorn in his side. Arias, quite simply, had not had time to put his plan into effect.

The explosives, however, were already in Panama.

Robles knew this. The only question was how much he would have to pay Viega to acquire them. "I am sure," he said, "that we can arrive at some mutually agreeable figure."

"Then, I am sure that I will be able to fulfill your requirements."

"I also require someone who can give me as much information about the construction of the canal as is possible. If I am to attack it, I need to know everything about it."

"Periera," Viega said without hesitation. "I will arrange a meeting. He is the man you want to see."

Viega stood and Robles knew that the meeting was over. He offered his hand, and Viega gave him a limp handshake. Robles felt as if he had something dead in his hand. It was all that he could do not to wipe his hand on his trousers.

"I can see," Viega said, "that you and I will be close friends. Together we will drive the yanquis out of my country."

Robles wondered if he would have to kill Viega before this was all over.

The first-class dining room of the *Bahia Grande* was rather small and meant to accommodate no more than a third of the ship's total passenger load. On this leg of the trip the *Bahia Grande* carried fewer than forty first-class passengers, which meant that the dining room was at only half of capacity. The first-class accommodations—dining room, lounge, and staterooms—had been refurbished when the Argentinian Passenger Lines acquired the ship from the original owners in 1935. The dining room and lounge had been redone in the manner of an expensive English hotel— dark mahogany paneling, plush, neutral-colored carpeting, and crystal chandeliers. The dining room steward and his waiters wore black tuxedos and moved with quiet efficiency. If not for the soft rolling of the ship and the quiet rumble of the engines, one might have thought he were dining at the Savoy in London.

The atmosphere aboard ship—at least for the first-class passengers—was one of luxuriant comfort. Air travel, although available to most destinations in South America, was not yet considered sufficiently reliable or luxurious. The aircraft available to most South American airlines—mostly Fokker Trimoters—were noisy, cramped, and of limited range. Such travel was for the adventurous. Most of these first-class passengers—an assortment of businessmen, diplomats, and other wealthy South Americans—would not even consider trading the comforts of a ship like the *Bahia Grande* for the vagaries of such travel.

On the first evening on board Harold Hollander, accompanied by his beautiful wife, arrived in the dining room at least twenty minutes after the other passengers had been seated. To the chagrin of everyone except himself, the obviously drunk Hollander loudly announced his presence to one and all as he and his embarrassed wife made their way across the dining room to their table. Those unfortunate enough to be seated at the same table gave each other looks of mortification as the Hollanders arrived. They were then required to suffer through an evening of crude jokes and mindless babble as the American insulted crew members and passengers alike. Every few minutes Hollander took a small swig from a silver flask he carried in the inside pocket of his dinner jacket. As his drunkenness grew, his already loathsome behavior deteriorated further, and after a short time in the dining room Hollander began to insult his wife, berating her for some imagined slight.

After dinner the Hollanders and most of the other first-class passengers moved into the first-class lounge, where there were several gaming tables. Here, Harry gambled badly and continued his heavy drinking and intolerable behavior. The other passengers kept as much space between him and themselves as possible. Fortunately for everyone, Hollander was apparently comatose by ten o'clock, and his wife had to call for the assistance of several crew members to assist him in getting back to his stateroom. During this disgraceful performance Mrs. Hollander struggled to maintain her dignity. Initially she spent much of her time apologizing and making excuses for her husband's behavior. Ultimately, however, even she sensed the futility of such protests. She sat in silence, eyes riveted on the far wall, as if to divorce herself from the evening's activities. Several times she covered her eyes with her hands as if to blind herself to her husband's actions, and it was obvious to all that

Mrs. Hollander was deeply embarrassed. Other than this small crack in her composure, she showed little, if any, emotion. It was as if she had long ago reconciled herself to these untoward displays of her husband's obnoxious behavior.

None of this went unnoticed by Max Greiser.

CHAPTER 18

The old man looked at Robles carefully. "And why have you come to me, my son?"

"Because I have been told that you can help me."

They were sitting in a water's edge café in Panama Harbor within sight of the giant breakwater that extended across the tidal mud flats to Naos Island. The harbor lay in a great circle that extended into the Bay of Panama. The Naos Island breakwater was more than three miles long. It protected the canal's entryway from the heavy current, and guided freighters into the narrow approach to the Panama Canal. Ships dotted the harbor awaiting their turn to pass through the approach for the short passage to the first locks at Miraflores and then on into the canal.

The old man was called Enrique Periera. He was more than seventy years old, but his voice was strong, his grip firm, and he sat with the posture of a younger man. His face was deeply lined and weatherbeaten from a life in the harsh tropic sun. "And the people who told you this?"

Robles made a gesture. "They are friends of President Arias. Men who are concerned with the welfare of Panama."

149

"Oh," Periera said. "Those men. And what about you? Are you concerned with the welfare of Panama?"

"Of course. I want to see the yanquis out of this country. Just as you do."

"I'm not so sure that you would not replace one evil with another."

"It is only the yanquis who wish to control Panama," Robles said. "Germany is concerned only with Europe . . . the Japanese only with the Pacific. Only the *norteamericanos* want to control our destiny."

"Your Spanish is excellent, señor," Periera said, "but you seem more European than one of us."

"My father's family has been in Argentina for a hundred years," Robles said proudly. "I was born and raised in Buenos Aires."

Periera noted that Robles had said nothing about his mother's family. "There are many Germans in Buenos Aires. Is it not so?"

Robles was silent. The old man was even wiser than they had told him.

"If it is not Panama that the Germans care about, it must be the canal."

"Germany has no wish to control the canal."

"Then," said Periera, "they must wish to destroy it."

"They said you were a wise man, Enrique Periera."

"It is customary, I suppose, to flatter those whose knowledge you wish to acquire."

Robles was certain that he could do the job alone, but with time short it would be beneficial to have the help of someone who could tell him everything he needed to know. "Will you help me, Enrique Periera?"

The old man looked at him for a long time before he answered.

In his younger days he had been an engineer from a wealthy Colombian family with extensive holdings in what was then the Colombian province of Panama. He remembered vividly the revolution of 1903 that, with American assistance, had wrested Panama from Colombian authority. It had been a revolution almost without violence. With

American naval vessels guarding the approaches to Panama City on the Pacific and Colón on the Caribbean, the Colombians had been powerless to thwart what amounted to a secession from their country of a sizable portion of their territory. The Panamanians, encouraged by the United States, had seen visions of the tremendous wealth that was to be theirs once the Americans completed their grand design for a canal that would link the Atlantic with the Pacific. They had seceded from Colombia but then had been forced to accept humiliating terms from the Americans, who wanted to build this canal.

The treaty between the new Republic of Panama and the United States had been negotiated in Washington between the American secretary of state, John Hay, and Philippe Bunau-Varilla, a citizen of France who had been involved with the earlier French effort to build a Panama Canal but had not set foot in Panama for eighteen years. The Frenchman was a major shareholder in the French company Compagnie Nouvelle, which had invested and lost millions of dollars in the first attempt to build a canal. Bunau-Varilla had convinced the leaders of the "republic to be" to appoint him as a special envoy to Washington because of his intimate knowledge of the workings of the American government and his promise to clear the way for the arrival of a special Panamanian delegation. Instead, Bunau-Varilla claimed, and his claim was accepted willingly by the American secretary of state, that he was the sole representative of the Panamanian government. He and Hay lashed out a treaty that gave the United States a firm grip on the land and affairs of the new nation. When the actual Panamanian delegation arrived in Washington—on the same day that Hay and Bunau-Varilla had signed the treaty—they were told that the treaty had been signed and that modification was beyond their control. Bunau-Varilla told the delegates from Panama, including the man who would be the new republic's first president, that they might as well go home. The delegation was outraged, but their protests fell on deaf ears. As far as the United States was concerned, they had signed an agreement with the duly recognized representative of the Panamanian government. This agreement had only to be ratified by the United States Senate to go into effect. The Senate approved the treaty by a vote of sixty-six to fourteen.

Under the terms of the agreement, Bunau-Varilla's company, the Compagnie Nouvelle of Paris, was to be awarded forty million dollars by the United States government. The fledgling Panamanian government was awarded ten million dollars and sent packing. For his efforts, supposedly on behalf of Panama, Philippe Bunau-Varilla had rescued himself and his company from a financial disaster. As soon as the treaty had been approved by the Senate, Bunau-Varilla informed the government of Panama that he was resigning his appointment as special envoy.

It had been thirty-eight years, but Periera remembered the indignity as if it had been yesterday.

To make matters worse, when Periera had applied for a job as an engineer with the Panama Canal Company, he was told that his services as an engineer were not required. This was at a time when the company was importing hundreds of engineers from the United States and Europe. Periera was offered a job as a common laborer. Since that time his hatred of the *norteamericanos* had burned with the intensity of a blast furnace.

"Why would I wish to destroy the canal? To drive out the yanquis, yes, but to destroy the canal is to destroy Panama. It is all that we have. It is our birthright."

"You and I both know that the canal cannot be destroyed," Robles said, unless we want to fill in the ditch with shovels. All that I want to do is to shut the canal down for a short time. I want you to tell me how to do it."

"A short time does not interest me," said the old man.

"I don't understand."

"You could destroy one of the interior locks and close the canal immediately. They would repair the damage and have the canal reopened in a month."

"That is all the time that I need," Robles said.

"Panama needs more time than that to get rid of the yanquis. Much more. When this war comes—and it will come soon, you are the proof of that—the Americans will leave if the canal is of no use to them. By the time the war is over, we—Panamanians—can repair the canal and go about our business without the presence of the *norteamericanos.*"

"You're talking about closing the canal for the duration of the war? That could be years."

"According to the yanquis, the reason they stay here is that in wartime the canal is vital to their national interests." Periera looked out to the harbor and the waiting ships. "If we can show them that only Panamanians have the power to allow access to the canal during wartime, they will go away."

"But how can we close the canal for such a long time? They would use every means available to repair the damage."

The old man sighed. "There are things that only time can repair. I will show you how the canal could be closed for five years. And nothing the yanquis do could repair it any sooner."

"Five years," Robles said. If this were true, he was in a position to truly alter the course of history. If the Americans could be denied access to the Panama Canal for such a lengthy period of time, their military strength would be diminished by half. Faced with enemies on two fronts and unable to move armies or navies quickly across huge distances, the Americans would be forced to divide their forces in order to face potential aggression from either direction. Suddenly a major military power would become a minor one, barely able to defend herself against the powers that were gathered against her. "How can we do this?" he said.

"Come back tomorrow," Periera said. "You and I will take a trip." The old man smiled. "Have you ever passed through the canal? It is a most pleasant journey, I can assure you, and one I think you will find most interesting."

While Robles was meeting with Periera, and Harry and Victoria were preparing to steal the German money, another Abwehr operative had arrived in New York City. His name was Dusko Popov, and he was a Yugoslavian who had been

*recruited by German Military Intelligence in Belgrade short-
ly after the commencement of hostilities. Popov was in his
early thirties—a tall, handsome con man who moved with
the self-assured swagger of a man who knew his way around.
He was equally as confident with the industrialists and
nobility of England, with whom he regularly met, as he was
with their daughters, whom he regularly bedded. Popov had
spent most of the past year in England sending back reports
on the military capabilities of the British to his bosses at the
Tirpitz Ufer. His successes in England had so pleased his
superiors in Berlin that he had been selected to initiate a new
spy network in the United States and to engage in an
apparently unconnected venture.*

*Popov carried with him a set of instructions, concealed in a
microdot, that if discovered by the BSC agents in Bermuda
would have been considered one of the greatest intelligence
coups of the war. The instructions went undiscovered in
Bermuda for the simple reason that Popov's baggage was
never searched. Popov's name had been included on a list of
those who would be allowed to pass through Bermuda
undisturbed. The list had been signed by William Stephenson
for the BSC in New York and by John Masterman represent-
ing the Twenty Committee in London.*

*The Twenty Committee was sometimes referred to by the
Roman numerals XX, and therefore sometimes known as the
Double-Cross Committee. The name was appropriate because the intention of the Twenty Committee was to deceive
the Germans by infiltrating their intelligence services, captur-
ing their spies and using them as double-agents. These
double-agents then fed the Germans a constant stream of
fraudulent information.*

*Dusko Popov was the most important agent in this double
cross system. He was presently on his way to the United
States, ostensibly to set up a new spy ring for Germany.
Actually he had already told his British controllers in London
about the German plan and was now on his way to meet with
BSC agents in New York, who were then to introduce him to
J. Edgar Hoover in Washington, D.C. Popov carried informa-*

tion about a sudden and very surprising German interest in
Pearl Harbor that the British were sure would be of great
interest to the Americans.

Even though the older man's expression never changed,
Wilfred Smythe could sense William Stephenson's disap-
pointment as Smythe told him about what had happened in
Panama.

"I tried to tell Trump that his plan was flawed from the
beginning," Smythe said. "But, of course, he paid little
attention to what I had to say."

Stephenson swiveled his chair so that his back was to
Smythe and he could look out from his office window high
above Rockefeller Center. "Doesn't surprise me very much.
Most of these fellows are a lot like the man who selects
them. . . . And Hoover doesn't listen to very much of what
we tell him."

"Anyway, this Fox chap went after the Germans," Smythe
said.

"Any chance of success?"

"I think he's more interested in avenging the death of his
friend than in recovering the money. Anyway, we probably
won't know anything for at least ten days. I've taken the
precaution of having some of our people waiting for the ship
to arrive in Buenos Aires. If Fox fails, we'll try to steal the
money as the Germans disembark."

"Not much chance of that," Stephenson said. "The
Germans will probably have an armed escort waiting." He
swiveled back to face Smythe. "How do you read Fox?"

"He's certainly resourceful. The counterfeit money was
absolutely outstanding. Even the FBI people, who see this
sort of thing all the time, were raving about the quality of
the bills."

"Trustworthy, d'you think?"

Smythe smiled. "Can't really say. He doesn't seem to be
the murdering monster that was pictured by Hoover and
Trump, but . . ." He was at a loss to explain what he felt
about Fox. "Who can say?" he added lamely.

"Perhaps we could use him when this operation is all over. We can always use resourceful people—especially Americans."

Smythe knew that Stephenson was generally reluctant to use Americans in any capacity. Whether this was from distrust, dislike, or merely apprehension about breaching the neutrality laws, Smythe could not say. "Perhaps," he said.

"In the meantime," Stephenson said, "I have another job for you. Once again, it will mean conferring with Director Hoover. I'm afraid there's no choice. Hoover could make things very uncomfortable for us if he thinks that we are withholding information from him. Our job here is to feed him information, let him take the credit, and hope that he'll be grateful enough to let us continue to operate."

"I thought that Roosevelt was firmly behind us." Smythe said.

"Yes, but Hoover exerts a powerful influence over a great many people in Washington—including the President. If he decides to make things difficult for us here, I'm not sure that we could continue to function."

"I'm sure you're correct."

Stephenson picked up some papers on his desk. "I'll want you to be in Washington tomorrow. The Twenty Committee people have sent someone over . . . fellow code-named Tricycle. He's a double agent who works for the Abwehr."

"Doubles for them or for us?" Smythe asked.

Stephenson smiled. "Hard to tell with some of these people, but Double-Cross seems to thinks this fellow is legitimate. Apparently, he's been feeding a lot of false but rather juicy misinformation to the Germans for the better part of two years, and they seem quite happy with the quality of the information. They're so impressed with his capabilities that they've actually sent him to America to set up a new spy network. But first they want him to make his way to Hawaii as quickly as possible."

Smythe didn't see where he fit into all of this.

"Before they sent him—and this is where it gets rather interesting—the Germans gave him a list—a sort of a questionnaire, actually—of things they'd like him to accomplish. Much of it is the usual sort of thing . . . aircraft production, shipbuilding, coastal defenses . . . but interestingly a fairly large portion of the questionnaire concerns American naval defenses at Pearl Harbor."

"Pearl Harbor? Now, why should that interest the Germans?"

"According to speculation by the Twenty Committee, the Germans have been asked by the Japanese to pass along a long list of very specific information about Pearl Harbor. And they want the information in a hurry."

"The Japanese," Smythe said. "Now, that makes more sense."

"I thought you'd think so."

"Does anyone seriously think that the Japanese would dare attack the Americans at Pearl Harbor?"

Stephenson said, "I don't think so—at least, no one has expressed that opinion to me. However, having this information does present somewhat of a dilemma for us."

"How so?"

"We've spent a great deal of time and effort in trying to persuade the Americans that the real threat to them is the situation in Europe. In that endeavor we've been largely successful. We don't want to tell them now that the Japanese constitute a more immediate threat—especially if we're not sure that it's true."

"Then why don't we just send Tricycle back to England on the next plane? There's very little chance that the Japanese would be bold enough to attack Pearl Harbor, and if we succeed in alarming the Americans, we'd make ourselves look like fools."

"And what if the unlikely happens, and the Japanese actually do attack Pearl Harbor? When the Americans discover that we had this information all along, everything we've worked to accomplish here would go up in smoke. Then everything that Roosevelt's critics say about us would be true, wouldn't it? That we care only about saving our own skin . . . that all this talk about a world made safe for democracy is merely a pack of lies. They would be perfectly justified in abandoning us the moment they discovered that we had held back this kind of information."

"So what do we do?"

"The only thing we can do. We send Tricycle to the FBI and let him tell Hoover everything. Your job will be to explain to Hoover that Tricycle is a double agent of questionable loyalties—which is absolutely true. That way we provide the information, but we don't accept the responsibility for its authenticity. Hoover will be free to do whatever he chooses with the information. If he chooses to alert the President, so be it. Perhaps the Americans will decide to bolster their forces in the Pacific . . . perhaps not. Tell Hoover that if he wants to send Tricycle to Hawaii we will see to it that he passes along to the Germans whatever bogus information the director chooses."

"In other words, give Hoover the information but do not vouch for its authenticity."

"I don't think that we can vouch for its authenticity. It seems rather improbable."

"When would you like me to leave?" Smythe asked.

"Director Hoover is expecting you—and Tricycle—tomorrow afternoon."

"Do I give him my disclaimer before he sees Tricycle? Or after?"

"I think before would be preferable . . . don't you?"

CHAPTER 19

Off the coast of Colombia, November 20

Maximilian Greiser could not keep his eyes off the elegant woman who was the wife of the very wealthy, very influential, and very obnoxious Harold Hollander. She and her husband sat two tables away from him in the first-class dining room. Her name, he had soon discovered, was Victoria Hollander, and she was perhaps the most beautiful woman Greiser had ever seen. He also saw something else. Beneath the air of elegant reserve, Greiser sensed a smoldering passion.

Greiser considered himself a man who could detect the slightest hint of availability in a woman. More often than not he was correct, and credited many of his conquests to this singular talent. Although the signs were very subtle, and he was certain that only he could detect them, this woman exuded a palpable electricity of desire. He found it difficult not to stare at her. Several times in the course of the evening their eyes met and held for just a moment. Greiser detected the slightest hint of a smile on her lips. Once she raised an eyebrow in his direction, and he felt a faint stirring in his groin.

Her husband, an industrialist of some kind or other, was a typical American buffoon—loud, profane, and offensive. He wondered what it was about wealthy Americans that made them so obnoxious. Even the English with their superior airs were not as disagreeable as the Americans.

Perhaps there was some jealousy involved, but Greiser found this American particularly odious. How, he wondered, did a man so obviously despicable merit such a splendid woman? There was, of course, a simple answer to his question. Money, he reasoned, had its benefits. He thought of the three and a half million dollars, safely locked away in the purser's vault, and wondered what life would be like if that money were his. Perhaps then this magnificent golden-haired creature would give him more than a momentary glance.

Greiser resented those who made arrogant displays of their wealth. He was the son of middle-class parents, his father a butcher, his mother a schoolteacher. Educated at the University of Würzburg, he had joined the Foreign Service in 1936 and served in a variety of foreign posts. At that time the Foreign Service was staffed mostly with upper-class Germans, and Greiser felt that he was often slighted because of his middle-class background. His resentful attitude toward his superiors had made it difficult for him to gain regular advancement, and when war came in 1939, he had requested and been granted a position with the Abwehr, where he felt his talents would be more appreciated. Since 1940 he had been stationed at the German Embassy in Buenos Aires as the assistant to the station chief of the Abwehr.

This night, the second night out from Colón, was similar to the previous evening in that Hollander, already drunk before dinner, had continued drinking heavily in the lounge after dinner. In addition to losing large sums of money, he berated everyone within earshot, demanded prompt service from waiters who brought an endless stream of drinks to his table, and, in general, made an ass of himself. Greiser watched as Mrs. Hollander, a small stricken smile on her face, tried to reason with her husband, but he would have none of it. If anything, he grew more boisterous, and his wife looked around the lounge as if pleading for help from the other passengers or perhaps, and this Greiser felt was more likely, as if she were looking for an avenue of escape.

Greiser despised this miserable excuse for a man and thought that he would like to go over and slap the American's face. He had even begun to develop a small fantasy about himself and the American couple in which he would approach their table during one of Hollander's particularly abominable moments and demand that the American act with some civility toward his wife and the other passengers. Hollander would be shocked into silence and skulk away like the coward he was. The wife and the other passengers would give Greiser grateful looks as he returned to his seat.

Emerging from his daydream, Greiser was startled to notice that the American woman was looking in his direction. He could not be sure, but he imagined that she had given him a barely perceptible nod as if she had read his mind. Momentarily flustered, caught in his imaginary transgression, he looked away.

A voice nearby failed to penetrate his thoughts. "I said— looks like he's dead drunk again," Blaskowitz repeated.

"Sorry," Greiser said. "My mind was miles away." He looked over at the Hollanders' table and saw that the American was slumped forward, his face flat on the table. "Disgusting," he said.

Blaskowitz chuckled. "If I were married to that one, I'd stay sober long enough to give her a good hard dick every night." He looked at Greiser. "She looks like that's what she needs . . . don't you think?"

"As usual, Blaskowitz, you manage to reduce everything to its crudest level." He looked at Victoria Hollander again, then smiled. "This time, however, I feel that you might be right." For the tenth time that evening he imagined her naked.

At that moment Victoria Hollander looked up, and their eyes met again briefly. This time it was the American woman who looked away. There was such a look of anguish on the woman's face that even Greiser felt sorry for her. But not for long. His instincts were predatory. When he sensed weakness and vulnerability, he prepared to strike. It had been a long time since he had seen a woman as vulnerable as this one. He could feel the excitement in his groin as he watched her sit quietly while the chief steward and two of the waiters helped Hollander to his feet and began to escort him to his cabin. Mrs. Hollander, her eyes damp, held her head high as she followed her husband from the lounge. She was the picture of the faithful, long-suffering wife, Greiser thought, but he sensed that her facade was about to crumble.

Harry Fox sat up in bed. He was fully clothed.

Vicky was pouring coffee into a cup. "Feel okay?" she asked.

He rubbed his temples. "I don't know how long I can keep this up," he said. Even though he was drinking much less than what the other passengers assumed he was consuming, he still had to drink much more than he was used to in order to convince everyone that his drunkenness was genuine.

"I think we should get this thing going tonight," Vicky said. "Another night of this and you won't be much good to anyone. You're sure that neither one of these men is the one who killed Ernesto?"

"Positive," Harry said. "These are the two couriers. I saw them at the hotel. The other one—the one who shot Ernesto—must have been the man they delivered the money to."

"And he's not on board?"

"No. I won't forget that face."

"Then let's get this thing over with and get back to Panama."

"You think we're ready?"

"I've seen him watching me," she said. "I don't know about us, but I know that he's ready."

He looked at her. "I want you to be careful. He might decide to take what he wants if you push him too far."

"Don't worry. I can handle him."

Harry watched her in the mirror. He never tired of

looking at her. "The first order of business is to find out where the money is ... chances are it's in the purser's vault."

"And if it is?" she said, dabbing perfume behind her ears.

"That's a problem," he said. "We'd have to place our counterfeit money in the vault, get a key, and get inside to make the switch."

"Can you do that?"

"Maybe. But it would be a lot easier if the German had the money in his cabin."

Victoria nodded. "Okay. If the money is in the purser's vault, I'll get him to bring it to his cabin."

Harry laughed. "Just like that?"

"I've seen this guy looking at me," she said. "I know the look. If he thinks I'll let him have what he wants, he'll promise me anything. The easy part is getting him to do what I want. The hard part is to keep him from getting what he wants."

Harry knew that she was right. Some men, he thought, would do anything—lie, steal, cheat, maybe even commit murder—for a woman like this. Such a woman was part of every man's fantasy, a fantasy which promised that sometime in every man's life there was a woman like this waiting for him. Harry smiled. His fantasy had come true.

She finished applying a touch of lipstick and turned to face him. "Here I go," she said. "Wish me luck."

"I ought to wish the German luck. He doesn't stand a chance."

She gave him a wink as she went out the door.

Harry waited a few minutes, then he left his stateroom and wandered somewhat aimlessly down the hallway. He knew that at this time, the cabin steward was usually in the process of turning back the sheets in the bedrooms. He came to an open cabin and knocked. Sure enough the cabin steward appeared. He was a slightly built young man of perhaps seventeen, with dark hair and smooth-cheeked features. He seemed surprised to see Harry and looked at him with some trepidation. His friends in the dining room had told him about the crazy *norteamericano* who was making everyone miserable at dinner.

"Can I help you, señor?" he said, in halting English.

Harry spoke to him in Spanish. "I seem to have locked myself out of my room. I wonder if you could let me back in?"

"Of course, señor." The steward reached into his pocket and removed a key, then stepped past Harry into the hallway and moved toward the American's stateroom, which was only a dozen doors away. Harry fell into step beside him. As they walked the steward was thinking that this man who was supposed to be so drunk at all times didn't seem very drunk right now.

At Harry's cabin the steward inserted his key in the lock and opened the door, then stepped back to allow Harry to enter. Harry pressed a twenty-dollar bill into the steward's hand as he walked past. "Thanks," he said.

The young man took a discreet peek at the bill. Twenty dollars for opening a door! He was almost speechless but managed a brief word of thanks as Harry turned to face him. Then the words came in a torrent as if he was afraid that the American would think him ungrateful. "If I can be of any further service, señor, please do not hesitate to ask for me. My name is Miguel."

"Thank you, Miguel. I'll remember that." He started to close the door.

"I'll be back soon to turn down the beds, señor."

Harry closed the door. He chuckled at how easy it was to make new friends. Every new venture, he thought, demanded new friends.

Greiser was surprised when Mrs. Hollander returned to the lounge. On the first night when her husband had been carried off by the waiters, she had chosen to remain in her cabin. Probably getting a little bored watching the drunken bastard sleep it off, he thought. He watched her as she approached the chief steward and spoke softly to him. Probably apologizing for her husband. The steward smiled pleasantly, nodding several times in agreement with whatever it was that she said. Mrs. Hollander reached into her purse and removed something. Even though she kept whatever it was hidden in her hand, Greiser was certain that she was preparing to give the chief steward money. His suspicions were confirmed when the steward looked around the room, and then with the practiced perfection of one who has done this sort of thing for many years, accepted the money and slipped it into his pocket in one graceful motion. Now he was smiling and nodding reassuringly, obviously telling Mrs. Hollander not to worry about her fool of a husband, and that he and his waiters would take care of him. She'd be better off, Greiser thought, if she had bribed the chief steward to dump her husband overboard.

The chief steward touched the bill of his cap, and Mrs. Hollander nodded, then turned away. She went to the door of the lounge and then stopped as if hesitant about returning to her cabin. She turned and looked back, then took a deep breath and went to the closest empty table. She sat, her eyes lowered as if afraid to meet the stares of the few passengers who were still in the lounge. When she did look up she looked directly at Greiser, letting her eyes hold his for barely a fraction of a second before she looked away.

Greiser did not waste a moment. He went to her table and stood across from her. "Good evening, Mrs. Hollander," he said. "I wonder if you would mind if I joined you in a drink?"

Victoria looked up cautiously; the boldness of a moment ago had vanished completely. "I was just going to sit here for a while," she said. "I didn't feel like going back to my cabin."

"Of course," Greiser said. "If you would prefer to be alone, I will not bother you any further." It was a calculated risk, but one that he felt he must take.

"No . . . of course. Please sit down, Mr . . . ?"

"Forgive me," he said, sitting down across from her. "I am Maximilian Greiser."

"Victoria Hollander," Vicky said, extending her hand across the table. "My friends call me Vicky."

Greiser took the offered hand and gave it what he was sure would be felt as a reassuring squeeze. "I would be delighted if you would allow me that privilege."

Victoria lowered her eyes and looked away. "Of course."

"And you must call me Max." Greiser signaled to a waiter and ordered drinks. "You are American?"

"Yes," Vicky said. "Houston, Texas."

"I wondered where your wonderful accent came from. I must confess I find Americans most agreeable . . . and the women are the most beautiful in the world."

Vicky allowed her eyes to meet his. The eyes held each other for a moment, and then she looked away again.

Although her obvious shyness was most appealing, Greiser could feel her longing. He had to force himself to go slow. He was certain that this kind of flirtation was a new experience for her, and he did not want to frighten her away. "As you might have guessed," he said, eager to keep the conversation going, "I am originally from Germany . . . Hamburg. My mother was Dutch. I have lived in South America for almost ten years."

"Well . . . Max," Vicky said, as if it was difficult for her to use his first name, "what brought you here to South America?"

"I own a small but profitable business in Buenos Aires"— he shrugged—"export-import. . . . I am glad to be away from the madness that has engulfed Europe."

"And your wife?"

Greiser saw the image of his plump wife waiting for him in Buenos Aires. "There is no one," he said without hesitation. "I have never been fortunate enough to find the woman to share my life." Lying was part of what he did for a living.

"I can't believe that some woman hasn't dug her claws into an attractive man like you."

Greiser could feel the sexual tension in the air. The woman's attraction to him was obvious. This was going better than expected. "I'm afraid that I have spent most of my time building my business," he said. "I have never had time for a home or a family."

"I'm afraid my husband would say the same thing. Why he bothered to get married, I'll never know."

"I deeply regret my decision not to marry," Greiser said. "Perhaps if I had met the right woman." He paused and Vicky thought he was going to add, "A woman like you," but he did not. He merely said, "Things would have been different."

Vicky wet her lips with her tongue and for one brief, wonderful moment Greiser thought that she was going to offer herself to him. He could sense the reluctance in her voice when she said, "I think I had better be getting back to my cabin. My husband might wake up and wonder where I am."

She is begging me to change her mind, Greiser thought. She wants me to tell her not to go. He smiled. Not tonight, Mrs. Hollander. It is too soon, and there are other nights. "I understand," he said. "Shall I walk you back to your cabin?"

She seemed horrified by the thought, and he knew that she would keep this meeting a secret from her husband. "No . . . thank you. I'll be just fine."

"Perhaps we could meet again, tomorrow evening," he said. "I have enjoyed our conversation."

Vicky smiled. "So have I . . . Max. I'm not sure . . . I mean, I don't know if I will be able to."

Greiser stood up and bowed. "I understand, Vicky. I understand completely."

She hurried off, as if hopeful that no one would notice that she had been there. Greiser watched, marveling at the motion of her hips and the absolute perfection of her legs. Again, he imagined her naked in his bed. He drew in his breath sharply at the thought. At the door she turned and gave him one long lingering look before she disappeared into the hallway. Greiser smiled. This, he thought, is going to be wonderful. She was as ready to be seduced as any woman he had ever met.

In the passageway, on the way back to her cabin, Vicky smiled to herself. I've been hit on by experts, she thought. This is going to be like taking candy from a baby.

CHAPTER 20

Panama City, November 21

The next morning in a driving rainstorm, Periera and Robles boarded the tramp steamer *Gabriella* at the loading docks off Avenida Norte in Panama City. Periera nodded to the ship's captain but made no attempt to introduce him to Robles. The ship, a small vessel of some two thousand tons, was one of many that passed through the canal delivering cargo from one side of Panama to the other. By special arrangement with the Panama Canal Authority, such ships, operated locally by Panamanian concerns, were given a special passage rate through the canal. It was often cheaper for the larger freighters to deliver their cargoes to Panama City where it would be reloaded onto these smaller vessels and carried through the canal to Colón, where it would be reloaded onto larger vessels for the Atlantic portion of the voyage. This was one of the few concessions that the American-controlled Panama Canal Authority had made to the local inhabitants. It cost the authority little and provided much needed employment to the Panamanians.

An American soldier, one of the transit guards who now traveled with every ship that passed through the canal, came aboard. His job was to check the cargo and to make sure that there was no contraband aboard. Some of the larger vessels carried as many as ten of these transit guards. The American made a brief inspection on deck and then, anxious to get out of the rain, went below into the cargo hold.

The small ship fell into line behind a larger freighter and prepared to piggyback its way into the canal at the Miraflores Locks. The locks at the canal were more than a thousand feet long and big enough to hold the largest ships then afloat. They were big enough in fact to hold a large freighter and one or more of the small Panamanian tramp steamers. It was this piggyback ability that enabled the Canal Authority to justify the reduced rate for the smaller ships' passage.

Periera and Robles, sheltered from the rain by the overhang from the bridge, stood on deck as the two ships passed inside the first lock gate at Miraflores. The two men, both engineers, could not help but marvel at the magnificence of the structure. It was somewhat ironic, Robles thought, that he, who so admired this technical achievement, had been selected to destroy the greatest engineering feat of this or perhaps any other age. He looked at Periera, who nodded his silent appreciation of Robles's predicament.

"It is indeed marvelous," Periera said.

At the time of their construction the locks at the Panama Canal were considered among the wonders of the modern world. Each lock chamber was an immense concrete trough one thousand feet long and more than one hundred feet wide and eighty-one feet deep with gigantic steel doors at either end. At the time of their construction, each individual chamber if stood on its end would have been the tallest structure in the world. There were twelve such chambers in the lock system of the canal. In order to facilitate two-way traffic, the twelve chambers had been built in six side-by-side pairs.

The gates, huge double doors at either end of the locks, weighed several hundred tons apiece. They swung open or closed on huge bull wheels, twenty feet in diameter, that were hidden within the concrete walls of the chambers and were operated by electrical power that was generated by the falling water at the Atlantic side of the canal.

The gates closed behind the *Gabriella,* and almost immediately the water level in the lock began to rise. The sensation was that of rising in a slow-moving elevator, and Robles could not help the smile that crossed his face as the two vessels rose like toy ships in a bathtub. The sensation of motion ceased, and the forward doors swung open, leading them into the second of the Miraflores Locks. The procedure was repeated and the ships rose again until they were at fifty-four feet above the level of the sea. At the far end of the lock, they could see the control house, a concrete structure that sat between the two chambers, from where the locks were operated by a single engineer.

"One man," Periera said, "operates all of this." He pointed to the control house as the *Gabriella* sailed through the gates and into the man-made Miraflores Lake. "The other two that you see are guards." From this point it was only a brief mile and a half journey to the next set of locks at Pedro Miguel. "Until three months ago," Periera continued, "the control houses were unguarded. One man, with the properly placed explosive, could have shut all of this down in an instant. It still could be done if one were willing to die."

Robles did not think much of that idea, but it was one that had to be considered. "How long would the canal remain closed?"

"A week . . . maybe two. Spare parts would be brought in immediately."

Although not enough to satisfy Periera, a week or two might be suitable for his own purposes, Robles thought. The control house, although guarded, was so exposed that a determined assault would probably prove successful. Escape was another matter. He scanned the surrounding area looking for an avenue of departure. There were soldiers everywhere, and although they did not look particularly vigilant at the moment, he was sure that the sound of gunfire and explosion would stir them from their lethargy. It seemed impossible that one could plant explosives and get away without being overwhelmed by reinforcements. Robles preferred being alive so that he might reap the fruits of his heroics.

"What about the lock gates themselves?" Robles asked. "If I could heavily damage one of the doors, surely they could not be replaced in such a hurry. That should take months—at least."

"But you would have to simultaneously damage another gate in the other chamber. One of the weaknesses of this type of canal is that if one of the locks is damaged the entire operation is shut down."

"Exactly."

"But the twin chambers allow this canal to continue operation. Traffic in the locks would be reduced to one-way, but unless you were able to blow another gate in the other chamber, traffic would continue to move through the canal."

It had stopped raining and Robles went to the rail and inspected the gates as inconspicuously as he could. He need not have been so careful. No one gave him a second glance.

The *Gabriella* passed through the locks at Pedro Miguel, which raised the ship an additional thirty-one feet. They were now eighty-five feet above sea level, ten miles from Panama City, and heading into the narrow, winding passage known as the Culebra Cut. The cut was nine miles long and less than two hundred feet wide. It had been excavated in a slender valley that lay between the three highest points on the route of the canal. The high points were hills— Contractor's, Gold, and Culebra—between five and six hundred feet high. The three hills were uncommonly steep and the earth had been made unstable by the deep trench that formed the canal. Mudslides were common. Of all the monumental tasks in the construction of the Panama Canal, this one had been the most incredibly difficult. Periera shuddered as he recalled the torture of the more than seven years it had taken to gouge out this narrow strip of earth. "Culebra," Periera whispered to himself. "The Snake."

For seven years there had been not a moment's cessation of the clamorous noise in what came to be known as the Culebra Cut. Night and day the gigantic earth excavation machines, which weighed several hundred tons and stood over thirty feet tall, had gouged huge shovelfuls of dirt from the slopes of the hills. In some months the great shovels removed more than two million cubic yards of dirt from the cut. The work—digging, blasting, transporting—went on endlessly. The problem was that the deeper the cut became, the more unstable was the surface of the three hills that loomed above the work site. When the rains came, the hillsides loosened and millions of cubic yards of mud and rock simply slid into the site of the excavation. On some occasions a single slide would obliterate three months of digging. At other times the slides would be so gradual that they were only enough to fill in the work that was being done at that time. The great earth shovels—as many as sixty-eight of them at one time—would plow the earth, their huge buckets lifting tons of dirt and muck and dropping it into the waiting railroad cars, which then would race off and deposit the accumulation and return for more. At the end of such a day the slides would fill in everything that had been done. It was as if the builders of the canal were struggling against the tide.

The three hills—Contractor's on the west side, and Gold and Culebra, or Snake, on the east—loomed above the *Gabriella* as the small ship made her passage through the cut. The angles of incline were steep, with Culebra's at least sixty degrees. The impression was of the sheer face of a cliff rather than of a hill. In the rainy season, only the thick vegetation held the surface in place.

Other than the locks themselves, this was easily the narrowest place in the canal. Navigation was extremely difficult in the cut, and it was obvious that when larger ships—battleships and aircraft carriers—passed through the cut, traffic in the slender channel would be reduced to one-way. Even smaller ships could barely scrape past each other in the narrow confines of the cut.

Robles smiled. The Culebra Cut was a natural bottleneck, and with the properly applied amount of explosives he could see that the bottleneck would become a logjam.

"Just three years ago," Periera said, "there was a minor slide that blocked the canal for a week. It took two months to fully clear the passageway. There have been many such slides since the canal opened."

Robles surveyed the hillsides. It would not take a great amount of explosives to bring any one or all of these hillsides rushing down to fill the Culebra Cut. The sides were precipitously steep and obviously unstable. The vegetation would provide cover for whatever had to be done. It was perfect for his purpose. It amazed him that nothing, other than encouraging the growth of vegetation and some minor attempts at terracing the hillside, had been done to prevent the possibility of these canal-blocking slides.

"Is this the place you promised me?"

"You could close the canal here, but for how long . . . a few months?"

Robles was not so sure. "The excavation machines that dug this trench don't even exist anymore. It would take several months—maybe more—to bring similar machines from America. I would be surprised if they could clear this channel in anything less than a year."

"Slides here are frequent," Periera said. "Dredging equipment is constantly in use. The cut would be cleared in a month—perhaps in a few weeks. Be patient," he said. "Soon, I will show you what you came to see."

By now they were out of the narrow Culebra Cut and into the waters of Gatun Lake, the great lake that had been created when the Chagres River had been dammed. It was twenty-three miles from this point to the final set of locks at the Atlantic end of the canal. "This is how the Americans succeeded where the French failed," Periera said. "The French tried to dig a trench across Panama as they had done at Suez. But the task was too much for them. The Americans built a series of locks on one end and another series at the other. Then they built a dam and flooded half the country with this lake. Then they connected their locks to the lake and"—he made a gesture with his palms up—"we have a canal."

"Ingenious," Robles said.

"Ingenious, yes. But how many of my people were dispossessed by the waters of this lake? There was no compensation. They were told to pack up and go . . . or drown."

Robles and the old man were silent for the rest of the trip across the lake.

As the *Gabriella* approached the triple locks at Gatun for the descent back to sea level and the final exit into the Caribbean side of the canal, Periera nodded to the young man at his side and pointed at the giant Gatun Dam that connected at the eastern end to the Gatun Locks. The Gatun Dam was an immense wall of earth extending for a mile and a half across the valley formed by the Chagres River. Here the builders of the canal, with marvelous economy, had brought everything that they had dug from the rest of the canal and created a huge embankment that was more than a thousand feet thick at its base. It was this dam that held back the waters of Chagres River and formed the huge lake that was the cornerstone of the Panama Canal.

"Without this dam," Periera said, "there is no Gatun Lake. Without Gatun Lake, there is no Panama Canal."

"You are not suggesting that it would be possible to destroy this dam? The thickness is incredible. It would take weeks of constant blasting to make even a minor dent in the surface. This is not possible."

"Every structure has a point of weakness."

Robles looked again at the gigantic structure. For a moment he would not allow himself to even consider that it was possible. Then he saw it.

"The spillway," he said softly.

The old man nodded.

The spillway at Gatun Dam was a dam within a dam, a thick barrier of concrete several hundred feet wide that allowed the Canal Authority to discharge water from the lake whenever the levels were too high. The spillway sat astride a deep channel that had been dug into Gatun Dam and allowed controlled release of excess water from the lake. It was immediately apparent to Robles that, if enough explosives were used, a large hole could be blasted in the spillway.

"I'd have to know exactly how thick it is," he said. "How deep the water is at the base." His mind was racing. If he could breach this dam—even a fairly small gap of ten or twenty feet—the force of the escaping water would gouge out huge amounts of dirt from the dam itself. Once the dam was breached, the process was irreversible and inevitable. The escaping water would widen the break until the opening was an uncontrollable chasm. The process would feed on itself—the lake was eighty-five feet higher than the land on the other side of the dam and the immense pressure of such a body of water would create an irresistible force that would inevitably destroy the dam that contained it. The wider the hole, the more water would rush out. The more water, the wider the hole. The size of the breach would grow rapidly, and in a very short time the rushing water would become a tidal wave that would destroy everything in its path.

"I remember this valley," Periera said, "before the lake covered the land. I remember the day the dam was completed and the waters began to flood everything."

"How long did it take to create this lake?"

"Five years."

"That means . . ."

"Yes. If you destroy this dam, the waters will seek their natural level. And even when the dam is repaired it will take years for the lake to reform. For that length of time the Panama Canal will be useless."

Robles barely heard the old man. Five years, he thought. Five years! In five years the world would be a vastly different place, and he, Carlos Gunther Robles, would be largely responsible for the makeup of that world.

The old man did not interrupt the younger man's reverie. It was enough for him to know that he had found the man who would convert his dreams to reality. There had been others, who had talked about ridding Panama of the yanquis, but they were mostly talk. They wanted to negotiate with the Americans. The thought made him furious. There was something about Robles, however, that filled him with confidence. This one did not seem like a man who liked to negotiate anything. The long wait, Periera was certain, was finally over.

CHAPTER 21

Off the coast of Venezuela, November 21

That evening when the waiters escorted the drunken Hollander back to his room, Greiser tried to catch Victoria's eye as she was leaving the lounge. She did not look in his direction, but kept her eyes straight ahead. He wondered if this meant that she had decided not to speak with him again. For the next twenty minutes he waited expectantly. This would be the test, he thought. If she came back, it meant that she was eager to continue their relationship. If she did not return . . . well, he thought, nothing ventured, nothing gained.

Less than twenty minutes later Greiser smiled when he saw Victoria Hollander standing in the doorway of the lounge. She had changed her clothes, he noted. She wore a flower-print dress, tight around the hips and cut low in the front. He drew in a sharp breath at the sight of her.

Victoria stood in the doorway, scanning the lounge. Every eye in the room was on her, and she was sure that very soon rumors of a shipboard romance between her and the German would be on everyone's lips.

Greiser stood and approached her. Every eye followed him. "I hope," he said, "that you have returned to join me."

"I shouldn't be doing this," she said. "Everyone's watching us."

Greiser smiled, happy that she had inadvertently acknowledged the clandestine nature of their meeting. "You must not let provincial minds disturb you," he said reassuringly. "If two friends choose to have a drink together, why should anyone take notice?"

"It's silly, I know, but I'm very uncomfortable."

"Perhaps," Greiser said, "you would like to take a walk around the promenade deck?"

"I'm not sure," she said, "I really shouldn't have come."

"It's a beautiful night. It would be nice to get some fresh air."

"It is rather smoky in here," she said.

Without hesitation, he took her elbow and led her into the hallway that led past the dining room and onto the promenade deck. He was aware that every eye in the lounge was on them. He smiled, knowing that the men were beside themselves with envy, while the women were passing knowing glances around the room. Let them think what they like, he thought. They'd probably applaud the man who cuckolded Hollander.

A short time after Victoria left her stateroom to go to the lounge, there was a quiet knock at the cabin door. Harry went to the door and opened it. In the passageway stood the cabin steward, Miguel.

"You said you wanted to see me, señor," he said softly.

"Yes," Harry said. "Come in."

The steward stepped into the room. He looked around.

Harry took a twenty-dollar bill from his pocket and gave it to the steward. "Miguel, I need a favor."

Miguel looked at the money but was reluctant to put it in his pocket. He did not yet know what this favor was.

"I need to find a discreet place to take a young lady for the evening," Harry said. "A young lady, I might add, who is not my wife."

Miguel put the money in his pocket. This was not an unusual situation aboard ship and one which occasionally afforded the crew an opportunity to make some extra money. "I'm sure that something could be arranged, señor."

"What I was thinking," Harry said, "was that there must be several empty cabins."

"This is true. I would be glad to arrange for accommodations for the gentleman and his lady."

Harry smiled. "Perfect." He took out another twenty but did not offer it to Miguel. "Now I don't care how large the cabin is," he said, "but I would like to have it on B deck. It would enable me to maintain the necessary discretion."

"There are several empty cabins on B deck," Miguel said, his eyes on the money. "I could have one ready for you at any time."

"Perhaps there is one available in the passageway directly below us?"

"Yes."

"And I could borrow your passkey for several hours this evening?"

"That would not be a problem, señor." All of the keys to the unused rooms were held by the chief steward, but Miguel had his passkey which opened any cabin.

Harry patted Miguel on the back and slipped the twenty into the breast pocket of the steward's white jacket. "You and I are going to be very good friends, Miguel. And I always take good care of my friends."

"Thank you, señor," Miguel said as Harry guided him to the door. "Give me a half hour to prepare the room, and I will be back with the key."

"I'll be right here waiting," Harry said.

Once in the hallway Miguel could not believe his good fortune. He had more than he could make in a month already in his pocket, and there was the promise of more to come. He gave a quick thanks to the Blessed Virgin and hurried off to prepare the cabin.

Outside, the night was pleasantly warm. The sea, dark and unusually calm, made soft soothing sounds as the ship plowed through the gentle waves. Victoria and Greiser walked, side-by-side, in silence for a short time, then stopped. Victoria leaned on the railing and watched the waves below. Greiser stood next to her and began to talk softly about what a beautiful evening it was and how happy he was that she had returned. Victoria recognized the implication in Greiser's tone and made only soft noises of assent and compliance. She knew that this was what he wanted to hear.

She let him ramble for a time and then turned to him and said wistfully, "There's no moon tonight."

Greiser smiled. This was going to be easier than he thought. "Are you disappointed?"

"No . . . I just thought it's such a beautiful night, that it would be nice if there were a moon." She averted her eyes and watched the rolling waves. She felt him move closer.

"You're right," Greiser said. "It would be nice if there were a moon." His elbow touched hers.

She did not move away. He moved closer. Victoria made a half turn to face him. "I know what you're thinking," she said. "But it can never happen. I have always been faithful to my husband."

He put an arm around her waist and pulled her closer.

"I don't want you to do that," she said. She looked up into his eyes, and he moved his face closer to hers. "Please don't," she said. He pinned her against the ship's rail and they kissed. His hand moved down her back.

"Max," she said. "Not here. Not now."

"Let's go back to my cabin," he said, his voice husky in her ear.

She hesitated. "You'll never know how much I want to," she said. "But I can't. I mustn't." She pushed him away, both palms on his chest.

For a moment he considered using force, but he was still confident that he could persuade her. If not now—later. He was, as always, the patient predator. "Why not?" he asked.

"If my husband ever found out, he'd divorce me in a minute."

"How could he find out? He's probably dead drunk right now."

"Don't underestimate him. You don't know him. Nothing ever escapes him. He's a very resourceful person . . . drunk or sober. Besides, I couldn't take the chance of his ever leaving me."

"I'd think it would be the best thing that could happen to you. He cares nothing for you—you've told me so yourself. He's nothing but a drunken fool."

"But a very rich drunken fool."

"Is money so important to you?"

"I hate to admit it, but money is everything to me." She looked out to sea, as if her thoughts were far away. "I grew up dirt poor on a farm in Texas. Since then I've grown accustomed to the finer things in life. I'm afraid that I love all of the things that money can buy. I love the look of money . . . even the smell of it." Vicky was pleased with herself. This was one of her finest performances. She had played a small part in a movie where Joan Crawford had said something very much like this. "I'm the kind of woman who needs a man to take care of her . . . preferably a very rich man. Hollander treats me as if I were a part of his art collection . . . something he owns, something to admire, something that's precious to him because only he can possess it. If he ever thought I'd been unfaithful to him, he'd leave me in a minute. And I own nothing," she said. "He'd see to it that I was left with exactly that. He has always made it quite clear that I am a wealthy woman only so long as I am his wife."

"If I had a woman like you," Greiser said, "I would shower her with gifts."

Victoria touched him on the cheek. "You're very sweet. But I've got to get back before he misses me."

Greiser's voice could not disguise his disappointment. "I had hoped that you could stay longer."

"Perhaps tomorrow."

He brightened. "Till tomorrow, then."

He moved toward her, and she let him kiss her lightly on the lips before she pushed him away. "If I stay any longer, there's no telling what I might do," she said.

He watched her as she hurried away from him as if his presence were too much for her to bear. When she was gone, he leaned on the rail and watched the waves. So, he thought, the lovely Mrs. Hollander loves the look and the smell of money. His thoughts went to the three and a half million dollars in the purser's vault. What would it harm to put that money to some use before he delivered it to Buenos Aires?

Harry was waiting for her when she got back. "How did it go?"

"You should have seen me, Harry. I don't think I've ever been better."

"You think he went for it?"

Victoria smiled confidently. "Tomorrow we'll find out everything we want to know." Then the smile slipped from Victoria's face. "He's a first-class creep. He makes my flesh crawl. Every time he looks at me I can feel him undressing me with his eyes." Her body gave an involuntary shiver.

Harry took her in his arms. "I'm sorry," he whispered. "I know this isn't easy. Are you going to be okay?"

Vicky rested her head on his shoulder. "Yes, Harry, I'll be okay." She let herself melt into his body. "Just hold me for a little while. Just make me feel good."

He knew she needed to be held, to be protected. For the first time he really thought about what it was that he had asked her to do. He had wanted to punish the Germans for what had happened to Garcia. He had wanted to steal the money to show Trump that he could do it without the help of the FBI. And he had involved Vicky, even though none of this had anything to do with her. He had asked her to play a part just as she had done in the movies. But this time the villains were real. The Germans weren't playing a role. No director would yell "Cut!" If the plot unraveled. If things went badly, it was conceivable that the Germans would try to kill them both. Vicky, however, would be their first and most vulnerable target. He held her in his arms, hoping that he could protect her from that.

They held each other, without speaking, for a long time.

183

CHAPTER 22

Off the coast of British Guiana, November 22

Victoria managed to avoid Greiser for most of the next day. Although Greiser anxiously awaited an opportunity to speak with her, she seemed never to be alone. Hollander clung to her as if she were a prized possession and he was afraid to let her out of his sight. Occasionally, once when she was out on deck with Harry, another time when they were having an early drink in the lounge, she would turn and see that the German was watching her. She, however, played the dutiful wife, anxious that her husband would not notice that another man was paying her special attention. Once in a while, as if she found it impossible to stop herself, she would look at Greiser and the two would exchange long, meaningful looks. Harold Hollander, like the drunken dullard he was supposed to be, noticed nothing.

Late in the afternoon Hollander made a great commotion about going back to his stateroom for a nap. He did not seem to mind when his wife decided to stay in the lounge.

As soon as Harry had gone, Victoria went to Greiser's table. She did not sit down. "Let's go for a walk," she said brazenly.

Greiser almost leapt to his feet. "As you wish," he said.

Outside, Vicky led him to a quiet spot on the promenade deck. "It was hell today," she said, "knowing that you were there and not being able to talk with you."

Greiser was ecstatic. He could feel himself on the verge of conquest. "It was awful for me, too," he said.

"But I'm afraid that we can't continue to meet like this."

Greiser's heart flipped. "I don't understand."

"I think my husband suspects something. Last night he wanted to know where I've been going."

"He's too drunk to suspect anything. He probably sleeps like a baby."

"Yes, but if he wakes up and wonders where I am . . ." Her voice trailed off. "He might even have me followed. He'd do such a thing." She looked around her, as if someone might be watching them.

Greiser could feel things slipping away from him. What had been a sure thing only moments ago was fast becoming a lost opportunity. "I don't want you to go," was all he could manage.

She touched his cheek. "And I don't want to go," she said. "But I'm afraid of what might happen to me if he found out about us. I'm not proud of why I stay with him, but there's nothing I can do about it."

Greiser's mind was racing. He knew that he had been very close to having this exquisite creature in his bed, and he was not about to spare any device that would accomplish that end. "Leave him," he said suddenly, the words racing ahead of the thought. "When we reach Buenos Aires, you will leave with me. I want you to be my wife."

"Don't be foolish, Max. I've told you that I am a woman of very expensive tastes."

"I have told you that I own my own business . . ."

"My husband," she interrupted, "owns corporations. He is worth millions."

". . . I, too, am very wealthy, and I would be glad to support you in the manner in which someone as beautiful as you deserves."

"You're very sweet," Vicky said. "I'll always remember you for saying that."

"I'm serious," Greiser said. "I can give you all of the riches that you deserve.

She turned away from him and looked out to sea. After a while she said softly, "I wish that I could believe that." He did not respond so she turned to face him, her eyes full of doubt. "I really want to believe it."

"I can prove it to you."

"How?"

He smiled. "How much money does a rich man carry with him?"

"I don't understand."

"How much money does your husband—the fabulously wealthy Mr. Hollander—carry with him."

"I don't know. A few thousand perhaps. Maybe more."

Greiser chuckled. "I have just completed a small business transaction in the United States and have in my possession, at this moment, almost four million American dollars." He paused. "That, of course, is only part of my personal fortune."

Greiser, Vicky thought, wasn't very much different from the Hollywood and Vegas sleazes who were always trying to impress women with money they did or didn't have. The theme was always the same—go to bed with me and I'll take care of you. "Lots of men claim to be wealthy," she said. "How do I know you're telling me the truth?"

"I can show you the money, if you like." He hoped that she would say that such a demonstration would not be necessary.

"When?" she asked.

Bitch, he thought. Behind the beautiful facade she was just another whore who demanded money for her services. He would take that greed and use it to his advantage. He smiled thinking of how he would enjoy seeing the surprise on her face when he abandoned her in Buenos Aires. When he finished with her, she would have no husband, no money, and no illusions about her value.

"Tonight?" Vicky asked.

"Surely you don't think that I would keep that kind of money in my cabin?"

"Of course not." She paused. "My husband keeps his valuables in the purser's vault."

"I will speak with the purser after dinner," Greiser said. "Tonight you will come to my cabin . . . after your husband leaves us for the evening."

"And you'll show me this money?" she said excitedly.

"Yes."

"All of it? Almost four million dollars?"

He smiled. She was almost like a child—a greedy child—who had been promised an expensive new toy. Well, he would teach her a lesson about greed, and about trusting the wrong person.

"Talking about money gets me excited," she said, and he was beginning to hope that he would not have to wait until tonight. "But I've got to get back to my cabin before my husband misses me. If he does, we can forget about tonight." She touched his face. "I can't wait," she said, and then she was gone.

Greiser watched her go. It was almost pathetic, he thought. Some women were so gullible. This one is so anxious to leave her husband, and so anxious to find another wealthy man to support her, that she is willing to believe anything. Once again he imagined her naked in his bed. They were seven days out from Buenos Aires, and after tonight he would have her whenever he wanted her. He smiled. It was going to be an interesting seven days.

"It's in the purser's vault," Vicky said.

Harry was laying out his clothes for the evening. He dropped his tuxedo on the bed. "That's where we figured he'd have it," he said. "Did you convince him to take it out of there?"

She unbuttoned her dress and let it drop to the floor. "Tonight in his cabin, I get to see the prize." She stood in front of him in her slip.

"Be careful," Harry said. "I have a feeling that these guys can play rough if they don't get what they want."

"Don't worry, Harry," she said. "I'm being very cautious."

"We have to make sure that he can't return the money to the vault after you've seen it."

"The vault is closed from eight P.M. until morning," she said. "As long as we wait until after eight, there's no way that he can put the money back. He'll have to keep the money in his cabin overnight."

"This might be the only chance we get," he said.

"I'll try to keep him busy for a while," Vicky said.

"Remember, he's dangerous. You'll have a tough time keeping him under control."

"It's sweet of you to worry so much." Vicky stepped out of her slip and did a pirouette in her underwear. "What do you think?"

He patted the bed. "I've been waiting for you."

She reached back, unsnapped her bra and threw it on the chair. "Just let me jump in the shower," she said. "Then I'll be right back. Guys like Greiser make me feel dirty," she said. "I have to wash that away." She went to him and kissed him and rubbed her breasts against him. "I'll be right back."

He heard the shower running and thought about her and Greiser. He wished that he could share her confidence that she could handle the German. The best thing to do, he thought, was to switch the money as quickly as possible and get this over with. Tonight they would get the money, and tomorrow they would leave the ship when it docked in Paramaribo.

CHAPTER 23

That evening Harry arrived in the dining room apparently even drunker than usual. He complained loudly to one and all that his drinks were watered down and proceeded to spike his martinis from the sterling silver flask that he carried in his inside jacket pocket. Each time, as he added more gin to his glass, Hollander took an extra swig from the flask.

As Harry raised the flask to his lips for the second time, a large, middle-aged woman who sat across from him with her pint-sized husband, glared at him disapprovingly. Harry smiled drunkenly in her direction. "Where are my manners?" he said, and reached across the table to offer her the flask. "Have a swig, honey. It'll loosen you up a bit." He gave her husband a huge wink.

The woman turned to her husband as if he might rescue her from this monster, but he seemed well aware that even in his drunken condition Hollander would be more than a match for him. The husband was content to register his disapproval with a disdainful sneer.

"Can't even be nice to some people," Harry said.

Victoria stood up and announced quietly, "I need to get some air." She quickly left the table before her husband could stop her.

Hollander raised himself out of his chair and then slumped as if the task were too much for him. "To hell with her," he mumbled to himself but loud enough for all to hear. He took another swig from his flask and returned to his dinner.

From the other side of the dining room, Max Greiser watched all of this with interested anticipation. The seat next to him, usually occupied by Blaskowitz, was empty. The American was, as usual, making an ass of himself. Only this time he was making a bigger ass of himself and doing it sooner. Greiser looked at his watch. It was only a little past eight o'clock, and Hollander was well on the road to oblivion. Greiser felt a surge of anticipation in his groin. Tonight he would pay Hollander the ultimate insult. When he was done with Hollander and his wife, he wanted everyone on board ship to know what had happened.

Greiser waited a moment and then followed Victoria. He found her out on the promenade deck, standing by the rail. Her head was bowed and her body shook as if she were crying. She looked so incredibly vulnerable, so impossibly helpless that he felt a sudden surge of passion. The urge to dominate was strong in him and never more strong than when he sensed powerlessness. He was certain that this woman was ready to do anything that he asked.

Victoria turned, startled at his approach. "Oh," she said, "it's you."

"You were, perhaps, expecting your husband?"

"No."

He put an arm around her waist, but she pulled away from him. "Not here," she said. "We might be seen."

"I have something I want you to see in my cabin."

"Now?" she said, alarmed at the thought. It was far too early to begin. Harry's plan required that the ship be quiet, that the passageways be almost deserted. "I have to get back to the dining room. My husband will miss me soon. He'll come looking for me."

"He's not in any condition to go looking for anyone," Greiser said. "Besides, it will only take a moment," he insisted. "I just want to show you the money, and then you can go back to the dining room. Later, when you have tucked your husband in for the night, you can come back to my cabin." He was confident and self-assured, and she responded in the only way that he knew she could.

"All right," she said.

He escorted her back inside and down the passageway that led away from the dining room and toward the passenger cabins, which were grouped on three decks in the stern section of the ship. Greiser's cabin was on B deck one deck below the cabin occupied by Harry and Victoria.

They arrived at his cabin and instead of using his key, Greiser knocked twice. "It's me," he said.

The door opened partially and half of Blaskowitz's beefy face appeared in the opening. The single eye went from one to the other, and then the door closed as he released the chain. In a moment the door opened and Blaskowitz stepped back so that they might enter. Blaskowitz's face was impassive but he could not hide the hostility behind his eyes. It was obvious to Victoria that he did not approve of Greiser's using the money to seduce her. Equally obvious was the fact that his enmity was focused, not on Greiser, but on her. Victoria also noted that Blaskowitz held a pistol in his hand. He saw her look at the weapon, and he quickly slipped it into a shoulder holster beneath his jacket.

Greiser, too, saw her look at the gun. "This much money needs protection," he said, by way of explanation, then turned to Blaskowitz. "Wait outside, Helmut," he said, and when Blaskowitz hesitated, he added, "It will be all right."

The stateroom was really two rooms in one. The first room was a small sitting room with a couch and an upholstered chair with a cocktail table between them. Through a door was the bedroom, two single beds flanking a nightstand.

When they were alone, Greiser led her to the bedroom. "Would you like to sit down?" he said indicating the bed.

"I can't stay," Victoria said nervously. "I have to get back to the dining room. My husband is probably looking for me already."

Greiser wanted her now—immediately—but was wise enough to realize that she was far too concerned with her husband to give him the kind of obedience he desired. If he were too insistent, she could hardly be expected to passively submit to all that he wanted from her. He wanted her to give him her full compliance. He would wait until she was not concerned about her fool of a husband. "I understand," he said pleasantly. "I only want you to be comfortable."

Victoria sat on the bed across from him, and Greiser reached under the bed and pulled out one then another large suitcase. He lifted them onto the bed. Each case was held closed by a leather strap and a small padlock. Greiser took a key from the nightstand and opened both locks. With considerable flourish he opened the leather straps and flipped open the cases to reveal the money.

"Oh, my God," Victoria whispered. "I've never seen anything like it." She looked at him. "And this is all yours?"

"All of it."

"What about Blaskowitz?"

"He works for me. When I travel with such large sums of money, I need someone to protect my person and my property."

Victoria had eyes only for the money. The two suitcases were almost full, and she noted that the money was still in the Bank of Mexico wrappers and that all the bills were facing, neatly, in the same direction. Harry would want to know that.

Greiser mistook the intensity of her scrutiny. He assumed that she, as he did, found the presence of so much money intoxicating. "You may touch it if you wish."

She licked her lips. "I'd like that," she said suggestively and then ran her fingers lightly over the top layer of money. She drew in a sharp breath through clenched teeth as if she were caressing bare skin.

Greiser felt as if she had touched him. He twitched as shivers of pleasure darted throughout his body.

She saw the effect that her calculated move had had on him, and she removed one of the money packets from the suitcase. Greiser could not tell that she was estimating the thickness of the packet. She waved it in front of her face, fanning herself. "Is it me, or is it hot in here?" she asked.

Just as Greiser began to think that he might abandon his earlier patience, Vicky stood up. She dropped the money back into the suitcase. She knew that it was now too late for Greiser to return the money to the purser's vault. "I have got to get back," she said. "Later, when my husband is . . . retired for the evening, I'll come back." She ran her fingertips across his cheek. "Is there anything special you'd like me to wear?"

Greiser's throat was dry. The anticipation of that moment was almost too much for him. He could only shake his head and mumble, "No."

"Be patient," she whispered. "It won't be long." She took one last look at the money. "I hope the money will still be here," she said. "There's something about money that is so very exciting. Don't you agree?"

He looked at the money as if in a daze. "It will be here," he said. "Don't worry."

"Later, then," she said and went quickly to the door. Greiser was too paralyzed to follow.

In the hallway she took a deep relieved breath before she realized that Blaskowitz was there, and for the first time she realized how immense this man was. His body filled the passageway, easily blocking her path. He eyed her coldly, saying nothing. "You can go in now," she said pleasantly, hoping somehow to blunt his malevolence.

Blaskowitz ignored her pleasantry. He continued to watch her, fondling her with his eyes. She felt his icy touch and gave an involuntary shiver. Blaskowitz smiled, but it was a smile that came from the sewer that was his soul.

Keeping as much distance between them as possible, Victoria squeezed past him and hurried down the hallway. Behind her she heard what might have been soft laughter.

* * *

Harry paced their stateroom, his head bowed, his hands linked behind his back. He stopped his pacing. "So you think that was all of it?" he asked.

Victoria sat on the bed, her shoes off, her feet up. "Two suitcases, almost full," she said.

"Suitcases under the bed . . . wrappers still on . . . bills facing in one direction," he murmured, cataloging what she had told him.

"Don't forget the key to the padlocks in the night table."

"From what you've told me about the padlocks, I'd be able to open them easily even without the key." But knowing where the key is will make things a lot easier."

"How much time will you need?" she asked.

"No more than ten minutes. You've got to get him out of that room for at least that long."

"Don't forget the other one," she said. "Blaskowitz. He has a gun and he scares me. I'll have Greiser send him away when I get there, then I'll tell him that we have to go outside for just a short time. You'll have to work fast. I don't think I can keep him away from that money for very long."

"I'll be ready," Harry said. "I have to see the steward to get the passkey for the room across the hall, but that should be no problem. I'll be there before you arrive at Greiser's cabin. From there I'll be able to see you and him leave the cabin. As soon as you go I can get to work. I'll be back across the hall before you return. When you do come back, I'll come back here with the money, then I'll play the irate husband and come rescue you. Do you think you can hold him off until I get back?"

"I'll be all right."

He still wasn't certain, but he let it go at that.

She crossed her fingers. "Now we wait."

She thought of Blaskowitz, aware that her confidence in her abilities did not extend to him.

CHAPTER 24

Viega's driver gave two sharp beeps on the horn, and in moments the double doors of the old warehouse building swung open. Viega gave Robles his gap-toothed smile and ordered his driver forward. The car moved slowly into the warehouse, and the doors behind them swung closed. The driver leaped out and opened the car door for Viega. Robles did not wait. He opened his door and got out on the other side.

"This way," Viega said, and Robles followed him.

They walked past rows of crates marked with the ports of origin from around the world. Robles could only guess at the contents of these crates.

Viega waved a hand at the crates in passing. "Most of these items are from South America," he said. "They are brought here to Panama City and warehoused until they can be shipped to Colón or to the Far East."

Robles knew that many of the South American freighters dropped off and picked up cargo in Panama City. Much of this cargo would never pass through the Panama Canal. It would be railroaded to Colón and then loaded onto freighters for the voyage to Europe. That way the owners would save the ninety cents per ton that was charged by the Panama Canal Authority. "And all of this is yours?" Robles asked.

"The warehouse is mine," Viega said. "Everything that you see here is merely stored here for a short time." He smiled. "There are some things that you do not see that are mine, however."

They stopped in front of a long row of merchandise, and Viega waited while several men pushed aside a number of crates. When the area was cleared, Robles saw that there was a large trap door on the floor. The men looped a cable through a steel ring on the trap door and attached it to a pulley on an overhead crossbeam. The heavy door was hoisted open, revealing a stairwell at least six feet wide.

"Come," Viega said and moved to the stairs.

Robles followed and Viega led him down into a large underground room. The ceiling was low and supported by heavy timbers so that Robles had to be wary of bumping his head. Here, too, were crates stacked in every corner. Robles saw that some contained liquor and assumed that Viega had a thriving, illicit liquor business. Other cases were unmarked. Viega pointed to one of these, and his men pried open one of the cases. It took two men to lift the opened case from its place at the top of the stack and place it at the feet of Robles and Viega.

"You are welcome to inspect the merchandise," Viega said.

Robles stepped forward and looked down into the open case. He reached down and removed what looked like a thick candle wrapped in dark red waxed paper. The dynamite felt heavy and solid in his hands. He felt the covering carefully to assure himself that it was not moist and that the material on the inside was perfectly stable. The paper was dry.

"How long has this been here?" Robles asked.

"Less than four months . . . all is perfectly fresh, I assure you."

Robles felt the inside of the case for the telltale moistness that would tell him that the nitroglycerine was leaking and that the dynamite was no longer stable. The case was dry. He held the dynamite stick up to the light where he could read the lettering on the wrapping. He nodded his satisfaction that the product was of a high explosive grade of the kind used in most mining applications. It was also of comparatively recent manufacture.

Viega pulled back a tarpaulin to reveal another stack of cases. "As you can see, I have a great deal of other types of explosives."

Beneath the tarp were stacked cases marked as Nitramex, an explosive only recently developed by the DuPont company and quite difficult to obtain. "You need Nitramon primer for detonation," Robles said.

Viega nodded to one of his men who uncovered several cases of primer.

"None of this came from Germany," Robles said. "I was told that you had German military explosives."

Viega led him behind the first row of cases. There his men uncovered a second row. There were at least fifty cases of Cyclotol, a high-grade military explosive used in Germany. The British and the American military still used an explosive called Amatol from the last war that was about half as powerful as this.

"Do you think this will be sufficient to do the job?"

Robles nodded. There must have been two hundred cases in the room. Enough, he thought, to wreak havoc in the canal. If Arias and his people had decided to blackmail the Americans with threats of violence against the canal, they had certainly stockpiled enough explosives to do the job.

"There is more, if you require it," Viega said. "In other locations. Perhaps not as much as this, but still a considerable amount."

Even though Robles's job as a construction engineer had made him intimately familiar with large explosive excavations, there were more explosives in this room than he had ever seen in one place. In one fell swoop Viega had solved what might have been his biggest problem, acquiring the amount of explosives needed to do the job. He now knew that he had the material to attack the Panama Canal on several fronts. Now he only had to plan that attack. And, he thought, negotiate with Viega for the dynamite. He looked at Viega and could tell by the expression on the man's face that he was already thinking about money.

"Perhaps," Robles said, "we could come to some agreement about price."

Viega's eyes darted quickly to the men who stood nearby, and Robles knew that Viega would not want to discuss price while others were in the room. "We are brothers," Viega said, as if he were insulted by the inclusion of such a tawdry topic. "We have the same goals, the same principles, the same desire for freedom. Let's not worry about money. My people wish only to be compensated for the amount they spent in acquiring this material." He smiled. "I am sure we can come to some mutually agreeable amount."

Robles did not return the smile. This, he was sure, was going to cost him plenty.

CHAPTER 25

Off the coast of British Guiana, November 22

It was well past eleven o'clock, and Greiser's impatience was beginning to show. He tapped his fingers nervously on the tabletop, checked his watch every few minutes, and several times had left the lounge to pace back and forth on the promenade deck. Under his breath he muttered obscenities that were directed toward the object of his resentment. That object, Harry Hollander, seemed as drunk as usual, but tonight, for some reason, had managed to avoid his normal early-evening comatose state for much longer than usual.

Hollander drank and laughed and told vulgar jokes to anyone who was within earshot. Between drinks he drank from his flask. Most of the other passengers tried to smile politely. The several other Americans on board shunned him with obvious embarrassment. Americans like this gave them all a bad name.

Greiser had started the evening with feverish anticipation. He was certain that by ten o'clock his long-awaited moment would arrive, and he would finally have Victoria Hollander in his bed. His last few evenings had been spent in restless sleep while he imagined the ecstasy of his conquest. Victoria had changed her hairstyle since dinner, gathering her hair on top of her head, exposing her neck and shoulders as if making herself more vulnerable to his predatory glances. As the evening wore on, Greiser's frustration became evident. At one point he had snapped at a waiter who was slow in bringing him a fresh drink. Every time he had looked in Victoria's direction, he was painfully reminded that that beautiful expanse of naked skin—and more—was his for the taking. Once or twice he was aware that Victoria would look in his direction. Whenever she felt that they were unobserved, she gave a minute shrug. There was nothing to do but wait.

Finally, at about a quarter to midnight, Hollander began to show signs that he was feeling the effects of his constant intake of alcohol. The uninterrupted stream of conversation and bad jokes had ebbed, and Hollander rubbed at his eyes with his knuckles. His eyes were droopy and his head bobbed forward and snapped back as he fought to keep himself awake. The battle was soon over, and the man surrendered to sleep. At first his head fell forward and his chin rested on his chest, but soon he had completely capitulated, and his head was cradled in his arms on the table.

Greiser breathed a sigh of relief when Victoria summoned the waiters to perform their nightly ritual of escorting Hollander back to his cabin. Greiser waited only a short time before returning to his cabin to await the arrival of Victoria Hollander.

As soon as Greiser entered his stateroom, he knew that something was bothering Blaskowitz. Blaskowitz was a simple creature who found it impossible to mask his displeasure. His face was indeed a window to his inner self. That inner self was usually teeming with some amorphous anger and accounted for his normally ferocious expression. Tonight, Greiser noted, the expression was troubled.

"What is it, Helmut?" he asked.

"I don't like this," Blaskowitz said.

"Don't like what?" Greiser was well aware of what it was that his colleague did not like.

Blaskowitz looked at him, his huge paws clenched into fists. "You using the money to get this woman into bed with you. If anything happens to it, we will both pay. It should be kept in the purser's vault."

"Nothing will happen to the money. It will not be left alone for an instant, but what harm can it do to benefit from the money before we turn it over to the embassy?"

Blaskowitz went immediately to his next point of contention. "I don't like this Hollander woman. There's something about her that doesn't seem right. Can't you just screw her and be done with it?"

Greiser thought he detected a note of jealousy in Blaskowitz's protest. After all, it had been Blaskowitz's crude comments that had started him thinking about Victoria Hollander. Now he was asking Blaskowitz to share the risk—if there was indeed any risk—but not the spoils. He liked to think of himself as a fair man. "Perhaps, Helmut," he said, "you would like to have your fair share of the conquest? When I am finished with her—perhaps in a day or two—I would have no difficulty if you chose to also avail yourself of the bountiful charms of Mrs. Hollander."

A sly smile spread across Blaskowitz's face. "Do you think she would agree to such a thing?"

Victoria Hollander's acquiescence was of little concern to Greiser. "You'll just have to convince her."

Blaskowitz knew there was only one way he could convince a woman like that. "She could make a lot of trouble for us."

"How? Who would she complain to? Her husband? What would she say?" Greiser mimicked a woman's voice. "Well, yes, I did go to his cabin two nights in a row and had sex with him. But on the third night his companion raped me." He laughed. "I don't think that is very likely. If Hollander found out that she came to this cabin of her own free will, he would divorce her in a minute. She has confessed as much to me already. No, my friend, she will say nothing of what happens to her while she is with us."

Blaskowitz nodded. "I suppose you are right." The sly smile was back.

Greiser laughed, pleased that Blaskowitz had already forgotten his concern about the money. "Of course I'm right. Tomorrow night, after I'm done with her, you can come in. Then I'll leave you alone with her, and it will be up to you to persuade her. I'm sure you can."

Blaskowitz imagined the scene and licked his lips.

"Look," Greiser said reassuringly. "By tomorrow morning the money will be back in the vault, and for the rest of the voyage we both have some fun. Where's the harm in that?"

Thoughts of Victoria Hollander, naked in his bed, crowded out any remaining anxiety Blaskowitz might have felt about the money. "I don't suppose it would do any harm to keep the money here for one night," he said.

"Ready to go?" Harry asked.

Victoria sat in front of the mirror at her dressing room table applying the finishing touches to her makeup. "Almost."

There was a knock at the outer cabin door and Harry held a finger to his lips. "Be right back," he whispered. He closed the bedroom door behind him, then opened the outer door and saw the deck steward, Miguel, standing somewhat nervously in the hallway. "Come in," Harry said.

The steward took a quick look up and down the hallway before entering. He spoke in Spanish. "How may I help you, señor?"

Harry took two one hundred dollar bills from his pocket and placed them on the table. Miguel swallowed hard and said again, "How may I help you, señor?"

Harry touched a finger to his lips and aimed a thumb in the direction of the bedroom. The steward nodded. "I need that room again this evening, Miguel," Harry whispered. He winked. "I'm meeting my lady friend a little later."

Miguel could not keep his eyes off the money on the table. He did not make that much money in half a year. On the other hand, he could lose his job if anyone ever found out what he had done. "I don't know, señor," he said. This *norteamericano* made him nervous. He never understood the rich, and he supposed that he never would. This one was cheating on his wife, and according to his friend Paco, who worked in the main lounge, his wife was spending a lot of time with one of the Germans on B deck.

Harry picked up the money and rubbed it between his thumb and forefinger. He took one of the bills and stuck it into the breast pocket of the steward's linen jacket. "One now . . . one later."

Miguel touched his hand to the pocket. He imagined that he could feel the hundred dollars beneath the fabric. He decided quickly. "Very well, señor."

Harry touched him on the shoulder. "Good boy."

Somewhat reluctantly, Miguel removed his passkey from his pocket. Giving a passkey to a passenger was an offense for which he could be fired. He had another key but hated to surrender this one to anyone. "I must have this back before morning," he said, handing it to Harry.

"I only need it for a few hours," Harry said. He could have said that he would return the key in half an hour. Miguel turned to leave, and Harry said, "One more thing."

"Yes."

"I want a bottle of your best champagne . . . on ice . . . waiting in the room."

Miguel smiled. "I understand, señor. It will be chilled and waiting." He turned to go again.

"One last thing," Harry said. "I'd like these suitcases taken to the room." He pointed to two large suitcases that sat by the door. "I have some special things I want to give to my . . . lady friend." He winked again at Miguel as if this were something that two men of the world would understand.

Miguel understood nothing. This yanqui was getting stranger by the minute. He would never understand these rich *norteamericanos.* He wondered who was the mysterious lady that this one was meeting. He was certain that it must be the daughter of the Argentinian businessman in stateroom seventeen. She had been making eyes at half the crew. "As you wish, señor," he said. He picked up the suitcases and was surprised by the weight. The yanqui was giving her something heavy.

Harry closed the door and went back to the bedroom. Victoria was still fussing with her hair. "Everything's ready," he said. "We go in ten minutes."

"I'm worried about the time you'll have to spend in that cabin switching the money."

"I've decided," Harry said, "to bring the money across the hall to my other cabin. I'll make the switch there."

"But won't you have to go back and forth twice that way?"

"Yes. But I'll still only have to carry the suitcases on one of those round trips. On the other trip I'll just be another passenger walking down the hallway. Don't worry. It'll be easier this way."

Victoria wasn't convinced, but she decided not to press him.

Fifteen minutes later Harry was in the cabin on B deck, down the hallway and across from the Germans. He quickly checked that the padlocks on his suitcases had not been tampered with, then removed the locks and left them on the table. He opened the champagne and poured it down the sink. When it was empty he read the label. "Good year," he whispered and put the bottle back into the ice bucket. He returned to the suitcases, opened them and methodically began to remove the money. He stacked the bills on the coffee table, making sure that all of the pictures faced the same way. When the cases were empty, he left them open on one of the beds and covered the money on the table with a blanket from the other bed. Now ready, Harry checked his watch and turned out the lights. He opened the door just a crack. From his vantage point he could watch the door of the Germans' cabin.

A few minutes later Vicky appeared. She looked in his direction and smiled, then checked herself with her compact mirror. She knocked gently on the door. It opened and she disappeared inside.

Harry lit a cigarette and tried to relax. Won't be long now, he thought. In just a few minutes he would know how things were going.

"Don't you look lovely," Greiser said, his eyes running hungrily up and down her body.

Victoria managed a pleasant smile. "Good evening," she said. Blaskowitz was in the room also, and even he seemed somehow less hostile than he had been before. She wasn't sure if that was an improvement, because the way he was looking at her made her skin crawl.

Greiser kissed the back of her hand, managing to make the gesture obscene. "I've been so looking forward to this night," he said.

Victoria tilted her head toward Blaskowitz. "We are going to be alone, aren't we?"

"Of course," Greiser said. "Helmut was just on his way out. He will be spending the evening in the lounge. Won't you, Helmut?"

Blaskowitz dragged his eyes away from Victoria. "What? . . . Oh, yes . . . of course. I was just on my way out when you arrived." He grinned lasciviously and went to the door. "Have a pleasant evening," he said and was gone.

Victoria shivered. "I find him quite unpleasant," she said.

"He can be," Greiser agreed, "but I think you will find that many women find his type quite attractive."

"Not me."

"Perhaps not," Greiser said, "but then one never knows what one will find stimulating." He quickly changed the subject. "I have some wine chilling," he said. "Would you care for some?"

"I'd love some," Victoria said, relieved that Greiser was not trying to rush her into the bedroom.

They sat on the sofa and Greiser poured the wine. He made a small toast and they clinked glasses. "To us," he said. "And to pleasure.

"To us," Vicky responded.

Greiser drained his glass and poured himself another.

Across the hall Harry watched Blaskowitz leave the room. The big man paused outside the door for a moment, looking around to make sure that no one was in the passageway. He pressed his ear against the door and listened for a short time; then, hands stuffed into his pockets, he walked down the hallway. At the stairs he looked back once, and went up toward the lounge.

Greiser's eyes kept drifting to her breasts, and Vicky knew that soon he would move closer. He did, sliding over so that his knee touched hers. He finished his wine and placed the glass on the table, took her half-empty glass from her hand, and placed it on the table next to his. He moved even closer, his eyes locked on hers. "I have been anticipating this moment forever," he said.

"And so have I," Vicky said, placing her hand on his knee. She could feel his body twitch at her touch.

"Shall we move into the bedroom?"

Vicky stood up. "Yes, but first I must check on my husband."

"But, I thought . . ."

"Don't worry," she interrupted. "I'll be back in ten minutes. I gave my husband a sleeping pill before I left. I told him I'd be right back. I want to make sure he is asleep for the evening."

He could not bear the thought of her leaving. He had been so close to his dream. His blood was racing, his heart pounding. He was ready now. He stood up. "I don't want you to go," he almost whined.

"And I don't want to go, darling," she said. "But I won't be able to relax if I think my husband is awake and wondering where I am." She gave him her best wanton look. "And I'm sure you want me to be relaxed."

"Of course," he said, "but . . ." He could think of no rejoinder. Once again she had rendered him helpless by bringing him to the brink and then slamming on the brakes. He was stunned by this unexpected turn of events.

"You're not afraid that I won't come back, are you?"

It had not occurred to him, but now that she mentioned it, the thought pierced him like a dagger. "No," he said doubtfully.

Vicky took his hand. "Come with me, then," she said pulling him toward the door. "I'll check on him, and we'll be back in a minute. It's just upstairs."

He was almost to the door when he remembered the money. "I can't leave," he said. "The money."

"We'll be back in a few minutes."

Greiser's eyes went to the bedroom, and Victoria knew that he was thinking about the money. She began to fear that she had lost him. "I understand," she said. "I just thought that if you came with me, we might have some fun." She grinned wickedly. "I'd like you to do it to me while the bastard is asleep in the next room." She stepped back. "But it's all right," she said, the disappointment evident in her voice. "I'll go now and try to get back."

"Try," he stammered, the word hitting him like a thunderbolt. His ardor told him that if she left now, he would never get another chance.

"There's always tomorrow, darling," she said. "We don't have to rush."

All of his plans were turning to disaster. He had to decide quickly. The wine . . . the heat . . . this woman; all combined to make thinking difficult. His brain struggled against his passion. He was a jumble of indecision. Passion won. "If I go with you, we can come right back?" he asked.

Vicky took his hand and led him to the door. "Right back," she said. "In no time at all."

Harry Fox watched them come out of the room. Greiser looked carefully up and down the hallway, and several times checked that the door was locked before following Vicky to the stairs. Harry waited until he was sure that the hallway was deserted then quickly went across to Greiser's room.

The door opened easily, and he slipped inside. He closed the door behind him, flipped on a small flashlight, and paused to get his bearings. The room was just as Vicky had described it: sitting room with couch, chair, and table, and coat closet to the left of the door. The bedroom door was to his left. He went immediately to the bedroom, reached under the bed on the left and pulled out both suitcases. He took the key from the nightstand and slipped it into his pocket noting that there was a Walther automatic pistol in the back of the drawer. He carried the suitcases into the other room, listened for a moment at the door, then, confident that all was quiet, opened the door, scanned the hallway, and swiftly carried the bags across to the other room.

Victoria placed a finger across her lips as she opened the door to her stateroom. "Wait here for just a second," she whispered and slipped inside. In seconds she was back and beckoned him to enter. Again she motioned for him to be quiet. "He's not quite asleep yet," she said. "But it can't be more than a few minutes before he is out cold. The sleeping pills usually work like a charm. I think he's too drunk for them to take effect."

Greiser looked worried. He had had time to start thinking about the money again. "I'd better go back," he said. "Meet me in my cabin when you've finished here."

"Don't be silly," Victoria said. "Soon we can make love here."

"I really think I should go."

"Maybe you don't really want me to come with you," she said.

"Of course I do," Greiser said through clenched teeth. "It's just that I—"

"Wait here, then," Vicky interrupted. "I'm going to give him another pill." She disappeared into the bedroom.

Greiser clenched his hands into fists. This was taking much too long, but he was afraid that if he left now, she would not follow him to his cabin. He knew that what he was doing would be considered a severe dereliction of duty, and if Blaskowitz discovered that he had left the money unguarded, there would be hell to pay. The last thing he needed was a subordinate who held incriminating evidence against him. Especially someone like Blaskowitz. He could hear Victoria Hollander talking soothingly to her husband and wanted to shout out at her to hurry up. But he held his silence, and, increasingly frustrated by the delay, he waited.

Once inside the other cabin, Harry threw the bags on the bed and went to work. Using the key from the nightstand, he removed the padlocks, thankful that he did not have to waste time picking the locks. He opened the first suitcase, checked to see which way the bills were facing, and how they were stacked, then dumped the contents on the bed. He placed the empty case on the floor and began to count out the number of wrapped packets of bills. There were two hundred packets in the first suitcase—exactly two million dollars.

Now he turned to his stack of counterfeit money which he had placed in rows of ten packages each. Working quickly, but carefully, he filled the suitcase with two hundred packets of counterfeit bills, making certain to place them in the proper order. He closed the first suitcase and turned to the second. Again he counted out the wrapped packages. This time there were one hundred and fifty—one and a half million dollars. Now he knew how much had been handed over to the man in the hotel room in Colón. He whistled softly. Someone was in Panama with half a million dollars.

Harry counted out the required number of counterfeit packets and placed them in the second case. He checked his watch. It had been slightly less than ten minutes since he had crossed the hallway to Greiser's room. Even though everything had gone like clockwork, he was still running behind schedule. He had told Vicky to keep Greiser busy for ten minutes. They should be returning at any moment.

Working as quickly as he could he closed and padlocked the suitcases and went to the door. Damn! Someone was in the hallway. He waited. Several passengers were engaged in boisterous conversation. Seconds seemed like hours. While he listened to the voices, he dumped the real money and the remaining counterfeit into his two suitcases and locked them. Finally the voices passed, and he opened the door cautiously. Empty, but he had lost precious minutes. He raced across the hallway, opened the door to Greiser's cabin and went inside. In moments the suitcases were back under the bed, the key in the nightstand and he was back at the door. He opened the door a crack. More voices. People were returning from the lounge. He checked his watch. He was out of time. If the hallway was not cleared in thirty seconds, he would have to risk being seen. If he casually left the cabin, he might not be noticed. He listened. Silence. He opened the door a crack, peered out and saw Greiser and Victoria coming down the hall.

Harry made his decision in an instant. He locked the door, made his way to the small coat closet in the sitting room. He stepped inside and closed the door behind him. Seconds later he heard the key in the door and the sound of voices as Greiser and Victoria entered the room. Through the louvered door Harry could see the lower half of their bodies.

Greiser immediately disappeared into the bedroom, and Harry assumed that he was checking that the suitcases were still there. In seconds he returned.

"I told you we'd be back soon," Victoria said.

"Yes," said Greiser. "And now perhaps we could—"

"I'd love some wine."

"Wine?" Greiser asked, his voice taking on a frantic note of frustration.

"It would help me to relax."

In spite of his predicament Harry grinned. Victoria was taking this guy for quite a ride. It was obvious that the German was at the end of his tether. She was handling the situation perfectly, he thought, and wondered how she would handle the knowledge that he was still in the room. He had to let her know. She was the only one who could get him out.

He heard the tinkling of glasses and imagined that Greiser

was pouring wine. Through the louvers he could see that the German's back was to the closet. He opened the door just enough to stick his head out, saw Victoria's eyes bulge, then closed the door again.

There was a long pause.

"What is it, my dear," he heard Greiser say. "You look white as a sheet."

Momentarily Victoria had lost her composure. She struggled to speak, to say something—anything—but the sight of Fox had completely unnerved her. Finally she managed, "I'm all right. Perhaps it's the wine."

"You look better already," Greiser said, the hope evident in his voice. He was deathly afraid that another chance was about to pass him by.

Victoria closed her eyes and gritted her teeth. She had hoped to avoid the next step. Now she could see no other way. She looked up at the anxious Greiser with a seductive smile. "Perhaps we should adjourn to the bedroom. I'm sure I'll be fine once I get out of these clothes."

"Oh, yes," Greiser said. He almost added, Thank you.

Harry heard them go to the bedroom, heard Victoria say in a loud voice, "Let's close this door," heard the thump of the door. Seconds later he was at the outer door, peering out into the hallway. All was quiet and he swiftly exited, closing the door quietly behind him. He paused and took a deep breath and then headed across the hall for the other cabin. Before he got there he heard a noise at the end of the passageway and turned to see Blaskowitz staring at him. Harry froze for a moment then turned quickly and walked past his cabin. He kept going. Behind him he heard Blaskowitz pounding on the door of Greiser's room. Harry had a sinking feeling that things were coming apart and that Vicky was in trouble. He didn't think she would be able to explain his presence in the hallway.

Greiser was naked, already in bed, while this woman seemed to be taking forever to undress. Perhaps, he thought, she imagined that this slow striptease would drive him to new heights of passion. Instead, her procrastination had only served to increase his frustration. She was still in her underwear, slowly removing her stockings, and he was about to reproach her for this unnecessary delay when he heard the pounding on the door.

Victoria had dragged out the undressing as long as she could. She had not heard Harry leave, but was sure she had given him enough time to do so. Her task now was to somehow extricate herself from what had become a very ticklish situation. Experience had taught her that once a man like Greiser gets to the undressing stage he is usually beyond listening to lame excuses. At this point the "I have a terrible headache," routine was just not going to work. She was just about to feign a sudden onslaught of nausea when, to her delight, she heard what she assumed was Harry pounding at the door.

Victoria and Greiser both had the same thought at the same time. "My husband," she said with undisguised relief, while he reacted to the same information with consternation.

Then they heard the voice. "Blaskowitz," Greiser said, more puzzled than angry. "What the hell does he want?"

Victoria did not reply. She had already begun putting her clothes back on.

"Wait here," Greiser said, pulling on his trousers. He went to the door and let Blaskowitz in. Before he could say anything, Blaskowitz interrupted. "I saw him in the hallway . . . outside."

"Who?"

"Hollander."

At first Greiser did not understand. "What are you talking about. Hollander is in his cabin. I've just come from there."

As he said it, the realization hit both of them at the same time. "The money," they said in unison and dashed to the bedroom.

Greiser pushed Vicky down onto the bed. "See that she does not leave," he said. Blaskowitz clamped a meaty paw around Vicky's arm and pulled her roughly to her feet. Greiser pulled out the suitcases and breathed a sigh of relief when he felt the weight. "Still full," he said. "Everything seems in order."

"Open them," Blaskowitz said.

Greiser was unaccustomed to taking orders from Blaskowitz, but he did not delay. He opened the cases and slumped forward in relief when he saw the money. Vicky held her breath until he said, "It's all here. Everything is in order." He closed the suitcases and pushed them back under the bed. He looked at Victoria, puzzlement and anger mixed on his face.

"What the hell is going on?" Vicky said. "I don't understand what is wrong."

Blaskowitz spun her around, crushing her arm in his grip. "Your husband was prowling around in the hall outside this room."

"Are you sure it was him?" Greiser asked.

"Positive. I was no more than twenty meters behind him. He saw me and kept walking."

Greiser turned his stare to Vicky. Her tactics were suddenly clear to him. He had almost been duped by this woman. His anger overwhelmed him. "You dragged me off to your cabin, didn't you?" he said savagely, the words exploding in a shower of spittle. "You tried to give him time to get the money. He wasn't even there when you played your little charade."

"No. He must have followed us here," she offered lamely.

Greiser's face was beet red, his anger barely contained. "You said he was fast asleep. You said you had given him a sleeping pill."

"Maybe it didn't work . . . maybe he woke up and wondered where I was," Vicky said, trying to maintain a tone of wounded innocence.

"He knew where you were, bitch," Blaskowitz said. "That's why he was here. You and he were after the money."

The enormity of what might have happened hit Greiser in the pit of his stomach. He gasped for breath, and his knees almost buckled. His face was a tortured mask. Although his career had been saved by inches, he realized that he would spend his life under obligation to Blaskowitz. If that moron ever told anyone what had almost happened, he was finished. "I should kill you for this," he said and smashed his palm across Vicky's face.

"I don't know what you're talking about," she protested. An ugly red welt spread across her cheek.

Blaskowitz clamped a hand across her mouth. "Shut up," he said. She was helpless in his grasp.

There was silence for a moment, and Greiser allowed his anger to subside. He took several deep breaths and seemed well on the way to regaining his composure. In a moment he even managed a small smile, and Vicky began to hope that she might escape unscathed. Greiser soon shattered that illusion. "Take off your clothes," he said quietly.

Vicky tried to shake her head, but Blaskowitz would not permit it. Her eyes were wide with fear. This was going to be bad.

"If I give him the word, Blaskowitz will snap your neck like a chicken's," he said.

As if to demonstrate his ability, Blaskowitz began to twist her neck. Vicky gave a muffled protest and started to unbutton her blouse.

She did not move quickly enough to suit Blaskowitz. Right hand still clamped across her mouth he ripped open her blouse with his left. "I'm going to enjoy this," he whispered in her ear.

"We are both going to enjoy it," Greiser added.

"I guess that makes three of us," Harry said from the doorway to the bedroom.

Greiser, his mouth agape, was stunned into inactivity, but Blaskowitz, his arms still round Victoria, whirled to face the intruder. When he saw Harry standing there, left shoulder on the door jamb, right hand on hip, as if he might have been a late arrival at a cocktail party, Blaskowitz bellowed in rage and sent Victoria spinning across the room. He reached for the pistol in the shoulder holster inside his jacket.

Victoria barely had time to shout a warning before Blaskowitz's hand emerged from beneath the coat with the pistol. He flicked off the safety with his thumb as he raised the weapon to aim at the man in the doorway. Before

Blaskowitz could bring the pistol to firing position, Harry took one quick step forward and lashed out with the blackjack that had been concealed in his right hand. The small club struck Blaskowitz on the wrist just above his thumb. The German felt a sharp, electric pain run up his arm, and the hand went instantly numb. He looked at the hand in surprise as the pistol began to slip from his fingers, then looked up just as Harry unleashed a fist into his midsection. The air exploded from Blaskowitz's lungs in a tortured gasp, and he doubled over. He barely felt the blow from the blackjack that hit him across the base of his skull and dropped him to the floor. Blaskowitz moaned once and then lay quietly, facedown, on the carpet.

"Fun's half over," Harry said to Greiser.

Greiser dived across the bed for the nightstand. He wrenched the drawer open and reached inside for the pistol, but Harry was too quick for him. He kicked the drawer closed, momentarily pinning Greiser's hand inside, then struck him across the wrist with the blackjack. Greiser yelped in pain and fell back across the bed.

Harry removed the pistol from the drawer and put it in his pocket as Greiser, arm hanging limply at his side, struggled to his feet.

"You'll have to kill me to take the money," Greiser said.

Harry looked from him to Victoria and back. "I came here for my wife, you son of a bitch," he said scornfully. "Why would I want your money? I buy and sell cheap bastards like you every day."

Greiser's expression went from fear to puzzlement. He looked at Vicky, his perplexity growing. Was it possible that he had misjudged the situation?

"I tried to tell you," Victoria said. She turned to Harry. "I was on my way out to get some fresh air, darling, when this gentleman offered me a drink. I . . ."

Harry grabbed her roughly by the arm. "Don't take me for a fool, you bitch," he said. "I've been watching you and this guy trying to make a fool of me. I was never as drunk as you thought." He pushed her against the door. "I'll deal with you later." He waved the blackjack in Greiser's face. "Stay away from my wife. Next time I won't be so lenient." Harry dragged Victoria to the door and pushed her out into the hallway. He draped his jacket over her shoulders, and they went quickly down the passageway and up the stairs to the next deck.

"D'you think he bought it?" Victoria asked in a trembling whisper.

"As far as he knows, he still has the money," Harry said. "He figures if I were after the money, I would have taken it then and there. I don't think he wants to think about anything else."

They were back at their stateroom, and Vicky sat down on the couch. She was still trembling. "I was scared, Harry. I didn't think you were coming."

"I had to come back here first." He held up the blackjack. I thought I might need reinforcements." He sat next to her.

"You're pretty handy with that thing," she said, resting her head on his shoulder.

His arm went around her, and she snuggled closer. "You don't run a bar in Kansas City without learning how to use the bouncer's best friend," he said.

They sat quietly for a while until Victoria's breathing had returned to normal. Then she looked up at him with a smile. "I want to see the money," she said.

"I don't have it," he said.

She pulled away, her eyes wide in alarm. "You mean it's still there? You never got it out?" All she could think was that this had been for naught.

He laughed. "I got it out all right. But it's in the suitcases in the other cabin." He pulled her back to him. "I'll return Miguel's key later and have him deliver the luggage here. That way no one ever sees me dragging suitcases up and down the stairs."

Victoria kissed him on the lips. "You're something, Harry," she said. "You're really something." She kissed him again and rested her head on his chest. He put both arms around her. She felt safe with him, safer than she had felt in a long time.

CHAPTER 26

Paramaribo, Dutch Guiana; November 23

On the morning of November 23 the *Bahia Grande* slid silently into her berth in Paramaribo, near the mouth of the Suriname River. November is the start of the second rainy season in Guiana, and with the morning temperatures already into the seventies and destined to climb higher, the day promised to be hot and sticky. The early morning dockside noises were many, men calling, machines humming as cargo was hoisted aloft, the clang of metal on metal.

Harry Fox awakened slowly, the noises of men at work drifting slowly into his consciousness and prodding him to wakefulness. Victoria was pressed against him, as if for protection, still deep in sleep. Gently he disentangled himself from her soft embrace and slipped quietly out of bed. For a moment he looked back at her. In sleep she seemed incredibly beautiful and somehow younger. Sleep had stolen the tension from her face and let him see the country girl who had gone to Hollywood to follow some ephemeral dream. Fox was filled with a momentary sadness that was just as quickly replaced by resignation. No one gets out unscathed, he thought. All we can do is huddle together until the light chases our fears away.

He dressed quietly and went out on deck. The noises were louder now. Men scurried about the wharves while cranes lifted cargo out of the holds of the several ships that were tied alongside the *Bahia Grande*. Behind him was the blue-green water of the river and the lush tropical green mountains of the opposite bank. Harry leaned on the ship's rail and looked down on the wharf and the corrugated roofs of the low storage sheds that lined the entire dock area. In the distance, shrouded in the morning mist, he could see the ring of mountains on the south side of the city.

This, Harry thought, was as good a place as any to get off. There was no reason to continue to Buenos Aires. His job was done. Even though it was unlikely that the Germans would discover what had happened to their money, he did not want to be around if they did. The FBI would be waiting for him in Buenos Aires, and he smiled thinking of the expression on Trump's face when his agents reported that Harry Fox was not on board ship when they arrived to collect the money. Three and a half million dollars would go a long way in South America—damn, three and a half million would go a long way anywhere, he thought. He knew people who could find him a new identity, and there were plenty of places in South America where a man could live like a king with this kind of money. He had done his part—the important part. The Germans would be denied the use of the money, and their agents would be exposed as soon as Chiari's money started to change color. The Englishman, Smythe, would be satisfied. He had gotten what he wanted. He might even be glad that Fox had duped Trump and the FBI. He hadn't seemed too pleased that the FBI had claimed the entire amount for itself. Only Hoover and the FBI would be deceived, and what the hell, that would be half the fun.

The only thing that stopped him was the fact that he had not found the man who had killed Ernesto Garcia. For all he knew the man was still in Panama. He could still go back and find him without handing over the money to the FBI.

The idea had barely begun to crystallize when he saw the black limousine turn onto the wharf and pull to a halt in front of the *Bahia Grande.* He knew right away who it would be, but he waited until the two men climbed out of the backseat and looked up at the ship before he stepped back from the rail and headed toward his cabin. It was nice, in a way, to know that the FBI was not as stupid as he had imagined.

By the time the knock came on the stateroom door, Victoria had dressed and she and Harry were expecting their visitors. Harry opened the door. "Yes?" he said.

The two men were dressed almost identically—dark gray summer-weight suits and navy blue ties—and Harry wondered if the FBI only hired one person and had him duplicated in one of their Washington labs. One was a little older than the other. Both carried leather briefcases. "Harry Fox?" asked the man closest to the door. Harry nodded and the man showed his identification and walked in without waiting for an invitation. "I'm agent Withers," he said, "and this is agent Stone." Neither man made any attempt at any kind of greeting. It was obvious that they did not care to deal with the likes of Harry Fox. Stone, however, found it difficult to take his eyes off Victoria. "I believe you know why we are here," said Withers.

"Excellent timing. We just got the money last night. Things worked out pretty well, if I do—"

"Where is the money?" Withers interrupted. "I'd like to verify it immediately."

"In the bedroom . . . in the two suitcases under the bed."

"Get it," Withers said to Stone, but the younger man was watching Victoria and did not hear. "Get the money, Stone," Withers said, his voice betraying his anger.

"It's under the bed," Harry added helpfully.

When Stone left the room, Harry said, "How did you know I'd have the money?"

"We didn't, but Trump figured that it's three days to Rio and four more to Buenos Aires. If you had any ideas about leaving with the money, now would have been the most opportune time."

"And what if I had gotten the money earlier and decided to jump ship in Caracas?"

"We've had people waiting at each of this ship's scheduled stops. Just to make sure that no one disappeared into the night."

Stone returned with the suitcases and placed them flat on the cocktail table. Harry gave Withers a key, and the FBI man opened the two locks that secured the bags. He flipped up the latches, opened the top of the first case, and whistled when he saw the money. He looked around, his smile suddenly genuine as if the sight of so much money had made him forget his role as J. Edgar Hoover's man in Dutch Guiana. "Sure looks pretty, don't it?" he said in a soft Southern drawl. Stone, wide-eyed, was silent.

Withers left the case open and opened the second. Again he whistled softly. He paused for a second, and Harry could see him gather himself into his FBI role again. "I'll have to verify that this is the money . . . and that it's all here," he said.

"I'm sure that Trump told you some of the money was distributed in Panama," Harry said.

"But no one knows how much."

"There was a half million missing," Harry said. "So I guess that's how much was given out earlier."

"Then there should be three and a half million here."

"Right again."

"And you should have a half million left over in counterfeit currency."

Harry's shoulders slumped momentarily and Withers' face registered his triumph. He'd been sure that Harry would try something. A half million in excellent counterfeit would be a nice payoff for a job like this. "I want the counterfeit also," Withers said.

Harry looked at Vicky. "It's in one of her bags. Better get it for them, Vicky."

Victoria went to the bedroom and returned with a leather bag. She opened it and reluctantly dumped the contents onto one of the stuffed chairs that flanked the cocktail table. She stepped back.

Withers bent over and picked up one of the packets of counterfeit bills. "Sweet Jesus," he said. "Will you look at this stuff, Stone?" He fondled the package, inspecting the contents carefully. "This stuff looks like the genuine article."

Stone concurred. "Best-looking counterfeit I've ever seen."

Harry laughed. "In about two weeks it'll change color. It won't be hard to pick out then."

Withers turned to Stone. "Count it . . . carefully. There should be three and a half million in the suitcases and a half million here on the table. Don't mix them up," he added. "Keep the counterfeit separate."

Stone nodded and knelt next to the money and began the task of counting.

"I've been authorized to conduct a search of your other belongings," Withers said. "Just in case there is more money than you claim."

"Go ahead," Harry said. "You've got everything."

"I'll start in the bedroom," Withers said.

As he started to leave Harry said, "What about the money I've been promised?"

"I don't know anything about that."

Harry grabbed Withers by the arm. "Trump promised me a hundred thousand for this job. I think I've earned it."

Withers looked at Harry's hand and waited until Fox released him before he spoke. "Then maybe you'd better take that up with Agent Trump when you get back to Panama City." He went off to begin his search.

When the search and the count were finished and the FBI men had verified that the money was accounted for and that there was no other money in the cabin, Withers wrapped the counterfeit in a towel and placed it in the suitcase with the other money. He closed the suitcases and gave Harry his locks back. He removed two larger locks from his briefcase and grinned. "These locks will not be opened until this money is safely back in Panama." He looked at his watch and turned to Stone. "Let's get going. The army is standing by with a plane to get me and the money back to Panama."

Stone picked up the suitcases.

"What about us?" Harry asked.

"What about you?" replied Withers.

"You got room in that plane for us? We'd like to get back to Panama, too."

"I have no orders that say that I am to provide transportation."

"Look," Harry said. "I just gave you and the FBI three and a half million bucks. That ought to be good enough to pay for a plane ride to Panama."

Although the army DC-3 had plenty of room, Withers could think of no reason why he should offer Harry a ride to Panama. Then he looked at Victoria and thought that it might not be bad to have a beautiful woman along for the ride. "Plane leaves in three hours," he said. "You may each bring one suitcase."

"What about the rest?" Vicky said.

"Have the ship crate it and deliver it to Panama on the return voyage." Withers turned to go. "If I don't see you at the airport in two hours and forty-five minutes . . . it's been nice doing business with you."

When the door closed, Harry said, "Pack two bags and let's get going. I want to get back as soon as possible." He started for the door. "I'll arrange to have the rest of our stuff crated and brought back on the return voyage," he said and was gone.

CHAPTER 27

*J. Edgar Hoover immediately distrusted Dusko Popov. The
FBI director didn't trust easily, and the Yugoslavian was
everything that Hoover detested in a man. Popov was smooth,
suave, charming, and handsome. He carried himself with a
bold self-assurance that instantly called attention to him as
someone to be wary of.*

*Of course, the lukewarm benediction he received from the
British might have had something to do with Hoover's
attitude. After talking with Smythe about Popov, and having
received absolutely no assurance that Popov was a trusted
British agent, Hoover decided to delay the meeting and have
the Yugoslavian watched. Perhaps if Popov was an untrust-
worthy double agent, Hoover reasoned, he might associate
with other fascist sympathizers. This would prove that he and
his information were not to be regarded seriously. The
director ordered that listening devices be planted in Popov's
hotel room and assigned several men to follow him.
As always, Hoover's men did this kind of work exceedingly
well.*

What was found was not perhaps what had been expected, but something that in Hoover's eyes made Popov's credibility equally suspect. The Yugoslavian, it was discovered, could not spend a single evening without the company of a woman. The FBI listening devices in Popov's hotel room recorded the incredible events that transpired there, and Hoover's men dutifully reported this information to their chief. Hoover, perhaps the most prudish man in America, was shocked.

When the director finally summoned Popov to his office, it was not to question him about the possible significance of the remarkable list of questions about Pearl Harbor that had been provided by the Germans, it was to denounce him as a sexual libertine. The meeting lasted less than a minute before Hoover, as if afraid that he might be contaminated by Popov's associations with licentious women, banished him from his office.

Hoover informed the British that the Yugoslavian's character was suspect and therefore his information must be considered likewise. The information, according to the FBI director, was "too precise to be believed. If anything, it sounds like a trap." Hoover refused to allow Popov to travel to Hawaii or to have anything further to do with him.

In any event, it was already too late for Popov's mission to have any effect on coming events. He had been delayed by the British, then further delayed by Hoover. The Japanese plans were already in motion, and they had decided they could not wait any longer.

It is not recorded that the British did anything to dissuade Hoover from his opinion that Popov was an unreliable double agent. Satisfied that they had done their duty, and convinced that the real menace was already on the loose, the British were content to let the matter drop. As far as they were concerned, with Hitler less than thirty miles from British soil, the Japanese seemed too far away to be of consequence.

Popov, amazed that such vital information could be so casually disregarded, returned to Britain, where he continued to serve the Twenty Committee throughout the war.

Bogotá, Colombia; November 24

Except for a refueling stop in Bogotá, Colombia, the long flight from Paramaribo to Panama was uneventful. Withers spent most of the time buried in paperwork with only an occasional glance at Harry and Victoria, who spent their time talking quietly and watching the dark South American jungle slip slowly beneath them. By the time they reached Bogotá, night was falling, and Withers informed them that the pilot did not want to cross the Andes in the dark.

"We'll spend the night here," Withers said, "and leave at first light."

While the craft was refueled, Harry left the plane and sent a telegram to Roberto Garcia in Panama. "I want someone to meet us as soon as we arrive," he explained to Victoria.

They spent the night inside the aircraft, Harry and Victoria on cots and Withers sitting up in a seat with the money on the seat beside him. In the morning the pilot brought coffee and sandwiches aboard, and in the early morning camaraderie Withers, for the first time, dropped his FBI persona and became friendlier. He wanted to know how they had managed to trick the Germans out of the money. Vicky told him, giving Harry most of the credit, but Withers was no fool and realized the risk she had taken.

Withers looked at Harry. "It's fortunate that you got back to the Germans' cabin when you did," he said. "Otherwise, Miss Gansell would have been in a great deal of trouble."

Harry knew that there was a subtle reprimand in Withers' statement.

"Harry had everything under control," Vicky said. "I knew he'd get back in time."

"I'm sure," Withers said.

Harry Fox looked away. He had made Vicky take a terrible risk without ever asking her or explaining the dangers to her. At first he had only been concerned with revenge against the men who had killed his friend. If either of the men on board ship had been the murderer, he might have killed them both. Instead, he had satisfied himself by taking the money. And in all of that he had never once stopped to consider that he had asked Victoria to risk her life, never once stopped to consider his desolation if anything had happened to her. And she, fully cognizant of the danger, had never once protested or accused him of indifference to her interests.

Harry watched while she finished telling Withers the rest of the story. She laughed and gestured as if it might have been a game. He realized at that moment that no one had ever loved him as purely as she had. With that came the realization that he loved her more than he had ever loved anyone. The thought that he had put her life at risk made him shiver.

"You okay?" Vicky asked.

He put his hand over hers. "Just a sudden chill," he said. "I'm fine now."

She gave his hand a squeeze and kissed him quickly.

They were underway as soon as they finished breakfast, and as soon as they were airborne, Withers retreated once more behind his G-man mask. Their pilot coaxed the aircraft over the three ranges of the Cordillera Mountains while Withers stared silently from the cabin window. Vicky, bewildered by Withers's changed attitude, looked to Harry. Harry smiled and touched her hand. "Don't let it bother you," he said softly. "He just forgot himself for a little while. Hoover's boy is back at work."

The last leg of the trip was over the Pacific, and as they approached Panama City, the sea-level entrance to the canal, glittering in the late-morning sunlight, was a silver slash across the dark green landscape. The Bay of Panama was dotted with the usual small fleet of ships awaiting passage through the canal. The Naos Island Breakwater was directly below them and straight ahead were the Miraflores Locks. Just beyond the small Miraflores Lake was the single lock at Pedro Miguel, and then the passage narrowed as the canal sliced through Culebra. The cut itself was hidden by the menacing hills that surrounded it as if the channel had been swallowed by the jungle. Glistening on the horizon and spreading as far as the eye could see was Gatun Lake. At the far end of the lake, dark specks against the horizon, were the Gatun Locks and the dam, and beyond that, half hidden in the haze, were the twin cities of Cristobal and Colón.

This, thought Harry, is my whole world. Everything I am, and everything I've done for the past seven years, is directly below me and visible in one panoramic view. Suddenly his world seemed smaller than it ever had before. Maybe, he thought, it's time to get out of here. Maybe it's time to go home.

When the DC-3 landed at the Army Air Corps airfield at Albrook Field in the Canal Zone, Roberto Garcia was waiting with a car, and Harry Fox and Victoria left as quickly as possible. Now that the money had been recovered, Harry Fox did not trust the FBI to honor the temporary truce that had been declared between them.

Harry rode up front with Roberto while Victoria had the back to herself. As soon as the Canal Zone was safely behind them, Harry said, "The man I was looking for was not on the ship."

Roberto nodded. "I know."

"How did you know?" Vicky asked.

Roberto watched her in the rearview mirror. "The word is that someone is in Panama with a lot of American money."

"Five hundred thousand dollars," Harry said.

Garcia whistled at that bit of news. "I figure that whoever killed my father is the one with the money."

"That's what I figure, too," Harry said. "Have you been able to track any of the money back to him?"

"Not yet," Garcia said, "but some of the money has been passed through Viega or his men."

"Narciso Viega?"

"Yes."

"That fat pig," Harry said. "I should have figured that sooner or later he'd get his filthy fingers into this." It made sense, Harry thought. If the Germans were going to do something in Latin America, the most logical place for them to begin was Panama, where the American presence was greatest. The Panama Canal was, perhaps, the most strategically vital—and tactically vulnerable—military installation in the world. And if Panama was indeed the location of choice, then it made sense that they would align themselves with some of the people of the deposed President Arias. And Viega represented the worst of that group.

When in power, President Arias—as might have been expected—represented an amalgamation of disparate political views in Panama. Arias had risen to power on a wave of anti-Americanism that was as natural to Panama as tropical weather. Americans, who liked to think of themselves as the kindly big brother to the rest of the continent, were universally despised in Latin America. As far as Harry was concerned, it was easy to see why this was so. Americans were patronizing and condescending to the citizens of every country in Latin America. Behind the kindly smile and the helpful hand there was always the threat that if one did not do things exactly as the Americans wanted, the U.S. Marines would land and tell you what to do. Nowhere in Latin America was this more true than in Panama.

In Panama the United States had appropriated a ten-mile-wide strip of land that effectively cut the country in half. This Panama Canal Zone, a source of tremendous irritation to the Panamanians, was considered by the "Zonians" to be American territory, and the American flag was flown everywhere. When the Panama Canal was first proposed, it was thought—even by those who opposed the American presence—that this engineering marvel would bring prosperity to Panama and to the average Panamanian. What happened, of course, was that the Panama Canal had brought prosperity, not to Panama, but to the Panama Canal Zone and to those who resided within its limits. The Canal Zone government was an independent agency of the United States and was operated under the supervision of the U.S. secretary of the Army. The governor of the Canal Zone was an American army officer, and the zone was operated as if it were an enormous army facility—commissaries, housing, recreational and medical facilities. Everything that was required for the comfort of those within the zone was imported. The zone, of course, was populated almost exclusively by Americans, whose standard of living was far above anything that Panamanians could ever hope to achieve. Those Americans who resided within the zone were the beneficiaries of tremendous privileges—low-cost food and housing and recreational activities. Those on the outside could only press their faces against the imaginary barrier between them and seethe with a bitter and ever-growing resentment. To make matters worse, the Americans tended to look down on the Panamanians. All of the important jobs inside the zone went to Americans; all of the menial jobs went to Panamanians. The Americans had turned Panama into a nation of servants and gardeners and laborers.

As if this were not enough, the United States had assumed unto itself an absolute authority over, not just the Panama Canal Zone, but over all of Panama. The original Panama Canal Treaty between the American Secretary of State John Hay and the self-styled representative of Panama, Philippe Bunau-Varilla, had given the United States the right to acquire any property outside the Canal Zone that the Americans deemed necessary for the operation and protection of the canal. In the case of public lands the United States merely notified the Panamanian government and took over the land. In the case of private property the United States had been given not only the right of eminent domain but the right to acquire such properties at pre-1903 prices, when Panamanian property was almost worthless. Despite vehement protests by the Panamanians, the Americans had continued this unpopular policy for almost twenty years.

Part of American policy was that anything—civil disturbance, national elections, natural disasters, or anything else—that threatened the operation of the canal was America's business. The will of the people of Panama was secondary to America's desire to protect its interests in the canal. American influence and, from time to time, American troops were used to keep Panama in line. An American garrison of twenty-eight thousand troops stationed at six different army posts inside the Canal Zone helped ensure that the Panamanians did not stray too far from what Washington decreed was the proper course. This proper course was always firmly in line with the best interests of the United States. In Panama, as might have been expected, resentment against the American presence was rampant.

Although many of these punitive agreements had been altered in a new treaty in 1936, most of the resentment remained. Arnulfo Arias had taken this resentment and turned it into a political movement. The basis for his popularity with the average Panamanian was his outspoken anti-Americanism. His countrymen, who had never accepted the Hay–Bunau-Varilla Treaty nor the partition of their country, were more than willing to support someone who promised to get rid of the hated yanquis.

But there was a darker side to this nationalistic fervor of the Arias movement. If Arias had done little more than declare his opposition to the policies of the United States, the benevolent giant to the north might have looked the other way and pretended that he was no more than a minor irritant. Arias, however, had declared his affinity with the policies of Adolf Hitler and fascism. There were whispers among some Panamanians that Arias had assumed dictatorial powers and that he was determined to stamp out any and all opposition to his rule. His party even had its racial policy, which was directed against the black West Indians who had been brought to Panama during the construction period of the canal. Despite the promise of the Americans to expatriate these workers when the canal was completed, most of the West Indians had stayed on and made a life for themselves in Panama. Now, a quarter of a century after the opening of the Panama Canal, the West Indians were a sizable minority of the population. There were many in Panama who resented their presence, and Arias had been able to utilize this racism as another of his rallying cries. This was another of the ills for which he blamed the United States. Under a new constitution Arias had been able to strip many of the West Indians of Panamanian citizenship.

He had made threats about "resettlement" of what he called the "nonindigenous population." To many who had heard Adolf Hitler talk about the resettlement of the Jews, these threats seemed uncomfortably familiar.

Harry knew many decent Panamanians who supported Arias, although they had reservations about some of his policies, because they agreed with his attempts to rid Panama of the overwhelming American presence. These were the Panamanians who wanted to establish a Panama that was independent of American influence and who saw Arias as a means to that end. But there were others who were less interested in national autonomy and more interested in the power they could derive from Arias's fascist policies. Narciso Viega was at the top of that list.

Viega, a career soldier, had been rumored to be one of the most powerful figures in the criminal underworld of Panama when Arias elevated him to the position of chief of the Panamanian National Guard. Even before his elevation to a prominent position in the Arias government, Viega had tried several times to bully Harry into offering him a partnership in the Panama Club. Viega, it was said, had been heavily involved in gambling, prostitution, and trafficking in illegal drugs. In a nation where corruption was considered a way of life, Viega had quickly made corruption the cornerstone of the Arias administration. In addition, he and his henchmen in the National Guard had been well on their way to establishing a police state in Panama, modeled after that of Nazi Germany, when the American-inspired coup had toppled the Arias government. The new government, with the backing of the American military presence, had quickly removed Viega from his powerful position. Although out of power, Viega still commanded the loyalty of many in Panama, and as long as Arias remained in exile in Cuba, Viega was the titular head of the opposition party.

If Viega is involved in this, Harry thought, it will not be easy to stop him.

"What happened to the rest of your luggage?" Roberto asked Harry, interrupting his train of thought.

"It's been crated and will be delivered to Colón when the ship makes the return voyage in about two weeks."

"You want me to arrange to have it delivered to the Panama Club when it arrives?"

"Yes."

Garcia smiled. "I will speak to my cousin who works with the Customs Department."

Harry smiled. The Garcias had cousins everywhere. "So," he said, "have you heard anything at all about the man we are looking for?"

"Not yet. But I will," Roberto said. "I've got a few contacts inside Viega's organization. Sooner or later someone will slip up."

Harry nodded. Roberto had closer ties to some of Viega's people than Harry would have preferred. "Keep on it," he said. "Whatever is going to happen will happen soon."

"We've got to get him, Harry," Roberto said softly. "I can't let him get away."

Harry saw the look of determination on his friend's face. He touched Roberto on the arm. "We'll get him," he said. "That's a promise." He looked away, watching the slums of Panama City roll past his window. He wondered how he could make good on such a promise.

CHAPTER 28

Washington, D.C., Navy Dept.; November 25

The Navy Department Building at Eighteenth Street and Constitution Avenue, a gray granite building in what might be called the pseudo-classical style, had been intended to serve as temporary quarters for the U.S. Navy during the last war. Although totally inadequate to the requirements at hand, it, along with its duplicate, called the Munitions Building, which occupied the space next to it and now housed the offices of the Department of the Army, was still in full-time use in the fall of 1941.

On the second floor of the Navy Building—called the second deck—were the various departments of the Office of Naval Communications (OP-20) that were responsible for cryptology—the sending and receiving of coded messages within the U.S. Navy—and cryptanalysis—the interception and deciphering of coded messages sent by an assortment of foreign powers.

Approximately a year earlier American cryptanalysts had managed an incredible achievement by reconstructing the cipher machine used by Imperial Japan to send its most critical messages. From that point on, the Americans were privy to a veritable avalanche of secret information about Japanese intentions. The decoded messages were known— perhaps because of the sorcery involved in their procurement —as Magic.

The Japanese machine was known as the Type 97 and was an incredibly complex piece of electronic machinery—more complex even than the Enigma deciphering machine that was used by the Germans and which had been compromised by the British. It was inconceivable to the Japanese that such a machine could be duplicated and its messages intercepted, and despite evidence to the contrary they continued to use the Type 97 to relay important messages to their military and diplomatic outposts around the world.

At that particular time the greatest effort of the Office of Naval Communications was expended in intercepting and translating the Japanese diplomatic codes, which were called Purple. OP-20-GZ, which was that part of the department that concentrated on the translations of intercepted messages, was undermanned and overwhelmed by the volume of the intercepts. Most of the time was spent in reading the Japanese diplomatic messages that passed between Ambassador Nomura and his superiors in Tokyo. Ambassador Nomura and special envoy Kurusu were at that time involved in intricate negotiations with Secretary of State Cordell Hull. It was felt by all who participated in these negotiations that failure to arrive at some compromise could only mean war between Japan and the United States.

By late November, 1941, the Office of Naval Intelligence had been made aware that large elements of the Japanese Imperial Navy, particularly Carrier Division 1 and Carrier Division 2, were no longer in home waters. It was obvious that Japan was on the verge of initiating hostilities. The question was, however, where would these hostilities begin? The best guesses at the time were that the Japanese would strike to the south, perhaps Singapore or Burma or the Dutch East Indies. The oil-rich Dutch colonies were seen as a natural target for the Japanese, who were being starved of the oil they required to survive as a major power. Already there

*had been reported sightings of large naval forces south of
Formosa and it was thought that Japanese forces were
moving into the region in preparation for the initiation of
hostilities. No one ever seriously considered the possibility,
nor did the deciphered messages ever suggest, that the
Japanese would be bold enough—or foolish enough—to
attack the American Pacific Fleet at Pearl Harbor.*

*Earlier in the year a report from American Ambassador
Grew in Tokyo had been sent to the State Department and
forwarded to Naval Intelligence. Ambassador Grew's report
stated that his third secretary, Max Bishop, had been informed by the Peruvian envoy in Tokyo, Dr. Ricardo Rivera
Schreiber, that the Japanese were planning a surprise attack
on Pearl Harbor if the current negotiations between the U.S.
and Japan did not go well. The report was not regarded
seriously in Washington and was forwarded to Admiral
Kimmel in Hawaii with an evaluation by Naval Intelligence
that refuted the allegations of Japanese preparations.*

One of the few who did take the report from Ambassador
Grew seriously was Lieutenant Commander Will
Thorensen, a career navy officer and head of OP-20-GX,
that part of Naval Communications responsible for the
handling of interception and direction finding and traffic
analysis. Thorensen's job was, in short, to determine
through radio intercepts the location and movement of
Japanese naval vessels in the Pacific. By inference he was
also to determine the intention of such Japanese naval
forces by the concentration of vessels and by the direction of
movement. Thorensen was well aware, as was everyone else
at Naval Communications, that the Japanese were very
definitely on the move.

Thorensen picked up the decoded messages from the
basket on his desk. The first to catch his attention was from
the office of Twelfth Naval District Intelligence in San
Francisco, whose job it was to collect, collate, and interpret
reports from commercial shipping in the Pacific and from
the wire services that operated in that area. Over the last

several days the San Francisco office had been passing along reports of some small but unexplained radio traffic in the northern Pacific. Cross bearings indicated that the transmissions were coming from the Kurils, an island group north of the main Japanese islands. From the report it was obvious that the operators in San Francisco were concerned about these low-level radio transmissions from an unidentified source. The tone of the message made it clear that those in San Francisco were worried that the radio transmissions might be from the missing Japanese carrier forces.

By this time the Pearl Harbor strike force, known as Kido Butai, had already assembled at Hitokappu Bay on Etorufu Island in the Kurils, one thousand miles north of Tokyo. The Japanese were awaiting the results of the negotiations in Washington, but, as Ambassador Grew had intimated earlier, they were prepared to strike if those negotiations were not resolved to their satisfaction.

Although aware of Japanese naval movement, the ONC staff seemed preoccupied with the ongoing interception and translation of the Japanese diplomatic messages as if everything that was of importance was contained in these dispatches between Tokyo and its emissaries in Washington. Thorensen, although not alone in his concern about the movement of Japanese naval units, felt that his department had been relegated to the back burner.

Thorensen, a small, intense man with dark hair and black expressive eyes, was a student of Japanese language, culture, and history. He was well aware of the Japanese penchant for initiating hostilities with a massive blow that was intended to neutralize any opponent. He had studied the Japanese surprise attack of 1904 on the Russian Fleet at Port Arthur, an attack from which the Russian Far Eastern Fleet could not recover. The Russian Baltic Fleet was rushed to the aid of their comrades, but this fleet, too, was surprised by a Japanese attack and destroyed. These twin defeats rendered the Russians unable to continue the war, and only the mediation of the United States had saved the Russians from further disaster. Thorensen knew that the surprise attack had followed six months of intense negotiations between the two parties, and he was certain that if the Japanese were to initiate hostilities, they would attempt the same sort of assault against the United States. There was only one place where an attack would have the same devastating effect. Thorensen felt certain that the Japanese would strike against the American naval forces at Pearl Harbor.

Thorensen picked up the message from San Francisco and walked across the hall of the Navy Building to the office of Commander Walter Blair, who was the aide to Admiral Noyes, the chief of Naval Communications. Noyes reported directly to Admiral Hart, the chief of Naval Operations. Thorensen had been badgering Blair of late about the northern Pacific reports, and Blair gave a brief sigh when he spotted Thorensen at his door.

"Come on in, Will," Blair said pleasantly, glancing at his watch. "What'cha got?"

"Same old thing. More reports of Japanese movements in the Pacific."

"Anything definite this time?"

Blair should know as well as anyone that intelligence was not a game of definites. "No. Only that they're definitely on the move."

"South?"

"South . . . but I've got a report here from the Twelfth in San Francisco about unusual levels of radio traffic in the north Pacific."

"Call letters? Ship names? Commanding officers?"

"No," Thorensen said. Blair knew, of course, that he had none of that information, or he would have gone directly to Admiral Noyes—or even to Hart. All he had were hunches, which were keeping him awake long into the night while he went over in his mind every message that came across his desk. His intuition was on alert and providing a steady drumbeat of adrenaline to his system. "But maybe you'll pass along my concerns to the admiral?"

Blair sighed. "Sure thing, Will." Blair looked at his fellow officer, and for the first time in some time, he felt a pang of sympathy for Thorensen. It was obvious that the man was working himself too hard and that he might be on the verge of a breakdown. The missing Jap carrier forces had become an obsession with him. "You look like you could use some sleep, Will," he said.

Thorensen nodded. "I can't sleep at night," he said. "I see Jap carriers in my dreams." He looked down at the floor, and for a moment Blair thought that Thorensen might burst into tears.

"You've got to pull yourself together."

Thorensen smiled and went on as if he had not heard. "I see them rounding Diamond Head." He shook his head to clear the vision. "Isn't that crazy?"

Blair turned paternal. "Don't worry about that," he said with a smile. "If the Japs were crazy enough to try to attack Hawaii, they'd be spotted before they got within a thousand miles. The entire U.S. Pacific Fleet would be waiting for them." Blair's smile broadened, "They're not that stupid."

"No, they're not," Thorensen agreed.

"We all—the admiral included—agree with you that the Japs are preparing to move, but it seems more than likely that they'll go after the British in Singapore or the Dutch oil fields. Don't you agree?"

Thorensen nodded reluctantly.

"Right now," Blair said, "they are trying to select a suitable target that will give them maximum gain with minimum risk."

"You're probably right," Thorensen said. "I'm just letting my imagination run away with me."

"Don't think you're alone in your concerns," Blair said. "I assure you that Admirals Noyes and Hart share your concerns about the movements of Jap naval forces in the Pacific."

Thorensen brightened immediately. "You've passed along my reports?"

"Of course," Blair said. He did not say that neither Noyes nor Hart put much stock in Thorensen's theories about Japan's intentions. A Japanese direct attack of a major U.S.

naval base was beyond credibility. Blair didn't care how many books about Japan Thorensen had read. Those runty little yellow men would never dare challenge the United States directly.

"Then Pearl will be alerted?" Thorensen asked.

"Pearl is on alert, at this very moment."

This was true. Admiral Kimmel at Pearl Harbor had been alerted, but merely to caution him about the possibility of sabotage. Nothing had been said about Japanese naval activity. As far as Kimmel knew, the Japanese were moving into southeast Asia and were of no immediate threat to his forces in Hawaii.

Thorensen sighed and slumped back into his chair. His relief was palpable.

"I'll tell you something else that will make you feel better," Blair said. Thorensen looked up expectantly as Blair got up from behind his desk. He went to the door, closed it, and came back to his seat. "Admiral Hart has decided to move some of the most modern elements of the Atlantic Fleet into the Pacific to be ready to counter Japanese moves anywhere in the region."

Thorensen clenched his hands into fists. This was the best possible news. "The fast battleships, also?"

Blair nodded reassuringly. "Both the *North Carolina* and *Washington*. The fleet is gathering now. As soon as they are joined by the *Hornet* and *Wasp*, they will head for the Panama Canal and on into the Pacific, where they will join up with Kimmel's forces."

Thorensen felt as if a great weight had been lifted from his shoulders. The *North Carolina* and the *Washington* were the U.S. Navy's biggest and most modern warships. Both were armed with nine 16-inch guns and heralded a new generation of fast, heavily armored battleships. Neither Thorensen nor Blair were aware that the Japanese Imperial Navy boasted two battleships that were twice as large as those upon which the Americans relied.

"That's great news," Thorensen said. He stuck out his hand, and Blair, somewhat awkwardly, shook it.

"I thought you'd think so," Blair said.

"I was beginning to think that no one was paying any attention to me."

"No fear of that, Will," Blair said, guiding Thorensen to the door. "The admiral is well aware of what you've been doing, and, believe me, he appreciates all of your hard work."

Blair watched Thorensen move down the hallway. He was somehow saddened by his colleague's vigorous step. The man, unfortunately, had an uneven temperament. The pressures of this job, he thought, were too much for some people. Thorensen, unfortunately, was one of them. Blair knew at that moment that Thorensen had probably advanced as far in the Navy as he ever would.

CHAPTER 29

Roberto Garcia was a young man of conflicted loyalties. Although he had known Harry Fox for most of his life and considered the American an older brother, he was like most Panamanians in that he despised the American presence in his country. As a young man he had never thought of Fox as an American but only as his father's closest friend. Since he had grown to manhood, his feelings about Harry had grown ambivalent. In many ways he had come to regard his and his father's relationship with Harry Fox as something of a betrayal of Panama.

He had talked with his father many times about the necessity of driving the Americans out of their country. Ernesto Garcia agreed with his son that Panamanians should have the right to determine their own course of action, but he refused to see that Harry Fox was a part of that particular problem. "Harry is not a yanqui," he would say. "Harry is a brother."

Roberto's inner conflict had caused him to seek acceptance among those who most despised the American presence. This was not a difficult task, and for the past several

241

years Roberto had worked closely with several political groups who were working toward a Panama free of American political influence. To the credit of Panama and its people, most of these groups were nonviolent and believed that a political settlement could be achieved with the Americans that would result in their eventual departure from Panama.

In the face of American intransigence, however, some of the groups inevitably had turned away from peaceful negotiation. Several of these quasi-political organizations were loyal to the deposed President Arias. Roberto, eager to prove his loyalty to his people, had aligned himself with one of these groups.

Now that his father was dead—and his death had been caused by his devotion to his friend—Roberto's internal conflict was even more troublesome. He had pledged to revenge his father's death, to kill the man who had pulled the trigger, but sometimes when he imagined the face of the killer, he saw Harry Fox.

Since the day of his father's death, Roberto had relentlessly pursued the identity of Ernesto Garcia's killer. None of his usual contacts seemed to have any useful information, and most of his queries were met by blank expressions. But occasionally he was able to gather a small snippet of information from someone who might have heard something from someone else. The man, it was said, was not Panamanian. He worked for the Germans and had been picked up by submarine, or had escaped into the mountains, or been flown to Colombia by one of the many German sympathizers who had worked for Scadta, the Colombian national airline. In any event, the word was that the man was gone. Roberto did not believe that for a moment.

During the course of his inquiry, he heard much that he did not believe was true—that the Germans were preparing to invade some unspecified South American country, or that the Americans were prepared to place all of Panama under martial law—and much that did not interest him. But the one thing that he did hear several times—and usually from sources that he regarded as reliable—was that Narciso Viega knew who this man was. It was not unusual to hear such things. Viega's reputation was such that most people in Panama believed that if he was not personally involved in whatever illegality was under question, he at the very least knew who had performed the crime.

Through a mutual friend he arranged a meeting with the son of Narciso Viega, a young man of about Roberto's age. His name was Antonio, and he and Roberto had attended school together. The two young men were little more than casual acquaintances who had not traveled in the same social circle then or now. Their only common ground was that both belonged to groups dedicated to removing American influence from Panama.

Antonio had agreed to meet Roberto in a café on Balboa Avenue, a short distance from the American Embassy, and on a Tuesday afternoon Roberto Garcia went to the café—being careful to arrive early—and settled down to wait for Antonio Viega.

Roberto saw the two men enter the café and knew that they were with Viega. The men—burly types who, despite the heat, wore jackets to conceal the weapons they wore below their armpits—looked around the room with practiced eyes. Neither one looked at Roberto. When they were quite certain that all was as it should be, one of them left and was soon followed into the cafe by Antonio.

Antonio Viega was tall and strikingly handsome. As the son of an important man in Panama, he was accorded a somewhat guarded respect by most of the people who came in contact with him. He did not, however, engender the affection of very many of his countrymen. He was cool and aloof and had never been hesitant about using his father's influence to acquire whatever he wanted. Sometimes it was money, and at other times it was beautiful women, for which it was said he had a rapacious hunger. He was the kind of man who was popular with a certain kind of young woman who did not know any better and who would soon regret that she did not. But he was not well liked by other men unless they happened to be part of his entourage, in which case they followed wherever he went and fed on the remnants of his voracious appetite.

Antonio walked directly to Roberto's table and sat down. "I am told that you wanted to speak with me," he said perfunctorily.

"Yes," Roberto said. "And I am very grateful that you have granted my request for this meeting."

"What do you want?"

"You have heard that my father was killed last week."

"Yes," Antonio said.

"I am told that your father knows the identity of the man who killed my father."

"I am told that your father was working for the yanquis when he was killed."

"He was helping his friend."

"Ah, yes. Fox. The yanqui. Garcia worked for him, didn't he?"

"They were partners. My father was a part owner of the club."

"Then you must be a partner now."

"Yes," Roberto said uncertainly. He and Harry Fox had not discussed this.

"If something should happen to Fox, you would be owner, no? You are indeed fortunate, Roberto. Fox lives a very dangerous life. I am told that it is just a matter of time before someone eliminates him. That would make you a wealthy man, no?"

Roberto smiled. "Yes, it would."

"And that is as it should be," Viega said. "Why should this *norteamericano*—and the others—suck our blood?"

"Panama for the Panamanians," Roberto said.

"Exactly." Antonio leaned forward. "I have been to the club several times," he said. "It's very nice."

Roberto knew that Narciso Viega had several times expressed an interest in becoming a part owner of the club. For his part ownership Viega offered protection from police and government harassment. Harry and Ernesto had resisted Viega's approaches.

"Perhaps," Antonio said, "you will invite me there sometime . . . as your guest?"

"Of course. You are welcome anytime."

"I have seen the new woman who sings in the lounge." Antonio's eyes danced. "She is very special."

"Yes," Roberto said. He knew what was coming.

"Perhaps you would introduce me to her on my next visit?" Antonio smiled, showing his gleaming white teeth, and adding, "I would consider it a great favor."

"Then consider it done," Roberto said.

"Now, what is it that I can do for you?"

"I have heard that your father can help me find the man who killed my father."

"I can't imagine who told you such a thing."

"People will talk."

"I am certain that this is not true," Antonio said. "But as a favor to you, I will ask my father about this matter." The sly smile was back. "Perhaps tomorrow—or the night after—I will come to your club and tell you what I have found out."

"That would be most gracious," Roberto said.

"And you could introduce me to the beautiful lady?"

"Of course. I am sure she will be pleased to meet you."

Antonio Viega gave a nod of satisfaction. "Until then," he said.

"Until then," Roberto said. He watched Viega saunter from the room and wondered how he was going to explain to Victoria that he had just promised her to the most notorious womanizer in Panama.

"You did what?" Harry said.

Roberto looked at the floor. "I told him that I would introduce them."

They were in Harry's office, Harry behind the desk, Victoria sitting on the couch across from them, and Roberto seated in front of the desk.

"Forget it," Harry said. "Victoria doesn't want anything to do with this guy."

Roberto looked up, his face full of resentment. "Viega

knows who killed my father. I want Antonio to find out for me. This was the only way I can get him to help me."

Harry, remembering with pain the risk that Victoria had taken with the Germans, would have none of it. "No way," he said. "I don't want Vicky involved with this guy."

"Why not?" Roberto shot back. "Because you are afraid for her . . . or afraid for yourself? Afraid that you might lose her?"

"Roberto . . ." Harry began. This was the first time that the two had ever had a confrontation of any kind.

Roberto sensed his advantage. "And what about my father's ownership of this property? Do I now assume that partnership?"

"As a matter of fact, legally I assumed one hundred percent ownership after your father's death—just as he would have done had I been the one who died first. If anything happens to me, ownership would go to you. But that's not how it has to be . . ."

Roberto leapt to his feet interrupting Harry in midsentence. "Very convenient, Harry," he said, his voice trembling. "You send my father to do your dirty work. He gets himself killed, and you wind up with everything." He moved to the door. "I see how it works now."

"Roberto," Harry said gently. "Come back here. We need to talk. I have something I want to tell you."

"No need to bother, Harry. I'm just a Panamanian. You don't have to worry about me." He yanked open the door and stomped out.

Harry looked at Victoria. "I was going to tell him," Harry said, "that I want him to have his father's share in the business."

"Then go after him," Vicky said. "Tell him now."

Harry looked at the open door. "He'll be back."

"I'm not so sure, Harry. He seems very confused right now. He blames you for his father's death."

Harry looked at his hands as if he might somehow see evidence of his guilt. "Maybe he's right," he said softly. "I put his life at risk, and he was killed. The best friend I ever had, and I got him killed."

"Don't do that, Harry. It wasn't your fault."

"Just as I put yours at risk. I was lucky that you weren't killed, too."

"Ernesto loved you, Harry. He was willing to share the risk. I love you, too. And I feel the same way."

Elbows on his desk, Harry covered his face with his hands.

Victoria went to him, sat on his lap, and put her arms around him. "Oh, Harry," she said. "I was wondering when you'd start to feel the loss of your friend."

He buried his face in her shoulder. "I guess I didn't really believe he was gone until we got back here and he wasn't there to meet us."

Victoria held him, stroking his hair. "It'll be all right, Harry," she whispered over and over again.

CHAPTER 30

A few days after Harry and Victoria returned from Guiana, Special Agent Trump arrived at the Panama Club. He was alone. Harry would have preferred to deal with Smythe, but agreed to see Trump in his upstairs office.

The two men eyed each other warily, like two animals prepared to do battle over territory. Trump, sweating in his light suit, fanned himself with his hat and sat in front of Harry's desk. He rearranged the strands of hair across his head. "How about a drink?" he asked. "It's so damn hot in this country."

"You bring something for me?" Harry asked.

"Like what?"

"My pardon? My money?"

"Not quite."

Harry was not surprised. He had never believed that Trump would make this easy. "What then?"

"How about that drink?"

Harry pointed to the bar. "Help yourself."

Trump went to the bar and began fixing his drink. "You?" he asked over his shoulder.

"Tell me about the pardon and the money," he said.

Trump came back to his seat and sipped at his drink. "You really should have one," he said. "I make an excellent Planters Punch."

"I thought we had a deal," Harry said.

"If you remember, the deal was for the recovery of four million dollars."

"And three and a half wasn't good enough?"

"There is still a considerable amount missing. We'd like to have that returned."

Harry lit a cigarette. "I didn't think I could trust you—or Hoover." Harry was surprised at the depths of his disappointment. He hadn't been aware of how much he had counted on being able to go home. Even though he had never held any illusions that Trump or the FBI would honor their commitment, somewhere in his subconscious he had somehow hoped that he might be wrong. He shook his head, angry with himself for hoping. "I don't know why I bothered to listen to you."

Trump pretended to be hurt by Harry's accusation. "I don't think that you should be the one to talk about trust, do you? We are willing to fulfill our end of the bargain. All you have to do is fulfill yours."

"You let the five hundred thousand get away, and now you want me to find it?"

"My information is that the man and the money are still in Panama."

Harry, suddenly interested, leaned forward. "What else do you know about him?"

Trump's smile was triumphant. "Still interested, huh?"

"When I find him, I'm going to kill him," Harry said. "I don't give a shit about your money."

"We are still willing to honor the deal."

Harry laughed. "I recover the other five hundred thousand and turn it over to you, and you give me fifty thousand. Is that how it works?"

"Something like that."

"Maybe this time I'll just keep the money . . . if there's any left."

"You could do that . . ." Trump paused. "But what about the pardon? I think it's time you got out of this godforsaken place and went home—don't you, Harry?"

"I'm not so sure, Trump," he said. "At least here I know who the crooks are."

"I'll leave you the name of a man. Our informants say that he might know the name of the man you are looking for." He placed a small business-size card on Harry's desk, finished his drink, and stood up.

"I want this man more than you do," Harry said.

"Maybe," Trump said, moving to the door.

"But I'm puzzled about one thing. Why don't you have your people follow this up?"

Trump smiled. "You're closer to the criminal element than we are. I thought you might have more success. Besides, we're trying to keep out of this, remember?"

When Trump had gone, Harry picked up the card and looked at the name Trump had written. "Rafael Dominguez," he read aloud. Dominguez was a small-time hoodlum who occasionally did work for Narciso Viega. He probably knew nothing but would do or say anything for a few dollars. Harry dropped the card on the table.

There was a knock at the door, and Roberto stuck his head into the room. His face still wore the resentment of the previous day. "Trump's gone," he said. "He tell you anything?"

Harry knew he meant about his father. He shook his head. "Nothing." He wanted desperately to engage Roberto in conversation. The card on his desk caught his eye. "D'you know this Rafael Dominguez character?" he asked.

"Small-time nobody." His words were curt, leaving Harry without an opening to continue the conversation.

Harry thought for a moment. "Can you get word to him that I want to see him? He might know something."

Roberto seemed uninterested. "Guys like this one can be hard to locate. When do you want to see him?"

Harry picked up the card and flipped it over. It had Trump's embassy number on the other side. "As soon as possible," he said. "Tell him to meet me here."

Roberto nodded and left without another word. Harry sighed and shook his head sadly. This thing with Roberto had gone on too long.

Narciso Viega picked a piece of cigar from his tongue, looked at it for a moment, and then flicked it out the window of the automobile. He looked at his son, who sat next to him in the backseat. "So how did the Garcia boy hear I was involved in this matter?"

"He didn't say you were involved, only that people had said that you knew who killed his father."

Viega looked out the window as the car moved slowly through the narrow streets of the Caledonia district, one of the many slum sections of Panama City. Most of the people in this section were black—descendants of the West Indians who had been brought to Panama to work as laborers on the canal. Viega watched them as he passed. Old men sat in doorways, shabbily dressed children played in the streets, listless women went about their endless chores, and everywhere the signs of poverty were evident. The houses were inevitably dilapidated, some of them little more than shacks created from scrap lumber. The streets were littered with the debris of shattered lives. Every vacant lot had been claimed by families who lived in tents or fragile cardboard structures whose existence seemed as precarious as the lives of the families who occupied them. Sad eyes watched with interest as Viega's car passed.

"Look at these Chomas," Viega said, using the term as an epithet for the West Indians of Panama.

"I don't have to look," Antonio said. "I can smell them."

Viega laughed. "Don't worry. When we are back in power, we will get rid of all of this filth."

"It won't be soon enough for me."

"What's the matter?" Viega said. "The women too ugly for you?" He laughed again. He was proud of his son's prowess with beautiful women. He considered himself a man of the world, but was often envious of the way women flocked to his son. "You like them blond and alabaster, eh?"

Antonio smiled. He knew how proud his father was of him.

"Like this *norteamericana* at Fox's club?" the father asked.

Antonio looked at his father in surprise. "Who told you that?"

Viega slapped his son playfully on the knee. "I know everything that you do, little boy." He flashed his rotting teeth. "I know all about your little escapades with the women. Nothing escapes me."

Those goddamned bodyguards, Antonio thought. They must tell him everything.

"That's why you bring me this bullshit about Roberto Garcia, is it not? You want him to fix you up with the girl."

"Perhaps," Antonio said.

"Perhaps, my ass," Viega said. "Tell him nothing, Tell him I know nothing. Tell him you know nothing."

"Now that his father is dead, Roberto is a part owner of the Panama Club," Antonio said. "If something were to happen to Fox, Roberto would become the owner."

Viega, suddenly interested, turned to look more closely at his son. "Go on."

"If something did happen to Fox, a boy like Roberto would need a partner to help him run that place."

Viega smiled. "And you would like to be that partner?"

"It might be of interest to me."

Viega thought for a moment. When he wasn't chasing women, the boy spent most of his time in saloons and casinos anyway. Maybe this would give him something to do—keep him out of trouble and out of his hair. The boy's mother was always pestering Viega to find something for the boy. In addition, Harry Fox had long been a thorn in his side. This situation might provide the perfect solution to a number of problems. "I'll tell you what," Viega said. "You tell young Garcia that I, too, have heard some things about the man who killed his father and that I will try to discover more. In the meantime, you try to find out what he and Fox know about this affair. I'm not worried about the boy, but if Fox is determined to put his nose into this, something will have to be done." He smiled and sucked on his cigar. "Perhaps young Roberto will be needing a partner sooner than he thinks."

CHAPTER 31

Robles unrolled the large engineering survey map and placed it on the table of his room. The map showed the dimensions and specifications of the spillway at the Gatun Dam and had been acquired for him by Drexler and his contacts at the Hapag-Lloyd Steamship Company in Balboa. Robles was not aware that some of the material had come from the German legation in Colón. It had surprised him that the Germans had had this and other technical information about the canal. Drexler had offered him maps and surveys of many of the installations of the Panama Canal, which according to the German had been collected over the past several years by an assortment of German spies or sympathizers who until this year had had easy and almost unlimited access to the canal.

"These items are hard to acquire now," Drexler had told him. "The Americans don't seem to realize that the horse is already out of the barn."

Ludwig Brack, a native Ecuadorian who had been trained by the Abwehr in the early thirties, and now worked with Drexler, had worked as a mule driver at the Gatun Locks for almost four years. The mules were the small but powerful locomotives that were used to pull the large freight ships through the locks. Before the threat of war Brack —and anyone else who worked at the canal—had had access to any area within the Canal Zone. Brack had used his familiarity with the Canal Zone personnel to photograph key locations along the waterway and to acquire a host of maps, surveys, and technical information about the canal. And he was not the only one. It seemed that Drexler and Erika Schreiber had an almost limitless supply of persons, both foreign and native, who were willing to provide them with whatever information they required.

Robles weighted down the corners of the survey map with a book and his coffee cup. He found that he was drinking more and more of the dark, South American coffee to help him remain alert. His schedule now was such that he spent most of the evening hours at the canal, then returned to his room for a few hours of restless sleep, and then was back planning for the next phase of his operation. He estimated that he was sleeping no more than four hours each day. Narciso Viega had commented that he looked like a man who needed an alarm clock. Robles was not certain what he had meant until Viega presented him with a supply of cocaine to keep him awake.

He looked at the dresser drawer where he kept the cocaine, but after a moment's hesitation decided against its use. He wanted to keep a clear head. There would come a time when he would need the drug, but for now he wanted to go on without it.

The survey map was large, and Robles was amazed at the detail of the specifications about the Gatun Spillway. Not only did the map give him the details of the height, length, depth, and width of the spillway, but also a detailed schematic of the inner gates that were used to lower the level of the water in the dam and even the comparative strength of the poured concrete that had been used to form the structure. A side view of the spillway showed that, as with most structures of this type, the dam was much thicker at the base than at the top. In this view the structure looked much like an inverted Y.

The inverted Y was solid concrete, eighty-five feet high, more than three hundred feet across, and, at the base, almost one hundred feet thick. The bed of the lake rose in a gentle slope so that on the inside the dam was sixty-five feet above the lake bottom.

Robles measured the distance from the surface of the water to the point where the bed of the lake contacted the base of the spillway. He assumed that over the years there would have been a considerable accumulation of mud and debris at the base of the dam, so he therefore subtracted ten feet from his calculations. He knew that it did not really matter where he breached the dam, so long as the breach was deep enough and wide enough. The resultant pressure from the escaping water would do the rest. He had earlier estimated that within fifteen minutes of a major structural crack in the concrete, a major breach would occur that would, within two hours, drop the level of Gatun Lake to a point below where the locks would be operable. Within thirty-six hours the lake would have lost more than eighty percent of its capacity. By then any ships remaining in the lake would be stranded for what might be several years.

An additional bonus to his plan was that all three U.S. Army bases on the Atlantic side of the canal, in addition to France Field and the navy base at Coco Solo, were below the dam. The resultant tidal wave would more than likely devastate all five American military bases as well as flood major portions of the twin cities of Colón and Cristobal. He held no illusions about the amount of damage that would be caused to these military installations. Fort Davis, the closest installation to the dam, would more than likely be completely destroyed. The others at varying distances from the coming flood would probably sustain no more than heavy damage that would render the facilities inoperable for at least a short time. Robles was sure that the Abwehr and especially the Führer would be more than satisfied by the amount of damage that he would inflict on the American presence in Panama.

Once again Robles went back to his diagram. He measured down the face of the dam to the point just above where the base began to thicken. At this point the dam was thirty-three feet thick and fifty-five feet below the surface of the lake. He made his calculations in a small notebook. He knew that under normal circumstances he would need an enormous amount of explosives to blast a hole through such an immense thickness of concrete. But, for several reasons, these circumstances were anything but normal.

In the first place the fact that the blast would take place beneath the surface of the lake would be tremendously beneficial to the explosive effect. An underwater, as opposed to an open air, explosion contributes mightily to the dynamic effect of the resultant explosion. The water would prevent, to a great extent, the dissipation of the force of the explosion, and the reverberation of the shock waves in the water would do almost as much damage to the dam as would the force of the explosion itself. The effect would be similar to that of an earthquake, where tremendous stress is placed on any structure in the vicinity of the shock waves. In order to maximize the power of the explosion, Robles knew that he would have to make certain that the explosive charge was snuggled against the wall of the dam. Any deviation from this, even by as little as a few feet, would more than likely result in failure.

In the second place, unlike a building or some other massive structure that had to be destroyed, a dam has certain inherent disadvantages. Even though this particular dam was built to withstand far greater pressures than any building of comparable size, it would have been much more difficult to bring down a building. Robles had studied the effects of bomb damage on cities earlier in the war and knew that it was much more difficult than it had been supposed to destroy buildings. Old, poorly constructed buildings, of course, tumbled down like a house of cards after the initial blast and many such structures were so severely damaged that they had to be pulled down. But modern buildings, those with heavy concrete foundations and thick walls or steel framing, had been able to withstand incredible amounts of punishment. A bomb blast had to be sufficiently large to destroy its target in the first millisecond of the explosion. If the structure survived the initial blast, there was an excellent chance that it would not fall.

A dam, on the other hand, is already struggling against the enormous force of the water that it holds. This force sometimes exerts millions of pounds of pressure against the thick concrete walls. Add to that force a small but significant additional force—in the form of an explosion—and all sorts of things start to happen. Unlike the building, the dam need not be destroyed or breached in the initial blast. Little more than moderate structural damage is all that is required. After the explosion, cracks appear in the surface—perhaps accompanied by a deep gouge at the focal point of the blast. Weakened, but still intact, the dam must struggle against the incredible force of the water it has been designed to hold. But now, with its structural integrity severely impaired, the dam can no longer maintain its designed function. What in another structure might be considered minimal structural damage is fatal. In minutes, or hours, or days, the dam gives way.

Robles completed his calculations. Four thousand pounds of dynamite, he thought, would do the job. To destroy a similarly constructed building would require at least ten times that much. He would, however, not take any chances. He would double the amount of explosive and hit the dam in a series of smaller explosions. The accumulated pressure, like a succession of hammer blows, would guarantee the success of the operation.

All that remained was to decide how he would place the charges at the dam. He grinned. He had known from the beginning how he would do that.

CHAPTER 32

In 1941, Panama City was one of the world's most open and exciting cities, providing every conceivable form of entertainment—legal and illegal. Every enterprise in the city was directed toward attracting those who lived and worked inside the adjacent Panama Canal Zone. Although everything was supposedly provided for the welfare of those who resided within the boundaries of the Canal Zone, the Zonians were drawn to Panama City because they could not find this kind of excitement anywhere within the American-controlled zone. In a country where poverty and hunger were the norm, those who lived and worked inside the ten-mile strip that divided the country were well fed, well paid, and well off. But because the zone was operated as if it were a gigantic army camp, the Zonians had money to spend but very little that was entertaining on which to spend it. There was, of course, an abundance of wholesome recreation in the zone typical of U.S. military establishments everywhere. If one wanted to play golf or tennis or go sailing, there were ample opportunities. There were enlisted men's clubs, officers' clubs, and residents' clubs that catered to most of the recreational activities deemed acceptable by the military governor of the zone. But most of the men, especially the military personnel, within the zone were young and single and looking for the kind of entertainment that young, single men usually looked for and that official army policy usually discouraged. For those pursuits they came to Panama City or to Colón at the Atlantic end of the canal.

To the Panamanians, whose average annual income was about what a lowly U.S. Army private made in two months, most of the refugees from the zone seemed fabulously wealthy, and there was, of course, a wide range of establishments dedicated to relieving them of that wealth. Most of these establishments catered to the enlisted men who nightly roamed the streets of Panama City and Colón. Most of the enlisted men were young, and away from home for the first time, and anxious to show that they were just as rough and tough and worldly as their brethren who had been in Panama for perhaps a few months more than they had. Some of these establishments were little more than residences by day that were converted to whorehouses at night, where for a few dollars a U.S. serviceman could have his sexual frustrations relieved and be back out on the street in ten minutes. Others were somewhat more sophisticated: a bar, a backroom for gambling, and upstairs rooms where the prostitutes plied their trade.

Then there were the places that catered to most of the same vices but to a wealthier clientele who liked their vices wrapped in a prettier and obviously more expensive package. Most of the clubs in Panama City fell into this category. There were relatively few establishments, outside of the major hotels, where a man might feel equally comfortable in the company of his wife—or his girlfriend.

Harry Fox's Panama Club was one of the most refined and easily the most popular of this small group of better establishments. The club offered dancing, food, and entertainment—in addition to the usual drinking and gambling—and attracted American military officers, civilian engineers, and Canal Zone administrators, along with

Panamanian government officials and local businessmen. The place was festive, casually elegant, and relatively safe from the kind of violent outbursts that were known to plague many of the other lesser establishments. It was also less stodgy than the large hotels, which provided its major competition.

It was well known that Harry did not allow prostitutes to work his club. If a patron preferred to bring a young lady of questionable reputation with him, that was his business, but the ladies of the street knew that they would be politely escorted to the door if they arrived sans escort. The drinks were expensive enough to discourage most of the military personnel who roamed the nearby streets in search of an evening's entertainment, but Harry had never refused to admit any U.S. serviceman who was sober and felt that he could afford to pay the going rate. The gambling tables were strictly for the high rollers and only those who could afford to lose ventured there. Harry had long ago learned that low-stakes tables attracted a boisterous element that he preferred not to encourage. Small-time gamblers, he thought, created more problems than they were worth.

Harry looked down to the main floor from his second floor office. The club was crowded with the usual assortment of Zonians, military officers, and wealthy Panamanians. He smiled and let the curtain fall back into place. Since Victoria had started singing at the club, business had been exceptionally good. Harry looked at his watch and turned to her. "Almost time for the nine o'clock show," he said. "Looks like a good crowd again."

"Have you talked with Roberto yet?"

"Sort of."

"What does 'sort of' mean?"

"I tried to talk to him yesterday, but he didn't seem very interested." Harry made a gesture of futility. "Don't worry, we'll get back together."

Vicky was not convinced. "All he wanted was for me to meet some guy," she said.

"Not just 'some guy.' The son of one of the most dangerous men in Panama."

"I can take care of myself, Harry. I thought you knew that."

Harry didn't answer. He heard the band strike up her signature tune. "Showtime," he said.

Victoria shook her head sadly and went to the door. "Don't let this thing between you and Roberto go any further than it already has," she said.

The applause started as soon as Victoria stepped into the room and continued as she made her way to the bandstand. On the way she stopped to say hello to faces that she had seen almost every night for the past month. She saw Roberto and touched his arm as she passed. He nodded and gave her a smile, but it was a small smile that seemed infinitely sad.

Vicky took the microphone and began her repertoire of standards. Her voice was clear and strong, but somehow soft and vulnerable, and she had the ability to make a momentary eye contact that made each man in the room feel that she was singing this song just for him. She did the songs she did every night—"Stardust," "Am I Blue," "I Only Have Eyes for You," and several others—and added a few recently popular tunes so that her set did not become routine.

What had impressed Harry Fox from the beginning was how she sang her songs and how his customers seemed to hang on every word. He'd had other singers at the Panama Club, some with better voices, but none had ever been able to enthrall his customers the way she did. When she sang, the room fell silent, and most of the men sat mesmerized by her voice. Harry had to tell her to take more breaks during each show so that he could sell some drinks.

As she sang her next-to-last number before the first break of the evening, Victoria watched Roberto, who sat alone at a front-row table that was usually reserved for some of Harry's regular patrons. Roberto seemed agitated and kept looking at his watch and then at the door as if he were expecting someone. Sure enough, during her last number, Roberto rose from his seat and went to greet someone who had just entered. The man, who seemed about the same age as Roberto, smiled warmly as Roberto approached. They shook hands and Roberto led the way back to the front-row table, where they conversed in a low whisper, Roberto leaning over so that the man could talk into his ear.

As they talked the man shrugged several times, and Roberto nodded slowly, obviously not entirely satisfied with what he was hearing. The man made several conciliatory gestures and patted Roberto on the arm several times as if to say, "Don't worry." Roberto's disappointment was evident. During this conversation, the man never once took his eyes from Victoria.

Victoria finished her song, accepted her applause, and promised to be back in ten minutes. She stepped off the bandstand and walked over to Roberto's table. Roberto's eyes widened as she approached.

"This must be the gentleman you wanted me to meet," Vicky said.

Antonio Viega sprang to his feet. "It is indeed an honor, señorita," he said, kissing her hand. "I have wanted to meet you for some time."

Victoria sat between them. "Any friend of Roberto's is a friend of mine."

Roberto thanked her with his eyes, and Vicky gave his hand a squeeze.

They ordered drinks, and Viega peppered her with questions about America. To him America was a land of gangsters and movie stars, and he seemed more interested in the former. "Did you ever see John Dillinger?" he asked as if the infamous gangster were a heroic figure.

"No," Vicky said. "But I met Gary Cooper once."

After a short time Vicky stood. "It's been nice," she said, "but I have to get back to work." She smiled in Roberto's direction. "I don't want Señor Garcia to fire me."

Roberto's eyes showed his gratitude for her gesture.

In his upstairs office Harry Fox let the curtain fall back across the window. He did not like what he had seen and felt uncomfortable about Roberto's association with Viega. Harry would have preferred that Roberto give the Viegas a wide berth, but he knew that Narciso Viega was involved in this in some way. They had so few clues to the identity of the man who had killed Ernesto that they could not afford to overlook anyone or anything that might help them find the killer. Harry would have preferred to leave the Viegas out of this, but he knew that he could not. Involving Viega was merely asking for the kind of trouble that Harry would rather avoid.

He went to his desk, sat down, and slid open the lower drawer. He removed a hand-carved walnut case, then took a small brass key from the front middle drawer. He inserted the key into the lock in the case, opened it, and took out a small, two-shot derringer. The gun weighed less than twelve ounces, but he liked the feel of it in his hand. It was a top-break model, and he snapped open the barrel to make sure that the pistol was loaded. He sat for a while holding the small pistol before he returned it to the case and placed it back inside the drawer.

As Vicky started her second set, she saw that Viega was joined at his table by two other men who, until now, had waited at the back of the lounge. Their eyes never stopped moving, but they seemed more interested in watching the crowd than in Vicky's performance. Roberto looked very uncomfortable.

During the next break, Vicky went back to Viega's table. He was obviously pleased to see her. He did not bother to introduce her to the two new arrivals, whom she assumed were bodyguards. "So, Antonio," she said, "how do you like the show?"

"It is wonderful," he said seriously. "You are wonderful."

"It's always nice to be appreciated," she said.

"Perhaps we could go somewhere after the show?" Viega asked.

Vicky smiled. "I have another show at eleven."

"After that?" he asked hopefully.

Vicky shook her head. "I just can't. Maybe some other time."

Just then Harry appeared. He looked at Roberto. "Mind if I join you and your guests?" He pulled up a chair and sat down before anyone had a chance to say anything. "I hope you're treating your guests to nothing but the best, Roberto." He smiled at Antonio Viega. "Such important people deserve nothing but the best."

"Everything's okay, Harry," Roberto said.

"Good . . . good," Harry said. "I just thought I'd stop by and say hello. I haven't seen your father here in quite some time, Antonio."

"He's a busy man."

"I'll bet he is," Harry said.

Viega's eyes narrowed. "I'll tell him you asked for him. I'm sure he'll be pleased by your concern for his well-being."

Vicky could feel the tension between the two. "This is all very nice," she said, getting up from her chair, "but I've got to get back to work."

As she walked away, Viega—without taking his eyes from her—said to Harry, "That is some woman, Fox. A man would be lucky to have a woman like that. But he might find it impossible to keep her."

Harry forced a smile as he stood. "Enjoy the rest of your stay, gentlemen. Don't forget the gaming tables are still open." He gave Roberto a brief pat on the shoulder. "I'm sure that my partner will take good care of you."

Antonio looked at Roberto. "Partner?" he said approvingly.

Roberto recovered from his initial surprise in time to give Harry a quick smile.

Harry gave Roberto a wink and then made his way back to his office. As he went up the stairs, he heard Victoria singing, "What'll I Do." He did not look back.

CHAPTER 33

The storage shed was large but old and dingy. It leaned precipitously to one side as if it might at any moment collapse into a pile of rotting timbers, but it suited Robles's requirements perfectly. It had formerly been a storage depot for some of the temporary buildings that had been constructed along the site of the canal. These buildings had been taken apart and stored in various locations for many years after the completion of the canal, but after years of neglect most of these buildings had been appropriated by the West Indians who made their homes here on the Atlantic side of Panama. Until recently the storage shed was empty of all that might have been of any use to anyone.

The shed was another of Narciso Viega's secret storage depots for the explosives he had accumulated over the past year. When he had brought Robles here to examine another batch of explosives, Robles had quickly realized that this rotting storehouse was the perfect location for his purposes. At one time the building had been used as a kind of boathouse and had sat directly on the northern shores of Gatun Lake, where its large double doors had provided easy access for small boats to move directly inside. Sometime soon after the completion of the canal, however, the structure had been moved back from the shores of the lake and had become a simple dirt-floored storage space without foundation. Now the shed sat slightly beyond the one-hundred-foot zone that the U.S. claimed around the entire lake. There was a clear path, covered only by minor vegetation and a few trees, between the long-unused double doors at the back of the building and the lake shore. Just off-shore, testament to the destruction of the land, the lake was dotted with the trunks of dead trees that rose white and ghostly from the dark waters of the man-made lake.

By boat the shed was less than three miles from Gatun Dam.

Through Viega, Robles had obtained a much-used, but still serviceable, tow truck. This old-timer, a 1928 Dodge, had once been used to service damaged military vehicles in the Canal Zone and then sold to a garage in Panama City as surplus equipment. The truck had a powerful winch, a long metal boom, and a long length of cable. Robles used this vehicle to transport the materials he required to the storage shed. He did not bother to ask how Viega was able to acquire such a vehicle. He had made a specific request, and the next day Viega had produced the truck.

Robles had then purchased from separate suppliers: twenty old, empty fifty-gallon oil drums, several coils of heavy steel cable, various large bolts and connectors, and an old but still usable arc welder.

Most of these items were purchased from Americans who worked inside the Canal Zone. No one ever asked what he intended to do with these materials and Robles assumed that most of the items were stolen from stock intended for use within the zone. As long as he paid cash, no one seemed to care. Robles received considerable pleasure in knowing that the Americans were selling him the tools that he would use to destroy them.

The most important part of his equipment had been provided by Ludwig Brack, who had acquired an ancient tug that had been discarded as surplus by the Hapag-Lloyd

Line. The tug was a weatherbeaten dinosaur that had originally been used on the lake before the canal opened. Only one of the two engines was in running condition, but Brack assured Robles that he would have both engines running perfectly in time for the attack on the dam. He had brought the tug across the lake and built a camouflaged canopy to protect it from prying eyes. Brack had worked every evening, long into the night, on the old, but still powerful, engines until he was confident that they were almost as good as new. When Brack's repairs were completed, he and Robles took the tug out onto the lake for a test run. They found, to their satisfaction, that the tug was capable of surprising speed.

This was the kind of work that Brack did well, and it amazed Robles that someone who could repair automobile and boat engines with ease, and build whatever was required, was not more curious about what had to be done or why he had been chosen to do it. Brack never asked questions. Robles told him what to do and he did it.

Ludwig Brack found it easier to take orders than to think for himself. It seemed to him that whenever he made a choice, he chose the wrong thing, so he preferred to let others, wiser than he, make his choices for him. He was a rather ugly man, with a large upper torso, short, stocky legs, and powerful arms that seemed too long for his body.

Brack was in his late twenties and had been born in Ecuador of German parents. All of his life he had been told by his father that Germans were God's favored race. With the rise of Hitler, Brack had been sure that his father's words were true, and when he was seventeen, he had joined one of the many German clubs that had sprouted all across South America. These clubs proved to be fertile ground when the German Intelligence services were looking for agents to do their work in the new world. Brack had been recruited by the Abwehr in 1935, when he was barely twenty, and in 1937 he was brought to Germany for intensive training. A year later he was sent to Panama, where his mechanical skills made it easy for him to find steady work in and around the canal. He had been there, providing intelligence information to the Abwehr, ever since.

Robles had given Brack the task of bringing together all of the various caches of explosives that had been acquired from Viega. To his joy and amazement, Robles discovered that much of the explosives were RDX, an explosive generally used by the military that was several times more powerful than dynamite. As soon as enough of the material had been gathered, Robles began the job of cutting and preparing it for packing into the empty drums.

Robles made drawings of the steel racks that he wanted installed on the boat and gave them to Brack, who nodded and said that it would be taken care of. The next night Brack brought the steel and began to work. When that was done, Robles showed Brack the modifications that he required in the bow of the boat. Brack nodded and began to work immediately. They worked together, rarely exchanging a word, both intent on the immediate task. It was a perfect symbiotic relationship. Robles provided the order that Brack required, and if Robles needed anything he said a few words to Brack, who nodded or mumbled and went off to get it.

When all the materials were gathered, Robles began the work in earnest. His first task was to determine how many drums he required to hold the necessary amount of explosives. He had more than a hundred cases of explosives —sixty percent dynamite, the rest RDX. Both explosives were dense and extremely heavy, almost two pounds to a single stick and Robles calculated that he could get more than one thousand pounds of explosive tightly packed into a single drum. This was as large as any bomb that had as yet been dropped on any city in the war. Four drums would be sufficient to do the job. He decided to use twice as much and leave no room for doubt.

He worked with the drums on their sides so that they could be rolled aside when he was finished packing them full. When he finished one, Brack rolled it out of his way, and Robles began work on the next. He took the better part of two nights to complete the task. Neither he nor Brack said anything during this time, but when he was finished Brack reached under the seat of the truck and brought out two bottles of beer. They sat, backs against the wheels of the truck.

"To success," Brack said awkwardly.

They clinked bottles and drank. The beer was warm, but it tasted as good as anything that either had ever drunk.

Robles finished his beer in one long satisfied gulp. He was confident that things were going well. All that he required now was the special detonators that he had asked Drexler to order from the Abwehr. Drexler had promised that the devices would arrive by ship on the next diplomatic shipment to Panama. That, he said, would be within the next few days. By then Robles would be ready.

Rafael Dominguez was a small, slightly built man in his late fifties. He had gray hair, sunken cheeks, and eyes that never stopped moving. He gulped down the whiskey that the waiter had brought him and looked at Harry expectantly. Harry made a motion to the waiter and another whiskey appeared on the table.

"I'm looking for a man," Harry said.

Dominguez downed the whiskey, wiped his mouth with his sleeve, and said, "And I always thought you liked women, Harry." When Harry did not smile, Dominguez said, "What man?"

"The man who killed my friend Ernesto."

"That was a terrible thing," Dominguez said.

"Would you like another drink?"

"This information will cost you more than a few drinks, Harry."

"I'm willing to pay. Name your price. Tell me his name and where I can find him."

"Is it worth five hundred dollars to you?"

"Yes," said Harry without hesitation.

"Maybe it's worth more," Dominguez said.

"It is worth five hundred dollars. The next time you ask, it will be worth four hundred dollars, and the time after that it—"

"All right. All right," Dominguez said. "I accept your offer."

"Do you know his name?"

Dominguez hesitated and Harry gave an exasperated sigh.

"No," Dominguez said quickly, afraid that he might lose his chance at the money. "But he is an Argentinian, and he works for the Germans."

"Why is he here?"

Dominguez shook his head. "That I don't know, but I know he is buying things from Narciso Viega."

"Things?"

"A truck, a boat . . . other things." Dominguez laughed. "Viega is charging him a pretty penny for everything he wants."

"How do you know this?"

"I hear things. Viega's men laugh about it. And they have money—lots of money."

"American money?"

"Sure. Fifty-dollar bills."

Harry was sure now that Dominguez knew what he was talking about. "Where do I find this man?"

"I can find out from Viega's men," Dominguez said. "I see them all the time. They will know."

"When?"

"Give me a few days."

"I want to know now."

Dominguez nodded. "I'll do what I can."

Harry started to rise. "We'll meet here, then," he said.

"Not here," Dominguez said. "If someone sees me in here too often, Viega might get suspicious." He looked around. "His men are everywhere, Harry."

"Where, then?"

"I'll call you when I know something, then you can meet me at the Central Hotel. And bring the money." He winked at Harry. "Can I have one more drink, Harry?"

"Sure," Harry said sadly. He motioned to the waiter and left Dominguez to his pleasure.

CHAPTER 34

Robles was bathed in sweat. Despite the overhead fan the darkened hotel room was stiflingly hot. He had fallen into a fitful sleep sometime during the early afternoon, a sleep from which he had been awakened by a dream in which he was being pursued by a small army of soldiers. As he ran he could hear the pounding of their footsteps behind him and then the staccato rattle of machine-gun fire. He awoke, surprised to find the room in darkness. He had no idea how long he had slept.

He sat up in bed and swung his feet out onto the floor. He buried his face in his hands and tried to shake the cobwebs from his brain. The pounding footsteps of his dream began again and he realized with a start that the sound was real. Someone was knocking at his door.

Quickly he reached under his pillow for the pistol and padded barefooted to the door. After a brief pause the knocking continued. "Who is it?" he asked.

"Erika."

"What do you want?" he hissed, angered that she had

272

come here. After their first meeting here, he had told that it was too dangerous for her to come.

"I must speak with you . . . now."

He could think of nothing so important that she would have to come to his room. His first thought was that she had betrayed him and led the Americans to him, but then he immediately realized that if that were the case, there would be no need for her to accompany them. He whipped open the door and pointed the gun into the hallway, half expecting to find someone with her.

"I'm alone," she said, apparently unperturbed that he was pointing a pistol at her heart.

He stepped back, and Erika came into the room. After he had closed the door, she looked him up and down. "Expecting company?" she said, speaking German in a voice that was slightly contemptuous.

He realized how he must look. He wore only his underwear—shorts and an undershirt—and had not shaved in several days. "I've been busy," he said. Self-consciously he ran his fingers through his hair and went to the bed, picked up his trousers, and began to put them on.

"Don't dress on my account," Erika said, watching him with undisguised amusement. She sat at the table and looked at the unrolled survey map he had left there. "Interesting."

He moved quickly in her direction, so quickly that she recoiled, thinking he might strike her, but he merely glared at her and gathered up the maps. Now it was his turn to use German. "What are you doing here?" he said, putting the maps aside.

"Something has happened, and Heinrich said that I should contact you immediately."

Robles was surprised that Drexler would send Erika to see him. "He knows that I want as little contact as possible with you people. It's dangerous. You could jeopardize the whole operation."

"I've missed you," she said.

"I've been busy," Robles snapped. "Why have you come?"

"Orders," she said.

"From whom?"

"The Old Man."

"Canaris? I already have my orders."

"Your orders, apparently, have been changed."

"I don't believe you."

She laughed. "Perhaps, if you listen for a moment, you will."

He sat across from her. "Go ahead," he said. "I'm listening."

"Christ, it's hot in this room," she said. "Don't you have anything to drink?"

"There's water in the pitcher," he said, nodding in the direction of the bedside table, "but it's probably as warm as the room."

Erika went to the pitcher and poured a small amount of the tepid water into a handkerchief. She wiped the back of her neck and dabbed at her forehead, and then, with her back to him, wiped the moist cloth inside the front of her blouse. Even with her back to him, she could feel his eyes on her. "It's always so damn hot in this country," she moaned.

"My orders?" he said.

She came back to the table and sat. "Several days ago Heinrich radioed to Abwehr headquarters some information about American fleet maneuvers that I was able to find out through one of my contacts here in Panama. It seems that the Americans have decided to move major portions of the Atlantic Fleet through the canal and into the Pacific—this includes the battleships *North Carolina* and *Washington,* the aircraft carriers *Hornet* and *Wasp,* the cruisers *Augusta* and *Northampton,* and a sizable number of cruisers and destroyers."

Robles clenched his hands into fists. This was exactly the movement that his operation was designed to prevent. If the ships passed through the canal before he was ready, everything that he had done would be in vain. "Do we know when this will happen?"

Erika smiled confidently. "They are scheduled to pass through the canal on the afternoon of December eighth."

"How does Canaris know such things?"

Erika smiled.

"He knows because I told him."

"You?"

"Or should I say, I told Heinrich and he told the Old Man."

Robles looked at her as if he were seeing her for the first time. It was easy to see why men would find her attractive. In addition to her obvious beauty, she exuded a raw almost overpowering sexuality. "How did you get this information?" he asked, knowing the answer.

She smiled and coyly touched her tongue to her upper lip. "I have my methods," she said.

He was beginning to understand the nature of her attractiveness. She was mysterious and yet available; youthful— almost virginal—and apparently unworldly, but beneath the surface juvenescence lurked a smoldering promise of incredible passion. "You must be very good," Robles said.

"I thought you knew that already."

"I want to know exactly what you found out."

"Well," she began, "my young lieutenant, who is the adjutant for General Andrews, the commander of the Caribbean Defense Command, told me that I would have the opportunity to see a truly remarkable sight on December eighth. He said that the most modern units of the Atlantic Fleet would pass through the canal early that morning and that I shouldn't miss the opportunity to see them."

"And he mentioned the ships by name?"

"Oh, yes. According to him, the ships are already on the move. They will stand off shore on the evening of the seventh, then the canal will be cleared of all traffic, and they will move in at first light. They will use both sides of the locks and move through the canal as rapidly as possible. My lieutenant expects them to be at the Miraflores Locks sometime before noon."

"And all of this information was given to Canaris?"

"Yes."

"And he relayed a change in my orders?"

Erika nodded. "Your orders will be confirmed in the next diplomatic pouch. According to Heinrich, the Old Man wants you to trap the fleet inside the canal."

Robles laughed out loud. "That's not possible."

"They seem to feel that you can do the impossible."

Block the canal, yes. But trap a fleet of warships inside— that was something else. Even if he waited until the fleet was inside the canal to blow the Gatun Dam, the water level would not drop rapidly enough to prevent the ships from making the transit to the locks on the Pacific side. It would be at least three hours before the water level in the lake dropped enough to prohibit the use of the locks. Although normal transit time was longer than that, he was certain that under emergency conditions the Americans could move the ships through the canal in that amount of time. "I don't know," he said.

Robles went to his maps, selected one, and returned to the table. He unrolled it and spread it out, using the water pitcher and the pistol as weights at opposite corners to hold it flat. The map was a detailed topological survey of the entire length of the canal. He had studied it a thousand times and knew every measurement by heart. But now he wanted to be sure. He measured carefully, almost oblivious to the fact that Erika was following his every move.

He traced the route that the American battle fleet would take as it passed through the canal. From the locks at Gatun it was a mere sixteen miles to the other side of Gatun Lake. Add perhaps ten miles to this as the ships followed the twisting path over the bed of the old Chagres River Valley that formed the deep water path across the canal. Fast, modern ships could cover that distance in less than an hour. At this point the canal narrowed significantly as the ships entered what was known as the Gamboa Reach. The Gamboa Reach was about five miles long and, although narrow, was wide enough to permit a considerable amount of maneuvering. From here the ships would move into the Culebra Cut. Robles tapped the spot on the map with his finger and smiled. He looked up and saw that Erika was watching him closely; her breathing was deep, her eyes dancing in the dim light.

The Culebra Cut was nine miles long and less than three hundred feet wide. The cut was so narrow that once a ship entered there was no choice but to continue the journey. Five miles into the narrow stretch the ships would pass beneath the looming hills called Gold and Contractor's that were the highest land points anywhere on the canal. If there was any chance for success, it would be here. This, he knew, was where he could make his attempt.

He knew that the hills on either side of the Culebra Cut were notoriously unstable. If he could undermine that instability with several properly placed charges, he could send millions of tons of rock, dirt, and debris tumbling into the narrow waterway. He would have to wait for the procession of American warships to enter the Gamboa Reach before he detonated his charges at the Gatun Dam. Any sooner and they might turn around and race back to the Gatun Locks rather than risk the Culebra Cut. Once the ships entered the cut, they would be unable to turn around in the narrow passageway. If he could then undermine the hills above the cut, dropping millions of tons of dirt, rock, and debris into the waterway, so that he could block the forward progress of the ships, they would be trapped— permanently. Their only chance would be to back out of the cut, and that, he knew would take hours. By then the water level at Gatun would be too low for the warships to escape. If he could do this, he would single-handedly have removed the newest, most powerful, and most efficient fighting units from the U.S. Navy's fleet. The Atlantic Fleet would be trapped, like toy ships in a bathtub.

He stabbed his finger at the spot. "Culebra," he whispered.

Erika felt her heart pounding as if she somehow knew that she was part of something momentous. "Snake," she said. "It means *snake* in Spanish," she said.

He smiled. "I know."

"You have found a way?" she said admiringly.

"Perhaps," he said, unwilling to tell her anything.

"I knew you would."

He began to roll up his map, angry with himself for letting her watch him at work. Even though she knew why he was here, the less she knew the better off he would be. "I think you'd better go now," he said.

"I don't want to go just yet," she said. "I want to stay here with you."

His face hardened. "Why? So that you can go back to Heinrich and tell him what you have learned? I'm not like your American lieutenant. You will learn nothing from me."

Erika got up and sat on the table, one foot on the floor. "The first time I saw you," she said, "I knew everything that I needed to know."

He knew how she worked, knew what she wanted. Some women were not satisfied unless they had power over you. His eyes were dark and dangerous.

She touched the back of her hand to the stubble on his cheek. "You need a shave and a bath. Want me to shave you? Give you a bath?"

Robles grabbed her wrist and twisted her arm back so that she was forced off the table. He continued to twist, driving her to her knees in front of him. "What do you really want?" he said.

Her face gave no indication that she was in pain or that she was afraid of him. "You can hurt me if you want," she said. "Whatever you want is fine with me."

He released her. "I don't want anything."

She stood up, rubbing her wrist. "You are very strong," she said. "I like that." She began to loosen the buttons of her blouse.

"I said . . ." he began.

"I know what you said," she interrupted. "But I didn't believe you. And you don't, either." She dropped the blouse to the floor and unzipped her skirt. She stepped out of her skirt and said to him, "Aren't you going to get undressed? I have to be going soon."

He couldn't take his eyes from her. She was long-legged, and the muscles in her thighs rippled as she slipped off her underwear. Slowly, mesmerized by her, Robles unbuckled his belt.

Erika turned toward the bed. From there she watched as he continued to undress. He padded across the floor and climbed in beside her. For a moment they lay side by side, not speaking, barely touching, and then he rolled over on top of her.

"You are going to make history," she said as he entered her. "And I am going to help you. When the war is won, you and I will be famous."

Joined with her, he understood her for the first time. She would make herself a part of history in the only way that she knew. He rammed himself into her over and over.

CHAPTER 35

Lake Gatun, the 164-square-mile lake formed by the damming of the Chagres River, was the centerpiece of the Panama Canal. It could be said that the great lock mechanisms at either end of the canal, impressive as they were, served merely to lift ships to the eighty-five-foot elevation of the lake, where the bulk of the trans-Panama voyage took place. When the Gatun Dam was completed in 1913 and the waters of the newly formed Gatun Lake began to rise, an entire section of central Panama began to disappear. Small towns and villages in the interior of Panama, many of which had clustered around the original route of the Panama Railroad, simply vanished from the map. Other areas, landlocked for millennia, had found themselves reborn as the waters of the rapidly growing lake had created new lakefront communities.

Gamboa, a port town within the Panama Canal Zone at the southeast corner of Lake Gatun, was less than six miles from the narrow passage of the Culebra Cut. Twenty-five years earlier Gamboa had been a sleepy village in central Panama, its quiet existence relieved only by an occasional train on the Panama Railroad. Now Gamboa was a small but bustling shorefront community that catered to the growing export business facilitated by proximity to the canal.

In the early evening of December 2, Robles and two of Viega's men had traveled by small boat from Gamboa, down the Gamboa Reach, and into the Culebra Cut. Earlier in the day Robles had purchased the boat for what he was sure was an outrageous sum from a man whom Viega had recommended. The boat was small and old and in need of some renovation, but Robles could see that it was certainly serviceable enough for his purpose. To blow the Gatun Dam he needed something larger, but this boat would enable him to transport the explosives that he required for the job in the Culebra Cut. For this purpose he had acquired several topographic maps of the area showing in great detail the surface elevations of the three hills that dominated the narrow passage through the Culebra Cut. Although Gold Hill was the highest of the three, it did not take Robles long to decide that it was not the most advantageous target. Contractor's Hill was actually closer to the cut than either of the other two hills. In order to excavate the trench, the builders of the canal had cut away most of the base of Contractor's. This was, Robles realized, the main reason the slope was so unstable. It was as if someone were to remove two corners from the wide base of an Egyptian pyramid. The sheer weight of the material above the excavation would exert such an incredible downward force that the surface would inevitably begin to slide toward the base. And the sides of Contractor's Hill were much steeper than any pyramid.

Near the base of Contractor's the boat pulled over into the underbrush, where it was hidden from prying eyes aboard passing ships. They ran the boat aground and stepped out onto the marshy shoreline that was densely covered with trees and thick undergrowth. Both of Viega's men carried rifles in case they encountered any alligators, which were common to the area. Robles followed the men as they hacked their way through the heavy brush. Less than twenty feet from the edge of the canal they came upon the sheer face of the excavation at Contractor's Hill. The effect was of a wall of rock, forty feet high, that ran in both directions for as far as Robles could see in the rapidly fading light. The surface of the wall of rock was scarred by deep fissures that were filled with packed earth. Robles took his knife and dug into the dirt. He found that the depth of the fissures was at least as deep as his arm could reach. That was good. That was very good.

He could see immediately that there was no way to climb to the top of the wall so that he could inspect the slope of the hill. He and the two men tramped and hacked their way along the base of the wall for what seemed like more than a mile before they came to the far end of the excavation. Suddenly the perpendicular excavation came to an end, and Robles was standing next to a steep slope.

Immediately Robles began to climb. Before he had gone twenty feet he had disappeared into the thick growth, and the men who waited below could not tell how far he had gone. He soon found that he could not stand erect but had to go forward on all fours, his hands digging into the loose soil. He had not gone more than fifty feet when the steepness of the slope caused him to lose his footing and sent him sliding back. He caught himself and sent a small avalanche of dirt and rock sliding down. He dug in and tried again. This time he was able to hoist himself upward by grabbing the wiry brush that grew everywhere. He went higher until he found himself in a shallow hollow, probably the result of a minor dirt slide, that enabled him to stand erect and take his bearings. He looked out from beneath the covering trees and saw the Culebra Cut beneath his feet. He must have been seventy-five feet above the level of the canal. Across from him he could see the slope of Gold Hill that formed the opposite bank of the cut. These two hills—Contractor's and Gold—had been the principal source of the great earth slides that had plagued the builders of the Panama Canal.

He worked his way around the hollow and began to pull himself higher up the slope. He realized to his amazement that if anything the slope was becoming steeper. He was almost hoisting himself up an almost vertical cliff. If it had not been for the handholds afforded by the brush, he could never have maintained his position on the slope. The going was now very slow and he was afraid that if he lost his footing he would go tumbling all the way back down. He thought of the expressions on the faces of Viega's men when he plummeted out of the undergrowth to land at their feet. Another man might have smiled at the thought, but Robles was one who was not given to smiling.

Finally he was able to hoist himself onto another wide shelf that afforded him a place to rest. In front of him, about twenty-five feet from the edge of the shelf, was another near-perpendicular wall of earth and rock that was too steep to support anything other than scrub vegetation. This wall was at least fifty feet high and ran for as far as he could see along the side of the hill. He realized that he could go no farther. At first he thought that this wall was an attempt at terracing the face of the hill, but quick inspection of the surrounding ground eliminated that explanation. The sheer face of the section was, he realized, the result of an earlier massive slide. When the earth began to slide, it simply dug out huge portions of the hill, leaving the remnants even less stable than before.

One benefit of the slide, however, was that it had created the uneven but usable shelf, perhaps twenty-five feet wide running along the base of the wall, on which he now stood. Here he could find safe footing. Here he could find a place to do what had to be done. He was now more than a hundred feet above the canal, looking directly down into the cut. So steep was the slope beneath him that he almost felt that if he had had enough room to take a running start he could leap out and land in the canal.

The sheer face of the rest of Contractor's Hill loomed another four hundred feet above him. From the point where he now stood to the top of the hill, the slope was almost perpendicular—it was impossible to climb any higher without equipment. Robles looked up, bending backward to do so, and marveled at the precarious balance of the rock and dirt above him. It was a wonder that the cliff did not come tumbling down of its own accord.

He moved forward to inspect the texture of the cliff. Much of the face of the cliff was exposed rock that was deeply fissured. The fissures were filled with dirt. He scraped away some of the dirt and found that here, too, some of the cracks were wide and deep enough for him to thrust his entire arm inside. Robles smiled. He knew that he could pack these openings with explosives. Obviously the slope—if a near-vertical face can be called a slope—had achieved some precarious balance. It would not take much to upset that balance.

He had been worried that it would take massive amounts of explosives to bring down this mountain of dirt and rock, but now he knew that he had worried needlessly. What was required was a series of smaller explosions, precisely timed so that one would feed upon the other. He took a small notebook and a pencil from his shirt pocket and drew a quick sketch of the hill, marking the locations where he felt his charges would be most effective. The drawing was crude, but it would suffice until he could make a more exact plan. The first charges would be placed at the base of the lower wall—down where Viega's men waited for him. He would have Viega's men tunnel into the surface of the lower wall—removing the dirt from the rock fissures would be all that was necessary—at intervals of approximately fifty feet, and he would place his first charges there. The second row of tunnels would be at approximately the seventy-five-foot mark, and the third would be where he now sat, at the base of the second wall one hundred feet above the canal. He would blow the charges in sequence, the lowest, first, to undermine the lower part of the hill. Just as that section started to move, he would blow the second, and then perhaps two seconds later he would detonate the third series of charges. By systematically removing the lateral support, the slope would be unable to contain its own enormous weight. The sides of the hill would first buckle inward, and then, like a building with a collapsing foundation, the entire top three quarters of the hill would come avalanching down into the Culebra Cut.

He looked at his crude sketch with satisfaction and put the notebook back into his pocket. It was relatively simple, he thought. Any slope of this extreme degree is under constant pressure from the forces of gravity. Any simple mishap will encourage the slope to equalize that pressure. He would simply give nature a hand.

He went back to the edge and again looked down into the cut. He knew now, beyond a shadow of a doubt, that he could fill that narrow trench with a million tons of rock, rubble, and mud. He lowered his feet over the edge of the shelf, dug his heels into the dirt, and began, sliding on his backside, to make his way back down the hill.

CHAPTER 36

The sounds of the night rain were everywhere, hammering on the rooftops, bouncing from the sidewalks. It poured in great rivulets down narrow streets, turning roads into impassable rivers in a tumultuous torrent of water. Robles listened to the sound of the rain as he lay in his bed. This, he thought, was what had almost doomed the construction of the Panama Canal. Torrential rains that took solid ground and turned it into a shifting, sliding, dangerous mass of moving earth. Ironically, the rain was what had made the operation of the canal possible. The tropical rains that drenched Panama for nine months of the year provided the massive amounts of water required to raise and lower each ship that passed through the waterway. Fifty-four million gallons of fresh water were required for each and every passage. This, he knew, was the strength and, at the same time, the weakness of the canal. He would use this weakness to destroy it.

The rain did little to relieve the oppressive heat, and Robles lay inert, watching the shadow of the swirling ceiling fan above his head. He heard the car door slam outside, over

286

the noise of the rain, and instantly he was on his feet, pistol in hand. He went to the window and looked down into the street. Below he saw three figures, raincoats held over heads, dashing to the door of his building. He pulled back the slide of the pistol, chambering the first shell.

He heard them lumber up the stairs, cursing the rain, and knew that there was nothing to worry about. Men bent on destruction did not make such noise. He tucked the pistol into his belt and waited for them to arrive.

The pounding on the door was loud and arrogant as if they assumed some authority over the occupant of the rooms within.

At the first pause in the banging, Robles said, "Who is it?"

"Viega sent us," said a voice.

Robles opened the door, and the three men stepped inside. The rain dripped from their coats onto the hard, bare floor. All three glared at Robles through squinting eyes. The first man—the obvious leader—was short and beefy with a pockmarked face and dark, suspicious eyes. The others stood behind him as if for protection. He was the one to be concerned with, Robles thought.

"Viega wants to see you right away," the leader said. "Get your coat."

"I don't think so," Robles said.

"What's that?"

"I don't want to get wet," Robles said. "Tell him I'll come along later."

An asymmetrical smile split the man's face, and he turned to his companions. "He doesn't want to get wet," he said. He spun around, aiming a beefy fist at Robles's jaw, but his intended target was far too quick for him.

Robles blocked the punch, grabbed the man's arm at the wrist, and then drove his open palm into the exposed elbow. There was a sucking sound at the point of dislocation, and the man screamed. He dropped to his knees, the arm dangling uselessly beside him. By then Robles had his pistol in his hand, aiming at the other two, who had not moved a muscle since the beginning of the fleeting confrontation.

"Help him up," Robles said, "and get him out of here."

As the three struggled to the door, Robles said, "Tell Viega I will be there later this evening."

The three men were in too much of a hurry to respond. Robles heard them bumping their way down the stairs while the man with the dislocated elbow gave an occasional short scream and cursed at them to be careful.

Narciso Viega pounded a fist on his desk. "Who the hell does this bastard think he is?" He turned his fury on his messengers. "Incompetents!" he screamed. "Get out of my sight!"

When they had gone, he sat back and tried to compose himself. He lit a cigar and puffed deeply, allowing the thick, acrid smoke to fill his lungs. After a while his pulse returned to normal, and he was able to think clearly. He reached into his desk drawer and removed a small stack of fifty-dollar bills that he had acquired from Robles as partial payment for the explosives and for his men. He examined the bills carefully for what must have been the hundredth time that evening. They looked perfect, felt perfect. He compared them to a bill he knew to be genuine and could detect no difference. Perhaps he was mistaken. It was still possible that he had judged Robles too quickly. But why then had the bastard refused to come to him? If the bastard really had tricked him, he would see to it that Robles suffered before he had him killed.

There was a soft knock at the door and a head appeared cautiously. "He's here."

"Who?"

"Robles."

"Show him in."

Robles was led into the room, a man on either side.

"I'm sure," Viega said, "that you would not mind if my men searched you for weapons."

Robles shrugged and raised his arms. "I am unarmed."

One of the men frisked Robles and nodded to Viega that he was indeed weaponless.

"Sit," Viega said, waving his visitor into a chair. He took

the cigar from his mouth and blew foul smoke toward Robles. "If you try to leave without my permission, my men will kill you."

"Why would I want to leave?" Robles said. "And why would you want to kill me?"

"Why does any man want to kill another man?" Viega said. "Either for women or for money." Viega tapped his fingers on the stack of bills. "I'm getting too old to be worrying about women."

"Then, I assume that this is about money."

"You're damn right it's about money."

"I thought we had agreed on a price for your merchandise and your help. I don't know that I want to renegotiate the terms of the deal at this point."

Viega chuckled. "You've got guts. I'll give you that. At one word from me, my men will take you outside and let you look at your own intestines." He puffed on his cigar. "It takes a long time to die like that. I think I would enjoy watching."

"Maybe you'd better tell me what is going on," Robles said.

Viega pushed the money closer to Robles. "This is what is going on." he said, watching Robles' face carefully for any reaction. There was none. "I have been hearing many rumors lately. Rumors that disturb me a great deal. Rumors about German money."

"I don't understand."

"Let me help you," Viega said. "For many months now, it has been common knowledge that the Germans in South America had run out of money and that the British had made it next to impossible for them to get more." He stubbed out his cigar in a vicious gesture as if he were burning the faces of those who would dare do such a thing. "People had to be paid with promises. Then, recently, money was suddenly available again, and all debts were paid and new ventures begun."

"Doesn't sound like much of a problem to me," Robles said.

"All of the debts were paid with crisp, new fifty-dollar bills," Viega said. He picked up one of his bills. "Like these that you gave to me."

"And?"

"There are rumors that the money is not real, my friend. There are whispers that it is counterfeit. Apparently, after a few days or weeks it changes colors."

Robles grabbed the money on the table. "This is real," he said. "Look at it."

"It looks real," Viega said, "but how can I be sure? How do I know I can trust you?"

"Do you think I would come here—unarmed—knowing that I had given you counterfeit money?"

"Who knows? I told you, you've got guts."

Robles inspected the money carefully while Viega watched him. "This money is real," Robles said. "It's too perfect to be fake."

"So," Viega said sarcastically, "I am to believe that your fifty-dollar bills are real, but the others are fake?"

Robles placed the money back on the table. "I don't know about the other money," he said, "but this money is real."

"I was told that someone tried to steal the money in Colón."

Robles was not surprised. Viega's sources were usually impeccable. "That's right," he said.

"Perhaps they did steal the money, and you and your friends decided to replace it with counterfeit?"

"I got out with my share intact. And so did the others. I'm positive of that." Robles thumped a fist on Viega's desk. "I killed one of the bastards who tried to get the money. The rest ran like scared rabbits."

"Garcia," Viega said softly.

"What?"

"Ernesto Garcia. He's the one you killed. If he was involved, then it's certain that Harry Fox was involved, too. I should have known."

"Who is Harry Fox?"

290

"An American here in Panama." Viega laughed, a sudden violent explosion of mirth.

"What is it?"

"Fox has got the money."

"What are you talking about?"

"They tried to get it in Colón, but you were too smart for them. You killed Garcia and got away with your share."

"And?"

"Fox somehow got the rest and switched it for counterfeit. That's why your money is good and the rest is bad."

"That's impossible," Robles said. "I don't believe it."

"How much money was there?" Viega asked.

Robles pictured the suitcases. "I'm not sure," he said. "Two, perhaps three or four million."

Viega's eyes lit up. "Let me tell you about Fox," he said. "The reason that he came to Panama is that some years ago he swindled some American businessmen out of a great deal of money."

Robles did not see any connection. His face was blank.

Viega's face broke into a smile. "He paid them off using counterfeit money and got out of the country before anyone found out."

Robles's face did not change expression, but it was suddenly clear to him that this could have happened. If he had not been there in Colón, all of the money would have been stolen. Those two incompetent fools who had been assigned to guard the money had obviously lost it somehow. Someone had known about the money, and this Fox— whoever he was—had been sent to steal it. Replacing it with counterfeit was a touch of genius. No one would suspect that the money had been taken until it was too late. He nodded to Viega. "What you've said makes a great deal of sense."

"At least I know that your money is legitimate," Viega said. He smiled, knowing that later he would have the money checked for authenticity. "Now we can be friends again."

"And if it had not been legitimate?"

Viega's face was sad. "My men have already been instructed to kill you on the way out."

"Perhaps you would be good enough to tell them that that will no longer be necessary."

Viega roared with laughter. "You've got guts, amigo." He called out in a loud voice, and almost immediately the door opened. Viega said to the man who stood in the doorway, "Our friend will be going back to his hotel. See that he arrives there safely."

"If you don't mind," Robles said, "I'd prefer to get back to the hotel on my own."

Viega was a prudent man, and he admired the same quality in others. "As you wish, amigo."

Robles nodded and was gone.

Viega sat for a while, puffing on his cigar. As soon as possible, he thought, he would have the money that Robles had given him checked by experts. But that had suddenly become a minor matter. If the Germans had been foolish enough to lose this much money, there were now much more important considerations. He couldn't be certain that Fox had the German money, but he would find out and make sure that he got his fair share. As always, Viega's fair share was one hundred percent.

Things were going rather well, Viega thought. Since Arias had been forced into exile and he himself had been removed from office, he had managed to maintain a certain amount of authority. He still had men who were loyal to him, and there were many in Panama who looked upon him as the leader of the opposition to the puppet government that had been put in power by the Americans. He would bide his time until the Americans were forced out and President Arias made his triumphant return. In the meantime, there were certain things that he could do to make the wait worthwhile. He would help Robles with this business at the canal in the hope that it would hasten the departure of the Americans. Then there was the matter of Fox and the German money. If Fox did indeed have the money, he would take it from him. He would assign his son Antonio to keep an eye on Harry

Fox and the Panama Club. Viega smiled. He had finally found a job for which his son was amply qualified. Soon Antonio would be the proprietor of the most successful club in Panama City, and he, Narciso Viega, would be in possession of a very large sum of American money.

CHAPTER 37

Alois von Schleicher, special assistant to the German ambassador to Argentina, was dictating a letter to his secretary when his desk telephone rang. He and his secretary, a young German named Werner Ott who was on his first diplomatic assignment, looked expectantly at each other, wondering who should answer the telephone. Von Schleicher raised an eyebrow, and Ott quickly picked up the phone.

Ott listened for a moment, his face showing some distress, then, placing a hand over the mouthpiece, he turned to von Schleicher. "Herr Hoffmann demands an immediate audience," he said in a loud whisper.

Von Schleicher was the ranking Abwehr officer in South America and a member of the German aristocracy, but he was rapidly growing accustomed to the increasing frequency of the demands of Gestapo officers such as Friedrich Hoffmann. He did his best to stifle a sigh of resignation and said, "Then, by all means, show the Oberführer in."

Ott went to the door, opened it, and Friedrich Hoffmann stomped into von Schleicher's office. He jerked a thumb at the door and spoke to Ott without looking at him. "Wait outside."

As Ott moved toward the door, von Schleicher stood. "Just a moment, Werner," he said.

Ott stopped and turned expectantly to face his superior. Von Schleicher said nothing. He merely stood behind his desk smiling at Hoffmann. Ott looked from one to the other, his discomfort growing with the silence until, finally, having made his point, von Schleicher said, "You may go now, Werner."

Ott bolted from the room and closed the door behind him.

"Please, be seated," von Schleicher said, and Hoffmann approached the chair in front of the desk. Von Schleicher remained standing, not as a show of respect but as an act of domination. At six feet three inches, he towered over the diminutive Hoffmann. Where, he wondered, does the Geheime Staatspolizei find such disagreeable little men? He smiled. "How may I be of assistance, Freddi?"

Hoffmann bristled. He knew that von Schleicher was, as usual, being deliberately disrespectful. He almost smiled, knowing that soon he would wipe the smile from the face of this aristocratic fool. "It's about the American money," Hoffmann said.

Von Schleicher gave an impatient snort. "Again?" Ever since the American money had been delivered to the Abwehr, Hoffmann had been beside himself with jealousy, and von Schleicher had found himself explaining over and over again that the money had been assigned to the Abwehr —and not to the Gestapo—by personal order of the Führer.

"My dear Hoffmann," von Schleicher went on, "I find this persistence on your part extremely distasteful. I understand that the Gestapo has financial problems in this theater of operations, but I'm afraid that is not my concern. When our financial fortunes were at a low point, the Abwehr did not turn to the Gestapo for assistance. Nor do I recall that you offered any."

Hoffmann started to speak, but von Schleicher interrupted him. "I have promised you and your department a full accounting of all monies spent and operations undertaken. Although I feel that this accounting is an unwarranted intrusion into the affairs of a sister agency, I have agreed to provide this information as a display of respect and cooperation between us."

Again Hoffmann tried to speak, but von Schleicher silenced him with a wave of his hand. "I have already provided you with information about projected operations against the British outpost in the Falklands. The saboteurs are highly trained members of the Argentinian armed forces, and we have the support of the Argentinian government, who are as anxious as we to remove the British presence from the area. It should be quite clear to you that if we can destroy the oil-storage facilities in the Falklands, the Royal Navy will be unable to operate in the South Atlantic."

Hoffmann nodded and settled back into his chair. Once von Schleicher got going, there was no stopping him.

"Our real target in this area, however, will be the Americans. When war comes to this hemisphere, it will be the Americans who pose the greatest threat to our interests. When that happens, they will be surprised at our level of preparedness. We have already made contact with a group of dissident Cubans who—at our signal—are prepared to mount a series of attacks upon the American naval base in Cuba. There are Mexicans who are prepared to infiltrate the American borders and perform acts of sabotage throughout the American Southwest. Prime targets will be bridges, dams, and the rail network throughout the area, as well as the port facilities on the Gulf Coast."

"I am well aware of your agency's wonderful work in this area," Hoffmann said. "Just as I am aware of your careful infiltration of the pro-German clubs here in Argentina and in Uruguay." He paused dramatically. "These are very expensive undertakings."

Von Schleicher smiled. "As you are aware, the Füher has seen fit to provide us with ample funds."

Hoffmann reached into his inside jacket pocket. "Exactly," he said. "And the reason for my visit." He withdrew an envelope from his pocket and placed it on the desk in front of von Schleicher. "Yesterday, one of your paid informants registered a complaint with one of my men."

"Complaint?"

Hoffmann ignored the question. "Of course, I thought nothing of it until this morning when I received a call from Señor Humberto of the Banco de la Nación."

"Pedro Humberto?"

"He seemed quite distraught. Apparently, he is the bank officer who has been assisting you in exchanging American currency to that of several Latin American countries. I assume that he—and perhaps you—have been making a small profit on the rate of exchange."

"Now see here, Hoffmann! If you think you can come in here and accuse me of some ridiculous charge—"

"Forgive me, von Schleicher. It is not my intent to embarrass you over such a trivial matter."

"Then, what is it? Why are you here?"

Hoffmann opened the envelope and removed two fifty-dollar bills. "Humberto sent these over just a few moments ago."

Von Schleicher snatched the bills out of Hoffmann's hand. "What is it?" he said, almost desperately. "What's wrong?"

Hoffmann was smiling broadly now. Von Schleicher knew that he was in trouble, and Hoffmann was determined to enjoy it to the fullest. "The first thing was something about the color," he said. He watched gleefully as von Schleicher stared at the bills. "It seems that a sharp-eyed clerk at the bank noticed that the color was not quite right."

"There's nothing wrong with these bills," von Schleicher said.

"Apparently, there is a suspicious tint of blue to the usual green color of the American money."

"It looks fine to me," von Schleicher said, wiping a small accumulation of sweat from his brow.

"Señor Humberto thought that it looked fine, also. But just as a precaution he had one of the clerks check the money that you had exchanged at the bank." He stared at von Schleicher. His smile had been replaced by his official Gestapo stone face.

Von Schleicher was almost whining now. "And?"

"Look at the serial numbers."

Von Schleicher looked. His eyes widened and his heart sank. The numbers were the same. The bills trembled in his hands. "I don't understand . . ."

"Of the more than one thousand bills you exchanged at the Banco de la Nación, twelve of them were duplicates. The money is counterfeit. According to the bank, there is a chemical process taking place that is changing the color of the paper."

"Oh, my God."

Hoffmann smiled again. "I am sorry to be the one to tell you this," he said insincerely.

"This is not my fault," von Schleicher said. "You can see that, can't you? Someone else is responsible."

"Who?"

Von Schleicher's eyes rolled wildly. "Those two idiots who delivered the money. It's their fault. It must be."

Hoffmann got out of his chair and went to the door. "Someone will pay for this, my friend. I only hope that it isn't you."

Von Schleicher buried his face in his hands. His career was ruined. The Abwehr network in South America was ruined. The news about this money would spread like wildfire. No one would do business with him or his agency. He was finished. He would be recalled to Germany soon. If he was lucky, he would be given an assignment on the Eastern Front. If he was not, he would be shot. His shock was gradually replaced by a growing anger. He would not suffer this alone. He flicked the switch on his intercom, and when Ott answered he said, "Find Greiser and Blaskowitz and tell them to come to my office immediately."

CHAPTER 38

Antonio Viega walked into the Panama Club, his two bodyguards by his side. He paused at the entrance and looked around with the haughty demeanor of one who was supremely confident of all he surveyed. He liked what he saw: the bar was busy as usual, the casino was filled with wealthy gamblers, and there was a buzz of expectant conversation from those who had come to see the floor show. Antonio briefly imagined what it would be like when all of this was his. He could not help but smile at the thought.

Roberto Garcia greeted Viega warmly and led him to what had lately become Antonio's regular table. Since his meeting with Victoria, Antonio had returned to the Panama Club every night to take in the last show of the evening. His father had instructed him to take an interest in the club and in Roberto Garcia, and to find out everything that he could about Harry Fox and the operation of the Panama Club. It was an assignment that young Antonio welcomed. It gave him an opportunity to continue his pursuit of Victoria Gansell, whose polite refusal of his invitations had worked him into an amorous frenzy.

Usually Antonio saw something that he liked and he took it. He was used to getting his way—particularly with women—but Victoria Gansell brushed aside his advances with an infuriatingly enigmatic smile. Rarely had he met a woman who seemed so unwilling to cooperate, but he was arrogant enough to assume that one day soon he would get what he wanted. He knew that Victoria was Harry Fox's woman, but that merely made her more desirable.

Antonio knew that his father planned to eliminate Harry Fox, take his money, and take over his club. Antonio wanted to take his woman, but he wanted her while Harry was still around.

"Maybe we should go someplace and have a talk," Antonio said when Roberto joined him at his table.

"Sure," Roberto said. "Let's go to my office."

They went into the office that had been Ernesto Garcia's and had lately been taken over by his son. It was rather plain, with a desk, several chairs, and a few filing cabinets. There were no windows and the walls were badly in need of a fresh coat of paint.

Antonio looked around and twitched his nose as if he had detected a foul odor. He was always ready to taunt Roberto. "I'll bet," he said, "the yanqui's office doesn't look like this."

"No," Roberto admitted. "It doesn't."

"You should be upstairs in the big fancy office," Antonio said. "Not the gringo."

"Is that what you wanted to talk about?"

"Among other things."

"I thought you might have news about the man who murdered my father," Roberto said.

Antonio sat behind the desk in Roberto's seat and put his feet up on the desk. "The man you are looking for is still in Panama," he said casually.

Roberto was instantly alert. "Where?"

"Don't worry, we will find him. My father has men looking for him now."

"I want to know who he is."

"All in good time, amigo. First we should talk about your future and the future of this club."

Roberto frowned. "I'm not sure I follow you."

"Fox says that you are his partner, but look at this office." Antonio looked around the room shaking his head. "Why should the best club in Panama City be owned by a *norteamericano?* This place should be yours, Roberto. You could be a big man in this town."

Roberto was wary. "I agree with you," he said, "but how?"

"I'd say that the best way would be to buy Fox out. But . . . there is a rumor going around that Fox has recently come into a lot of money." Antonio waited for some confirmation of this, but when Roberto said nothing, he went on. "If that's true, it might take some other method of persuasion to get him to give up this place." He smiled. "My father might be willing to talk with him."

"Why would you do this for me? What's in it for you?"

"When we get rid of Fox, we will share the profits. You and me together, amigo. Partners in this place. Fifty-fifty."

"Harry would never give this place up."

"Everybody has his price. What is it the yanquis say"— Antonio smiled wickedly—"you can't take it with you?"

"I'd like to own this place," Roberto said, "but I don't want anyone to get killed."

"Whatever you say, Roberto. I'm sure Fox can be persuaded that it's time for him to look for a healthier climate."

Roberto thought for a moment. "Fifty-fifty?"

"Fifty-fifty. Except for one thing. I want Vicky all to myself."

"And I get the name of the man who killed my father?"

Antonio stood and offered his hand. "Whatever you say, partner."

Harry Fox sipped his drink and then spoke to Vicky, who watched at the window. "They still in there?"

"Yes."

Harry inspected his drink as if expecting to find things

floating in the glass. "They sure have a lot to talk about, don't they?"

Vicky left the window and sat across from him. "I thought you said you talked with Roberto. I thought things were okay."

Harry shrugged. "I did talk with him. I thought everything was okay. He say anything to you?"

"Not really. He's friendly, but distant."

"The Viegas worry me," Harry said. "With Ernesto gone, they think they can get to me through his son."

"Roberto would never go for that."

"I used to think so," Harry said. "But now I'm not so sure."

"Roberto would never go over to the Viegas."

Harry nodded. "The Viegas are in this up to their dirty necks." He stood and moved out from behind his desk. "I think it's time to press the issue."

Vicky moved between Harry and the door. "What are you going to do?"

"Just ask Antonio what he's after."

"Just like that," Vicky said. "And he's going to tell you?"

"Maybe I can be a little more persuasive than that."

"A fight between you and Antonio—and those goons he travels with—won't accomplish anything."

Harry clenched his fists. "I've got to do something. The Viegas are linked to the man who killed Ernesto. I've got to get to him through them."

"And you think that provoking Antonio will accomplish that?"

"No, but it'll make me feel a helluva lot better."

"What about this Dominguez character? Wasn't he supposed to get back to you?"

"I think he's stalling me. He called yesterday and said that I should meet with him on Saturday." Harry shook his head disgustedly. "I don't think he knows anything."

"Maybe it's time for me to talk to Antonio."

"I want you to stay out of this," Harry said.

"He likes to brag," Vicky said. "And he wants to impress

me with what a big shot he is. Maybe he'll tell me what we want to know."

"Forget it," Harry said. "It's too dangerous."

"It's too dangerous not to," Vicky said. "I can handle him, Harry—no problem."

Harry was silent for a moment. He stared at her, but her eyes did not waver. "You don't understand people like the Viegas," he said. "They're not like anyone you have ever known. They kill people who get in their way. I've already risked your life once," he said softly. "I don't want to do that again."

"This will be different, Harry. I'll be right here. You can watch over me every minute."

"That won't work. Antonio won't be satisfied just talking. He'll want you to leave with him," Harry said.

"I won't leave. I'll tell him I can't."

"Guys like Antonio aren't easy to discourage," Harry said. "Besides, there is something that we haven't considered. The Viegas might try to get to me through you." He opened a desk drawer and took out the walnut case. He placed it on his desk and opened it. "Ever carry a gun?" he asked.

"No," she said, alarm beginning to spread across her face.

He opened the hardwood case and took out the derringer. "Very small . . . light . . . fits in the palm of your hand." He held it out to her. "It'll fit easily into your purse. No one will even know you're carrying it."

Vicky recoiled from it. "I don't want that," she said. "I don't need that."

"Might come in handy." Harry held up a small key. "I keep the key to the case right here in my desk. If you ever feel the need . . ."

"If I need a gun to protect myself from a little weasel like Antonio Viega," Vicky said, "then I might just as well give up and go back home."

Harry put the derringer back into the case. "That might not be a bad idea," he said. "It might be safer if you went back home until this whole thing blows over."

She reached out and touched his hand. "You're not going to get rid of me that easy."

Harry put his other hand over hers. "I have a feeling," he said, "that things are going to get very bad. Very soon."

After her show Vicky went to Antonio Viega's table. "Buy me a drink," she said.

Viega was full of himself. Here he was with the most beautiful woman in Panama—an American—and he imagined that he was the envy of everyone at the Panama Club. He snapped his fingers arrogantly and a waiter appeared almost immediately.

"Planter's punch," Vicky said.

Viega took a good look at her. The dress that she wore for her show was skin-tight and cut low in front. He licked his lips hungrily. He had never seen such a woman. Perhaps tonight would be his lucky night.

The waiter arrived with her drink, and Vicky took a long swallow and set the glass down on the table. She smiled at Viega. "Did you like the show tonight?"

"It was wonderful," he said truthfully. Antonio leaned forward. "Some friends of mine are having a celebration tonight. Lots of important people will be there. I was hoping that you might like to come with me."

"I don't think Harry would like that."

Viega shrugged. "Don't let him bother you. He's only a minor distraction."

Vicky shook her head. "You don't know him like I do," she said. "He is a very dangerous man."

Viega scoffed. "He's nothing to worry about."

Vicky looked down at the table and spoke in a very small voice, "Not for you, maybe. But if he ever found out that I was with you, I'd be in a lot of trouble."

Viega's face hardened as if the mere thought were an affront to his manhood. "Leave him," he said. "He wouldn't dare touch you if you were with me."

Vicky was silent for a moment as if she were considering Viega's offer. "I enjoy working here at the club," she said.

"It's what I want to do. This tension between you and Harry is making everything very difficult."

Antonio sensed that things were finally going his way. "Don't worry about Fox," he said. "Take a week or two off. Relax . . . enjoy yourself. Soon enough things will be back to normal."

"I don't understand."

Viega looked around and then leaned even closer. "In a very short time—a week or two—you'll be able to go back to work at the Panama Club without having to worry about Fox."

Vicky seemed puzzled by his vagueness. "How?"

Antonio smiled. "I'm not at liberty to say, but Panama can be a very dangerous country. It is always possible that Fox will soon be persuaded that the climate here in Panama is not good for his health."

Vicky allowed the recognition to spread slowly across her face. "You mean there might be new management at the Panama Club?"

"There is always that possibility."

Vicky smiled as if that prospect pleased her. "And let me guess—you might be part of that new management."

Antonio was encouraged by her attitude. "Very definitely," he said. He grinned lecherously. "How would you like to have me as your boss?"

Vicky ignored the question. "But what about Roberto?"

"We would keep him around," Viega said with a shrug, then added, "For a while anyway."

"When does all this happen?"

"Who knows?" Viega said smiling. "Things happen unexpectedly."

Suddenly Vicky's eyes widened, and she sat bolt upright in her seat.

"What is it?" Antonio asked.

"Harry is on his way over here."

Viega looked up to see Harry Fox approach their table. Antonio smiled insolently. He was going to enjoy this. "Well, Harry," he said, "would you like to join us?"

Harry Fox did not even look at him. He was glaring at Victoria. "Getting a little too friendly with the customers, don't you think?"

Victoria moved slightly in her seat, instinctively distancing herself from both of them. "Just having a drink, Harry. It's no big deal."

"Go up to my office," Harry said, his face expressionless, but his voice menacing. "I'll talk to you later."

Vicky started to rise, but Antonio grabbed her by the arm and pulled her back down onto her seat. "Perhaps the lady would prefer to be with me, Harry. Why don't you just go about taking care of your business—while you're still able to," he added mischievously.

Harry turned to Antonio as if noticing him for the first time. "What does that mean?"

Viega shrugged. "Just what I said. Maybe one day soon you will lose your desire to operate a place like this."

Harry turned back to Victoria. "I told you to go," he said, but Viega had a firm grip on her arm.

"Please," she whispered to Viega. "Let me go. I don't want to make a scene."

Viega hesitated and then released her. "All right," he said. "But only because you ask me. Not because of him."

Vicky scampered away. She kept her head down until she got to the stairs, and then she looked back to see that Harry still hovered over Viega. Now there were two others—Viega's bodyguards—standing near the table. Harry had been right, she thought, about the Viegas' desire to take over the Panama Club. She wondered if he had known all along that they might try to kill him.

"What are you going to do, Harry?" Viega said. "My friends and I are wondering."

Harry eyed the bodyguards nervously. His own security people were beginning to gather, but he waved them back to their posts with a movement of his hand. "We don't need any trouble here," he said.

Viega laughed. "You've already got trouble, Harry. You just don't know how much." He lit a cigar, and Harry was reminded of how much this boy was like his father. Viega blew smoke at Harry. "Enjoy your place, Harry," he said. "Enjoy your woman . . . enjoy your money. But remember that I am going to take it all away from you. If you were a wise man you would pack your things and run off like a thief in the night, thankful that you still had your life."

"Don't count on it," Harry said.

Viega rose from his seat. "I won't," he said. "A wise man knows when it is time to leave the gaming tables; a foolish man waits until he has lost everything." He smiled. "I think you are one of the foolish ones, Harry Fox."

Viega nodded to his men, and they made a small procession—one in front, one behind him—as they went to the door. It had been a very good night, Antonio thought; soon he would have Fox's woman, and shortly after that he would have everything else.

Harry watched until they had gone and then turned and headed to his office.

"He's gone?" Vicky asked when Harry entered the office.

"Good riddance," Harry said. "That kid makes my flesh crawl. I want you to stay away from him. I don't even want to think about—"

There was a light knock on the door, and they looked at each other. Vicky went to the door, opened it, and Roberto came in. The young man shuffled his feet nervously as if he were embarrassed to be here.

"What can I do for you, Roberto?" Harry asked.

"I came to tell you to be careful, Harry."

Harry looked at Vicky. "Careful of what?"

"The Viegas," Roberto said. "They want to take over the club. I don't think they would hesitate to kill you to get it."

"Doesn't surprise me."

"Antonio offered me fifty percent of this place."

"He'd have the other fifty percent?"

Roberto nodded.

"The Viegas don't give anybody fifty percent of anything,

Roberto. They'd keep you around long enough to take over here and then . . ."

Roberto nodded. "Don't worry, I know how they work," he said. "Another thing. He talked about a rumor that you had come into a lot of money lately."

Harry, puzzled, looked at Vicky. "Now, where the hell would he get that idea? Narciso knows about the German money, but why would he think that I've come into a lot of money?"

"He couldn't possibly know that the money was switched," Vicky said.

Harry thought for a moment. "Unless some of the counterfeit has started to show up."

"Antonio also wants Victoria," Roberto said.

"I think he's made that perfectly clear," Harry said. "I don't want her playing along with him. He's too unpredictable."

"I don't think she's in any danger while you're still around, Harry. He'll make a play for her, but he'll be very careful if he thinks you're looking out for her."

Victoria watched them. They were like two friends who had had something come between them and were struggling to get back to what they had been. "I'm glad you came to us, Roberto," she said. "I appreciate it."

Roberto flashed her a smile and looked tentatively at Harry.

"Your father was like a brother to me," Harry said. "I know how you feel about what happened, and I want you to know that I would give my right arm to have him back with us."

"I know that, Harry," Roberto said. "My father always told us that you were the best man he had ever met."

Harry seemed embarrassed by the sudden display of affection. He coughed once or twice. "The other night— when I said you were my partner—that's exactly what I meant. Your father and I had always agreed that someday the Panama Club would be yours. When my pardon comes through," he said, "I'll be leaving Panama—for good. I guess this place is going to be yours sooner than any of us had planned."

Roberto's eyes were moist. He started to speak a few times but could not.

"But before then," Harry said, "we are going to have to deal with the Viegas, or they'll be dogging your heels like the hyenas they are."

"Don't worry about me, Harry," Roberto said. "Right now it's you they're after."

Harry smiled. "I guess the climate in Panama is about to get even hotter than usual."

"For you, at least," Vicky said. "Antonio mentioned something about Panama being a very dangerous place."

"Have you heard anything at all from Dominguez?" Harry said to Roberto.

"Not a word. You?"

"One phone call. Nothing else. Could be a dead end. Maybe it's time that I met with Narciso."

"You think that's a good idea, Harry?" Roberto said, alarm spreading across his face.

"We're not getting anywhere. If we're ever going to find out who killed your father, we're going to have to take the initiative. Tell Antonio I want to negotiate. That'll catch Narciso's interest. He's always looking for the easy way out. He thinks that if I get scared enough, he can buy me out cheap."

Roberto was dubious. "You can't trust him, Harry."

"Tell him we'll meet someplace of my choosing. I'll tell him I want the name of the man who killed Ernesto as a prelude to any negotiations."

"It's too dangerous, Harry," Roberto said.

Harry Fox leaned back in his chair as if he had not heard. "I want to get this thing over with . . . soon. Tell Antonio I want to see Narciso."

Roberto looked to Vicky, hoping that she might protest, but she was silent. Roberto shook his head. "Whatever you say, Harry. Whatever you say."

When Roberto had gone, Victoria went to Harry and put

her arms around him. "I'm glad that you and Roberto are back together," she said. "And I'm glad that this place will be his."

"Ernesto and I had always agreed that the Panama Club would belong to Roberto." He shrugged. "It's the way it should be."

"I think I love you more right now than I ever did." Vicky said, kissing him. "I'd like to grow old with you, Harry Fox."

He returned her kiss and held onto her. "Let's hope that we get the chance."

CHAPTER 39

Under cover of darkness Robles led the men to the base of Contractor's Hill. There were six of them, including Robles, and each carried a long-handled shovel. Robles carried a long steel rod with a pointed end. Several of the men carried hooded flashlights, but there was enough light from a quarter moon so that the artificial lights were not necessary. Each man also carried twenty sticks of dynamite in a canvas sack around his neck. They moved as quietly as possible, but it was inevitable that in the dark, moving through the underbrush, they would make a considerable amount of noise. Robles was not concerned that someone might hear them. Although there was much activity by the Army Corps of Engineers during daylight hours, as soon as it was dark the construction crews reported back to their barracks. After dark parts of the canal were virtually undefended.

Robles had been told by Erika Schreiber that the Americans had bolstered the garrison at the canal by another three thousand men. There were now more than thirty-one thousand American troops in the Canal Zone. This number was in addition to the five thousand construction men who had been brought in by the Corps of Engineers. Most of these men, however, were engaged at both ends of the canal in a desperate effort to modernize the antiquated defensive systems at the locks. It was well documented that the Americans assumed that the canal was most vulnerable to a coordinated air strike at the locks, and this was where they anticipated that any attack would be directed. Robles had already seen the aircraft warning systems that had been installed near the Pacific and Atlantic entrances. He assumed that the systems had been copied from similar systems that the British had used against German air raids. Barrage balloons hung listlessly in the sky for the entire length of the canal, and the Gatun Dam and the three lock systems of the canal now bristled with antiaircraft guns. The gunnery crews were on round-the-clock alert. Similarly, the American soldiers were on constant alert for saboteurs at the locks. All ships were searched before transit, and what were called transit guards were stationed on all ships as they passed through the canal. Robles had also noted the presence of powerful motor torpedo boats patrolling the waters adjacent to the two entrances to the canal.

The Americans were obviously determined that no possible threat to the canal escaped their notice. Their attempts at defense were directed toward the sky or toward the ships that approached the canal. Most of their efforts were apparently intended to protect the fragile lock system. In an attempt to bolster those areas of the canal that were thought to be most vulnerable, the Americans had left the interior portions of the canal almost defenseless. What they did not know, Robles thought, was that the greatest threat to their sacred canal had already penetrated their belated attempts at defense.

At the base of the hill his men unslung their satchels and awaited his orders. Robles drove a stake into the dirt that filled the crevices between the rocks about three feet above the base of the hill and indicated to the first man that this was where he should begin to dig. A few inches below the surface the dirt was compacted like clay. This was all that kept it from collapse.

"Here," he said, pointing. "As deep as you can and this wide." He held his hands apart to show the measurement. When the first man started to dig, Robles paced off the distance to the next site. "Here," he said to the next man. Then he paced off the distance to the next location.

When all of the men were working and he could see that the digging was going well, Robles took the long steel bar he had brought with him and started to climb the face of the hill. He was able to use the rod to assist him in his climb, driving it into the ground to hold him in place as he moved upward. Finally he reached the spot where he had determined to put his second row of charges. On his last trip he had noticed that one of the previous slides had revealed the rock below the thick covering of dirt and vegetation. That rock was deeply fissured, and several of these cracks were wide enough for him to insert a stick of dynamite. Now he wanted to know how deep were these fissures.

He approached the exposed rock and felt along the surface until he found the rift he was looking for. Then he inserted the steel rod, which was six feet long, and about the same diameter as a stick of dynamite, into the crack. The rod slid all the way into the rock. He withdrew the rod and tried it at several other locations. At several of his test sites the rod did not penetrate more than a few feet, at some only inches, but there were enough deep locations for him to place an adequate number of charges. He was certain that he need only remove the surface dirt to reveal similarly fissured rock all along this part of the hill. He would return the next night, alone, and place his charges here in the fissures. With his charges placed deep into the surface rock, he felt confident that he could bring the entire structure rumbling down into the narrow waterway below.

He rubbed the clay from his hands. "Tomorrow," he whispered.

He made his way back down the hill and found that his men were still working at the holes. He peered at his luminous watch and knew that they would have to work harder if they were to dig as many holes as he wanted before dawn. He went to the first hole and drove the steel rod deep into the clay loosening the soil at the base of the hole. The man inserted the long-handled shovel and removed a shovelful. Robles drove the rod in again and then moved to the next hole. Soon he found himself, like a man possessed, moving from hole to hole driving the steel rod as deep as he could. The men seemed to take inspiration from his efforts, and soon the holes were as deep as they could be made.

Robles staked out another six locations and started the men back to work. While they worked on the new holes, he went to those already dug. He took the dynamite from the satchels and placed one charge next to each hole. Earlier that day he had taped five sticks together in a single charge. Now he inserted a detonator cap into the center and ran his wire to each stick. He slid the dynamite down into the hole, leaving enough wire so that it protruded from the end of the hole, and, with a shovel, began to refill the hole. He packed the dirt back into the hole, and when he was done felt for the protruding wire. Even in daylight this wire would be virtually invisible to someone standing only a few feet away. When he was finished he moved to the next hole and repeated the process until he had set his charges and refilled all of the holes that had been dug.

Before morning he would repeat this process twenty-four times in twenty-four separate holes. By first light, when traffic resumed in the canal and the soldiers had assumed their guard posts at various locations along the waterway, Robles and the men who had worked with him would be long gone.

CHAPTER 40

On Saturday evening, as Harry was preparing to leave for the Central Hotel for his meeting with Dominguez, there was a commotion down in the bar. Harry looked through the window and saw that his patrons were standing up and looking in the direction of the front door. The focus of their attention was just beyond Harry's view. Many of the women had their hands in front of their faces as if unwilling to look at whatever it was that had caused the disturbance.

Harry raced downstairs and was met by Roberto, who had obviously been on his way to get him. "What the hell's going on?" Harry said.

"A car dumped somebody at the front door," Roberto said. "He dragged himself inside the foyer."

Together they raced to the front door, and as soon as Harry saw the figure on the floor he knew that it was Rafael Dominguez. A small crowd had formed a semicircle around the man, who lay facedown on the floor.

Harry pushed his way inside the circle. He rolled the man over onto his back. The barely recognizable form on the floor was indeed Dominguez. He had been badly beaten and had obviously lost a lot of blood, but he was still alive.

"Anybody call an ambulance?" Harry said.

No one responded, but one of the doormen scurried off to the telephone.

"Don't worry, Rafael," Harry said. "The doctor will be here soon."

Dominguez's eyes fluttered briefly as he tried to talk. His nose was like raw meat, and his lips were split in several places. He coughed and blood poured from his mouth. Most of his teeth were gone. "Harry," he whispered.

Harry leaned closer. "What is it?"

"They told me to bring you a message," he groaned, his words barely comprehensible.

"What is it?"

Dominguez struggled to remain conscious. "I don't know," he said. "They wouldn't tell me. They just kept hitting me."

Harry knew who "they" were, and looking at Dominguez's shattered face, he knew what the message was, also. "Just take it easy," he said. "We'll have you at a hospital in no time."

"I'm sorry, Harry," he said through shattered lips. "I couldn't find out where the Argentinian is."

"That's okay. Don't worry about it."

"But his name is Robles."

Harry patted him on the shoulder. "Good work, Rafael."

"Can I still get the money?"

Harry almost laughed. Dominguez had been beaten to within an inch of his life, and he was still worrying about his money. "Sure," Harry said. "The money is yours."

"Hang on to it for me, Harry. I trust you." Dominguez closed his eyes and slipped into unconsciousness.

"It'll be right here waiting for you," Harry said, touching him on the shoulder.

An ambulance screeched to a stop at the door, and two uniformed attendants came rushing inside with a stretcher. Behind them, at a somewhat more leisurely pace, followed an older man in a dark suit. He was, obviously, the doctor.

While the attendants unfurled the stretcher, the doctor knelt next to Dominguez. He examined him roughly. A sharp moan from Dominguez did not change his manner. "What happened to him?" he asked Harry.

"He staggered in here like this," Harry said.

"This didn't happen here?"

"I don't allow this kind of thing at my club, Doctor. You may ask anyone here."

The doctor directed the attendants to move Dominguez onto the stretcher. As they lifted him, Dominguez seemed to drift back into consciousness. His eyes fluttered open, and he whispered, "Harry."

Harry bent closer.

Dominguez's tongue darted out between his shattered lips. The attempt was to moisten the blood-caked lips, but the effect was somehow reptilian. "Robles," he began, struggling with the words, "is buying lots of explosives."

The doctor motioned to the attendants, and they hustled Dominguez out to the ambulance. As they pulled away, siren howling, Harry went back inside. Most of his patrons had long since gone back to the bar or the gaming tables. "That's it," Harry said absently to the few who remained.

Harry made his way back to his office, ignoring the questions of a few inquisitive patrons. This beating, he knew, was a message to him to mind his own business. He thought of Robles, putting the name with the face of the man he had seen at the Washington Hotel in Colón the night that Ernesto Garcia had been killed. Viega's people were protecting this man. Why? Money was the obvious answer. Everything Viega did was for money. Robles worked for the Germans, was getting help from Viega, and was buying explosives. There was only one thing in Panama that was worth blowing up. The canal.

He quickened his step a little. He had to get in touch with Trump to let him know that that was why Robles was here in Panama. The Germans wanted to destroy the canal.

CHAPTER 41

At 2:26 P.M. on Sunday afternoon, the broadcast of the Giants-Dodgers football game was interrupted by the news that the Japanese had attacked the American naval base at Pearl Harbor in Hawaii. Most Americans had never heard of the place. Moments before the 3 P.M. broadcast of the New York Philharmonic concert, CBS reported the catastrophe to the rest of the nation.

In Washington the reaction was one of stunned amazement. The nation's capital seemed momentarily immobilized by the news that few had thought possible. Most of the nation's military commanders were enjoying the weekend, like almost everyone else in Washington, and absent from their posts.

In Annapolis, Maryland, Lieutenant-Commander Will Thorensen, who was at home, heard the news on the radio. He immediately changed into his uniform and began to prepare to leave for the Navy Building, where he knew his staff would be gathering. His wife, Louise, helped him pack an extra uniform because both knew that he might not be back for several days. Louise, a small, handsome woman, had worried excessively over the past several weeks about her husband's mental health and was now concerned that the confirmation of what he had feared most would push him over the edge. She was surprised to find, however, that the news had had an almost opposite effect. Thorensen was calmer than she had seen him in months. When she kissed him good-bye at the door, he held her a moment longer than usual and said, "Don't worry, Lou, we'll take care of those bastards."

Panama City

It was already past three o'clock in the afternoon in Panama when word began to spread rapidly that something catastrophic had happened in Hawaii. At first the residents of Panama City knew only that the streets of their city were swept instantly clear of the military personnel who were an almost constant presence. Army vehicles traveled the city, loudspeakers loudly blaring the message that all American military personnel were to report immediately to their respective bases. Soldiers and sailors, confusion and alarm on every face, grabbed every available means of transportation back to their posts. The scene was chaotic—servicemen rode ten to a taxi, some of them sitting on the outside clinging to doors, others standing on running boards. Buses were rerouted, passengers discharged, to take the Americans back to their bases inside the Canal Zone. Nothing was certain but the panic on the faces of the American soldiers.

The soldiers left behind them a flood of rumors—most of them ludicrous: the Germans had landed in Florida; the Japanese had landed in California. None of the rumors was as devastating as the truth. The Japanese, in one incredible strategic masterpiece, had almost completely destroyed the entire U.S. Pacific Fleet. Of the nine battleships at anchor that December morning, five had been sunk and the others mortally wounded. The balance of power in the Pacific had suddenly and irrevocably swung to the Japanese.

Although the citizens of Panama and the military personnel in the Canal Zone would not discover the true extent of the catastrophe until much later, it was not long before word of what had actually happened began to spread like wildfire around the zone and Panama City. In the zone the reaction was near panic. Rumors of an anticipated Japanese attack on the canal coupled with an invasion of Panama were everywhere. Someone in the Army Corps of Engineers gave the order to activate the smoke screens that had been devised to protect the locks at Gatun from air attack, and in just a few hours the entire area was covered with a thick, choking pall of smoke. This, of course, fueled further rumors that the canal would soon be under attack.

The Panamanians, who had no particular animosity toward the Japanese and assumed that the Japanese felt the same about them, took secret delight in the panic-stricken reaction of the Americans. For the first time they saw a hint of impotence in the American military. For the first time they saw the look of fear on the faces of the haughty *norteamericanos*. They saw the panic, despair, and helplessness, and knew that no matter how long it took, things in Panama would never be the same again.

Once the Americans had returned to the Canal Zone, a curious calm descended upon Panama City. The streets and shops were almost deserted. Commerce came to a virtual standstill, as everyone gathered around radios to listen to the latest news. The Japanese, it seemed, had not only dealt a mortal blow to the Americans in Hawaii, but had also attacked major American bases in the Philippines as well as those of the British in Hong Kong and Malaya. Secretly many Panamanians were exhilarated by the audacity of the Japanese and applauded the news of their victories. They were inspired by the fact that the Americans—and the British—had been revealed as the paper tigers they really were.

Carlos Robles also spent the next several hours in front of the radio. What he heard amazed, but at the same time dismayed, him. The Japanese attack thrilled him as much as it did the Panamanians, but he realized that it had made his job infinitely more difficult. The Americans would now redouble their security efforts in the canal. Yesterday he might have easily accomplished his goal. Today was a different story. Now it was doubly imperative that he stop the American fleet that was on its way to reinforce the fleet at Pearl Harbor. He'd have to move swifter before the Americans recovered from their initial, inevitable panic.

It was clear now that his task was part of a coordinated effort between Germany and Japan to eliminate the Americans as a major military force. He expected a German declaration of war against the United States at any moment. If, as the radio reports intimated, the Japanese had destroyed the Pacific Fleet and occupied the Philippines, the Americans were no longer a major power in the Pacific. If he could shut down the Panama Canal, the Americans would be helpless against the combined onslaught of Germany and Japan. His contribution, particularly if he trapped the Atlantic Fleet inside the canal, would be immeasurable.

He called Drexler, and the two agreed to meet at the Pier Balboa in an hour.

Drexler arrived looking nervous and tired. "It's incredible," he said. "I've been in contact with the German Embassy. They have been given instructions to destroy all classified materials no later than tomorrow."

"This means war," Robles said.

"Without a doubt." He looked at Robles with a sudden and all-encompassing respect. "I feel that the Führer is waiting only for your destruction of the canal before he declares war." Drexler stiffened and Robles thought that the German might salute him, but Drexler merely grasped him by the arm. "What you are about to accomplish will be heralded in the annals of German history for a thousand years." He made a brief, almost imperceptible, bow. "I salute you, and I envy you, and I offer you my unqualified support. Whatever you require, you need only ask."

Robles smiled at this reversal of sentiment. Drexler's cooperation had been reluctant, but now that glory was at hand, he wanted to be a part of the enterprise. "I may call upon you," Robles said, "to perform a vital service. One that entails considerable risk."

"I am ready to lay down my life," Drexler responded, "as is Brack."

The Germans, Robles thought, would be more reliable than the Panamanians. He had known that Brack would assist him, but Drexler's offer relieved him of a troubling uncertainty about how he was going to attack two points on the canal with only one man to help him. He did not want to rely on Viega or on any of his men. Now he did not have to. "I will contact you tonight," he said. "Be ready to move at a moment's notice."

Drexler grabbed his hand and shook it gratefully. "I will be ready," he said. "Duty is everything."

Robles watched Drexler walk away. By this time tomorrow Drexler would more than likely be dead.

BSC Agent Wilfred Smythe had left Miami at 10 A.M. on the morning of the seventh on the regularly scheduled Pan Am flight to Panama City. One hour out from Panama the captain had informed the passengers that the Japanese had attacked the naval base at Pearl Harbor. The other passengers fell into a stunned silence for the remainder of the flight, but it was all that Smythe could do to hide his elation. The Americans were in it now. The British were no longer alone. He felt as if a tremendous weight had been lifted from his shoulders.

As soon as his plane landed, Smythe headed for the American Embassy, where he had an appointment with Special Agent Trump. At the Embassy gates he was stopped by a suddenly cautious Marine guard who would not allow him entry until one of the Embassy staffers appeared, to verify his credentials. The situation inside the embassy was as close to panic as anything that Smythe had ever seen. Everyone seemed to be running around in circles with no apparent purpose, and it was several minutes before he was able to find someone to direct him to Trump's office.

When Trump's secretary announced that Smythe was in

the outer office, Trump came to the door. "What the hell do you want?"

"We had an appointment," Smythe said.

"Don't you know there's a war on?"

"Oh, yes, it's been on for more than two years."

Trump scowled. "What was it that you wanted?"

"I have a report to pass along to you about the counterfeit money situation."

"I can't be concerned with that now," Trump said. "There are other more important things going on."

Smythe nodded agreeably. "I understand, of course, and I will not take up any more of your time." He started to leave.

Trump suddenly relented. "Come in," he said. "But make it fast."

Smythe followed Trump inside his office. It was fairly large with a view of Balboa Avenue and Panama Bay. Papers were strewn everywhere as if someone had emptied every waste basket in the embassy on the floor.

Trump plopped himself into his chair behind the desk. "There's a report going around that a reconnaissance plane out of Albrook spotted a Jap invasion fleet three hundred miles out."

Smythe, who was more familiar with the nature of such sightings, said, "Probably a couple of fishing boats."

Trump looked at him sharply as if he were impugning the reliability of the American military. "I'm busy," he said. "Tell me what you came for and let me get on about my business."

"The reports are merely preliminary from one of our outposts in Argentina, but apparently some of the counterfeit money has started to show up. A German attempt to sabotage British oil-storage facilities on the Falklands was thwarted because the saboteurs were paid in counterfeit money. When they discovered the deception, they turned in the Germans to the local police. German Military Intelligence has been running a thriving spy ring out of the embassy in Buenos Aires. Argentinian government officials had ignored—and in some cases collaborated with—this German activity, but apparently some of these same officials were also paid with counterfeit and decided that the Germans had overstayed their welcome."

"That's great," Trump said. "I'm glad this whole thing has worked out for you, but I'm kind of busy."

"Apparently, an attempted attack on an American installation in Cuba was also prevented when——"

"Look," Trump interrupted, "the Japs are hitting American installations all over the Pacific. With real bombs, and planes, and troops. Not just a bunch of wetbacks running around with a few sticks of dynamite. The Panama Canal is a logical next target"—he pointed to his window and to the bay—"and there just might be a Jap invasion fleet over the horizon." He stood up. "So if you'll excuse me . . ."

Trump escorted Smythe to the door. "Look," he said, "why don't you call me in a day or two. When things calm down a bit, I might have more time."

In another minute Smythe was out on the street wondering what he should do next. He could think of nothing other than to visit Harry Fox.

Harry seemed about as happy to see Smythe as had Trump, and the Englishman was beginning to think that perhaps the whole trip had been one gigantic mistake. After all, the world situation had changed dramatically since he had left New York on Friday, and there were probably lots of things for which Stephenson needed him back at BSC headquarters at Rockefeller Center. It was doubtful, however, that he would be able to get any kind of flight out of Panama for at least several days. Smythe was familiar with the kind of panic that usually accompanied the news that the Americans had suffered through today, and knew that every American who did not have to remain in Panama would be battling to get out on the next available flight. He did not have to call the Pan Am terminal to know that bedlam would reign there today.

"I just thought you'd like to know," Smythe told Harry, after listing several of the operations that had been stymied because of the currency switch, "that your efforts have resulted in a considerable amount of trouble for the Germans."

Harry's expression barely changed.

Smythe went doggedly on. "And we expect to reap a considerable harvest of information in the very near future." He smiled pleasantly, hoping to alter Harry's dark mood. "It's very possible that this operation could result in the elimination of every German spy network in South and Central America."

Harry lit a cigarette without offering one to Smythe. "That's great," he said. "I'm glad for you."

It was clear to Smythe that Fox wasn't glad at all. He had to remind himself that the American's view of the Japanese attack was completely different from his. To the Americans the attack on Pearl Harbor had been a tremendous shock. The idea of a sneak attack, of beginning a war without notice to the enemy, ran counter to the American sense of decency and fair play. The British had suffered through two hard years of war, and their cherished sense of fair play had been put aside for the duration. As far as Smythe was concerned, this morning's attack had brought the Americans into the war and perhaps saved the British from defeat.

He tried another tack. "I also want you to know that my government will honor any and all commitments made to you."

"That's more than I can say for my own government."

Smythe smiled, happy to receive any kind of positive response. "As soon as I am authorized by my office, I will inform my embassy here to turn the money over to you."

"I won't hold my breath," Harry said.

Smythe ignored the cynicism. "Any luck with finding the man who killed your friend?"

"He's still in Panama," Harry said. "I'm sure of it. Some of his money—the real McCoy—has been showing up."

"If I can be of any help, let me know."

"I'll find him myself," Harry said. "You and Trump haven't been much help up to now."

"I've been back in New York and Washington," Smythe

said defensively. "Dealing with some very important matters."

Harry ignored his attempt at explanation. "I think he's here to sabotage the canal."

Smythe's eyes widened. "Why do you think that?"

Harry told Smythe about Dominguez.

"Did he tell you anything else?"

"Only that the man is Argentinian . . . and that his name is Robles."

The color drained from Smythe's face. "Are you sure that was the name," he said.

Harry nodded. "Why?"

"There is very real possibility," Smythe said, "that the man you are looking for is one of the most dangerous saboteurs in the world. We've been after him for some time."

"What makes you think he's the same one?"

"Last month an Argentinian who is suspected of working with the Germans passed through Bermuda. We should have detained him when we had the chance, but we couldn't be certain he was the man we wanted. Apparently, he murdered a young woman who worked for us in Bermuda, but that was not discovered until after he had been allowed to leave. We tried to find him, but we lost him when he got to the States." Smythe sighed. "Since then we have come to believe that he is the man responsible for some of the most incredible feats of sabotage of this—or any other—war. We only know that he was headed for South America somewhere. Perhaps he is here in Panama." He shook his head disbelievingly. "The name he used was Robles."

They stared at each other for a moment until Smythe said, "Have you told Trump what you have learned about this Robles?"

"I tried to contact him last night, and I've been calling all afternoon. He doesn't return my calls. Things are a little chaotic around here."

"Keep trying," Smythe said. "Trump has got to know." He was up and heading to the door. "I've got to get back to my embassy." He stopped at the door. "Don't do anything on your own. We want this man alive."

"I want him dead," Harry said.

Smythe was about to protest but thought better of it. "Talk to Trump first," he said. "I'll contact you as soon as I can."

Trump's voice came on the phone. "This had better be good," he said.

"I think the guy we're looking for is after the canal." Harry explained what he had heard from Dominguez and Smythe.

"We've got enough real problems to worry about," Trump said. "I don't think we have to worry too much about one man running around with some explosives. Right now the defense forces in the Canal Zone are on twenty-four-hour alert. The only way a saboteur could damage the canal would be to plant explosives at the locks, and security there is tighter than a drum. It's impossible to get near them."

"Smythe thought this could be serious."

"What the hell does he know."

"He seemed pretty concerned that—"

Trump cut him off. "I'll be sure to pass along your concerns to the military," he said and hung up.

Harry sat for a while, thinking. If Trump wasn't concerned, then maybe he shouldn't be, either. Anyway, his problem wasn't the Panama Canal. Let Trump worry about that. His problem was finding Robles before he left Panama.

Roberto Garcia came in. "Antonio Viega is downstairs. Says he wants to see you."

"You've told him I want to see his father?"

"Yes."

Harry nodded. "Let's go."

When Fox arrived at Viega's table, he saw Viega's bodyguards sitting on either side of him.

Viega grinned when Harry approached. "I understand you had a little problem here last night," he said.

"Nothing I can't handle," Harry said.

Viega laughed. "Sometimes little problems just keep getting bigger and bigger, and sometimes a man begins to lose everything he has—little by little. Sometimes he doesn't know when to give up and get out."

"Don't worry, son," Harry said as he sat down at the table, "I'll know when to get out."

"I hope so, Harry. Things are going to get real hot around here . . . for all of us. Looks like the Japanese are going to keep you yanquis busy for a while. Maybe," Viega said grinning, "you'll find out what it is like to have your country occupied by a foreign power."

Harry ignored him. "I want to meet with your father."

"When?"

"Right away. The sooner we get this thing settled the better."

"Tonight, then. I will speak to him. Come to our house at ten o'clock. He will be waiting for you."

Harry hesitated.

"You're not afraid to meet there, are you, Harry?" Antonio said.

"I'd rather he came here."

Antonio sighed in mock exasperation. "Was it not you who asked for this meeting? Besides, your friends will know where you are going. It would be rather foolish of us to try anything. Don't you think?"

Harry nodded. "I'll be there," he said.

CHAPTER 42

Panama Canal Zone; December 7, 6 P.M.

The heat inside the storage shed was like a living creature that wrapped itself around their bodies making it difficult for them to breathe. Ludwig Brack was stripped to the waist, sweat glistening on his chest, as he struggled with the oil drums that Robles had told him to move. Each of the drums had been loaded with more than one thousand pounds of high explosives, and Brack grunted and groaned with the strain of rolling the drums across the dirt floor. It would have been easier to use the winch on the truck, and he had suggested this to Robles, but the Argentinian had not wanted to start the truck until it was absolutely necessary.

"There may be American patrols on the lake," Robles had said.

The discussion ended there. Brack moved the heavy drums by hand and used an overhead pulley, slung across the roof timbers of the shed, to raise them to a standing position.

When Brack had finished moving the drums to where Robles wanted them, he watched Robles carefully while the latter inserted the detonators into the explosives that had been packed inside the fifty-gallon drums. "When I am finished," Robles said. "I want you to weld the drums shut."

"Weld?" Brack said fearfully. "Won't the flame ignite the explosive—or the detonators?"

Robles laughed. "Don't worry. Heat has no effect on the explosive, and the detonators are pressure-set. They will only ignite at the preset depth."

Brack remained unconvinced. Although he had been trained in several methods of murder, explosives were not a part of his training. To him explosives were an unknown quantity and something to be feared.

"Just do it," Robles said. "I will be right here with you. I have no intention of being blown to pieces. I have important work to do."

Brack mumbled something and went to the welder.

Darkness was already falling when Robles and Brack finished the work and winched the oil drums onto the bed of the truck. When all nine drums were in position and secured by cables, Robles opened the back doors of the shed, and together he and Brack began to roll the truck outside. Once outside, the natural slope of the land made the job easy, and Robles jumped in behind the wheel of the truck as it began to pick up speed. He applied the brakes and slowly backed down to the lake shore. Brack, dripping with sweat, followed on foot.

Robles climbed down from the truck just as Brack arrived. Both went to the water's edge and stepped on board the old tug that was partially hidden in the dense foliage that surrounded the lake. They peered out into the growing darkness. There was nothing except the sounds of the forest and the creatures of the lake.

"No patrols," Brack said softly. "The fools expect nothing."

Robles looked at Brack, but said nothing. He, too, had expected some kind of naval patrol on the lake after the attack on Pearl Harbor, but apparently the entire focus of the American defenses was directed outward. The rumors of a Japanese fleet were everywhere, and apparently the Americans viewed the threat seriously enough to disregard any potential internal threat.

"Okay," Robles said. "Let's start bringing the explosives aboard."

Brack was like an excited child. He ran to the truck and jumped inside the cab. The engine coughed once and started immediately. Brack listened to the soft hum of the motor and felt the satisfaction of knowing that he had done a good job refurbishing the ancient engine. In a moment he was back at the power winch on the truck bed, starting to unload the drums onto the boat.

Robles guided the drums onto the steel racks that Brack had made and fitted to the bow section of the tug. There were three of these racks, only inches above the deck, and placed like tracks aimed at the bow. The drums lay on their sides so that they could roll along these tracks, which were slightly higher toward the front end and closed at the rear so that the drums rolled to the rear, where they were held securely by metal chocks. One by one, slowly and laboriously, they placed the nine drums—three to each rack—into position until the racks were filled. Robles then placed metal chocks at the front so that the rolling motion of the boat would not cause the drums to roll forward.

By the time they were finished, the darkness was like a heavy blanket that enveloped them. The two men inspected the work, and Robles was satisfied that all was well. Robles went to the bow where earlier, Brack had completely sawed through the timbers of the bow section from just above the deck level. The bow had then been reattached using a soft wood and nails so that from a distance all seemed normal. Robles was certain that one firm blow would entirely remove the bow section from just above the deck so that the drums would have clear passage as they rolled forward.

There was a rumbling of thunder in the distance, and they knew that rain was not far behind. Suddenly there was a noise from back at the shed, and both men looked at each other. Robles dashed to the truck and pulled out the pistol that he had placed under the seat. Both men moved into the foliage as they heard footsteps approaching, and soon a figure appeared out of the darkness.

"Are you there?" they heard Drexler call.

Robles stepped out from hiding. "Keep coming," he said. "We are right in front of you."

Drexler approached, looking first at the truck and then the boat. "Everything ready?" he asked.

"You're late," Robles chided. "All the work has been done."

"I had to wait. Erika has been trying to contact her lieutenant all day. To make sure the American ships were still coming," Drexler explained.

"And?"

"Apparently, the Japanese attack has forced the Americans to advance their schedule. The ships are scheduled to arrive at Colón in the early morning and, as a precaution, move through the canal under cover of darkness. They are expected at the Gatun Locks at three A.M."

Robles smiled triumphantly. "That makes our job easier."

"What part do I play in this?" Drexler asked.

"Come," Robles said and led him to the boat. They stepped on board. "Your job will be to aim the boat at the Gatun Dam."

Drexler eyed the drums on the boat. He seemed nervous in the presence of so much explosive power. "I'm still not sure how all of this works," he said.

Robles sighed. He had explained it all before. "We will wait until the American fleet enters the canal," he said patiently. "After the ships enter the Gamboa Reach, I will signal by flare, and you will bring the boat out into the lake and steer directly for the center of the Gatun Dam. You will lock the helm so that the boat will sail in a straight line, and then you will slip over the side and swim to shore."

"What happens if the boat veers slightly off course?"

Robles rolled his eyes. "I have already computed the drift and the target will be lined up accordingly. The spillway is three hundred feet across, giving us a margin for error of one hundred fifty feet on either side. You will not miss."

Drexler persisted with his annoying questions, and Robles knew why he preferred to work with Brack. "What happens when the Americans see the boat heading at the dam?"

"At first they will assume that it has gone off course and do nothing. By the time they react and start firing, it will be too late. None of the heavy antiaircraft weapons on the dam can fire at targets in the lake. Everything is aimed at the sky. Only the light machine-guns and small arms can be trained on objects in the lake, and they could fire at this boat all day without doing any appreciable damage."

Brack nodded. This he knew was true.

Robles went on. "As soon as the bow of the ship touches the dam, the small charges I have placed in the hold will detonate. If this does not happen, Brack will wait five seconds and use the radio-controlled detonator. This charge will blow a large hole in the bow section, just below the water line. As the tug takes on water, it will settle by the bow and when it reaches the proper angle, the drums will roll forward, smash through the bow, and roll into the water at the base of the dam. At a depth of thirty-five feet the drums will explode against the side of the dam. When that happens, nothing the Americans can do will save the dam from destruction."

Robles knew that now would be the perfect time to attack the dam. Under cover of darkness they could approach the dam and destroy the spillway before the Americans could react. If he had been forced to attack during daylight, he had planned to blow several charges around the lake. This he hoped would trick the Americans into thinking that they were under attack. Earlier that afternoon he had seen the smoke screen that, when activated, had covered the Gatun Locks, dam, and miles of the lake with a thick, acrid smoke. That defensive system would certainly hide the locks from any air attack, but it would also obscure the vision of any defender. If he could make the Americans activate the smoke screens, Drexler would be able to approach within fifty yards of the dam without being seen.

"And where will you be when all of this happens?" Drexler asked.

"I will be waiting for the ships to pass inside the Culebra Cut." The thought made him smile, but no one noticed in the darkness. "Once they are inside, I will bring a mountain down on top of them."

The three were silent for a moment as if the impact of what they were about to do had rendered them speechless. Drexler broke the silence. He stuck out his hand and solemnly shook Robles's hand and then Brack's. "We three," he said, "will be forever linked by this act. A hundred years from now they will remember our names."

Just then a flash of lightning illuminated the lake, followed almost immediately by a sharp crack of thunder. Somewhere to the left they heard a tree fall. Momentarily the three faces—tired, apprehensive, almost cadaverous in the harsh glare—had been caught and frozen as in a photograph that suddenly appears and then fades from view. Then the darkness enveloped them, leaving each man to his private thoughts.

The rain came, hard and sudden, without preliminary showers. They ran to the truck and scrambled inside, soaked to the skin in seconds. Robles looked at his watch. "We've got six hours to get ready," he said. "And I have to leave soon. Let's go back to the shed and go over everything in detail."

CHAPTER 43

The three of them watched each other; Harry behind his desk, Vicky pacing nervously back and forth, and Roberto sitting quietly in a chair against the wall.

"I think it's crazy," Vicky said. "You're just going to walk in there while they sit back and wait for you."

"I don't think they'll try anything," Harry said. "Viega is a bad apple, but he likes to do things the easy way. If he thinks he can scare me off or buy me off, he'll do it that way."

Vicky looked to Roberto for help. "Roberto said they might kill you."

"As long as you and Roberto know I'm in there, they won't try anything," Harry said. "Narciso Viega is a lot of things, but he's not stupid. I'm a well-known American businessman in this town. He's not going to invite me to his house to kill me. I'm probably safer there than I am on the street. He wants the Panama Club, and he thinks I'm ready to sell. I'll tell him that I want Robles before I even consider negotiations. Narciso would sell out his mother for the right deal."

335

"Then what?"

"We take care of Robles"—Harry looked at Roberto, who nodded his assent—"then we prove to the FBI that Viega has been working with a German spy."

"And how will you do that?" Vicky asked.

Harry thought for a moment. "According to Dominguez, Robles is buying everything from Viega—probably the explosives, too. I'll bet if the police raided Viega's place they'd find some of that German money. The new government is looking for an excuse to put Viega away, and the FBI would be glad to help them get rid of anybody who deals with the Germans or who tries anything that threatens the operation of the canal."

"So you . . . take care of Robles, have Viega arrested, get your money and pardon from the FBI, and we all live happily ever after?" Vicky said.

"Sounds good to me," Harry said.

"Too good," Vicky said. "I don't think any of this is going to work."

Harry looked at Roberto. "Got any better ideas?"

Roberto shook his head.

"I've got a better idea," Vicky said. "Let's just forget about the whole thing before you wind up dead. Roberto will tell Antonio to take a hike, you tell his father to forget it, and we'll just ride it out until this is all over."

"It's too late for that," Harry said. "The Viegas sense blood. If we don't do something, they will."

"I've got a bad feeling about this, Harry. You can't trust these people. Couldn't you get Trump to back you up."

Harry nodded reluctantly. "I don't want him getting in my way, but if it will make you feel better, wait a half an hour after we leave, then call Trump and Smythe and tell them where I've gone." He turned to Roberto. "Roberto will wait outside, just in case they try anything."

"I'm ready," Roberto said.

"Nothing heroic," Harry said. "I just want you outside Viega's place. If I'm not out in twenty minutes, or if you suspect that things have gone wrong, bring the police."

Victoria covered her eyes with her hands. "You could be dead by then."

"Don't worry about me."

"Don't worry," she said sharply. "I love you. What's going to happen to me if you go and get yourself killed? Do I just go back to what I was doing before I came here like none of this ever happened?" The anger drained from her face and was replaced with a terrible sadness. "I don't want you dead, Harry."

"I love you, too," he said. "And I don't want you to worry about me. Everything will be fine. You'll see."

Victoria did not answer, and for a long time the room was in silence, then Harry said quietly to Roberto, "You ready?"

Roberto stood up and nodded.

"Then let's go," Harry said. He looked at Victoria, but she did not look up.

After they had gone, she sat for a long time without moving. This was her worst nightmare come true. She had found someone. Someone she cared about and who cared about her. Now it was all going to disappear for reasons that she could hardly begin to understand. At first it had seemed like a game, but now it had turned deadly serious. It was like a ticking time bomb, and there didn't seem to be a thing she could do to stop it.

CHAPTER 44

The rain came in a steady, unrelenting downpour that had already lasted for almost two hours. Harry Fox adjusted his hat and pulled the collar of his raincoat up against his neck before he climbed out of the car. The gate to Viega's estate was open, beckoning invitingly, and there did not seem to be the usual guards on duty at the entrance. Lightning flashed in the distance, and Harry could see Roberto's face illuminated by the suddenly bright sky. The face was worried. In a moment the worried expression disappeared into darkness.

"I don't like it, Harry," Roberto said from the driver's seat. "Let me drive you in. If it doesn't look right, we get the hell out in a hurry."

Harry leaned an elbow on the door and window. "I need you out here," he said. "Park up the street, out of sight. If you don't hear from me in twenty minutes, you can assume that I'm in trouble." He touched Roberto on the shoulder, turned, and started up the driveway. Behind him he could hear Roberto's car pull away. He felt suddenly very alone.

The driveway was long and moved in a gentle curve toward the house. There were high trees on either side, and in the dark it was like walking in a tunnel. Harry expected someone to jump out from the trees at any moment, but there was nothing, and he soon found himself standing at the front door. Still there were no guards. He didn't like that.

He rang the bell and heard the sound echo around the house as if all the rooms were empty. In a short time the door opened. It was Antonio Viega.

"Come in," Antonio said pleasantly. "My father is waiting for you."

Harry stepped in, and Viega looked out into the driveway. "No car, Harry? It's a long walk. Especially in the rain."

"Someone dropped me here," Harry said. "He'll be back in twenty minutes to pick me up."

Antonio grinned as he took Harry's hat and coat. "You'd think you didn't trust us." He quickly frisked Harry for weapons.

"You'd think you didn't trust me," Harry said.

Antonio led Harry Fox across a foyer and into a large room, where Narciso Viega sat with his back to the door. The older man was feeding tropical fish in a large aquarium. He talked to the fish as one might to a child. He turned when Antonio and Harry entered.

"Harry," he said, as if the two were old friends, "it is so good to see you."

Harry nodded.

"You like fish?" Viega asked, nodding toward his aquarium.

"Sauteed with a little butter," Harry said.

Viega laughed. "You always were a funny guy, Harry. I'm going to miss that. When you leave Panama, I mean."

"I'm not leaving yet."

"But that's what we are here to talk about, no?"

"Maybe."

"Well, then. Sit down and let's talk." Viega indicated a seat close by him, and Harry sat. Antonio sat across from them, but it was obvious that he was only an observer.

The house was deadly quiet, but Harry could hear floors creaking, as if someone was walking on tiptoes upstairs or in a room next door. He adjusted his chair so that he could see the door. He did not want to be surprised by any sudden entrances.

Viega lit a cigar. "Harry," he said, "I think you have overstayed your welcome in Panama. It's time to think about going home."

"You and all the other yanquis," Antonio added harshly, but his father put a finger to his lips to silence him.

"But before you go, you have something that my son wants, and something that I want."

"I know what Antonio wants—the Panama Club. That's what I'm here to talk about. But what is it that you want?"

Viega chuckled. "The money, Harry. The money you took from the Germans. Someone made a switch, Harry. You're the only one who could have done it."

"You're right about the money, Viega. I did take it . . ."

Narciso Viega beamed. He had been right all along.

". . . but I don't have it anymore. It was an FBI operation. I had to hand over the money to them."

The smile drifted from Viega's face. "You expect me to believe that you worked with the FBI? That you handed over several million dollars?"

"Three and a half million dollars, to be exact," Harry said. "They offered me a pardon if I'd help them get the money."

"I don't believe you," Viega said.

"If I had that kind of money, would I be sitting here talking to you? I'd be long gone and you could have the Panama Club dirt cheap."

For the first time Viega seemed unsure of himself.

"I'm here," Harry went on, "because I want to sell the club. I want to go back to the States and I need money."

"Why should we pay you anything?" shot Antonio. "We can get rid of you and just take it."

"That could be messy," Harry said. "Even though I'm not very popular with my own government, I am an American citizen, and they might be unhappy that a prominent American businessman has disappeared."

"We might be willing to take that chance," Antonio muttered.

Harry ignored him and talked directly to the father. "You've got to remember that your side is out of power now."

"Not for long," Narciso said. "Between the Germans and the Japanese, I think you and your government will be gone from Panama soon."

"Maybe," Harry said. "But I'm willing to sell now. And if you give me the information that I want, I'd be willing to accept less than what the place is worth."

"What do you want?" Narciso said.

"The man who killed my friend."

Narciso laughed. "What makes you think that I know where this man is? He could be out of the country by now."

"He's still here," Harry said. "I know who he is and why he's here." Harry saw the surprise on Viega's face and decided to push even further. "And I know that you are working with him."

"As usual, Harry, you're bluffing."

"His name is Robles, and he's here to destroy the canal."

Viega's eyes narrowed menacingly, but he recovered quickly with a forced smile. "Then why don't you just tell your friends at the FBI to arrest all of us and pick this man up?"

"Because I want to kill him myself."

The tension in the room was electric, and Harry could feel that something was about to happen. He prepared himself to move quickly, but in a moment the feeling passed. Narciso Viega stared at him. Antonio avoided his eyes.

"And if I give you this man, you will sell me the Panama Club?" Narciso asked.

"Cheap."

Narciso nodded to Antonio, who went to the door. "Then I will give him to you," he said.

The door opened and Harry turned to see Robles enter the room. Harry recognized him instantly as the man he had seen on the stairs of the Washington Hotel in Colón on the night that Ernesto Garcia had been killed. Robles, never taking his eyes from the American, came and sat next to Viega.

"Were you listening?" Viega asked Robles, who nodded. "I told you that he was a man to watch carefully."

Harry's pulse was pounding, but he managed to maintain an outward calm.

"What do you want us to do with him?" Viega asked.

"Kill him." Robles said, matter-of-factly. He reached into his pocket and removed a knife, opened the blade, and said, "I'll do it now."

Harry sat quietly.

"Not in my house," Viega said sharply. "We will take care of this, but not here."

"As you choose," Robles said. "But take care of it right away." He looked at his watch. "I have to go. I have work to do." He nodded toward Harry. "I wish we had time to talk," he said. "I'd like to know how you took the money from the Germans."

Harry looked at his watch, hoping that Roberto might be here soon. If the police arrived now, they could capture Robles and stop the whole operation. "I've got time."

"I'm afraid you don't," Robles said and went to the door. He opened it. "I think your ride is here."

Harry turned to face the door, and two of Viega's men entered with Roberto between them. His clothing was torn and his face bore the marks of rough treatment. Roberto's hands were tied behind his back, and he stumbled as he was pushed into the room. Roberto's head was down. "I'm sorry, Harry," he said. "They were waiting for me."

Both men were armed. They stationed themselves on either side of the door to prevent any sudden attempts at escape.

"Good-bye," Robles said. "By this time tomorrow Panama will be on the road to freedom." He nodded toward Harry and Roberto. "Kill them both."

"Don't worry," Viega said. "I'll take care of them."

When Robles left, the room fell into an oppressive silence.

No one spoke for several minutes. Viega rested his chin on his fist as if he were considering what to do next.

"There are others who know that I'm here," Harry said.

"The girl?" Narciso said. "Antonio will bring her here."

Antonio grinned lecherously.

"Not just her," Harry said. "The FBI."

"I think you're bluffing, Harry," Viega said. "In any case, they'd have to find you first." He grinned. "There is so much jungle in Panama. It could take many years to find a body out there."

Harry knew that something had made Viega stop Robles from killing him on the spot. Something made him hesitate now. The Panamanian wanted something, and it could only be money—the German money. Viega thought that he still had the money that had been taken from the Germans. Harry knew he could use that fact to save their lives. At least he could buy some time.

"Can I buy my way out of this?" Harry said.

Viega smiled. This was what he had been waiting for. "It would take an awful lot of money, Harry." He raised his eyebrows meaningfully. "A lot of money."

"I just might have a lot of money. Then again I might not."

"Why don't you let me beat it out of him?" Antonio said.

"I don't think you could do it, Antonio."

Antonio stepped forward, ready to smash a fist across Harry's jaw, but his father stopped him with a word. "Wait."

Antonio paused, his fist poised to strike. Harry gave him a contemptuous look and turned away. "There's no way you're going to get me to tell," Harry said. "That money is the only thing that's keeping me alive."

Narciso Viega was not a stupid man, and he knew that what Harry said was true. He also knew that sooner or later he could make Fox tell him what he wanted to know, but with a man like Harry Fox he suspected that it would take a very long time. He looked at Roberto, who was wide-eyed with fear. He didn't know anything about the money. Why would Fox tell him? Who, then? "What about the girl," Viega said. "Maybe she knows where the money is."

Harry hoped to keep Vicky out of this mess. "She doesn't know anything," he said.

"Bring the girl here," Viega said to his son. "Let's find out what she knows."

"I'm telling you, she doesn't know anything," Harry said again.

Viega puffed contentedly on his cigar. "We'll just have to find that out for ourselves."

CHAPTER 45

It was well past midnight, and Harry was long overdue. Victoria Gansell was pacing the floor in Harry's office, smoking cigarette after cigarette, waiting for him to come back. She had not heard from Roberto either and knew that he would have contacted her if it were possible. She knew that something had gone wrong, and she had a terrible foreboding that she would never see either of them again. She tried to imagine her life without Harry, but all she could see was a black emptiness.

Earlier she had tried to call Trump to tell him that Harry was in trouble, but he had refused to take her call. In near hysteria she had told the receptionist at the American Embassy that this was a life and death emergency. The woman reminded her gently that the embassy was in a state of crisis, but did promise to pass along the information to Trump. He had not called her back.

She had talked with Smythe, but when she told him that Harry had gone to talk with Narciso Viega, he seemed disinterested. "Tell him to call me when he gets back," the

Englishman had said. "I'd like to know if he finds out anything about Robles."

Since that time she had tried to contact both men again, but Smythe was out and Trump was not taking any calls. Vicky could feel a rising panic.

When the phone rang, Victoria pounced on it before the first ring was finished. It was Smythe, calling to ask if Harry had returned from Viega's.

Vicky, almost in tears, said, "No. I'm sure something has happened to him."

Once again Smythe seemed distant. "I doubt very much that Viega would try anything foolish," he said. "Harry is too well known in Panama City."

"Then, why isn't Harry back here? Why hasn't he called me?"

Smythe had no answer for that. "I'm sure he is fine," he said lamely.

"Can you help me?" Vicky pleaded. "Go to Viega's with some of your people?"

"That," said Smythe, "is somewhat out of my jurisdiction. You'd have to call Trump for that."

"I have called Trump. He won't take my calls. He doesn't care what happens to Harry."

"Did Harry tell him about Robles?"

"He didn't care about that, either."

Smythe hesitated, as if thinking, then said, "I'm not really sure what I can do, but let me make a few phone calls."

"Phone calls?" Vicky shrieked. "We need more than phone calls."

"Sorry," Smythe said. "That's really all that I can do." He hung up before Vicky could say anything else.

Vicky paced back and forth, not knowing what else to do, hoping against hope that Harry and Roberto would walk in at any minute. Every few minutes she peeked through the curtains, looking down at the floor of the club, hoping to see them come in the front door. Nothing. Call the police, she thought. Then what? Tell them that Harry went to visit Viega and hadn't come back? So what? He had gone voluntarily, hadn't he? What evidence had she that Harry was in trouble? None.

So she paced and went to the window. She looked out and saw Antonio Viega talking to one of the waiters. They both looked up, and she knew that Viega was looking for her. Vicky closed the curtain, hoping that he had not seen her but certain that he had. Her first reaction was to run, but something told her that if she wanted to help Harry, she would have to let this one play itself out. She had to pull herself together, had to play the proper role. She went to Harry's desk and sat in his chair. She forced herself to be calm. She would wait for Viega right here.

Antonio Viega knocked on the door and waited until he heard her call before entering. He stepped into the room and saw her sitting calmly behind the desk. She wore a light-weight jacket over her dress and appeared to be working on some papers that were on the desk.

"What is it?" she said, barely looking up. "I'm busy right now."

Antonio was a little surprised by her brevity. "Fox sent me to bring you to him."

"Oh, really," Vicky said. "And I'm supposed to walk out of here with you at"—she looked up at the clock on the wall—"almost one in the morning? Now, why would I do that?"

Antonio shrugged. "We thought that you might be able to talk some sense into him. We want you to convince him to tell us where he is keeping the money."

"What money?"

"The money he took from the Germans."

Vicky thought for a minute. Obviously, the Viegas thought that Harry had the German money, and Harry must be using that fact to buy some time. She suppressed a sigh of relief. Harry was still alive. "Oh," she said. "That money. What makes you think he'll tell me where it is?"

Antonio was not as shrewd as his father. His methods were more direct. He pulled back his jacket to reveal the pistol in his shoulder holster. "If you want to see him alive, you'll find a way to convince him."

Vicky stood up. "Then, I suppose we'd better go," she said. She went to the door and was halfway down the stairs before Antonio caught up with her.

In the car on the way to Viega's house she ignored Antonio and watched the rain-soaked streets roll past her window. The rain had stopped and people were out. Just another night in Panama City, she thought. She knew that she was about to play the most important role of her life, and she had to decide just how to play it. Her mind ran through a catalog of parts and players. She wondered how Joan Crawford, or Bette Davis, or Vivien Leigh would play the role. Bitchy, she thought. Very bitchy. When they arrived at Viega's, she paused and took a deep breath before she went in the door.

Antonio brought her to his father's office. The two guards were still at the door; Roberto, hands still tied behind his back, sat in a chair across from Harry, whose wrists were tied to the arm of his chair. Vicky ignored them and went to Narciso Viega. "You must be the man in charge," she said.

Viega looked her up and down. He liked what he saw. She wore a cotton dress and a light jacket. Her hair was golden yellow, her skin creamy white, and she moved with the confident elegance of the beautiful. It was easy to see why his son had fallen for this one. She had the look of an American movie star. "Yes," he said, suddenly meek in her presence.

"Got a cigarette?" she asked.

Viega waved and Antonio came forward with one. Narciso lit it for her, and as he did, Vicky looked into his eyes.

She turned and looked at Harry. "Looks like your luck finally ran out, Harry," she said. "Could be the end of the line."

Harry smiled grimly.

Narciso came right to the point. "We were hoping that you might know where Fox keeps his money," he said.

Vicky took a drag on her cigarette. "No, but I've got some pretty good ideas."

Viega, suddenly the gentleman, said, "And how could we persuade you to share those ideas with us?"

Vicky stubbed out her cigarette in an ashtray and sat on the arm of an upholstered chair. "What's in it for me?" She put her hands into the pockets of her jacket.

Viega turned shrewd again. Beauty only dazzled him for a short time. "Better to share than to wind up with nothing," he said pleasantly, but his meaning was clear. "Don't you agree?"

Vicky smiled. "I see your point, but I think you have to agree that I have my own interests to protect. How do I know that you will allow Harry—or me—to leave after you have found the money?"

Viega gestured as if such a thing were unthinkable. "We want only the money. Nothing more."

"How can I be sure?"

"Perhaps," Viega said, "you might be willing to make a small gesture of good faith." His smile was friendly, but the eyes were dangerous. "And then we could reciprocate in some way."

Vicky removed a small key from her pocket and held it up between thumb and forefinger. She made sure that Harry could see it. "This is the key to a suitcase in Harry's office. I think you'll find that some of the money is in there." She held it out to Viega.

Narciso's eyes bulged as if he had seen the Holy Grail. He snatched the key hungrily from her fingers, a wide grin spreading across his face. He looked triumphantly at his son and held out the key. "Go," he said. "Bring back the money."

As Antonio stepped forward, Vicky pulled her other hand from her pocket and stuck the derringer behind Narciso Viega's right ear. He froze at the touch of the metal. "Don't anybody move," she said. She held onto the collar of his shirt with her left hand and used his body as a shield to protect herself from the possibility that the guards at the door might be foolish enough to start shooting.

"Jesus Christ," Narciso said, his body suddenly rigid, his voice trembling. "Be careful with that thing."

Antonio recovered from his initial shock. "It's probably not even loaded," he said, starting to advance on her.

"Stop!" his father screamed at him. "Don't anybody do anything to frighten her."

"That's right, Antonio," Vicky said, "don't scare me. I might get nervous and blow poppa's brains out."

Narciso Viega crossed himself and began to mumble a hasty prayer of contrition.

"Untie Harry and Roberto," Vicky said.

Antonio hesitated. "Do it," his father ordered.

Antonio reluctantly obeyed.

"He's got a gun, Harry," Vicky said.

As soon as Harry was free, he took the pistols from Antonio and the guards. When Roberto was freed, Harry gave him a pistol and then ordered Antonio and the guards to move into a corner away from the door. "Okay," he said to Vicky, "you can step away from Viega now."

Harry pushed Viega over with the others, and Vicky, relieved of her task, dropped the derringer on the table and slumped into a chair. Harry put the small pistol in his pocket. "You were great," he said, touching her shoulder. "You saved both of us."

She looked up at him, tears in her eyes. Now that the role had been played, her near hysteria had returned. "Don't ever do anything like that to me again, Harry."

"There's no way you can get out of here," Antonio said angrily.

His father gave him an angry look. "Fool," he said.

Harry told Roberto to keep them covered while he went to check the outside. He went to the window in the front hall and looked out. There were at least four armed men in the driveway. Others, he suspected, would be covering the other exits. He went back to Viega's office. "Armed men outside," he said. "How many more are there?" he asked Viega.

"More than enough," Viega said proudly. "They'll cut you to ribbons if you try to leave without my permission."

"We'll just have to take you with us," Harry said.

Viega sneered at him. "Do you really think you can make

it? In the dark? Surrounded by my men? Without a car?" He laughed. "You're still a dead man, Harry Fox."

There were three of them to get out, Harry thought, and he doubted that they could all make it using only Viega and his son as a shield. One of the guards was sure to get off a shot and hit one of them before they could get to the street.

They couldn't stay here. Robles was preparing to destroy the Panama Canal tonight. He couldn't let that happen, and he couldn't think of any other options. "Time to leave," he said. "We'll take the Viegas with us."

Narciso Viega went to a chair and sat down. "I'm not going anywhere," he said. "Unless you plan to carry me."

"Get up," Harry said. "I'll shoot you right here."

"I doubt that," Viega said. "If you shoot me, you're in worse shape than ever." He smiled, yellow teeth gleaming.

"Perhaps a bullet in the arm would convince you to be more cooperative?"

Viega scoffed. "At the first sound of gunfire, my men would be in here in seconds."

"I could kill your son if you refuse to help us," Harry said.

"If you must—you must, but that won't help you get away."

Antonio tried to shrink into the corner as Harry approached. "You're coming with us," Harry said to the terrified Antonio.

"Go ahead," Viega said. "I'll just sit here and listen while my men gun you down."

Harry knew that Viega was right. Their chances of making it to the street were slight.

Viega saw Harry's hesitation and chortled with glee. "Go ahead," he said. "My men are eager to have some target practice. It has been some time since they shot anyone."

As if on cue, the sound of gunfire erupted outside. They heard running and men yelling. One of Viega's men burst into the room, and Harry pointed the pistol at his midsection. The guard's jaw dropped in surprise, and he made no move to raise his rifle. Harry took it from him and pushed him over with the others.

The gunfire continued outside. "What's going on out there?" Harry snapped.

The man who had just come in said, "There are soldiers on the grounds."

"What kind of soldiers?"

"Yanquis."

Just then they heard the front door being smashed in and boots clattering across the foyer. Doors were being kicked in all over the house.

"Get down," Harry said to Roberto and pulled Vicky onto the floor.

Seconds later the door was smashed in and several U.S. Army soldiers poured into the room. They leveled their rifles at the wide-eyed Panamanians. The young lieutenant who led them wore the armband of the military police. He said, "We are looking for two Americans who are said to be held captive in this house. We are authorized by the military governor of the Panama Canal Zone to conduct a search of these premises."

The Panamanians were too stunned to speak.

"Over here," Harry said. He pulled Vicky to her feet. He quickly pointed at Roberto and said, "He's with us," then realized that he still held the pistol in his hand. The soldiers, none of whom was more than twenty years old, eyed him warily.

"If I were you, sir," the lieutenant said, "I'd put that weapon down."

Harry bent down and placed the pistol on the carpet.

"Who sent you to get us?" Harry said.

"There are two gentlemen outside in the car waiting for you."

Harry put an arm around Vicky and led her outside. Roberto followed. There were about thirty American soldiers on the grounds, and several of Viega's guards had been wounded. Most of them, apparently, had surrendered their weapons without putting up much of a fight. An American Embassy staff car had pulled up into the driveway in front of the house, and as Harry and Vicky came out of the house, the back door opened. Trump stepped out and looked around. Smythe stepped out behind him.

"I guess we're too early," Trump said. "You're still alive."

Harry ignored the sarcasm. He was glad to see even Trump. "What brings you here—with the army?" he asked.

Trump jerked a thumb over his shoulder at Smythe. "Someone apparently got the British ambassador to persuade the American ambassador that there was some merit to your story about an attempt to sabotage the canal."

Smythe gave a small, casual salute. "Nice to see you're still alive, Harry," he said.

Vicky went to Smythe and gave him a kiss on the cheek. "Thanks," she said. "For listening to me."

The Englishman was embarrassed.

"I was ordered to find you," Trump said. "Now why don't you tell us what this is all about."

"Why don't you have your driver take Vicky back to my place," Harry said. "Then we can go inside and talk to Viega. He's the one who can tell us what we want to know."

They found Narciso Viega sitting behind his desk, his men lined against the wall behind him, the American soldiers standing guard. Viega was defiant. "This is an outrage," he said. "My government will protest this unwarranted intrusion of my personal property."

Trump flashed his FBI badge. "The United States is in a state of war, Mr. Viega. Under treaties signed by both our governments, we have the right to protect the Panama Canal by any and all means necessary. We have reason to believe that you are involved in a plot to destroy or damage the canal. If that is the case, then I, as an officer of the Justice Department of the United States, will authorize the military governor of the Canal Zone to execute you tomorrow morning."

Harry Fox was quite sure that Trump was overstating his authority, but the recitation was given so confidently that Viega was stunned. His eyes bulged at the mention of the word *execute*.

"You have no authority to threaten this," Viega said.

"We're going to hang your fuckin' ass," Trump said, abandoning his usual formality. "Then we'll argue about who has the authority. Either way, it won't make much difference to you."

Viega's eyes darted around the room, but he saw only the impassive faces of the Americans soldiers, every one of whom would have been glad to carry out the sentence right then and there. Viega sank back into his chair.

"Your only hope," Trump said, "is to tell us everything right now."

Viega fidgeted nervously, his hands fluttering across the desk. He turned to look at his son and his men behind him, then turned back to face Trump. "I will tell you nothing," he said. "I will not betray my country."

"That's it, then," Trump said. "Take him away."

Viega's shoulders sagged as the lieutenant stepped forward to take him into custody, but Harry Fox intervened. "I think we can persuade Mr. Viega that it is in his and his country's best interests to talk with us," he said.

"How?" Trump wanted to know.

"Take his men outside, and let me talk with him alone," Harry said. When Trump hesitated, Harry added, "It couldn't hurt."

"Okay," Trump said. "But I stay here with you."

As soon as Viega's men had been herded outside, Harry sat in the chair in front of the desk. He leaned forward, his elbows on the table. "Narciso," he said, "you and I both know that you don't want to hang. Not for Japan, or Germany, or even for Panama. Your men are outside and no one will ever know what you tell us in here. So why don't you just give yourself a chance?"

Narciso Viega looked suddenly very old. "He said I would hang. Why should I tell you anything if they're going to hang me anyway?"

Harry looked at Trump, who said, "As of this moment the United States Congress has not officially made a declaration of war. That declaration is expected any moment. Until then any belligerent acts against the United States might not be regarded as treason or as acts of sabotage under military rule."

Viega was confused. He looked imploringly at Harry. "It may already be too late. The plan is already underway. I have no power to stop it."

Harry could feel Trump's agitation behind him. "If you cooperate now, Narciso, before the declaration of war," Harry said, "you could walk away from this one. If you wait too long, we can't help you."

Viega's surrender was complete. His face sank as if it had collapsed from the inside. "What do you want to know?" he asked.

"Everything," Trump said.

CHAPTER 46

Panama Canal, Gatun Locks; December 8, 5 A.M.

Since the completion of the Panama Canal in 1914, the size of ships in the United States Navy had been limited by the size of the locks in the canal. While the capital ships of other navies, particularly of the German and the Japanese, had no such restrictions, American ships were built so that they might pass through the canal. The locks in the canal were one hundred and ten feet wide. The width of the latest American battleships, the *Washington* and the *North Carolina,* was one hundred and eight feet.

Under cover of darkness the great ships, along with the other vessels that accompanied them on this frantic journey to Hawaii, had moved into Limón Bay and on into the approaches to the canal. Slowly, ponderously, the sister ships had been guided into the first of the locks at Gatun. The howling screech as the heavily armor-plated sides of the ships scraped along the side of the locks was like the shrill cry of banshees in the night. The first lock raised the ships twenty-eight feet, and then the gates opened and the mules, cables straining under the vast weight of the mammoth ships, slowly pulled the battleships forward into the middle locks.

As soon as the first locks were cleared, the escort vessels moved in. Behind them would come the cruisers and then the aircraft carriers. The sense of urgency was electric. Every man on duty that night, whether on board the ships or working to put them through the canal, was certain that this fleet was sailing to the rescue of the American forces on Hawaii. Rumor had it that an immense Japanese fleet had surrounded the Hawaiian Islands and that invasion was imminent. Sailors lined the decks of the navy ships, watching as the fleet squeezed through the locks. The silence was eerie. As each ship completed its journey through the triple set of locks and moved into Gatun Lake, the workers—line handlers and mule drivers and lock operators—waved a silent salute and hurried back to the task of moving the next ship through.

It went on for hours.

From his position across the lake, Heinrich Drexler could see the running lights of the great ships as they entered Gatun Lake. He was in awe of the size of the vessels and of his own responsibility. His palms were wet with sweat. He knew that the moment was soon to be at hand. He grasped his semiautomatic rifle and settled in to wait for the signal.

In the darkness the ships were forced to run at reduced speed and to follow the zigzag course that had been the valley of the Chagres River while they traversed the lake. At that rate it would take almost three hours to cross Gatun Lake and for the first ships to arrive at the Gamboa Reach. By then it would be daybreak, and the fleet would have to pass through the Culebra Cut in daylight. When the battleships arrived at Culebra, the last units of the fleet, more than ten miles behind the front runners, would already be inside the Gamboa Reach.

At midnight, acting upon Robles's orders, Drexler had moved the boat from its position near the storage shed and, closely following the contours of the shoreline, worked his way to within one mile of the Gatun Dam. It was fortunate for him that he had changed locations because by 4 A.M. the

U.S. Army, alerted by Trump, had discovered the storage shed and most of the equipment that had been left behind. By then most of the ships of the fleet were halfway across the lake, with the vanguard already arriving at the approach to the Gamboa Reach.

Despite the early hour the people of Gamboa were out in force to witness the awesome sight of the Atlantic Fleet slipping silently past their hillside homes. Most of the inhabitants of Gamboa were Americans who lived and worked in the Canal Zone, and they were used to the passage of great ships in the canal, but this was something that few of them had ever witnessed or were likely to witness again. In the chill half-light of early morning they stood and waved for hour after hour as the long procession of cold, gray, battle-dressed warships glided past. The citizens of Gamboa understood that these ships were all that stood between them and an enemy who had seemed remote but now might have been just over the horizon.

In the dim predawn light a light fog rose from the surface of the lake, and the ships were like gray ghosts that floated against a gray background. If not for the running lights they might not have been visible at all.

Across the reach from the town of Gamboa, just where the passage narrows, the ancient steam dredge, *Las Cascadas,* which had toiled almost endlessly since the opening of the canal more than twenty-five years earlier, blew three blasts on her steam whistle as the lead ship, *North Carolina,* pulled into view. The mighty warship gave a deep-throated reply as if to salute *Las Cascadas'* tireless efforts in keeping the channel open, and moved into the narrowing channel.

Hidden in the heavy foliage, Ludwig Brack watched the great ships slip past and disappear into the mist that shrouded the Gamboa Reach. This he knew was the point of no return. Soon the vessels would be into the Culebra Cut, where Robles was waiting. Brack readied his signal flare. When most of the ships had disappeared into the reach, he would signal Drexler and move to his next position.

From his position on Contractor's Hill, Carlos Robles heard the blast of steam from the battleship. He had watched the procession of lights move across the lake, and even he was awed by what he had seen. He trained his field glasses on the first ship and thought that he could perceive details of the superstructure. He smiled. The ships were inside the Gamboa Reach now. Very soon the first ships would enter the Culebra Cut. Once that happened, there was no way out. No matter what happened then, the American fleet would be trapped. He checked his watch. In less than twenty minutes he expected that Brack would give the signal that would start the mayhem.

Drexler, too, was looking at his watch. It would soon be full light, and he wondered why Brack had not yet given the signal. There seemed to be a lot of activity on the lake at this time that did not seem to have anything to do with the American fleet, and Drexler had the gnawing fear that small boats were in the lake looking for him. A half hour earlier he had heard motor noises, and a searchlight had swept the shoreline where he and his boat were hidden beneath a canopy of overhanging trees, but miraculously he and his boat had not been spotted, and the other boat, the voices, and the lights had disappeared into the darkness.

But still there was too much activity out on the lake. If Brack didn't give the signal soon, he would have to make his attack in daylight. Then he saw it. A high arching flare of light, off on the other side of the lake, that was his signal to proceed. Suddenly his nervousness vanished, and he knew that he would succeed. Drexler started the engines and brought them to a rumbling idle before he edged the throttle forward and inched away from the shore. Once he had cleared the treeline, he pushed the throttle forward, and the engines responded perfectly with a soft, growling roar. He kept the boat within twenty yards of the shore, hugging the overhanging trees for protection. Ahead was a small island, and he kept that between himself and the open lake.

Drexler was less than ten minutes away from the Gatun Dam, and he knew that he could make at least half of the journey partially hidden in the shoreline and the overhanging trees. Once he pulled within view of the dam, nothing could stop him. He could feel the flush of victory.

Around a bend he could sense light, and he knew that the dam was less than a half mile away. He pushed the throttle full ahead, and the tug surged forward at top speed, the powerful engines churning the waters of the lake to a frothy foam. He rounded the bend, and there it was—the Gatun Dam. In the center of this long, low, gigantic pile of packed earth and rock was—unmistakably—the concrete spillway, gleaming almost white against the dark background of the dam itself. To Drexler's surprise, the entire dam was lit from one end to the other. Searchlights swung to and fro, piercing the sky, dancing across the lake, slender fingers probing every corner of the darkness. He could even see figures running across the dam, hear the sound of motors on the lake. They are looking for me, he thought. It was too late to stop him now.

He was within five hundred yards of his target.

He aimed his boat at the center of the dam and locked the helm in place. Nothing could prevent him from striking the target. His heart surged as he raced across the lake, and he took one last look at the dam. All that remained now was to arm the contact fuse in the bow before he went over the side. Suddenly he was caught in the harsh glare of a searchlight. Instinctively, he ducked behind the wheelhouse just as a fusillade of machine-gun fire raked the deck of his boat. A column of water rose ahead of him and cascaded across the deck, then another just off the starboard bow. Someone was firing shells at him.

High above him a flare exploded, and the soft light of morning burst into a harsh, flashbulb intensity that sharply illuminated everything around him. Everything was suddenly bright white and dark shadow, like an overexposed photograph, and Drexler had to shield his eyes from the sudden glare.

Drexler peered out from his hiding place and saw fast boats approaching. He saw the dim outline of another, larger ship—a destroyer perhaps—firing at him from a greater distance. The destroyer was firing the shells that had exploded ahead of him. He looked toward the dam and saw that he was still several hundred yards away. The boats were gaining on him, but he doubted that they would be on him before he reached the dam. Drexler grabbed his semiautomatic and fired at the approaching boats, but they were still too far away for his shots to have any effect.

When he was within two hundred yards, a shell exploded dead ahead, and then another even closer. Drexler was drenched as an avalanche of water pounded the deck, and his boat paused, momentarily overwhelmed by the additional weight, and then shook herself free and plowed ahead. They were firing at him from the dam now. He could see figures running frantically across the road that topped the concrete structure. He crawled forward, keeping out of reach of the machine-gun fire that still peppered the deck. Inside the wheelhouse he flipped the switch of the contact fuse just the way that Robles had shown him. The explosive charge was now armed and ready. It was too late for him to escape now, and he realized that he would have to stay with the boat until it smashed into the dam. From the beginning he had known that this was how it would end.

But it was too late for them, too.

The pursuing boats, fast Motor Torpedo Boats of the 15th Naval District Command, were gaining on him rapidly. "Damn!" he screamed. They were going to catch him. Bullhorns ordered him to heave to, but Drexler remained hidden from view. As the boats pulled in closer, he could see that there were men prepared to leap on board. He fired a short burst at them to drive them back. He succeeded but his shots were greeted by a wall of machine-gun fire that ripped chunks from every part of the boat.

Drexler was hit several times but still managed to return fire. Another round of fire from the pursuers sent bits and pieces of his boat flying into the air. One of the MTBs attempted to circle in front of him to cut him off from his target, and Drexler maniacally rushed out on deck, firing wildly as if he could prevent them from blocking his path. A hailstorm of machine-gun fire knocked him back. His rifle went spiraling away, and he slumped to the deck mortally wounded but not yet dead just as a five-inch shell from the destroyer passed through the bow of his boat without exploding. Water rushed into the open bow, and the boat immediately slowed as the bow filled with water. In minutes the boat was down by the bow and shipping more water as the engines strained to push her ahead. The water of Gatun Lake rushed across the deck, reviving Drexler, who opened his eyes in time to see the drums begin to roll forward on the tracks. He screamed, not in fear, but in frustration because he saw that he was still a hundred yards from the dam. The barrels rolled along the tracks, smashed through the bow, and plunged into the lake. Seconds later Drexler and his tiny boat were lifted out of the lake, carried aloft on a rising cushion of rapidly expanding water, and then ripped apart as the huge explosion broached the surface.

The explosion, the largest that anyone there had ever witnessed, hurtled small pieces of the boat several hundred yards into the air. For several minutes chunks of debris dropped from the sky, sending the sailors on the MTBs scurrying for shelter. The noise was like a hailstorm as the debris slapped back down onto the surface of the water. The sound of the explosion reverberated across Gatun Lake. When it was finished, there was only silence and a circle of debris to mark the spot where the explosion had taken place.

Robles heard the noise and gave a silent cheer. He was certain that Drexler had succeeded. He had placed himself in a well-concealed position on a terraced slope cut into a lower hillside two hundred yards away from the site of his planned explosion. He and the wires he had run from his explosive charges were hidden from view by the dense jungle foliage. He knew that in moments the dam would give way and millions of gallons of water would begin to rush from the lake in a never-ending torrent. It was too late for the fleet to turn around. They were already inside the nine-mile-long Culebra Cut. At any moment he expected to see the sleek gray shape of the first battleship as it came around the slight curve of the cut just below Contractor's Hill. As soon as he saw the first ship he would blow his charges and watch the entire hill go rumbling down into the narrow passage.

It was almost full light now, and as he looked across the Culebra Cut he saw movement. There were several men silhouetted at the top of Gold Hill. What was going on here? Then he saw more, like ants crawling across the face of the hill. They were looking for something. Him? Impossible. But what, then? He stood up and looked out at Contractor's Hill. He saw them there, too. Soldiers. They had come from the far side of the hill and were now working their way down from the top, laboriously lowering themselves on ropes. He heard a muffled scream as one of the men slipped and went tumbling down the steep slope. There must have been fifty of them—perhaps a hundred. He had been betrayed, but it was too late to stop him. The soldiers would never reach him in time. They would have to die, too.

The soldiers were still far from where he had placed his charges, but he could wait no longer. He retracted the detonator arm on the plunger, checked that the current was on, and rapidly depressed the plunger. It made a whirring sound as it went into the box and made contact with the pinion and armature. Then there was only silence.

Robles stared at the box in disbelief. He checked quickly that the connections had been properly made, but knew even before he did so that they had been correct. He did not make mistakes like that. The wire must have been pulled loose at the base of the hill next to the first set of charges. That was the only explanation possible. The soldiers had not yet reached the spot where he had placed the explosives. He could still make it back there and reconnect the wire before the soldiers got there.

He saw the soldiers scrambling down the face of the cliff. They were getting closer. It was too risky. He could never make it there and back in time to escape capture. Then, out of the mist, moving so slowly that she barely rippled the water, he saw the *North Carolina* appear in the cut, ghostly quiet in the soft morning air. The ship was magnificent, awesome. In the narrow confines of the Culebra Cut, surrounded by land close in on both sides, the huge ship moved cautiously, making less than ten knots. She seemed larger than life and oddly out of place.

His mind was made up. It was worth the risk.

He threw his satchel across his shoulder and was up and running, plunging down the slope of the hill, following the trail of detonating cord that led to his explosives. Branches tore at his face, ripped at his clothing, and tugged at the canvas satchel. He slipped and fell, rolling head over heels down the slope. He tumbled for more than thirty feet before coming to a stop at the base of the hill.

Momentarily dazed, Robles shook his head and reached to pick up his bag, which had fallen nearby. He looked up directly into the barrel of a pistol.

"You look like you're in a big hurry to get somewhere," Harry Fox said.

Robles pushed himself to his feet. He brushed the dirt from his clothing. "You," he said in disbelief.

Fox kept the weapon trained on the middle of Robles's chest. "Me," he said simply. "Roberto and I cut your wires. I followed them here."

"How did you get here? How did you know?"

"Your friend Viega decided he didn't want to hang for the greater glory of Germany. He didn't know all the details of your operation, but he knew enough to put us on your trail. This jungle is crawling with soldiers."

"You're too late," Robles said. "The dam is already destroyed."

"Afraid not," Harry said. "The navy had patrol boats out all night looking for your friends. They would have had to fight their way past a small fleet. I doubt that they got within a mile of the dam."

Robles refused to believe that he had failed. "But I heard the explosion."

"What you heard was probably your friends saying a very loud good-bye."

Behind Fox, Robles saw the shape of the American battleship approaching. It seemed so close that he felt that he could reach out and touch it. In just a few minutes the ship would pass them. He saw something else in the jungle behind Fox. Perhaps it was not too late to block the canal. "I can still bring down this mountain," Robles said, "and block the canal for months."

"You'd have to go through me," Harry said. "If I were you, I wouldn't give me an excuse to kill you. If you're lucky the army will arrive before Roberto Garcia. He'll kill you on sight."

Robles smiled and Harry heard the click of the rifle bolt, behind him, as a shell slid into the chamber. He turned slowly and saw Ludwig Brack, his rifle aimed at Harry. "Drop the pistol," Brack said.

Robles stepped forward and took the gun from Harry's hand, then smashed him across the side of the head with it. Harry spun around and dropped facedown to the ground.

"Kill him," Brack said.

"No. The noise will attract the soldiers," Robles said. "As soon as you see the explosion of the hill, finish him and make your escape."

"What about you?"

"Don't worry about me. He reached into his satchel and removed several pencil-thin timing detonators. "There is only enough time to reset the charges. Not enough time to get away."

"There is still time," Brack said. "We can both get away."

Robles threw aside the satchel and put the detonators in his pocket. There was no time for sentimentality. "Perhaps," he said. "If so, I will see you again." He turned and ran into the jungle. In seconds he was lost from view.

In his frustration Brack wanted to kill Harry Fox at that moment. He didn't need to use his rifle. He pulled his knife from its sheath and viciously kicked Harry's ribs. Harry grunted with the force of the blow and lay still, facedown in the tangle of weeds and long grass. Brack knelt beside him, grabbed his shoulder and rolled him over onto his back. The knife went to Harry's throat as Brack prepared to slice him open. Brack saw that his victim's eyes were open, and for the briefest of moments he didn't realize that Harry held the derringer under his chin. Suddenly he felt the firmness of the metal against his throat, and he only had time enough to realize that he was a dead man as Fox pulled the trigger.

The small weapon, pressed under his chin, made barely any noise. Brack blinked his eyes once, then opened them wide. His surprise was complete, but it is doubtful if he ever saw anything, or heard the small, muffled sound. He pitched over and landed heavily on top of Harry Fox.

Harry pushed the heavy man aside and got to his feet. He turned to look into the Culebra Cut, The *North Carolina* was almost on top of him now. Several hundred yards behind the battleship, he could see the sister ship, *Washington*. He grabbed the rifle and plunged into the jungle after Robles, heading for Contractor's Hill.

Robles was at the base of the hill. He quickly reset his charges and inserted the pencil-thin ignitors. He twisted the timing caps, giving himself two minutes to escape. It would be close, but maybe it would be enough. The soldiers were less than fifty feet above him struggling to work their way down the hill. He was hidden from their view by the dense foliage and the sheer face of the hill that was like a shelf above his head. The soldiers would soon find themselves in the cut, he thought, although that would be beyond their concern.

Harry crashed through the trees. Vines and creepers grabbed at his ankles and shoulders. Leaves and branches slapped his face, and he covered it with his arms to protect his eyes.

Robles heard him coming from fifty yards away. He crouched behind the thick base of a mahogany tree, and when Harry rushed past, Robles stepped out and hit him across the back of the head with the pistol. Harry went sprawling, the rifle flying out of his hands and landing several yards away. He rolled over onto his back and raised himself on his elbows.

Robles stepped into the clearing, the pistol aimed at Harry's chest. "In one minute," he said. "This will all be over. Unfortunately, you have even less time than that." He walked to within five feet of Harry Fox and raised the pistol.

He wanted to be sure that he did not miss. He squeezed one eye shut as he sighted down the barrel. Harry closed his eyes.

The sound of the shot reverberated across the floor of the jungle and across the Culebra Cut. Birds squawked and took flight. Harry opened his eyes and saw Robles on his knees in front of him clutching his chest. Roberto stepped from behind the trees, a pistol in his hand.

He circled Robles warily and kicked away the pistol that lay in front of him. "You okay, Harry?" he asked.

Harry pulled himself to his feet. He wanted to check himself for bullet holes, but did not. "I'm okay," he said.

Robles looked up. A dark circle of blood was spreading across his chest from just below his right shoulder. His right arm hung limply at his side. "You're both dead," he said. "We're all dead. The whole mountain is going to come tumbling down on top of us." He gave a ghastly grin. "It's too late for all of us. The ignitors are set to go off in about ten seconds."

"These you mean?" Roberto said throwing several of the ignitors in front of Robles. "I saw you set them back there."

Robles looked at his ignitors and could see that they had been deactivated. He was finished. The look he gave Roberto was one of everlasting hatred.

Roberto held up one more of the thin detonators. "Interesting device," he said. "By twisting this cap on top, you can set the timer for anywhere between ten seconds and one hour. Or turn it off." He walked behind Robles and gave the cap a slight twist. "You have ten seconds to remember the name of Ernesto Garcia," he said, and dropped the ignitor down the back of Robles' shirt.

Robles screamed and clawed one-handed at the back of his shirt. He rolled across the floor of the jungle like a man tormented by hornets. His screams grew in intensity as his time grew short.

Harry looked away. A brief, muffled sound, like a firecracker tucked into a pillow, silenced the screams, and when Harry looked back, Robles lay still. He was on his back, sightless eyes staring wildly at the canopy of leaves that almost blocked the sky. A dark pool of blood soaked into the floor of the jungle beneath him.

Roberto said nothing. He walked to the edge of the trees, and Harry followed him. They stood at the edge of the Culebra Cut and watched as the ships passed by. Now the long line of ships extended back as far as the eye could see. The *North Carolina* had already passed them; the *Washington* was just abreast of where they stood. Harry felt he could touch the ship as it moved silently past. On board the battleship, out on the open bridge deck, a sailor spotted them. He waved a greeting, and Harry returned the wave. Roberto hesitated as if the wave could not have been meant for him, but the moment was cathartic and soon he too was waving. Neither knew which of them had been the first to start cheering, but a moment later the two of them were yelling their lungs out. They cheered until they were hoarse.

Epilogue

The United States Embassy in Panama occupies one of the most beautiful spots in Panama City. The embassy, a tight cluster of three- and four-story buildings, sits on the edge of Panama Bay on the wide, palm-tree-lined Balboa Avenue. Facing the embassy, just across Balboa, is a parklike esplanade that juts into the bay like the bow of a ship that has run aground stern first.

It was to this spot that Harry Fox and Victoria Gansell came on Friday afternoon, ten minutes before Harry Fox's scheduled appointment at the embassy. They had been told by Trump that the American ambassador himself wanted to present the Presidential pardon that had been granted to Harry for his work in depriving the Germans of much of the four million dollars and for his part in the capture of the Argentinian saboteur.

It was not until the appointed hour that Victoria was able to articulate the doubts that had gnawed at her since Trump had informed Harry about the appointment. "I don't like the way this whole thing has been handled, Harry," she said. "First of all, Hoover and Trump take all the credit for stopping Robles and saving the canal—there wasn't one mention of your name or of Roberto's in any of the newspaper reports."

"That's not important," Harry said. "Smythe told me that the FBI makes a habit of taking credit for other people's work."

"Smythe also told you not to trust them, didn't he?"

"Yes. He said not to believe anything that Trump said until I actually had my pardon in my hand."

"He also warned you against coming here to the embassy, didn't he?"

Harry nodded.

"Well?" Vicky said. "What are we doing here? Once you set foot on embassy grounds, you are in American territory. You could be arrested. Panama's not so bad. Maybe we should just stay here—for a while at least."

Harry put his arms around her. "We're going home. You and me—together."

"They could be waiting to arrest you, Harry."

"I can't believe that Trump or Hoover would try to arrest me now. Not after what I did for them. The public wouldn't stand for it."

"The public doesn't know anything about it. Hoover took all the credit. I don't think they're about to share it with you."

"Let them have the credit," Harry said. "I just want to go home. I've been here too long." He looked at the embassy across the street and the American flag waving in the stiff breeze off the bay. "I think we've all been here too long. It's time to let the Panamanians run their own lives."

Vicky sighed. "I don't think that's going to happen, Harry. Not now. Not till the war's over."

Harry's eyes and thoughts were on the piece of American territory that was less than fifty yards away from where he stood. "Let's go," he said confidently.

"You sure?" Vicky asked.

"There's nothing to worry about," he said, already heading toward the street.

Trump was waiting for them in his office, and when his secretary showed Harry and Vicky in, he offered them a seat and a cold drink. Things were much less hectic now than they had been in the frantic few days that followed the attack on Pearl Harbor, and Trump seemed almost happy-go-lucky as he sat behind his desk. The rumored Japanese invasion had, of course, turned out to be just that—a rumor. Even yesterday's declaration of war by Germany had been almost anticlimactic, something that everyone had expected, and it was received with a sense of relief when it finally came. The declaration was a puzzle to almost everyone.

Harry couldn't fathom why Hitler had been so foolish as to declare war on the United States. Germany was already embroiled in a massive campaign against the Russians that threatened to consume as much manpower as Germany could ever provide. The British, secure in their island fortress, were nipping at Hitler's heels like a pack of pesky dogs, forcing Germany to divert much needed men and equipment from the campaign in the East. It was an open secret that Roosevelt wanted to enter the war against Germany, but the American people were now consumed with exacting revenge against the Japanese. Congress might never have agreed to a declaration of war against Germany if Hitler hadn't obliged with a declaration of his own.

Only Wilfred Smythe had offered a possible solution to Harry's question. "It's possible that Hitler and the Japanese had intended the attack on Pearl Harbor and the destruction of the Panama Canal to be a massive, concerted strike against the United States. The Japanese succeeded in their part and the Germans failed in theirs. Perhaps Hitler felt obligated to stand with the Japanese, who after all had done him a tremendous favor by attacking an enemy who had grown increasingly belligerent toward him." It made as much sense as anything else that Harry had heard.

Trump did not offer any new answers. In fact, to Vicky's

growing discomfort, he did not seem to be ready to offer much of anything. The ambassador who was to present the pardon did not seem to be anywhere on the premises. There were, however, several FBI agents in attendance. They stood by impassively, hard eyes glaring at her and Harry, and Vicky was quick to note that they had all of the exits covered.

"Well," Trump said, after they had run through preliminary pleasantries. "How long has it been since you've actually been on American soil?"

"Too long," Harry said. "I'm anxious to get home."

"I suppose I should tell you at this point," Trump said, "that the President has been too busy to pay attention to this pardon business."

"Has he signed it yet?" Harry asked.

Trump grinned and Vicky felt her heart sink. The bastard, she thought; he's really going to do it.

"Actually," Trump went on, "the President doesn't know anything about it."

"Harry, let's get out of here."

Harry put his hand on Vicky's arm reassuringly. "Just wait," he said, then turned to Trump. "Just what does that mean?"

Trump looked at the four FBI agents who waited at the far wall, next to the door. His smile was conspiratorial, and they joined him as if they were in on the joke. "I should explain something to you first, Fox," Trump said. "The purpose of this operation was threefold. The first aspect was to help the British take the money away from the Germans. The second was to acquire this money for the U.S. Treasury. The third was to capture one of our most wanted criminals. Someone who had eluded us for many years."

"That would be me?" Harry said calmly.

"I don't believe this," Vicky said. "You're not really going to do this?"

"I'm afraid we are," Trump said. "The agents behind you are here to take Harry into custody."

"You bastard," Vicky said, but Harry put his hand on her arm again.

"I guess you get everything, then," he said to Trump. "You help out the British, get your money, and get your man."

Trump could not stop the happy grin that spread across his face. "Precisely."

Harry grinned back at him. "I guess you haven't returned the money to the Treasury yet?" Harry asked.

"The money is here in the embassy," Trump said, feeling for the first time a vague discomfort. "It will return to the United States on the same plane and in the same hands as the agents who take you into custody."

"I would check it very carefully before I hand it over to Mr. Hoover, if I were you."

Trump's smile was fading fast. "What's that supposed to mean?"

Now it was Harry's turn to smile. "Things aren't always what they seem."

"I don't believe you," Trump said. "You're bluffing."

"So, call my bluff," Harry said. "Check the money."

Trump barked at one of the men at the door. "The money is in the embassy vault. Check it right away."

The door opened and they could hear footsteps running down the hall. The import of what had happened hit Trump like a hammer blow. Harry turned to Vicky and gave her a wink, and for the first time since they had arrived in Trump's office, she began to think that everything was going to be all right. No one said anything for the ten minutes that the agent was gone. Trump drummed his fingers on the desk and fidgeted nervously with his tie while Victoria held Harry's hand.

The door opened and the agent came into the room, went to Trump, and whispered in his ear. The color drained from Trump's face, and Harry gave Vicky another wink.

"Where is it?" Trump said softly, almost pleadingly. He had already informed the director that the money had been recovered, and Hoover had planned a press conference when the money and Harry Fox arrived back in the United States. He did not want to be the one to make the director look foolish. He was well aware of what happened to those who did.

"It is in a very safe place," Harry said. "I thought it would be a nice gesture to turn it over to the ambassador when he presented me with my pardon."

"But it is safe?"

"Most of it," Harry said.

Trump swallowed. "Most of it?"

"My expenses were very high," Harry said, "and I thought I'd save you the trouble of paying me the money you promised me. I'll just take what you owe me before I turn it over to the ambassador."

"Leaving how much?"

"A nice round three million."

Trump closed his eyes and ran a handkerchief across his forehead. The director would have his ass for this. This operation, which was to have allowed him to return to Washington, would probably keep him stuck in the Tropics for another ten years. If he arrested Fox now, the Treasury would never see that money, and Hoover would never forgive him. There was no other way. He forced a smile. "Three million seems fine," he said. "After all, you did bear the brunt of the expenses on your own."

Harry got up from his chair. "When do you think I could expect that pardon?"

Trump looked at his calendar. "A week—ten days maybe. Certainly no longer than that."

Harry stuck out his hand and the weary Trump had no option but to offer his own. "Then, I guess I'll see you in about ten days," Harry said. "I'll show you where the money is once I get the pardon."

The men at the door looked to Trump for guidance as Harry and Victoria approached the door, but Trump had already turned away. He couldn't bring himself to watch as Harry walked out the door.

* * *

There was a cooling breeze off the bay, and when they left the embassy the two Americans walked arm in arm along Balboa Avenue. At some distance from the American Embassy they crossed to the center of the avenue, to the wide strip of lawn that separated both lanes of traffic. They found a bench and sat facing the bay. The entrance to the Panama Canal was less than two miles away, and they could see the ships in the bay, lined up, waiting to transit the isthmus.

"How did you do it?" Vicky asked.

"Easy. I had Chiari run off an extra four million for me. The only difference was that I had him use good ink for the second batch. He even duplicated the Mexican bank wrappers. When we switched with the Germans, I left the real money in the other stateroom and gave the FBI the second batch of counterfeit. The real money was shipped here in a crate with the rest of our luggage."

"You think of everything," Vicky said.

"I don't trust anyone," Harry said, putting an arm around her shoulders. "Except you."

"There's something you should know about me," Vicky said.

Harry looked at her. "I know everything I need to know. You don't have to tell me anything else."

Vicky shook her head. "No secrets," she said, determined to go on. "My name isn't Victoria Gansell," she said. "That's a stage name."

Harry's eyes widened in mock horror. "I can't believe it," he said. "How could you keep something like this from me?"

"My real name is Madge Waslewski," she said.

Harry could not stop the laughter. He put his head back and let it come as if the laughter could wash away all of the tension of the past month.

Vicky watched him, smiling. She wanted the feeling to last.

Harry looked at her. "I'll bet that name would look great on a marquee."

Vicky grinned. "It's so Hollywood," she said.

They laughed again and Vicky had a sudden pang of regret for what they were leaving behind. She wondered if things would always be the same for them. She looked out at the bay. "It really is beautiful here," she said. "Do you think you'll ever miss it?"

Harry laughed and pulled her closer. "We're going home," he said. "Nothing can ever be better than that."

SUSPENSE, INTRIGUE & INTERNATIONAL DANGER

These novels of espionage and excitement-filled tension will guarantee you the best in high-voltage reading pleasure.

43